Thorn Season

Thorn Season

KIERA AZAR

STORYTIDE
An Imprint of HarperCollins Publishers

Storytide is an imprint of HarperCollins Publishers.

Thorn Season
Copyright © 2025 by Kiera Azar
Map art by Nicolette Caven
All rights reserved. Manufactured in Harrisonburg, VA, United States of America. No part of this book may be used or reproduced in any manner whatsoever without written permission except in the case of brief quotations embodied in critical articles and reviews. For information, address HarperCollins Children's Books, a division of HarperCollins Publishers, 195 Broadway, New York, NY 10007.
www.epicreads.com

Library of Congress Control Number: 2025934270
ISBN 978-0-06-342779-2 — ISBN 978-0-06-346312-7 (international edition) — ISBN 978-0-06-346477-3 (special edition)

Typography by Laura Mock
25 26 27 28 29 LBC 5 4 3 2 1
First Edition

For my parents,
who fill my world with so much love.

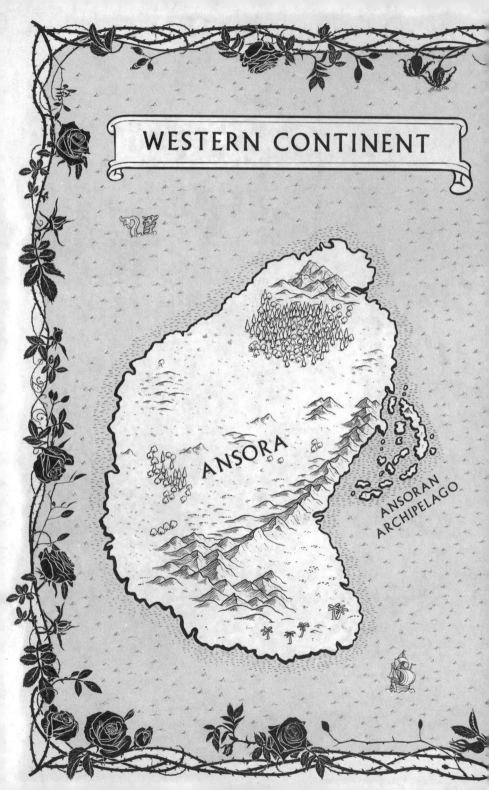

 **1**

Of all the treasonous acts I'd ever committed, this shouldn't have been the one to get me caught.

Red water streamed between my fingers with each frantic sponge-drag, but even my frothing assault of soap and vinegar wouldn't erase the Hunters' Mark on Marge's door. I was only spreading the paint around, making a mess of the rose pattern Marge had drawn above the door knocker last summer.

So much for preserving her memory.

Footsteps clopped behind me and I spun, heart racing. The air was still fuzzed and dewy as a morning peach, the jewel-toned houses barely flushed with color; I had to squint to see the figures through the haze.

I exhaled in a sharp blast. Not the guards. Just some children racing across the mosaic-encrusted road, too caught up in their laughter to notice me. They rounded the corner, and the street returned to its sleepy silence, the silver penny blossom trees rustling like sequins in the wind.

But a few streets away, the market was yawning awake and exhaling the stench of roses. Soon, the festivity of Rose Season would drag locals from their beds.

I was running out of time.

I dunked the sponge into the bucket and slapped it across the door once more, scrubbing until vinegar fumes stung my eyes. Marge had loved the first day of Rose Season. Last year, she'd gorged on so many syrup-steeped confections that we'd had to cancel our Double Decks game, and I'd brought her mint tea instead. I'd risen in the early hours of this morning and, remembering her sweet, grateful face, had known I couldn't leave the Hunters' Mark on her door one more day.

The tenth Hunters' Mark to appear in the kingdom of Daradon within the last two months.

The Hunters had never struck so frequently within such a short period, and the sudden, inexplicable increase had left me with a permanent chest-fluttering feeling.

It had made the locals nervous, too.

Another Wielder living among us all this time! I'd heard them whisper. *I once let her watch the children!* As if Marge hadn't also volunteered at the clinic, or salted the ice off her neighbors' doorsteps, or distributed lemon baskets when her potted trees had overflowed. As if her existence had been a scandal and her slaughter an inconvenience.

I clenched the sponge, water veining my olive-brown skin. Marge should've let them break their bones on the ice. I would.

Footsteps pounded again, and this time I recognized those long strides. I whirled as my best friend braced her hands on her knees, her black braid snapping around her hip.

"The guards," Tari said, panting. "They're coming this way."

I swore, hurling the sponge into the bucket. Our hands scrabbled to clean the evidence. Water slopped and wood clacked, and robins scattered at the noise.

"There!" Tari pointed across the street.

Three guards ambled up the pavement, their silver-stitched uniforms gleaming.

I dropped to the doorstep and mopped the water, red streaking under my sponge like a bloodstain. "How did they get here so fast? You were meant to be watching!"

She winced, bending to help me. "I got distracted." A green gem swung from her neck like a pendulum, flashing rainbows over her rich copper skin.

My eyes snapped up. "You left your post for *that?*"

"It was on sale!"

"It's fake!"

Tari faltered, then plucked up the gem. "Really?"

I stood, trousers soaked. "Do you understand what a lookout does?"

"Do you understand what a *cleaner* does?" She gestured at the mark, now bleeding down the door. "Gracious gods, it looks worse than when you started!"

"If my father finds out about this—"

The guards' voices halted me, now audible over our bickering. Father was the least of my worries.

I hefted the bucket, tipping water down my blouse. Murkier water ribboned downhill across the mosaic tiles; the guards would follow that trail to the perpetrators. Tari could outrun them, but I couldn't.

I looked toward Marge's door and swallowed. Houses were always locked up after a Hunting.

"Alissa, don't," Tari warned.

But the guards' eyes would land on us soon.

So, committing my second treasonous act of the day, I reached for my specter.

It reeled out of me like a thread from an internal skein, and I exhaled as the ever-present tightness eased within me. Though invisible to everyone else, my specter looked to me like a mirage-shimmer rising off hot concrete or the eddy of air above a flame—rippling faster today on account of my rapid heartbeat.

I breathed deeply, settling the urge to feed out more than I needed. There was a reason I'd never knowingly met another Wielder: to Wield was to risk exposure.

One strand would have to be enough.

I poured the tendril through the keyhole, reshaping it to fill the cavity—one of the first tricks I'd ever taught myself—and the lock clicked open.

I shoved Tari inside and hustled after her. I relocked the door as gloom engulfed us, my specter lurching in protest when I yanked it back beside my bones. Our breaths puffed into the silence, dust spiraling past our lips like vapor on a snow-frosted night.

My vision adjusted . . . and my blood chilled.

I'd imagined broken glass and upturned furniture—evidence of Marge's struggle before the Hunters had forced dullroot, the specter poison, into her veins to trap the power beneath her skin.

This scene was somehow more disturbing. Because the lounge was exactly as I remembered, with the paint-speckled table and four mismatched chairs—for Tari, Lidia, Marge, and me. Yet an unnatural layer of gray dust carpeted every surface, giving the impression of years of neglect. As though Marge was already long forgotten by the world.

"It's only been one week," I whispered.

Tari's angular face tightened with concern. "Are you all right?" she asked. Because she must have known how this room would affect me.

She knew my horror flowed alongside the deep, aching guilt of survival.

I shakily set the bucket down and approached the table. Once a month, Marge would shuffle the cards here for Double Decks. Tari and Lidia would pretend not to cheat while Marge and I would roll our eyes, and we would all trade town gossip over hot lemonade.

Now only one mug occupied the surface. Mold feathered in its center, Marge's burgundy kiss crusting the rim.

In a gut-wrenching flash, I imagined my own bedchamber deserted like this: a half-empty glass of pomegranate tea sweating onto my vanity, the dark strands of my hair straggling around a wide-tooth comb. The last pieces of me, outliving the whole.

"Remember last summer," Tari murmured, "when we moved the table outside? Lidia hid a pair of queens up her shirtsleeves, and they flew off..."

"But there was no breeze," I said softly. "I remember."

"Do you think Marge...?"

I'd asked myself similar questions all week: Had Marge ever Wielded her specter around us undetected? Had she, like me, suffered under the strain of constant confinement?

"She always hated when Lidia cheated," I said.

Sad laughter. "Only because she didn't know how to cheat herself."

My heart panged at the memory of Marge's eye twitching with every bluff. Had she tried lying to the Hunters when they'd come, hoping the eye twitch wouldn't give her away?

Tari shuffled closer, dust pluming under her boots. "Do you smell that?"

I inhaled. My wet blouse clung to my chest. "I smell only vinegar."

She shook her head. "It smells bitter. Like something burning."

I frowned at the hearth. The smell of a fire wouldn't have lingered unless someone had sneaked in more recently.

"The door was locked," I said.

"Locks only stop Wholeborns. Maybe Marge had family she didn't tell us about." Tari spoke with tentative encouragement, but I trampled my flaring hope.

Tari had spent her early childhood in Bormia, where the small Wielder population lived unprosecuted; though a Wholeborn herself, she'd already met more Wielders than I would knowingly encounter in my lifetime. I'd once petitioned Father to arrange for our passage there. But Bormia didn't accept refugees, he'd said, and even if it did, Daradon's ships couldn't cross the choppy waters into their territory.

Since then, I'd imagined finding a fellow Wielder in this prison of a kingdom. We could learn from each other, *confide* in each other. We wouldn't be alone.

But Marge had been here all along, and I'd never guessed that we'd been concealing the same secret. She'd always seemed so free with her laughter—so different from everything I'd expected to find in another Wielder . . . So different from me.

Even if I miraculously crossed paths with a Wielder again, it would lead to the same painful ending: I wouldn't recognize them as an ally until it was too late.

Swallowing a knot of emotion, I reached for Marge's dusty table—

I gasped, my specter heaving me backward at the first touch.

"What is it?" Tari asked.

I scrubbed my hand across my trousers, gaping. The dust hadn't felt like dust. And now my specter coiled deep inside me, squirming with the effort to get out, out, *out*—

A silhouette darkened the curtains. "Anyone in there?"

Tari and I shared a panicked look. Then we clambered under the table, elbows digging into ribs. The dust-flurry threatened to tickle up a cough, and my specter twisted again.

The door handle rattled. "Hello?"

"I'll go," Tari murmured. "Stay inside."

I grabbed her wrist. "No."

"It's fine. I'll feign parch fever."

"And do what? Sneeze all over them?"

She rolled her eyes. "Parch fever makes people disoriented. I've seen it at Mama's clinic."

"Disoriented people don't scrub Hunters' Marks off doors."

"No?" She flung a hand to her forehead, eyes saucer-round. "But I thought this was my house, sir." Her whisper pitched up and down in hysteria. "The vandals must've come overnight!"

I gave her a deadpan stare. "They'll never buy that."

"Then I'll spend the night in the town jail. It'll be my first arrest." A wicked grin. "My parents might throw me a party."

She wasn't exaggerating. Tari's parents would reward this rebellion the way my father might reward me for going a day without Wielding. Not that I'd ever lasted that long.

But I knew the real reason she didn't want the guards to catch me here. Because while Tari's crime began and ended at Marge's doorstep, my crime began at birth.

"Quickly," Tari said. "Before they bring the locksmith."

She tugged away, and my hand smacked the floor. Something nipped my skin, and I hissed. Tari paused as I turned my hand over.

Horror glued me to the spot.

Because stuck to my clammy palm was a human tooth.

The sharp points dug into my skin, revealing the pink, fleshy underside where the gum still plastered the root. I glanced farther down, and nausea choked me. Dark, dried spatter-marks covered the floor.

This was why there hadn't been signs of struggle elsewhere. Because Marge had crouched *here*, too frightened to face the Hunters. They'd found her anyway.

And they'd hit her hard enough to knock out a tooth.

Tari regained her faculties first, seizing the tooth and tossing it aside with a sickening clatter. But the indent remained on my palm—little dimples where the points had nearly broken skin. I blinked rapidly, trying not to picture the Hunters' faces. Trying not to guess which one of them had issued that tooth-loosening blow.

Had they unleashed a similar violence upon my mother before they'd killed her? Would they unleash the same upon me?

My ears rang as the guards' voices drifted away.

"They're leaving," Tari said, eyes glassy. "We should go."

I fought to steady my breathing, to settle the frantic thrum of my specter. Then we dashed out the door and into the street, the bucket wrapped in my sopping embrace.

I managed three steps before someone grasped my arm.

"All right, the fun's over—"

The guard broke off as I turned, my eyes already framed wide with innocence. I hoped he couldn't feel the nervous quiver down my limbs.

"Is there a problem?" I asked.

The guard dropped his hand, stammering. "Lady Alissa. I didn't recognize you."

I tilted my head, letting my face bronze in the first light of morning. The guard was young enough that my smile sent a shock of pink to his cheeks. "I hope you don't go around grabbing every citizen like that." My voice lilted between a flirt and a threat. The voice of a courtier.

His blush deepened. "No, my lady. We received a report that someone was destroying town property." He glanced to Marge's dripping door. To where I could still make out the two connected spires of the Hunters' Mark—a long, sharp *M* with a plunging center.

Father once told me the spires represented the two gods of passing, a symbol to honor the dead. But my first visit to court had taught me that those spires mimicked the two-tined crown of Daradon. Not a tribute to the gods—but to the vicious king who held the Hunters' leash.

And I'd just been caught scrubbing those tines away.

I readjusted my bucket, chin lifted. "That would be me."

The guard's eyes flicked to Tari and tightened on her tan waistcoat. "Are you sure, my lady?"

I gritted my teeth. The bucket was in *my* arms. *My* clothes were sodden with paint and water. Yet he'd seen Tari's lotus pin—the national Bormian flower—shining proudly at her breast, and he'd thought to accuse her.

Bormians were always labeled as sympathizers.

"What's your name?" I asked, fighting to conceal the bite in my tone.

He straightened. "Byron, my lady."

"*Byron.*" Names held power, and I said his like I would never forget it. "You're new?"

"Yes, my lady. I trained with the royal guard before coming to Vereen."

The royal guard. I could work with that.

"You must forgive my father, Byron. He should have warned the guards I'd be here. With the preparations for tonight's ball, it surely slipped his mind."

Byron frowned. "This was Lord Heron's idea?"

"It's the first day of Rose Season. People from across the kingdom have traveled to Vereen to see our famed craftwork." I leaned closer, confiding. "This street is so near the market. We don't want to drive away shoppers." When Byron looked unconvinced, I wrinkled my nose toward Marge's door. "And we certainly don't want to be associated with *their kind*."

I felt sick at the words. Felt sick that Byron's face softened with understanding. But nobody questioned cruelty the way they questioned kindness.

"My father didn't wish to draw attention," I said, driving in my final weapon. "He'll be mortified to hear I dragged you from your post on such an important day."

Bull's-eye. Having trained at the palace, Byron would've seen how royal guards were punished for their oversights. Vereen was nothing like the capital, but Byron didn't know that. And leaving his post to accost the lady of Vereen? That was a medal-worthy oversight.

He gulped, looking so ill that I almost pitied him. Then he said, as if doing *me* a favor, "Don't fear, my lady. I won't mention this to His Lordship."

He marched off, and I cut the strings of my puppet smile.

"How do you do that?" Tari mumbled as I glimpsed movement from Lidia's house across the street: curtains swishing, Lidia darting away.

"Lidia reported us," I said flatly. Lidia and Marge had been dearest friends, as close as Tari and me. Now Lidia wouldn't offer Marge the dignity of an unmarked door.

Of all the cowards on this street, she was the worst.

"She's afraid," Tari said. "*Everyone's* afraid. It doesn't mean they don't care."

I went to shout her down. Cowering under a table, being yanked into the open, feeling a tooth tear from its gum—*that* was fear.

But I stopped myself. Tari had no specter; she didn't understand what it was to be truly afraid. She might support me, worry for me, but I alone experienced the constant hum of dread that, at any moment, the Hunters could prune me from the world. I wouldn't be kindly overlooked if they discovered my specter, and I certainly wouldn't be spared.

After all, the Hunters' bloodline had to remain untainted.

And I was the thorn on their family tree.

 # 2

I walked the side streets home, avoiding the bustle-and-haggle of the market, ducking around every corner like the criminal I was. Though Byron had accepted my ugly excuse, Lidia had seen everything, and my steaming indignation was cooling into doubt.

Never show your power, Father had always taught me. *Never give them a reason to look.* And what had I done? I'd openly vandalized the Hunters' Mark, then inexplicably conquered a locked door. I may as well have taken the pink *Happy Rose Season!* banner from the square and waved it above my head.

It had been foolish. Reckless. Yet despite my churning anxiety, I knew it had also been *right*.

Some believed that the Hunters descended from the legendary Spellmakers of old, the only beings who could sniff out power like bloodhounds—and could even harness certain forms of power to forge indestructible objects.

My father knew the truth. His late mother, a Hunter, had married into nobility, and his inherited title had saved him from having to execute Wielders with the rest of the vast Capewell family. But though this had made Father an outcast among them—subject to both scorn and envy—he'd still learned how the Hunters truly found their targets. While the family didn't possess a drop of Spellmaker blood, they did possess a Spellmade compass.

A compass that pointed to Wielders, separating us from Wholeborns like chaff from grain.

The idea of such an object had always horrified me—but even more so since the rise in Huntings. Was this uptick born of sadistic boredom, or had it been a directive from the young king, wanting to reassert his power? Most importantly: Was the spike going to drop?

I'd implored Father to extract answers from the Capewells, but he'd looked so pained that I hadn't pressed again.

And now Marge was dead. Slaughtered by the same people who'd sent my father a premature condolence letter during my childhood bout of blueneck fever. The same people who spoke to him as though he wasn't worth half the space he took up in a room.

Father only tolerated the Capewells so they wouldn't look in my direction; he believed they wouldn't think to consult the compass around their own family members without cause.

But if I'd survived this long purely because of the fortune of my blood ties . . . how could I *not* use my extra time to wash the hateful mark off Marge's door?

The ruddy water was drying stiff to my blouse as I gusted into the foyer, inhaling the scent of the sesame biscuits Father toasted every morning. While Rose Season had ensnared the rest of Vereen, our staff knew to keep our manor rose-free—though they didn't know *why* I'd emptied my stomach when a new maid had arranged a vase in my chambers last spring.

To this day, I wouldn't discuss the root of my aversion. Wouldn't explain the dark months when I'd refused to leave my chambers, and the maids had wafted fresh-bread steam under my door just to get me to eat. Only Amarie knew about the old, rose-infused memory I still couldn't face; as our house manager and only live-in staff member, she was the only person my father trusted with every secret.

She was also the only person who scolded me like a child.

"I know, I know." I cringed at my boot-treads as she hurried toward me, her tawny hair jouncing in its bun. "I'll clean up—"

"Go back out," she said, hissing and shooing me toward the door.

The wide staircase creaked, and I scrambled backward. Father should've been in his study by now.

My hand was on the doorknob when someone said, "Alissa."

The voice twisted like a knife in my gut.

I hadn't seen Garret since the increase in Huntings, and I felt too raw for this meeting. Too weary. But when I turned, I knew that despite the vinegar fumes making me smell like a meat marinade, I looked just as composed and aloof as the boy coming down the stairs.

Not a boy anymore, I reminded myself. In a black waistcoat and blazer, his leather shoes polished to a mirror-gleam, Garret Shaw looked every bit the Capewell he'd promised never to become. Long limbs and sleek edges. A clean shave across his deeply tanned skin. The only token of his youth was the eight-year-old scar interrupting one eyebrow like a crack in a mask—a souvenir from headbutting a doorknob the night we'd swiped my father's brandy.

I hated that scar more than any other piece of him. It always reminded me of how hard we'd laughed that night.

"What are you doing here?" I asked, automatically scanning for the weapons he must have been carrying beneath his fine clothes. Weapons he hadn't yet used against me, despite being the only Hunter who wouldn't need the compass to know what I was.

I'd made the mistake of telling him myself.

"I had business with your father." Garret descended the last step and looked me over, that dark eyebrow lifting in cool amusement. "Been swimming?"

"Painting."

"You don't paint."

No—while my father had produced the peacock-colored spray of artwork along the mahogany walls, I could barely draw an apple.

"You don't do business with my father," I countered.

Garret's mouth flattened. Although they'd long ago given up the attempt, the Capewells used to proposition Father to join the Hunters' service, for the triumph of having him—a ruling lord—under their command. Father had always given the same answer: no.

Garret turned to Amarie, whose eyes flitted nervously between us. "Send word if Heron reconsiders our discussion. *Before* tonight's ball."

"Amarie doesn't take orders from you," I said.

"That wasn't an order." Garret smiled thinly. "Just a request."

He slunk toward me, the clasp of his steel bracelet flashing in the sunlight. Even after seven years, I shuddered at the sight of Garret's oath band.

Though still permissible by Daradonian law, the oath band was deemed archaic; it served as a shackle, only removable by the person to whom the wearer had sworn an oath. And if the wearer broke their oath—or the band—without permission, the law demanded they forfeit their hand from the wrist down.

Garret was the only Hunter who wore one of those bands. Probably because he was the only Hunter who hadn't been born into the role.

Garret's birth parents had been killed during the Starling Rebellion, when rogue Wielders had attacked Wholeborns in a gruesome attempt to balance the score of violence. Wray Capewell, my father's cousin, had known Garret's parents well, and he'd raised their orphaned child within the family of Hunters, treating Garret no worse—but certainly no better—than the many young Capewells squalling about Capewell Manor.

Now Garret stopped before me, as flinty-eyed as he'd been for the past seven years—since he'd been sharpened under the whetstone of the Hunters' influence.

Since he'd chosen them over me.

I refused to shrink back when he reached around me for the door handle. Then, because I could still feel the phantom dint of Marge's tooth, because I wanted to torture myself with one more reason to despise him, I asked, "Been to town recently?"

Garret paused, his arm outstretched behind me, his severe face inches above mine. His warm breath skimmed my cheek as he said, eyes narrowed, "Not for weeks."

It was the note of confusion that made me believe him. And though his answer changed nothing between us—though he'd killed countless other Wielders—I felt a stab of relief that he hadn't been the one to kill my friend.

He looked all the way down me then, and I tensed as his gaze landed on my red-stained fingers. "Mind that nobody sees you," he said carefully, "when you're . . . painting."

I glowered as he brushed past me, and with a tendril of my specter, I slammed the door behind him.

"You'll get a rash," I muttered atop the grand staircase, the heat-and-perfume haze pressing around me.

Father had been scratching his chest for the entire hour-long journey into Henthorn, the capital city. I couldn't blame him; city visits tested both our nerves. But Father wore his anxiety for all to see.

And courtiers saw everything.

They twirled in a sea of satin below us, music and laughter flowing as freely as the sparkling wine. Roses coiled up marble pillars and burst like sores between the archways, their petals weeping over the king's throne. And above the dais, shimmering in silver, were the symbols representing Daradon's five provinces: a carp for Avanford; a wheat stalk for Creak; a sword for the soldiers of Parrey; a book for the scholars of Dawning; and in the center of them all, a bejeweled ring for the craftspeople of Vereen.

"At least they have lemon cakes." I nodded toward the dessert table, where sugared tarts, brandied plums, and pistachio-crusted truffles tumbled from a pastry cornucopia. But the semolina lemon cakes—my favorite dessert—were a new addition and usually only found at Verenian bakeries. "How terrible can one night be with a lemon cake in hand?"

"Don't tempt the gods," Father grumbled.

"The gods don't care about lemon cakes. Now stop scratching, and be glad you don't look like you belong on a plate *beside* the lemon cakes."

Father eyed me and cringed. I'd heaped myself in Henthornian fashion this evening, with puffed pink sleeves hanging low off my shoulders and satiny skirts tenting below my corseted waist. I resembled a walking meringue—and my sweeping updo was the swirl of chocolate cream on top.

"You didn't have to wear that," he said.

"And miss the chance to trip over my skirts on the way to the dance floor? I was hoping to take a few centerpieces down with me."

Father's mouth barely twitched in amusement. He seemed especially fretful tonight. While Rose Season manifested at court as the annual social season—during which the nobles indulged in enough gossip, merriment, and rich foods to hibernate over the cooler months—its roots originated from a more formal tradition, which still held strong.

Every noble, upon their eighteenth season, would participate in a closing ceremony to swear fealty to the reigning monarch. Though appearance was only mandatory on the first and last nights of the season, these eighteenth-season nobles were encouraged—no, *expected*—to pass the six weeks leading up to the ceremony in a first stay at court.

And this year marked my eighteenth season.

I'd told Father I could handle court for six weeks, but he'd been adamant. Sending his Wielder daughter to live at the palace would've felt like sending a deer into a wolf's den, and he would only relax once these weeks of Rose Season had wilted off the calendar.

But with the festivity in full bloom tonight, he was on the brink of sweating through his coattails.

I grabbed his clammy hand and squeezed. "Back straight. Chin high. And by all the gracious gods, stay away from Rupert when he drinks. Last year, he breathed beside a candle and singed my eyebrows."

Father actually cracked a faint smile at that. Then he briefly touched my cheek. "What would I do without you, my girl?"

Sudden guilt stabbed at me. He would unravel if he noticed the tinge of red paint staining my fingernails.

Returning his smile a little tightly, I descended the stairs at his side, one meringue joining the others on the white tray of the ballroom floor. As the stench of roses swept over me, roiling my stomach, I inhaled the citrus-and-lavender perfume at my wrist. It was a trick

Tari had learned at her mother's clinic, and as usual, my nausea settled.

But it returned with a vengeance as I noticed Briar Capewell's straw-yellow hair swishing through the crowd.

Father subtly angled himself between us.

He and Briar were first cousins on his mother's side, and while Father and I had inherited most of our characteristics from the Paine side of the family—heavy brows, olive coloring, dark lashes around broody, almond-brown eyes—Briar presented a statuesque figure of creams and golds. But today, her high cheeks blazed with florid anger. The crisscross straps of her peach dress shifted with every violent footfall, threatening to reveal the Hunters' Mark tattooed over her heart.

A defiant outfit choice.

The Crown forbade the Hunters from revealing their true identities, claiming that faceless executioners produced a greater fear. But Briar Capewell, the head of the Hunter family, resented the powerlessness of anonymity. When standing over a Wielder's body, wearing the mask of the Hunters, she was horror incarnate.

But standing among the gentry, wearing the guise of a merchant, she was the bitter human equivalent of a lemon pith.

"The ship docked this morning, Heron," she said, stopping before us. "Were you aware?"

"Hello to you, too, Briar," Father mumbled.

"They've prepared the ambassadorial chambers." She laughed roughly. "They should've prepared the dungeons."

I frowned at Father. "An ambassador's here?"

Father hesitated, seeming oddly reluctant to speak around me.

Briar said, "His Majesty is hosting an Ansoran ambassador for Rose Season."

I fought to school my expression. Ansora, the Wielder-ruled empire across the sea, had always seemed like an illusion, glimmering at the map's western edge. While their ongoing conflict with our neighboring kingdom, Orren, had made their surrounding waters near impenetrable, the Ansoran mainland thrived with culture and prosperity, a haven for Wielders and Wholeborns alike.

And one of their ambassadors had journeyed *here*?

"The king should've refused," Briar said, popping my vision like a soap bubble. "Doesn't he understand the risk?" She picked at a hangnail, uncharacteristically fidgety. "You're a ruling lord. What's the point of having influence at court if you don't use it?"

"It's not in my interest to influence our king's political decisions," Father said.

Briar's lips thinned. "The Wielder will have free rein here. What if he gets his hands on your lovely daughter?"

Father tensed, but my specter was already rousing inside me. No wonder Briar looked so distressed.

"The ambassador is a Wielder?" I asked, breathless. "It's been confirmed?"

"No," Father said, his voice even flatter than his expression. This must be why he'd kept the news to himself. He'd wanted to avoid raising my interest, my hopefulness. He surely knew how much I wanted to meet another Wielder.

And he knew how dangerous that could be.

"All we know," he continued, "is that the Ansorans requested an invitation for this year's season. Their empress is known to be particularly vicious when affronted, and our king thought to preserve international relations."

"With *vermin*?" Briar spat.

Father flinched, and I almost flinched with him. The way most people said *Wielder* was usually insult enough. But now I imagined Briar spitting the word *vermin* at Marge and had to breathe deep to settle the spectral tug inside me.

A specter was said to be a natural extension of a Wielder's physiology—a gathering of power not only governed by its Wielder's intent but also deeply attuned to their subconscious. Their most primal and instinctive impulses.

Which was why, right now, my specter strained with my desire to yank Briar away by her hair.

"I suppose you know vermin better than anyone," I said, heat clawing up my neck, "after so many years of scavenging around court."

"Alissa," Father warned, inching further between us. Rankling a Hunter was exactly what I *shouldn't* be doing.

But even in her agitation, Briar seemed vaguely entertained. "Your daughter's tongue grows sharper each year, Heron. You should train her to keep it inside that pretty mouth before it gets her into trouble." She smiled at me, and there it was—the only secret we shared, dripping like acid into the silence.

Because this was the exact smile she'd given me ten years ago, after she'd whipped her palm across my face.

Back then, I'd been too afraid of her to tell Father what she'd done. But she was no longer the greatest monster I knew.

I opened my mouth, but Father spoke first, his expression hard. "Be quiet, Briar."

I startled, pride swelling in my chest. Father never risked standing up for himself against the Hunters. But he would always stand up for me.

Briar glanced at Father's silver brooch: a circlet of penny blossoms, the Paine emblem. At court, jewelry meant status. Rubies glittered from every corner, emeralds winked under crystal chandeliers, pink diamonds dripped from my own earlobes. And while Father's brooch sparkled with dark blue xerylites—coveted gemstones native to Vereen—Briar's only adornment was the Hunters' Mark over her heart. The tattoo she wasn't allowed to reveal.

Her cheeks became blotched again—an angry, resentful red. "My lord," she conceded with a mocking air, her entire face puckering as though from a nasty taste. *Lemon pith indeed.*

Father turned to me, eyes shadowed. "Why don't you go and find Carmen?"

With a glare at Briar, I departed. But as the ball raged around me, I didn't search for my friend. I began examining each garment for a rising sun, the Ansoran insignia.

I had to find the ambassador.

I wouldn't return here until the last night of Rose Season, and he might have left by then; I couldn't lose my only chance at meeting another Wielder. I wouldn't expose myself, of course. Despite Father's fears, I wasn't *that* reckless. But maybe just knowing of another Wielder's specter would be enough—more than I'd had with Marge.

I hastened, growing giddy with anticipation, when Lord Rupert of Creak planted a mustache-tickling kiss on my knuckles and started rambling about the vineyard he'd acquired in Avanford.

"Oh, you're not serious." I scrunched my nose just so. "Avanish wine is horribly tart."

"*Tart?*" Rupert adjusted his monocle. "Why, Fiona adored the stuff, gods rest her!"

I internally winced at the mention of Father's late wife, a Creakish noblewoman I'd never met, but whose name I exploited with my every breath. Lady Fiona's death had occurred so shortly after my birth that Father had been able to pass her off as my mother without raising suspicion. If these nobles discovered I was actually the bastard child from Father's secret love affair, they would want me stripped of my title.

And if they learned my birth mother had been a *Wielder*, they would want me dead.

"I'll make a connoisseur of you yet, dear girl," Rupert continued. "I'll send you a case for sampling. That ought to change your mind."

He puffed up as though he'd won the argument, and I slipped away as a Parrian merchant approached him, eager to offload a case of rum.

After twenty more minutes of searching, I collapsed against the dessert table and downed a flute of sparkling wine. I was raising another, surveying the crowd, when a familiar voice said, "He's not here."

I lowered the flute as Garret slid beside me.

"The ambassador," he clarified, his knowing gaze sweeping my face. "He's making his appearance tomorrow."

Hope flooded out of me as quickly as it had risen, leaving me hollow.

"It's your eighteenth season." Garret leaned back against the table and adjusted his bronze cufflink. "You're bound to meet him during your stay."

"I'm not joining court this year," I said, surprised at the bite in my voice. Even more surprised that it wasn't directed at Garret.

Each time I Wielded, I knew I scored another stress line into Father's forehead, spun another silver thread into his hair. And because Wielding was the most selfish thing I could never stop doing, I tried to appease him in everything else. I didn't push him to acknowledge the increase in Huntings; I didn't push him to talk about my birth mother; I didn't even push to join court for my eighteenth season.

But when I'd agreed to stay home, I hadn't realized he'd been keeping me from another Wielder.

"Shame." Garret's faint, genuine smile pierced me through the ribs; it made his face seem softer. Younger. "I saw that trick you pulled on Rupert."

It was Carmen, the princess of Daradon, who'd first taught me how to charm Rupert into sending me gifts. From there, I'd learned the secret to getting anything from anyone:

Never ask a person for what you truly want; wait until they offer it freely.

"You've always thrived here," Garret said. "It's your craft." I tensed, waiting for the insult. But he left the compliment as it was—an invisible hand reaching across the chasm between us.

I stood a little straighter. Smacked that invisible hand away. "That's what happens when you're born into nobility."

"Tell your father that." He nodded toward a dim alcove, and I went taut. Father usually spent these balls cloistered with the Jacombs of Dawning, his closest acquaintances at court. But tonight, he was still shrinking under Briar's tirade. Probably paying for having shut her up within earshot of the gentry.

My specter squirmed. With my next exhale, I let it breach my bare skin. I unspooled a tendril across the cool marble floor, feeling the satisfying stretch of release from deep inside me. Then I slipped it under a nobleman's shoe.

The man stumbled. And crashed right into Briar.

I chuckled under my breath.

Garret grabbed my arm, his soft smile gone. "Don't do that."

"Do what?" I wrenched away, all innocence. "I can't help that she's more sour tonight than usual. Though I'm surprised she has time to pout about the ambassador when she's so busy with her nighttime excursions." My tone turned bitter. "Ten Huntings within two months is bound to wear a person out."

"Lower your voice."

As Briar scrambled under the nobleman, I remembered her tight, anxious expression from earlier. And I understood what it meant.

"Oh," I breathed, smiling grimly. "Don't tell me the leader of the king's Hunters is afraid of one little Wielder."

Garret reached for my wine. "Maybe you've had enough."

I pulled back. "Maybe you shouldn't tell me what to do."

I was turning when Garret seized my wrist. He tugged me toward him and I gasped, stumbling into the space between us. Wine fizzled over our fingers.

"Is this fun for you?" he hissed. His stare bore down on mine, turning me rigid. "Seeing how far you can push before—"

"Before *what*?" I gritted out.

His grip contracted around my wrist.

Before I expose you, I waited for him to say. *Before I decide you're not worth keeping alive.*

My specter reared, and I was moments away from lashing it against him when he abruptly released me and dropped his gaze. A coiffed blond head crept into my eyeline, and my specter shriveled tight.

Then His Majesty King Erik Vard of Daradon asked, "Lady Alissa, may I have this dance?"

 # 3

Father used to read me fairy tales—stories of strapping young heroes who slayed monsters and rescued damsels, all without getting a speck of blood on their hands.

The gods had sculpted King Erik after those heroes. That same power and grace sang in his every movement—honed his knife-sharp bone structure, then generously softened it with romance: fair starburst lashes framing his frost-blue eyes and a lush mouth that flirted on the edge of swollen, like he'd either just returned from a heady kiss or was about to engage in one.

But it was those clean hands that cemented his fairy-tale image: never stained by the blood he'd spilled.

My skin crawled at the cold feel of them—one clasping mine, the other settling at the dip of my waist—as he led me in a dance. I hoped Father couldn't see us. The sight of me in the king's grasp would be hell on his rash.

"I felt it my duty to rescue you." King Erik smirked, his voice low and sultry. Dressed in his usual finery—silver-embroidered indigo, with a cape fastened at his shoulders—he stood out like a pillar against the twinkling pink backdrop. "You looked terribly affronted. That was one of Briar's boys, wasn't it?"

The king wasn't much older than Garret, but I knew what he'd meant. *One of Briar's boys.* As if she'd molded him herself.

"It was, Your Majesty."

"I hope he wasn't bothering you."

"No more than usual," I said, and regretted it instantly. Because Erik's gaze tightened over my shoulder, closing in on a target.

I didn't know what exactly compelled me to clunk forward, digging my heel into his polished boot. But I exhaled when his icy attention slid off Garret.

"My apologies," I said. "I rarely dance."

The king smiled, all warmth and tolerance. "You may step on my toes as often as you wish. You're saving me from dancing with Lady Perla." He whispered intimately, "It's like dragging a wet fish across the dance floor." At my false laughter, his smile grew sharper. More satisfied. "I'm fortunate you'll be joining court this year, Lady Alissa. I'm far too dependent on your trampling feet to let them wander off now."

Here we go. I'd grown accustomed to Erik's appreciative glances since I'd come of age.

I'd grown equally accustomed to batting away his flirtations like swatting flies.

"I'm afraid Your Majesty will have to manage without me," I said, laughing again. "Though I'm certain your shoes will thank me."

His head tilted—a predator prickling with awareness. "This is your eighteenth season, no?"

"Yes, Your Majesty."

"Then I assume you're unaware of Rose Season's origins. You see, the tradition began so each new generation of nobles could swear fealty to the Crown."

"Yes, Your Majesty." I maintained my smile. "I look forward to the ceremony at the end of the season."

"But you won't be remaining at the palace in the meantime?"

"No, Your Majesty."

He licked his lips, his wry smile glistening. "Forgive me, Lady Alissa. I feel myself growing offended, and I doubt that's what you intend."

My specter twitched at his tone—falsely playful, dark with meaning. The anxious thrum of my pulse grew palpable where my palm pressed his.

You've always thrived here, Garret had said. Because court had always enthralled me—the schemes and secrets, the verbal warfare that sent my specter zipping with a little thrill. In different circumstances, I might've joined court despite Father's wishes. But it wasn't court he wanted to keep me from.

It had always been the king.

"We have a large house, Your Majesty," I said, thick with apology. "I couldn't bear to leave my father alone in it for so long."

"By all means, tell him to join you."

"You wouldn't like that, Your Majesty." Another empty laugh. "You have enough Verenian nobles cluttering your halls for Rose Season. Craftspeople can be a fussy lot."

"Ah, that's why you don't stay? For fear of cluttering my halls?" He twirled me to a swell of music. My twisting skirts dragged me off-kilter, but he steadied me against him—a wolf keeping hold of its prey. "I'm relieved, Lady Alissa. My imagination had quite run away with me. I'd believed you were deliberately avoiding my company."

I faltered—just for a moment. Then I lowered my lashes. Plastered on a brave, wobbling smile. "You read me too well, Your Majesty, though it's not *your* company I wish to avoid. I hear you're hosting a Wielder at court this year."

He quirked an eyebrow. "I'm hosting an *Ansoran* at court."

"Aren't they mostly Wielders?"

"In this case, it's of no consequence. It would be against any creature's interest to lose control within my walls."

I clenched my jaw behind my smile. Allegedly, a specter's natural tendency was to extend outside a Wielder's body—like a plant moving toward light, or a muscle craving to be stretched. It was therefore argued that specters might execute their Wielders' desires even without conscious intention. That a specter's free-flowing nature made it uncontrollable. *Dangerous.*

And that, in being unable to manage such volatile power, Wielders were no better than beasts untethered.

So why, after two centuries of slaughtering Wielders under the Execution Decree, would the kingdom welcome a foreign Wielder now? If *this* was of no consequence, why did people like Marge still have to die?

"You mustn't worry yourself," Erik said, in true hero fashion. "The creature wouldn't do you any harm. And if it *tried*"—he twirled me again, dragged me firmly back—"where else could be safer than right here, beside your king?" His gaze dropped to my lips, heavy with suggestion.

I stilled. Flirtations were a regular part of the script. But the look in his eyes was something new . . . Something that made my blood spike with the threat of danger.

He gave a slow, curving grin. "I've startled you."

"No, Your Majesty." My chest fluttered rapidly, still trapped against his. I had to crane to meet his stare. "You could never startle me."

I already know what you're capable of.

Erik leaned down, and I fought the instinct to recoil. "My advisors are campaigning for Lady Perla." His breath rippled against my ear; his fingers splayed across my back. "But I believe they've overlooked another, far more pleasing option."

He pulled away, and I knew what he saw: the color draining from my face like wet paint dripping down a canvas. The young king *was* looking to reaffirm his power over the kingdom.

Because apparently, he was searching for a bride.

"Tell me, Lady Alissa." His thumb trailed down my spine. "Did you like the lemon cakes?"

My head emptied. And in the stillness, I finally heard the whispers. Finally saw the wide circle we'd created with our dance—an invisible barrier the other nobles hadn't crossed, but had pierced with their razor-sharp notice.

They had noticed what this dance had meant. And I hadn't.

"Your Majesty." I swallowed, heart racing. "You flatter me, but—"

"*But.*" Erik clicked his tongue, teasing. "Why must you follow that statement with *but?*"

Because I'm not a damsel in need of rescuing. I'm one of the creatures you like to cut down.

I wanted to run, or throw up—or shove my hairpins into his jugular—but just then, the noise in the ballroom abruptly ratcheted. We broke eye contact, faces snapping in opposite directions. Messengers weaved through the crowd, leaving open mouths wherever they passed.

The word bounced toward me, an echo layered in different voices.

Hunters, Hunters, Hunters.

Goose bumps lashed up my skin.

Distracted by the chaos, Erik relaxed his grip, and I used the excuse to feign a stumble. He reached out to steady me too late; the sudden swarm of people created a barrier between us, and I let myself get swept away.

I jostled between the bodies, devouring scraps of conversations, head swiveling to find my father.

"*They crashed through the estate.*"

"*A noble household!*"

Oh, gods.

The room became too stifling, my skin too tight. I could still feel the king's hands on me, and I was breathing fast, tasting roses on every breath—

Then Father's arm banded around my shoulders, towing me through the crowd.

"The estate," I gasped. "Amarie—"

"Not ours," Father murmured. "The Jacombs' estate." He looked to where the Jacombs were extracting the news from a messenger, their faces carved with horror. "Their staff."

My stomach turned. The Jacombs' household had two dozen live-in staff members.

"How many?" I whispered.

Father's neck tensed with a hard swallow. "All of them."

Two dozen Wielders. Two dozen deaths.

The misery in Father's eyes warred with relief—a relief that felt obscene in the wake of such slaughter.

I knew. Because I felt it too.

"I'll take her home." Garret appeared beside me, and my emotion kindled into rage.

"This doesn't concern you," I snapped.

But Father didn't dismiss him; his gaze had darkened on Garret's oath band.

"You worry too much, Heron." Garret tugged his blazer sleeve, smiling blandly. "She's perfectly safe with me."

Father cast him a sharp look of warning. Then he kissed the top of my head and urged me forward. I would've tripped if Garret hadn't grasped my elbow.

"I don't need an escort—"

"Please, my girl." Father's voice warbled, cracking my resolve. "I need to be here. I'll see you at home."

As Garret steered me toward an arched exit, I caught a final glimpse of the ballroom.

The king's eyes were searching the crowd.

 # 4

I'd first met Garret one blustery morning when his adoptive father, Wray Capewell, had visited our estate. Father had told me to play outside, away from the Hunter; while splashing in rain puddles, I found Garret shivering in Wray's lacquered carriage, forgotten. I invited him inside for cinnamon milk, and when Wray had scolded him for taking handouts like a street urchin, I "accidentally" tipped steaming milk down the man's trousers. Father had withheld my desserts all week, but it had been worth it for the grateful smile twitching around Garret's mouth. And when, months later, I told him about my specter, I hadn't glimpsed a lick of judgment in his awed reaction.

He judged me now.

As I twirled my mother's lucky coin over a tendril of my specter, Garret watched, tight-lipped and wary, as though it might shoot down his throat. My mother had been Hunted mere weeks after my birth, and this coin was all I possessed of her—lighter than real gold, with a chip on the circumference, as if a tiny person had taken a bite. Garret must have recognized it—or he simply didn't want to risk touching my *dirty specter*—because he didn't seize the coin like he probably should have.

Wielding an object was always dangerous; though I alone saw my specter, rippling like a heat wave around a fire, witnesses might see the coin held invisibly aloft, and I would be exposed. But right now, sweating in a heap of satin, heart beating faster than the clattering wheels over the Verenian roads, I needed the sense of release only Wielding could offer.

For eighteen years, I'd managed my fear, balancing on the knife's edge between guilt and gratitude. The Hunters' compass couldn't target Wielders beyond a certain distance, Father always assured me, and the Capewells had no reason to consult it in my presence. As long as I was careful, I was safe. But tonight had marked the eleventh Hunting in two months, with the largest body count yet.

And the background hum of my dread was quickly whirring into panic.

What had warranted this torrent of slaughter after two centuries of a drip-pace? Were the Capewells finally picking off the last of Daradon's Wielders? I'd never wanted my father to experience the pain of outliving his child. But if the Huntings continued like this . . .

Did I truly have as much time left as I'd wanted to believe?

My mother's coin spun faster, and Garret's fists tightened in his lap. Even he couldn't protect me if someone saw me now. More than that—I wasn't sure he would want to.

So, as the street festivities grew louder, I released the coin and forcibly withdrew my specter.

Garret exhaled. "So, Erik's in the market for a bride."

"*In the market?*" I shifted uncomfortably, hot-faced and agitated after an hour in the carriage. "I'm not a sack of grain. He's not trying to buy me."

"Isn't he?"

I opened my mouth, then remembered the lemon cakes and sank back.

"Everyone saw how he looked at you," Garret said. "They'll be lobbying for your favor."

"Is that why Briar sent you to the estate today? She wants me to endear her to the nobles?"

Garret lifted the curtain and looked onto the square, overflowing with music and dancers and syrup cakes, all glittering under the lantern-strung canopy. The light dappled his face in one long, moving streak. "That's not why I was at your estate."

I was about to probe when I saw him roll his wrist under the oath band, restless. As though he couldn't elaborate without breaching whatever vow he'd made upon joining the Capewells' service.

The vow he would have to cut off his hand to break.

We jostled onto a residential street, and his gaze tightened on the red smudge across Marge's door—the last vestige of the Hunters' Mark that Tari and I hadn't managed to erase.

"I heard the last Hunting in Vereen was close to your estate," he murmured. "I hadn't realized how close."

Too close. I fidgeted with my mother's coin, my specter twitching to spin it again.

"She was young," Garret continued. "Unmarried. She left nobody behind."

"Nobody to miss her, you mean?"

He dropped the curtain, stone-faced. "If they suspect a Wielder community here, they might search this area for the rest."

They. As if he didn't classify himself among them.

He wedged a little finger under his oath band. Swallowed. Then: "You should join court for your eighteenth season. The palace could be the safest place for you right now."

We rolled onto the paths of my estate, and I gathered my skirts.

I didn't know what range of distance the compass covered; my home might fall inside its boundary if the Hunters searched here again, and with Marge gone, I may well be the next Wielder in the vicinity.

But with the fresh memory of the king's eyes grazing over me, Garret had chosen the wrong night for his appeal.

"If you believe any place so near the king could be considered *safe*," I said, "then you don't know the king."

Not like I did.

I opened the door to a rush of air, and Garret captured my arm. He hesitated, eyes flicking between me and the house.

"What?" I bit out.

He frowned toward my white-knuckled hold on the door, then slowly withdrew his hand. "You don't have to end up like her."

My specter flared with my temper.

"She was my friend." I tumbled onto the drive. "And her name was *Marge*."

I went to slam the door when Garret said softly, "I wasn't talking about your friend."

I froze, breath snagging. He hadn't been alluding to the trace of paint on my nails but to the coin between my fingers.

My mother's coin.

You don't have to end up like her.

I glanced over my shoulder. With the nighttime flies whirring like rain-drizzle around him, Garret might have been that boy again, shivering and forgotten—if not for those guarded eyes, the grimly set mouth. A part of me would always mourn the loss of him. But tonight, that part was quiet.

"If you want to wait for my father," I said, pocketing the coin, "you're waiting here."

In a cruel mirror-reversal of the day we'd met, I left him on the drive, staring after me.

Amarie was waiting at the door, warm light streaming around her shoulders. "Your father?"

"Still in Henthorn," I said, heading for the kitchens. I was less hungry than restless, but that seemed a good enough reason to raid the pantry. "I fell sick from the roses, and he made me leave early."

Amarie would learn about the Hunting soon enough, and I couldn't bring myself to say the words. To acknowledge the feeling of the noose, slowly tightening around me.

Her steps clacked after me. "He sent you with *that boy?*"

"Yes, because between the absent ambassador and the king's proposal, I hadn't suffered enough."

Amarie grabbed my hand, halting me. Her wide eyes reflected the candlelight. "The king proposed?"

"Not outright." I sighed, extricating my fingers. "But my sudden exit won't go unnoticed."

"Your father won't like this."

"You can't tell him," I said, already cursing myself. Amarie had worked in this house since her teenage years—had grown up with my father—and she was too loyal to him to ever really serve as my secret-keeper. "By the time I return to Henthorn, Erik will have forgotten about me." Though my specter twisted in protest, I knew that even meeting the ambassador wasn't worth joining court. Nothing was worth the king's attention.

"Men like King Erik don't forget, Alissa. The longer he cannot have you, the more he will want you."

I went to object—*the king is fickle, shallow*—but true fear had deepened the groove between her brows. And suddenly all I could remember was the eagerness in Erik's eyes when I'd started to refuse him.

Reality hit me. I'd refused the king of Daradon. And now I was his challenge, a prize deer in a royal hunt. He didn't necessarily want *me*. He just wanted to mount my head on his wall. And if, while in pursuit, he discovered my secret...

Well, the head-mounting would take a more literal turn.

"Amarie," I whispered, horror rising, "what do I—?"

A crash shook through the manor, startling the words off my tongue. Then shouting—voices I didn't recognize. And among them—

Garret.

I didn't think. I was already running toward the thumping and yelling and shattering glass. My specter pulsed around my body, pumping me faster through the halls. My blood thundered with one name, one purpose. *Garret, Garret, Garret.*

I rounded a corner and smacked against him. The relief almost knocked me over.

But Garret pushed me backward, his breath hot on my face. "Run, Alissa." He looked to Amarie, who panted behind me. "*Run.*"

Time seemed to slow as I looked over Garret's shoulder and saw the glint of a battle-axe. For a moment, nothing existed but those wicked double blades. Nothing but the man's gloved fist, tightening around the handle. The roaring in my head.

Then Garret shoved me into the parlor, and time sped up once more. He slammed the door and pushed a desk across it, the screech singing in my teeth.

"Out the back!" He yanked me toward the opposite door.

And stopped short as three more figures stalked from that doorway.

All were hooded and weapons-strapped, with black masks concealing everything but their eyes.

I began to tremble.

This was really happening. The Capewells had finally found me out.

They prowled closer, and my breaths sawed out hot and fast, the scene taking on a nightmare quality. I'd expected royally embellished uniforms, indicating their service to the Crown. I'd expected to recognize individuals among them, even masked.

I'd been wrong on both fronts. I must've never met these particular Hunters, because I couldn't identify anyone amid this display of worn, armored leather and combat knives.

I would never know which of my family members had been sent to kill me.

Garret tugged me behind him. "Be calm, Alissa." He would reason with them—tell them they'd made a mistake.

But my stomach plunged when he dropped into a fighting stance. Like he knew he couldn't dissuade them.

Like he hoped instead to shield me from their blades.

Something collided with the door, rattling the desk, and my specter fed off my panic. The power curled in on itself—*shrinking*—as the figures dispersed around the parlor.

One figure by the hearth, where Amarie warmed her hands each night; one by the window, where Tari and I always watched the snowfall; one by the armchair, where Father's slippers poked between the legs. The slippers were old and shedding fabric, and a new pair sat wrapped in my closet for Father's birthday. And suddenly all I wanted was to fall to my knees and beg—not for my life, but for a moment to retrieve those slippers, because Father wouldn't think to buy them for himself and his feet would be cold once I was gone.

Once I was gone.

The thought lashed around me, near-choking. How would Father survive this? He would return to find the Hunters' Mark on our door, and it would break him—*kill* him.

I'd scrubbed the mark this morning. I'd brought this upon us both.

The door splintered under the axe, and Amarie screamed. The Hunters pounced on Garret in the distraction.

He moved fast—dodging one figure, punching another in the ribs. He was reaching under his blazer when the smallest Hunter landed a blow that sent him careening into the drinks table.

Crystal shattered and Garret's blood rained over the shards.

"No!" I stumbled forward, tripping against the table. I gasped as broken crystal sliced my palm, but I didn't feel the pain.

"Alissa." Garret's whisper sounded clogged with blood. "Don't show them. Don't—"

They yanked him away from me; forced him to his knees; twisted his arms behind his back. I lurched toward him again but the tallest Hunter blocked me, one palm on his sheathed weapon, the other rising—

I staggered back, my rapid breaths spinning me off balance. *Not here, please not here.* I didn't want Amarie to see them strike me.

I didn't want Father to find my teeth.

The door crashed open, stalling the Hunter's hand. It wasn't a mercy.

The largest of the four—the axe-wielding Hunter—eclipsed the threshold, muscles rippling under leather. His gaze locked on mine, and he advanced.

My specter coiled tighter with each pounding step, and I held myself rigid. Stripped bare of the jewels and the charm and the bloodline—of every tool that had ever saved me.

These brutes had violated my home. Yet I'd never felt more like a criminal.

The Hunter was a foot away when Amarie darted between us. The moment layered within a breath—his hand reaching for her arm, her face shying away, the fury sharpening my panic to a knifepoint.

My limbs unfroze. I pushed Amarie aside and shoved the Hunter—hard.

He stumbled back, blinking in shock. His armor glistened with a streak of my blood.

"You do not touch her," I snarled.

The room tensed, heavy breathing all around. The axe-wielding Hunter glanced darkly at the arm I'd stretched in front of Amarie, and I had a terrible premonition of him hacking it off.

But I'd promised myself I wouldn't shrink like a coward before the Hunters. I would face them with my chin high. So I didn't balk, even as my vision throbbed with my ragged pulse. Even as the man's hazel eyes flickered over me in grim assessment—and then, scowling, he drew a glass vial from his pocket.

Dullroot.

I'd always dreaded to learn how the poison would feel, stifling my specter and robbing me of any chance at fighting back. After eighteen years, I should've been ready to find out. But amid Garret's struggling, and Amarie's weeping, and my own racehorse heartbeat kicking against my ribs, there came the same crashing realization that every Hunted Wielder must have experienced before me:

I wasn't ready to die.

I felt far from my body—numb with disbelief—as the Hunter thumbed the cork off the vial and held it out.

"Drink," he ordered, low and guttural.

I stiffened, recognizing the too-sweet scent emanating from the cloudy liquid. This wasn't dullroot, the specter poison. It was nightmilk.

And I knew what that much nightmilk would do.

His leather glove groaned around the axe. "*Drink.*"

My ears rang, a more powerful dread seeping into me. This wasn't right.

Then the smallest Hunter raised a knife to Garret's throat in warning. And I took the vial, my shaky fingers smearing blood against the glass. Amarie sobbed her prayers as I brought the vial to my lips.

"Don't," Garret said. His eyes brimmed with sudden fear and regret.

But there was nothing to regret. Despite the bitter distance between us, Garret had tried to protect me tonight. They would hurt him for his disobedience.

I couldn't let them kill him for it.

Slowly, so my free hand appeared lost in the folds of my skirts, I reached for my mother's coin. I squeezed, feeling its face imprint my palm. Then I drew my hand behind me and dropped the coin to the carpet.

I didn't want the Hunters to bury it with me. To bury *her* again.

My eyes blurred on Father's slippers as I tipped the nightmilk into my mouth. I lasted four seconds before the vial slipped from my fingers. An arm looped around my waist to catch me.

No—not an arm—

Garret yelled my name. My knees gave way.

 # 5

Crackling torches. Flickering heat.

I inhaled the scent of earth and rotting wood, mingled with the saccharine aftertaste of nightmilk threatening to drag me back under. My eyes quivered open. Dark, rock-hewn walls curved around me, rippling with torchlight. An earth-packed floor sprawled at eye level, strewn with loose rocks that should've nipped my bare arms. But a thick quilt separated me from the ground, my head angled so the hairpins wouldn't bite into my scalp.

As the grogginess faded, guilt took its place. Heavy, smothering guilt that made me want to curl up and wait for the Hunters to finish the job.

What would I do without you, my girl?

My father would outlive his only child. He would come apart from the loss. Though he couldn't bear to talk about my mother's Hunting, I knew he'd only survived it because he'd had to be strong for me. But now . . .

My specter poured around me like the gauze of a death-veil—solemn, grieving—palpitating with the torch-flicker.

Then I jerked upright, blinking when my vision spun. Impossible, and yet . . . my specter flowed free, unhindered.

They hadn't dosed me with dullroot while I'd been unconscious.

I braced myself to stand, newly alert, but leaned too hard on my right hand and winced. A bandage wrapped my palm.

I unraveled it, confused—then remembered too late that I'd cut myself on broken crystal. Salve glistened along a shallow slice in my palm, slightly numbing the area.

The Hunters had tended my wound?

I hauled myself up, and my shoe connected with something round—an apple, now rolling across the ground until it *plonked* against a wooden door.

Heart slamming, I peeked through the keyhole. A torchlit passage stretched outside. Judging from the earthen walls, I had to be underground.

I pulled the door handle. Locked. I loosed a curl of my specter—then stilled it.

Don't show them, Garret had said. But hadn't the Hunters' compass already identified me as a Wielder? They wouldn't have brought me here unless—

A chill stole over me, my specter thinning out in open air.

The Capewells must have been waiting for me to unlock this door. I'd made a mockery of their family dynasty, and now Briar wanted me to sign the confession.

She wanted me to nail my own coffin shut before she buried me.

I could remain and plead innocent, using my confinement as proof. But could I stop them from torturing an admission out of me? The vicious image flashed: Briar shattering my bones—*enjoying* it.

If I possessed any chance of returning to Father, I had to take it now.

My specter jittered through the keyhole, producing a *click*; the door opened silently. I paused, listening for far-off movement. Then I bundled my skirts and staggered ahead.

The walls smeared past me, the torch heat drying my eyes. I counted the dead ends—three, four, five. Dirt burrowed into my velvet shoes, chafing my feet.

Six dead ends. Seven.

My breathing was growing frantic when voices trickled toward me.

I stumbled outside an earth-carved room, my shadow wavering. I pressed a trembling hand over my mouth and peered inside. The four Hunters sat around a rickety table, masked and hooded, their matte leather armor absorbing the torchlight.

"It was a mistake," the largest one said. I flinched, recognizing his graveled voice. The battle-axe ran along his spine, its twin blades curving like wings. This was the Hunter who'd handed me the nightmilk. "We should've taken the boy, too."

Another Hunter scraped back his hood and mussed his buttery-blond hair, the ends falling to his shoulders. "Keil only said the girl."

"Keil also said she'd be alone."

"You should be glad she wasn't." A husky female voice issued from the smallest figure—the one who'd punched Garret, then held a knife to his throat. "At least we had some fun before we left." She clenched her fists, brown skin straining over bleeding knuckles.

My legs nearly folded. How badly had they beaten Garret for his insubordination?

For a white-hot moment, rage clouded my fear, and my specter swelled inside me—

"Goren's just mad he got shoved that hard by someone half his size," the blond Hunter said. "Bad for his reputation, you know?"

The largest Hunter—*Goren*—glowered at him, and my specter

shrank again at the look. I couldn't place his name in what I remembered of the Capewell family tree. "The boy could get in the way," Goren said. "He could stop him."

The woman chuckled. "Then we'll start sending little pieces—"

"Great gods, Osana." The blond Hunter's eyes went wide. "You have a problem, you know that?"

"Oh, so you'd rather—?"

"Enough." The last Hunter gave the woman a stony look. Lean and long-limbed, he was the one who'd raised his hand to me in the parlor. "You saw the boy when we took her," he said quietly. "He won't get in the way."

"Dashiel's right." The blond Hunter stood and adjusted his bandolier—a sash spiked with black throwing knives. "You don't fight that hard for someone you don't care about."

I swallowed thickly. I couldn't interpret most of their conversation—couldn't recognize *any* of their names. But I understood that Garret had fought for me until the end.

It was the second time he ever had. And the second time he'd lost.

"Where are you going?" Goren demanded.

The blond Hunter grabbed a waterskin from the table. "To check on our guest. Make sure the way you drove that carriage didn't give her whiplash."

I jumped back and darted around the corner.

My strides were aimless—each frantic breath a rasp of dirt—but I couldn't stop when the Hunter was approaching my empty cell.

I understood now: They were toying with me before the true torment began. Goren would use his axe. The woman would delight in finer torture, cutting off pieces of me until my specter poured out, hot and thick as blood.

Vermin, Briar had said—because she'd made me a rat in these tunnels, scrambling for escape.

She would make sure I never saw my father again.

I was beginning to shake when I rounded a corner and smacked into something smooth and solid and distinctly human.

I skidded back—almost fell—when strong hands steadied me at the waist, gathering me against an armored chest. I gaped up into an unmasked face. Into brown eyes so light they were almost golden.

Those eyes dipped over me and widened. The man's grip went loose.

I lurched off his chest, a scream rising in my throat. My heels caught the back of my skirts. I sucked a sharp breath; my world tipped.

And I felt it. An embrace of power molding behind me, cushioning my fall.

A *specter*.

It thrummed against my skin with a steady heartbeat, familiar and foreign all at once. I didn't move—didn't *breathe*—as the embrace scooped me upright and my feet found solid ground.

A last graze of pressure, and the specter broke like a wave around my shoulders. The man inhaled deeply, smiling as if it filled him up.

"You're a Wielder," I breathed. Tears burned my throat.

His laughter was low and melodic. "Don't worry, my lady. We aren't half as terrible as the rumors claim." He winked. "Not all of us, at least."

My specter trembled, hands twitching to reach for his honey-bright skin—to grab his broad shoulders and *shake*, just to prove he was real.

He leaned back, a charming smile still playing around his mouth. "I could've sworn I locked that door."

The words doused me like cold water.

The absent dullroot, my captors' rugged attire, their unfamiliar names. *Don't show them*, Garret had said, because he'd known in the parlor what I hadn't yet understood. That my greatest fear had been warping reality. These people didn't know what I was...

Because they weren't the Hunters.

The realization crashed into me, and for one mortifying second, I thought I would collapse from relief—

Then the man's meaning sank in. If I hadn't been Hunted, I'd been kidnapped—and I could easily guess why kidnappers would target a ruling lord's daughter. This man—this *Wielder*—had brought me here as ransom. And he'd locked the door behind me.

A Wholeborn would not have gotten out.

I gulped, my mind racing as the silence stretched taut. "I picked the lock."

The man lifted an eyebrow.

"With my hairpins," I added, hoping the lie was half-credible.

He slanted his head, gold-brown hair almost tickling the curved ceiling. "I don't know many nobles who can pick locks."

My eyes narrowed. "I don't know many Wielders who kidnap nobles."

"Do you know many Wielders?"

"Do *you*?"

His smile deepened. "A few."

Before I could digest those words, footsteps pounded behind me. I whirled to find Goren storming through the passage, torch flames juddering in his wake. I staggered back toward the Wielder, my specter rising inside me.

Then Goren jerked to a stop. Another stride—and he pitched away again, as if an invisible wall stood before him.

My eyes widened, searching what seemed like empty space. The Wielder must have erected his specter in front of Goren, obstructing his path. But unlike with my own specter, I found no ripple-shimmer to betray its position. I didn't know how far this Wielder could stretch his power, or how he chose to mold it. It could be anywhere at any time—harmless under the Wielder's instruction, but so was a fist before it swung. And, invisible to all but its own Wielder, a swing from a specter was one that nobody would see coming.

I hadn't realized until now how unnerving that could be. How dangerous.

Goren rolled his neck. "We don't know how she got out."

"Apparently, our lovely friend can pick locks," the Wielder answered smoothly.

Goren shot me a glare. I fumbled another step, wincing as I hit the Wielder's armor.

The Wielder sighed, his chest grazing my back. "I'll handle this, Goren."

"She's seen your face."

My breath caught. I wasn't supposed to escape that cell—to know my kidnappers' faces. Now I was a liability.

"Yes, I noticed." The Wielder shifted behind me. "An unfortunate complication."

My muscles tightened to run, but I was caught between the men; moving away from the Wielder would mean moving toward Goren. And I did *not* want to move toward Goren.

"Can you draw, my lady?" the Wielder suddenly asked.

I spun toward him, and he reversed to allow room for my overflowing skirts. He looked a couple of years my senior, and, standing a whole head above me, with a powerful build and a golden, chiseled face, he should have made for an imposing figure. But his champagne eyes were soft and sparkling, his full mouth still curved with that disarming smile.

"Excuse me?" I must have misheard him.

"You're from Vereen," he said, "the province of craftspeople. Are you an artist?"

"No."

"Excellent. So, you're unlikely to render my face from memory."

"She's a noble," Goren said, with an odd note of significance.

"Well, we can hardly hold that against her."

"She could—"

"Thank you, Goren." The Wielder's expression remained amiable, but his voice deepened with warning. "You may go."

I angled sideways to glance between them, goose bumps prickling my nape as the tension thickened. Then Goren marched away, head stooped against the low ceiling.

And I knew who was in charge.

I was still exhaling when warm fingers brushed mine.

"Your hand."

I snapped out of the Wielder's reach, facing him fully in the same movement.

He paused, then retreated. Offered a gentler smile. "Forgive me. It was bleeding when you arrived."

The bandage. The salve.

My brows furrowed. "You tended it."

"I expected you wouldn't want to bleed all over your dress. And we truly never intended to cause you injury."

My stare hardened. People who didn't intend to cause injury rarely ventured into kidnapping.

Straightening to my full height, I summoned the haughtiest look in my arsenal and asked, "Who are you?"

"Keil, my lady." He sketched a perfect bow. "It's a pleasure to make your acquaintance, though I regret the circumstances."

"I doubt you regret them when you orchestrated them."

His eyes flared—with surprise and a little amusement.

"Amarie," I said. "And Garret. Are they—?"

"They're back at your manor." Keil leaned against the earthen wall and crossed his arms, the movement laced with easy confidence. "Your house manager is unharmed, but I hear the boy put up quite a fight for you."

The boy. The others had called him that, too. Like the rest of Daradon's citizens, my kidnappers didn't know who the Capewells truly were.

Which meant they'd beaten Garret for sport.

My skin heated, my specter teeming near the surface. "Your cronies attacked him for trying to protect me. From what I heard, they enjoyed it."

"Is that so?" Keil looked me over, contemplating. Then he said, with that infuriating smile, "I'll tell my *cronies* to be quieter when discussing their unsavory pastimes."

I clenched my fists. Keil's quick eyes tracked the movement, but he didn't so much as tense. Judging from the nicks and scratches across his matte black armor, he was a fighter as well as a Wielder. And *I* was . . . a walking meringue. He didn't see me as a threat. Yet.

I lifted my chin. "Do you know what you've done by bringing me here? My father is the ruling lord of the most affluent province in the kingdom."

"Then, may I suggest he invest in guards?"

"Oh, he doesn't have to. Do you know why? Because any fool knows that threatening a ruling family is the same as threatening the king. And *nobody* escapes the king's wrath." I dropped my voice, leaned closer. And though I hated myself a little for my next words, I said them without flinching. "It'll be worse for you, because of what you are. The king will give you to his Hunters. They will poison you, and bleed you, and show you no mercy. So if you're half as smart as you clearly think you are, you'll return me to my home before they make you wish you'd stayed in whatever hidey-hole you crawled out from."

A pause, to let his fear sink in. Then I stepped back. Waited.

Keil shouldered off the wall and unfolded his arms. "That's quite a speech," he said pleasantly. "I liked that last part especially, about the hidey-hole. Did you come up with it yourself, or does every noble learn to recite it for occasions such as these?"

I blinked. Though I wasn't a fighter, I knew how to aim my words—where to strike for impact, where to make it *hurt*. The threat of the Hunters should've buckled any Wielder in Daradon. So why was he still standing?

"Is this a challenge to you?" I asked. "You want to see how much gold or land you can get from my father?"

"Ransoming nobles for their fathers' lands . . ." Keil hummed. "I should have thought of that sooner. Now that you mention it, does it snow at your estate? I'm in the market for a winter home."

I gawked up at him. The Capewells had slaughtered Marge for existing. I couldn't imagine what they would do to a Wielder who'd committed kidnap and ransom. Keil was risking everything—his secret, his safety—and he was making *jokes*?

"I hope a winter home is worth a punishment worse than death," I said.

He chuckled. "I'd hardly call your company *a punishment worse than death.*" With that, he sidled past me, his body brushing my shoulder in the narrow space. "If you will, my lady." He made a sweeping gesture, one powerful arm outstretched.

"Is that the way out?"

"If I told you it was, would you walk with me?"

"I'm not going anywhere with you." I planted my feet. "I'm leaving. Now."

"As you like." Keil continued down the passage. "When your father arrives, I'll be sure to tell him you popped out for some air."

I wavered. Even if I found the exit, Father was on his way with whatever ransom Keil had demanded. What if I escaped, only to leave him at the mercy of my captors?

No. Running wasn't an option. I could be trapped here with Keil, or trapped alone.

At the thought of encountering Goren, I swallowed my pride and rushed after the Wielder.

6

Keil moved painfully slowly, sauntering like a predator who'd finished his hunt and was now enjoying the meal. He took several turns to confuse me, but it wasn't necessary. My thoughts revolved grimly around one scenario: whipping my specter against the back of his head.

For now, I would play the helpless Wholeborn noblewoman and await rescue. But what if Keil had demanded something Father couldn't give? What if they hurt him as they'd hurt Garret? I had to protect him, even though I couldn't tell how powerful Keil's specter was—or how powerful *mine* was in comparison.

Even though the idea of fighting another Wielder hollowed my stomach.

The rhythmic scrape of metal on metal drifted over our footfalls, and I paused outside another concave room. The woman, Osana, sharpened a dagger over a tabletop of weapons, her blade humming across the honing steel.

"Give it a rest," said the blond man, lounging in a chair. He was using a throwing knife to peel an apple in one long spiral. "You could fillet a sea serpent with that blade."

"At least I'm being productive while *you* have a picnic."

"You should join me, unless you want to be embarrassed at the exchange. Nothing intimidating about a growling belly."

Osana gave him a rude gesture and tossed her weapon to the table. Another dagger floated to take its place.

I heard a soft gasp—then realized it had come from me. My hand drifted across my waist. In the parlor, I'd felt a curling grasp as the nightmilk had taken hold . . . not an arm. The tendril of a specter.

It wasn't just Keil. They were *all* Wielders.

"Show-off," the blond man muttered.

A dagger shot at him like a dart. He caught the handle and twisted his wrist, slashing Osana's invisible hold. She hissed, recoiling. But she would recover quickly. Permanently tethered to their Wielders, specters coalesced after injury. There was only one way to amputate a specter from its Wielder:

The Wielder had to die.

According to old texts, all power began its life cycle in spectral form—born with the Wielder whose body housed it. But while Wielders brought power into the world, they didn't take it out with them. After a Wielder's death, the specter sloughed from the body like a snakeskin and remained within the world as a raw, intangible power—the exact power that had once been harnessed by the ancient Spellmakers.

My old tutor—a miserable woman who'd considered me a spoiled Wholeborn heiress—had therefore claimed that Wholeborn spirits passed happily to the next realm while Wielder spirits were forever chained here by their lingering specters.

When I'd sobbed to Father, fearing for my mother's chained spirit, he'd permanently dismissed the tutor. And though his face had grown weary with grief, he'd swallowed his pain to ease mine.

Taking my little hands, he'd reassured me that my mother was at peace, but that a part of her—the echo of power that had once been her specter—would always linger in this realm beside me. *Watching over us*, he'd said.

More curious than comforted, I'd enlisted Tari to come "digging" for molted specters with a garden fork. I'd used my specter to lift the fork by its sharp tines, and the steel had sliced ribbons through my spectral muscle like flesh.

I knew from experience: The injuries *hurt*.

Now the blond man groaned, reaching down. "You made me drop my apple." He palmed the fruit, then began lifting his mask as if to blow off the dirt.

Keil cleared his throat, and I jolted. I hadn't felt him come up behind me, so close that I could smell the leather of his armor. He watched me curiously, his strong jaw tilted to catch the torchlight. I'd seen the same look on Verenian clockmakers before they dismantled a timepiece to study its parts.

An *oops* sound returned my focus to the blond man, whose hand hovered over his mask.

But Osana had gone stiff, her eyes trained on me. And despite the power she'd displayed, I returned her glare before continuing ahead.

The man's sharp whisper trailed after us. "Don't give her that look. You'll scare her."

"Did she look scared to you?" Osana growled, and their voices faded from earshot.

My heart raced as we continued down the passage, panic and amazement battling for the greatest share of my agitation. *Five Wielders*. Four more than I'd imagined having to fight two minutes ago . . . but also four more than I'd imagined meeting in my lifetime.

How had they kept hidden, especially clustered together? Were there *more* of them?

A pulse-skip brought me to my senses. I'd better hope there weren't more of them. This group had kidnapped me, had *hurt* Garret. They were criminals first and Wielders second.

I couldn't forget it.

Keil stopped ahead of me, foot propped against the door of my feeble cell. I stormed past him, faltering when I noticed a chair in the earthen room, stacked with a cloak, a waterskin, and three new apples. All courtesy of the blond man, no doubt.

Footsteps shuffled behind me, and I turned to find Keil holding a long strip of white cloth. "Your hand, please, my lady."

I stepped back, wary.

He nodded to the fist I'd clenched around my skirts. "To rebandage your wound."

"That's not necessary," I said, concerned that he might try to bind my wrists instead.

"I really must insist. Leaving a wound open in this environment risks infection." He held his free hand out to me, palm open. "It won't take a moment."

The crackling of the torches filled the silence as I remained tense, unmoving. After a beat, Keil seemed to realize why.

"I mean only to dress the wound," he said, voice softening. "Truly."

I glanced skeptically between his broad palm and his bright, earnest eyes.

Slowly, I lifted my hand.

Keil met me halfway, his body shifting with the low groan of leather, his warm fingers taking mine. Cradling the back of my hand, he angled my palm to assess the cut. The salve shone in the firelight, and guilt flickered in his eyes.

Then, as promised, he began dressing the wound.

He worked quickly but gently, layering the bandage over and under my thumb, his fingers brushing my skin with every wrap around. He was securing the fabric at my wrist when he broke the quiet.

"I don't want your father's gold."

I glanced up at him but found no trace of amusement. Only a solemn shadow, passing like mist across his face.

"Something was stolen from me." His fingers paused, gaze still lowered to my hand. "This is the only way I know to get it back."

I startled, and only Keil's hold on the bandage kept me from tearing away.

"My father is no thief," I ground out.

Keil tied off the bandage in silence, his jaw flickering. He was still holding my wrist loosely in his palm when his eyes lifted to mine—searching, considering something.

Then he said, quietly, "He's a Capewell, isn't he? They're all thieves."

"The *Capewells* . . . ?" I blinked. Slowly shook my head.

It should've been impossible. The Capewells safeguarded their identities as the king's Hunters, even to their own displeasure. But from the way Keil was looking at me, with bleak confirmation . . . he knew exactly what the Capewells were.

My stomach plunged. *They will poison you, and bleed you, and show you no mercy,* I'd threatened. These Wielders surely wanted revenge against the monsters who threatened their existence.

And I might have just enticed them to start with me.

I ripped my hand away and stumbled back, heart pounding. It was too cruel—too ironic—these Wielders killing me because of my Hunter blood.

Keil took a backstep of his own, clearly sensing my fresh panic. "You're in no danger, my lady." He spoke measuredly, holding my stare. "I'm not in the business of punishing innocents for the misfortune of their bloodlines."

"No? Then why am I here?" My voice whipped out sharper than I'd expected. "You think the Capewells stole something from you—"

"I don't *think* anything."

"Yes, that much is obvious," I snapped. "If you'd given this kidnapping scheme two seconds of thought, you would've realized that my father and I are *Paines*. We have no interest in the Capewells or their business."

"You and the young Capewell seem concerned for one another. Garret, wasn't it?"

"Garret is . . ." Guilt stalled my tongue. *Garret is not a Capewell*, I'd almost said.

I told myself I wasn't defending the Hunter; I was defending the person who'd tried to protect me tonight. But Keil's Wielders had beaten Garret—had *enjoyed* it—for a reason.

Because Garret had deserved it.

"Garret is none of your business," I said instead, flushed with equal shame and indignation. "The Capewells won't give you whatever it is you want. Not for me."

"Don't feel too wounded, my lady." Keil crossed his arms. "I hear the Capewells wouldn't sacrifice a hot bath to save one of their own. But your father is one of the few outsiders who can access Capewell Manor. And now, the only one with incentive."

Capewell Manor.

I tasted bile.

"What you wish to retrieve is at Capewell Manor," I said. "You've ordered my father into the heart of the Hunters' territory."

"Yes," Keil replied, unflinching.

He was going to get my father killed.

My specter coursed fast, pooling at my fingertips. The bandage cushioned the bite of my nails as my right hand curled into a fist.

Again, Keil noted the movement. But this time, he uncrossed his arms and widened his stance. And I knew he wasn't waiting to intercept my fist. He was offering me easier access if I chose to strike him.

He was waiting for the blow.

I slowly inhaled. "You seek something from the Hunters," I said darkly. "You possess the uncommon advantage of knowing where to find them, as well as a team to confront them. Yet you would rather ransom an innocent man's daughter to get what you want." I forced my fist to uncurl, my specter to settle. "I will not bruise my knuckles on the face of a coward."

Keil's expression became unreadable. The torchlight sputtered behind him, gilding his armor and playing through the bronze in his hair. "Perhaps," he said slowly, "your father is not as innocent as you'd like to believe."

I drew up at the cruel accusation. Father had never involved himself with the Hunters. And he never would.

"Perhaps," I echoed, fury blistering over my better judgment, "whatever the Capewells did to you was no more than you deserved."

Keil went rigid, and my specter lashed inside me with self-reproach. I'd gone too far.

But rather than the anger I'd anticipated, Keil's face crumpled with something like sorrow. "You're not what I expected, Lady Alissa." He spoke tightly, as if the admission pained him. "I'm impressed."

I looked him over—the first Wielder I'd ever truly met—and blew out a breath of sour laughter. "And I am profoundly disappointed."

Keil offered a sad smile, then paused with one foot out the door.

A feather-touch trailed my scalp, and I gasped as my hair came loose, dark waves spilling like silk around my shoulders. My hairpins glinted through the air and assembled in Keil's waiting hand.

"Forgive me, my lady." He nodded to the keyhole. "For the lock."

My mouth was still hanging open when the door clicked shut.

 # 7

I paced between the curved walls, my skirts dragging dirt toward my heels. With each turn, my hatred for Briar Capewell grew.

Not only had she failed to conceal the Capewells' service to the Crown—a secret her ancestors had kept for two centuries—but the wretched woman couldn't even be content with executing my people. She had to steal from them, too.

And now these Wielders had entangled Father in her mess.

My specter throbbed, and I let it stream in ribbons around me to ease the internal strain.

Keil was wrong about Father. *I* stood a better chance of accessing Capewell Manor, and only because Garret had once sneaked me inside himself.

We'd been children—aged eight and ten—with a brash, heroic plan to steal the Hunters' compass and protect Daradon's Wielders from exposure. We made a game of it—pouring tar across the corridors, stringing twine between the walls to trip pursuers. We'd just reached Wray Capewell's office when Briar caught us snooping through her brother's belongings.

It should've been funny—her tar-squelching shoeprints, her blotchy anger. But suddenly, nothing about this was funny. Garret was braver than me, was actually opening his mouth to laugh.

Then Briar struck him so hard that he bit his own tongue.

I shrieked as her arm rose a second time—and Briar found the sound so aggravating that she whipped her hand across my face instead. I sobbed while she smiled down at me. Her hand lifted again, slowly, its shadow looming over me before the release.

And Garret's eyes took on a dark glimmer.

He pounced upon her back, took a fistful of her hair, and pulled. Tearing and biting and punching, he fought her, like a wild canine having broken out of its cage. Briar was bleeding, too, as she dealt him three more blows. Then we fled—back into the booby-trapped hallways and out through the manor's escape tunnel.

I told Father we'd tripped down the mosaic steps in town, and spent the evening pressing a cool cloth to Garret's bruises.

I won't let her turn me into a Hunter, he'd said that night, battered and proud. *I don't care what she does to me. She can't make me become like her.*

And for the first time, I'd imagined my life sprawling out beside his. I'd been too young to name or understand the feeling; I'd only known that Garret felt like home.

Then, three years later, Garret's adoptive father, Wray, had died. And at thirteen, Garret had been orphaned all over again.

I begged Father to take in Garret as his ward—to stop Briar digging her claws into him. But by the time Father relented and I summoned Garret to deliver the news, it was too late. My specter rushed out to meet him, flickering fast with my excitement.

And Garret recoiled from it. Stepped back.

A locked bracelet glinted at his wrist.

Put your dirty specter on me again, he'd said in a voice that was no longer his own, *and I'll cut through it, Wielder.*

He could have hit me in that moment, and it would've hurt less.

That quickly, my world had shifted. And I never put my specter on him again.

The wisps of power slid back to me now, quieted by the memories. Garret had fought for me tonight—had acted as the boy he'd been rather than the man he'd become.

I was still considering what that meant when a knock jolted me from my reverie.

A *knock*. As if this cell were a dressing room and I was busy primping myself.

The door opened and I tensed. Though I could only see the man's dark eyes framed by deep brown skin, I recognized his lean build.

Dashiel. The one who'd raised his hand to me in the parlor.

He approached, arm lifting again, and I inhaled sharply—

Then he stopped, one palm held up and facing out. Just as he'd held it in the parlor.

A retrospective lens slipped over the memory, bathing it in a new light. Dashiel hadn't raised his palm to strike me. In the chaos of my kidnapping, he'd shown his open palm in reassurance—to signal *peace*.

He must have seen my dread melting, because he now gestured to the door. "This way, my lady."

I tentatively approached, and a *swoosh* sounded from behind. I jumped as the cloak billowed from the chair and deflated around Dashiel's arm.

He held it forward. "You may get cold."

I stared wide-eyed, my specter humming at the display. Such free, careless Wielding—from all of them. How had this kingdom not beaten the impulse out of them?

How had it never gotten them *killed?*

"I'll be fine," I said shakily, and Dashiel led me away.

He slowed to accommodate my footwear, even offering his arm when the tunnels darkened. Then we approached a wooden ladder, and I bundled my skirts. Dashiel had the good grace to turn his head while I climbed.

The night-fresh air blasted hair into my eyes, so I wasn't prepared when warm hands encircled my waist to hoist me up. I gasped, automatically grabbing on to strong shoulders for purchase. I didn't let go until Keil—now masked and hooded—set me gently to my feet.

"My lady," he said in soft greeting, making sure I was steady before stepping back.

I skewered him with a glare he didn't return. He held my gaze a moment longer, infuriatingly calm, then turned toward a tree-lined path, ground lanterns spilling light across his boots.

A field sprawled around us, long grass combed to one side under the current of wind. Seated under a dip of grassland and tangled with shoots, the tunnel opening could've led to the burrow of a large animal. I was watching Dashiel emerge from it when a stronger wind ruffled my sleeves, carrying a familiar sour-noted fragrance.

My eyes darted to the trees. In darkness, the blossoms seemed pale as parchment. But come morning, they would glisten like fallen stars.

"We're still in Vereen," I said, half-dazed. Penny blossom trees were native to my province, where craftspeople crushed their silver petals into shimmering dyes.

Dashiel nodded, brushing off his trousers. "You know your land well."

I looked back toward the tunnel entry with new understanding. Of course these Wielders had stationed themselves here.

Vereen's underground hosted a wealth of ancient xerylite mines, many of which had been used as strongholds during the Starling Rebellion. While the coordinates had since been stricken from public files—with only my father holding the records—the tunnels had remained an emblem of defiance. Of Wielders, fighting back.

And apparently, their locations weren't forgotten.

I inched toward the entry, curiosity rousing my specter.

"Stay there," Goren barked, with the sternness of someone setting a naughty child on a countertop. I stumbled, not realizing how close he'd been standing. Or that he'd been glowering at me, biceps bulging as he scraped his ash-brown hair into a topknot.

I took another backstep. Keil may not punish innocents for their lineage, but Goren had made no such promises. And right now, the Hunters' blood felt heavier—more dangerous—than the specter under my skin.

"You won't be harmed, my lady." Dashiel shot Goren a disapproving look.

Goren grunted, snapping his hood down.

The grass rustled, and I turned to see the blond man swaggering toward us, twirling a throwing knife between quick fingers. "Hello, lockpicker." His bright green eyes betrayed a wicked smile. "I'm Lye. Lysander, really, but I don't expect anyone to bother with that many syllables."

"This isn't a dinner party," said Goren.

"It's not? Huh. That explains the lack of appetizers."

"Get in position."

"Oh, don't be grouchy in front of the lady." Lye sheathed the knife through his bandolier. "You're the one who said we didn't need to guard the door."

"And what would you have done if you'd caught her escaping? Offered her a map?"

"If she asked nicely." Lye threw me another eye-crinkling grin. "Good thing you didn't see *me* walking around without a mask. People have been known to swoon."

"*Get in position,*" Goren growled again.

Lye rolled his eyes and wedged between us. He leaned down, voice low with mischief. "I've never picked a lock with hairpins. Who taught you?"

I was spared from having to answer as footfalls thumped toward us.

"Rider sighted," Osana panted, slowing to a jog. "Prepare for conflict."

My stomach lurched. "Wait. *Conflict*—"

"Armed?" Keil asked.

Her eyes flicked to me and hardened. "Armed," she confirmed.

A beat of silence. Then the Wielders snapped into fighting stances, eyes forward and feet apart. Lye's throwing knives whistled from their sheaths; Keil moved to my other side. I bustled against them, hemmed in.

"*Wait,*" I said, blood rushing. "My father wouldn't be armed. She's made a mistake."

Osana shot me a murderous look, fingers twitching toward her dagger.

"Easy," Keil murmured, gaze fixed on the path.

"You have to listen to me," I pressed. "My father is not a threat—"

Wheels clacked on the path, silencing me.

Steel flashed as Goren flipped his axe. "We strike first?"

"No!" I said. I would fight these Wielders to protect my father, but gods—*oh, gods*—I desperately didn't want to.

Keil looked down at me—a brief, broad assessment—then frowned back at the path. "Let him show his hand. We retaliate if we must." He added, with a glance at Lye, "Keep her out of the crossfire."

Lye nodded, and I was caught halfway between relief and alarm—there was going to be crossfire?!—when an enclosed wagon rolled into view, and the air hitched in my throat.

Because riding at its seat was not Father.

It was Garret.

 # 8

Garret's face was darkly splotched and swollen, one eye nearly sealed shut. He held the reins rigidly, wincing as the seat jostled. Even after Briar's attack ten years ago, I'd never seen him so battered. And though this was a fraction of the suffering he'd brought to countless Wielders—the suffering he could easily inflict upon *me*—my specter rushed up, ready to reach for him. To lay itself like a poultice against his tender skin as if to draw his pain away.

Garret's cargo creaked to a stop and he unseated, his blazer drifting open. Double holsters sat tucked against his ribs, knife hilts angled for easy reach. *Armed*, as Osana had said—but she hadn't been talking about Father.

Dread seeped into me as Garret faced us. *Why isn't Father here?*

Keil stepped forward and the air grew charged. "You are not Lord Heron," he said, his voice harsher than I'd heard it yet.

Garret gave him a bleak look. "You're astute."

"Where is he?" I asked, heart rate climbing. If Briar had caught him at Capewell Manor—if she'd hurt him because of whatever these Wielders had demanded—

"I told him to stay behind," Garret said. My knot of worry tightened.

"He wouldn't have agreed to that."

"He didn't have a choice."

"Why not?" I pressed.

Garret cocked his head at Keil. "Do you let all your hostages lead their own ransom exchanges?"

"Answer the question," Keil ordered.

Garret released a strained, impatient breath. "Heron *complied* because he couldn't have accessed what you wanted without my help. How fortunate, then, that your acquaintances left me so generously intact."

Keil folded his arms. Even Lye tensed beside me.

Then Garret hissed as his blazer flapped wide. His knives scraped from their holsters and thudded to the grass. His waistcoat buttons popped open; his trousers rippled; his silk pockets turned out.

By the time Keil's specter finished disarming him, a scattering of weapons encircled Garret's feet, each blade a bright shard in the moonlight.

Garret raised his scarred eyebrow. "Satisfied?"

"Not nearly," said Keil.

My temper spiked. While they were out-posturing each other, Father awaited my return.

"This is ridiculous." I bunched my skirts and marched forward, shoes sinking into the grass.

I made it five feet before rebounding off Keil's specter.

The sensation was so shocking—sending tingles across my skin—that I almost didn't notice Osana and Dashiel shooting ahead of me. They skimmed around Garret, opened the wagon, and climbed inside. Dust swirled out in a flash of lantern light before the doors slammed shut.

My specter pulsated near the surface as Keil slunk beside me, his hood rippling in the breeze. He'd claimed the Capewells had stolen something from him; judging by the wagon size, it had to be some kind of weapon.

I couldn't imagine the depth of Father's terror tonight—and all for a *weapon*?

I went to bite out the accusation when I noticed that Keil's eyes had gone distant on the wagon. His fists contracted; his shoulders rolled. Was he . . . nervous?

Slowly, with my unbandaged hand, I reached in front of me. Keil and I jolted at the same time—him, at my unexpected touch. And me, as I met with his specter.

Having encountered various Wielders in Bormia, Tari once told me that specters weren't equal in strength. Some were as thin as organza—a film of power, comparable to a weak muscle. Others rippled with force, far mightier than any corporeal limb. My initial contact with Keil's specter had stunned me out of proper awareness. But now, I knew undoubtedly that his specter belonged in the latter category.

I could feel his energy within its contours, pulsing with a wild heartbeat, humming with inhuman strength. I drove forward cautiously, testing the resistance—the tensed spectral muscle barring my way.

Its rhythm flickered. Hesitated. Then I gasped softly as the power reshaped, molding like clay around my fingers.

Keil was reducing its solidity to allow me access.

He must have been watching me now—confused, curious—because the thrum of his specter slowed, the ripples lapping against me with a searching intent.

Being more accustomed to Wielding slim, sinuous tendrils that flowed unnoticed through the world, I rarely stretched my power this way. It was magnificent... *beautiful.*

My own specter strained, aching to break the surface.

The wagon door thwacked open, and my head snapped up. Keil's specter began peeling away.

No. I automatically grasped, clenching for a final touch. At my reaction, Keil paused. His specter enveloped my hand again, thin and uncertain, then pulsed gently against my fingers before threading past them in silent farewell.

I touched empty air and lingered, hollowed by a deep sadness.

Then the moment returned to me, as cold as the nipping wind.

Garret was looking grimly toward the vacant space I'd been exploring. But beside him, Dashiel was emerging from the wagon alone, moving stiffly as he closed the doors.

Something was wrong.

"He's short," Dashiel said, unleashing the wagon from Garret's horse. "By many."

I recognized Garret's too-fast blink, that slight straining of his neck. He was suddenly unnerved.

"Where are the rest, Capewell?" Keil demanded.

"I emptied the hold, as you asked." Garret's voice remained deceivingly calm. "We don't tend to... *store* our acquisitions. You were lucky we kept these for so long."

Dashiel stiffened further. *"Lucky?"*

I frowned toward the wagon doors—toward that hazy strip of light pouring from between them. How many *somethings* had the Capewells stolen, exactly?

"He's lying," Goren snapped from behind.

"Why should it benefit me to lie?" Garret asked. "Or to withhold from you that which I have no desire to keep?" He jerked his chin toward the wagon. "There are five there. Surely you found the one among them you really wanted."

Keil held his breath, waiting. Dashiel gave a hard nod, and Keil's chest deflated.

The reaction unsettled me.

"Well, then." Garret smoothed his blazer. "I've relinquished all I can. I suggest you let that be enough, since you can't relinquish a fraction of *your* leverage."

"Is that a challenge?" Goren's rough voice preceded the whoosh of his axe-flip.

Garret stared over my shoulder, his expression bored. Cold. "If you wanted to hurt her, you would have already. You wish to do so now, out of spite?" He smiled—a bruised, skin-splitting smile—and met my gaze as he said, "Go ahead."

I hated myself for flinching. I hated him more for having seen it.

Garret may have fought for me in the parlor, but he'd emerged unchanged—as ruthless as he'd been for the past seven years.

"No?" he probed when the Wielders made no move against me. "Then kindly relieve us all of each other's company. This has wasted enough of my time."

Wind whistled through the silence, my specter flaring with each shallow breath.

Finally, Keil turned toward me. He reached into his pocket, and Garret tensed in my periphery.

Then Keil withdrew his hand. My hairpins shone in his palm.

"Goodbye, Lady Alissa," he said quietly. His lashes fanned low, skimming the top edge of his mask. "I pray that you can accept my apology."

I held his gaze, struggling to decipher the heavy meaning in his eyes. I gathered the hairpins, and Keil's hand twitched when my fingers grazed his palm.

Pocketing the pins, I saw Garret drag his narrowed stare between us. My face flamed inexplicably as I crunched forward again.

My breathing heaved loud in my ears, and I entered that slant of foggy light oozing from the wagon—

And my specter lurched, rocking me back a step.

Goose bumps rushed up my arms.

My hand trembled into the light, dust freckling my fingertips. I crumbled the specks against my thumb, then hissed quietly at the writhe of my specter. At the deep, internal coiling as it raced from the surface. It had reacted the same way this morning, to the same strange dust in Marge's lounge.

Horror sank through my bones as I finally realized why.

This wasn't dust. It was *ash*. An ash that specters couldn't bear to touch—it felt vile, *wrong*—because it was a product of the only poison that could stifle a specter's power.

The ash of burnt dullroot.

"Oh, gods." My words wobbled on an exhale. Because there was only one reason why this wagon would contain dullroot.

"Walk, Alissa," Garret said, glaring at me. "*Now.*"

He drew the word out, chilling and thawing me all at once. But rather than stepping toward Garret, I stepped sideways. Toward the wagon.

"You don't want to do that," he said, now with a tinge of sympathy.

He was right. I didn't want to witness this atrocity firsthand. I didn't want to bear my kidnappers' grief alongside my own. But it wasn't just morbid compulsion driving me. It was guilt.

Something was stolen from me, Keil had said. Not something. Some*one*.

There were Wielder prisoners inside this wagon.

My specter was pumping wildly now, a second heartbeat against my ribs, and I couldn't keep from turning, from reaching toward the doors—

Garret's hand enclosed my wrist. "Let's go."

"Don't touch me," I snarled, trying to yank away. But he caught my other arm. Leaned over me.

"Don't do this," he murmured. "Not in front of them."

I barely understood him. I only knew that my specter was wringing me from the inside out, and this Hunter *was still touching me—*

"You want to get back to your father?" The words lashed me, drawing me taut in his hold. He said slowly, with a look so dark that my stomach clenched, "Then *let's go*."

My pulse hammered in my throat, a wild drumbeat urging me in split directions. I glanced toward my kidnappers, who watched Garret with barely restrained fury; toward Keil, whose particular gaze had darkened on Garret's grip around my arm; and finally, toward the wagon.

Toward the Wielders who'd been imprisoned for the crime I committed every day.

Sorrow gnawed at me, my specter squirming to the point of pain. But I tightened my internal fist around it. Garret knew me better than he had the right to.

He knew I would always choose my father.

In the midst of the thick, heaving hostility, Garret retrieved his weapons and I mounted his steed, the crunch and rustle of my gown obscenely loud. Before I could adjust the puff of satin, Garret mounted behind me, trapping my skirts under him.

The motion tugged me back against his body, and we both tensed at the abrupt closeness. His holsters bracketed my ribs, knife hilts skimming me with every movement. I heard his tight swallow as he encircled me, arms hovering awkwardly to avoid leaning on my thighs. Then he snapped the reins.

My hands trembled as we moved off, and I looked over Garret's arm for a last glance of the only Wielders I would ever meet. Keil was already reaching for the wagon doors—for the prisoner he'd so desperately wanted to retrieve from Capewell Manor.

My chest panged with the next lurch of the steed.

Keil's hands were trembling, too.

 # 9

The noise woke me.

Firewood popped and embers spattered and footsteps clicked, each sound a hammer strike against my temples. I opened one eye to a smear of stark color—white walls and an orange blaze from the fire. The world throbbed around me, squeezing too tight. I groaned.

"You're awake," Garret said from beyond my hazy eyeline. "Good."

"What did you do to me?" I mumbled, easing myself up. I was lying on a hard sofa, the miserable heap of my skirts puddling off the edge. Gods, whoever designed a dress with this much fabric wanted courtiers to die painful deaths.

I touched my forehead, and my arm grazed the open side of a blazer. *Garret's* blazer, draped like a stiff blanket around my shoulders.

I frowned.

"Other than rescue you from a group of brutes despite your own efforts to thwart me?" he asked. "Nothing. You fell asleep during the ride. Your body's still working off that nightmilk, so you'll feel bleary for a while." A pause. "The food should help."

My vision blinked into clarity. A teapot piped on the low table before me, alongside hot buttered scones and an herbed pie, steam ribboning through its lattice holes. Two pink sugar cubes had been prepared inside a teacup, the way I'd always liked.

And beside the food, reflecting the flames, sat Garret's unholstered knives.

I whipped my head around, suddenly over-alert. Cold memory crashed into me. It was all here—the white sofas under flat-weave rugs, the glass ornaments on the bookcase, the orange blossoms sweetening the air—as if Wray Capewell's office had been preserved in wax for a decade.

They say this will be mine someday, a young Garret had told me minutes before Briar had caught us here. *But they're wrong. I'll have run away by then.*

You can't just leave, I'd said. *Where will you go?*

With you, obviously. Where else would I go?

The past swirled away, leaving the bitter dregs of the present. Garret had brought me to Capewell Manor.

Into the Hunters' territory.

"You really should eat something." He was talking again. "That much nightmilk will produce a headache unless—"

My specter gusted free.

A *thud*, then a grunt as my power pinned Garret against the wall, rippling fiercely, keeping him *away from me* as I scrambled for the door.

Silver flashed between his fingers. "Alissa, wait."

I wrenched the door open—then *pain*, sharp as a blade on skin. My specter smacked back to my body, and my knees hit the floor.

I doubled over, whimpering. My specter quivered against my bones.

Through spotted vision, I saw Garret set a double-edged knife atop his desk. *Put your dirty specter on me again*, he'd once said, *and I'll cut through it, Wielder.*

I'd always hoped he'd been bluffing.

Apparently not.

"Be gentle, please," he said now, disapproving. He gestured to his face: the raw bruises; the nose gashed at the bridge; the left eye, puffed and bloodshot. "I just took a beating for you, if you remember."

"Why did you bring me here?" I growled.

"It was closer than your estate." His shoes clacked forward. "And holding you upright in that saddle wasn't exactly easy. Do you know how much that dress weighs?"

I recoiled as his shadow loomed over me. But he only shut the door, locked it, and pocketed the key. Then he offered me his hand.

I ignored it.

"You can't keep me here." My specter was already convalescing; in a few seconds, I'd be able to unlock the door myself.

Garret sighed, withdrawing his hand. "And they call courtiers dramatic." He turned toward the seating area. "If I wanted to keep you here, you would've woken in the hold."

The hold.

I stood as the scenes flipped through my mind: the wagon, the dullroot ash, the instinctive recoil of my specter.

"There were people in that wagon," I said with disgust. "*Wielders.*"

"Prisoners," Garret clarified. "Briar's prisoners." He took a medicinal jar from the low table and eased into an armchair. He wore just his dark shirt tucked into tailored trousers, and his edges appeared softer than usual. But he sounded sharper than ever when he said, "How do you think she'll react if she discovers your father freed them?"

My specter shuddered. It was exactly what I'd feared when Keil had ordered Father into Capewell Manor.

"You freed them," I said.

"That Wielder's ransom note suggests otherwise. It was addressed to Heron, after all." Garret set the jar on the armrest. Began unbuttoning his shirt. "Briar was called away on business tonight. But she'll return to the hold to find her prisoners gone, and that ransom note sitting in their empty cell. I expect she'll put the pieces together."

I gaped at him, blood rushing behind my ears. This was why he'd ordered Father to stay behind. So he could plant Keil's ransom note in the hold.

And frame my father.

My cheek smarted with a phantom pain—made worse by how small this room made me feel. Briar had hit me here, had *battered* Garret when he'd only been a child.

If she believed that Father had infiltrated her territory . . . she would tear him to pieces.

"Why are you doing this?" I whispered. "My father has done nothing to you."

Anger flashed in Garret's eyes. Then they iced over again. "I can retrieve the note before Briar sees it." He unscrewed the medicinal jar. "But I'll need a reason."

My specter bristled, and I was about to ask whether keeping all his teeth was a good enough reason—

Then I glimpsed his wrist. And my legs weakened.

Garret's oath band was gone. The vow he'd sworn to the Capewells, the promise that had bound him for seven years . . . He'd been released from it.

How?

He parted his shirt, wincing, and my gaze trailed down his torso: the Hunters' Mark tattooed over his heart, the hard planes of taut bronze skin . . . and then the angry red blossom across his ribs. He dipped his fingers into the jar, and spread the salve tentatively across the bruise.

I could strike him against his injury. I could unlock the door and run. But I didn't know where the Capewells kept their Wielder prisoners; I hadn't even realized they *kept* prisoners until tonight.

I wouldn't find that ransom note before Briar returned.

And Garret knew it.

I drifted toward the glow of the fire and sat rigidly on the opposite sofa, the low table creating a barrier between us. The collar of Garret's blazer skimmed my neck, and I shrugged it off, having forgotten I was wearing it.

He frowned when I tossed it aside.

"What do you want?" I asked, shaking despite the warmth.

Garret tipped his head back, shutting his eyes as he exhausted half the jar onto his ribs. I gritted my teeth at the insult; if he was closing his eyes, he didn't consider me a worthy opponent.

The column of his throat bobbed with the words "A thank-you would be nice."

"I'm sorry?"

"You should be. Do you know how hard it's been to keep Briar off your scent all these years? There are thousands of Wielders in Daradon, all practicing self-restraint. But *you* like to spin coins and trip nobles. You like to make my job that much harder."

I straightened, baffled by the claim that Garret had been actively protecting me.

Then his other statement took hold. And my specter tingled.

"*Thousands*," I breathed.

"The Avanish family on Laurel Street. The baker who runs the winter market." He opened his eyes, watching me through dark lashes.

A mocking smile ghosted his lips. "I have a list, if you like."

"Why aren't they—?"

"Dead?" He sat up and closed the jar, his torso gleaming. I suddenly wished I'd struck him before the salve had numbed the worst of the pain. "Two centuries ago, Wielders comprised a quarter of Daradon's population. Kingdom-wide tensions made it easier to pass the Execution Decree, but the Crown couldn't target them all at once. A single specter can be more physically powerful than ten Wholeborns, and even the weakest specters have the advantage of invisibility. Given the chance to fight, the Wielders would've won.

"Instead, the Crown anointed a group of mercenary brothers—your ancestors—as Hunters, and gifted them a Spellmade compass to track Wielders. These brothers targeted Wielders after nightfall, in every corner of Daradon, so nobody could predict the next victim. Two Wielders might have lived in opposite houses, one chosen for the Hunt, the other inexplicably spared. When enough Wielders are left behind, a phenomenon occurs. The Wielders count themselves lucky. *Grateful*, even. To preserve that good luck and avoid discovery, they stifle the only power that could save them. They slink into the shadows of society, and a civil war is avoided. After all, Wielders can't unite if they're hiding from one another. And those who *try* to unite . . . Well, they're dealt with harshly enough that none follow in their footsteps." He spoke these last words pointedly—with something like satisfaction.

There had only been one attempted uprising in recent history: the Starling Rebellion. While that rebellion hadn't lasted long enough to unite Daradon's Wielders, it had cost many Wholeborn civilians their lives.

Civilians like Garret's birth parents.

How had I never considered it before—his own quiet resentment? The personal vengeance that must have transformed each kill into a catharsis? Hunters had executed my mother . . . but Wielders had slaughtered both his parents.

"So, we *all* deserve it, then?" I asked, horror-struck. "Because of the crimes of the few?"

He looked at me, long and hard, the intensity prickling my scalp. And I realized I would rather be back in those tunnels with my kidnappers. I would rather be anywhere than in this room, with the happy little teapot and the sleepy heat kissing my brow. Because despite the seven years of frost between us, I'd never felt fearful of Garret.

Until now.

Now I felt like a Wielder alone with a Hunter.

"On the contrary," he said at last, voice pitched low over the fire crackle. "Evils require balance. Hunt too much, and we arouse rebellion. Too little, and we no longer inspire fear."

"You're talking about murder."

"I'm talking about business. Executing a handful for the good of all. You've benefited from that system, haven't you? You should be gladder than anyone for the way things are."

Guilt choked me, and I bolted to my feet.

"Why are you telling me this?" I spat. "To elicit my sincerest gratitude? Fine. Thank you for not driving a knife in my gut despite how much you clearly want to. Now retrieve that note from the hold. My father has suffered enough tonight because of your *business*."

Garret's cold laughter quickened my heart rate. "Has he?"

Then he stood and moved around the table. I lurched aside, banging my knee on its edge. He cast me a scathing look before kicking up the corner of the rug.

Acid scalded my throat. Dark blood encrusted the grooves of the white wooden floor—the ten-year-old evidence of Garret's beating.

A beating he'd taken to keep Briar's hands off *me*.

"Wray made me clean my own blood," he said quietly, "as punishment for provoking Briar's hand. But I never could get this out." His bare chest swelled with a sigh, his tattoo shifting. "Do you remember that day? The booby traps along the halls. Our sprint through the escape tunnel. All to find the Hunters' compass and protect you from exposure."

"We wanted to protect all Wielders," I said.

The slightest hint of a smile. "Maybe *you* did." He kicked the rug back down, the slap of air stirring my skirts. "We wouldn't have found it lying around here, you know. Spellmade objects are coveted, and their owners are deemed *keepers*. It's a sacred position."

Because Spellmakers were once considered gods-touched individuals. Neither Wielder nor Wholeborn, they were the only beings who could harvest the molted specter left after a Wielder's death to forge objects like the compass. And unlike Wielders, whose specters were connected to their being, Spellmakers had no allegiance to the power they molded.

So, to save themselves from persecution, Spellmakers had sold their services.

They'd become the pampered pets of monarchs, for they had tamed an inaccessible power. While Wielders were menaces, Spellmakers were silver knights. After all, power was only deemed dangerous when it couldn't be commandeered by those in authority.

But Spellmaking was allegedly so taxing on the body that each generation had grown more riddled with sickness, scarcely making it to reproductive age.

And the rulers who had once revered them eventually ran them into extinction.

"Wray was the keeper of the compass then," Garret continued, "and he kept it on him at all times." He met my gaze, his left side aglow with firelight. "Wray's death wasn't a random murder in a Henthornian alley as everybody believed. He was killed for that compass. It hasn't been recovered since."

I startled. Garret's adoptive father had died seven years ago. For *seven years*, the Capewells had been separated from their device to track Wielders.

It was all I'd wanted as a child—unbounded safety. So I said now, with all the venom I could manage, "*Good*."

"Is it?" Garret's good eye tightened. "Briar didn't tell King Erik about the theft at the time. Even when he was a boy of fifteen, she feared him, and she dreaded what he would do to the Capewells if he found out. Since Erik's reign began, we've Hunted Wielders on information alone." He inhaled slowly—an archer pulling back the bowstring before the release. Then: "Who do you think supplies that information?"

For a brief, blessed second, the words wouldn't penetrate.

Then they pierced deep enough to hit bone.

Perhaps your father is not as innocent as you'd like to believe, Keil had said.

It had been years since the Capewells had propositioned Father to join their service. Because they'd accepted failure . . .

Or because they'd already succeeded?

"Your father's position allows him to gather reports from the entire kingdom," Garret said. "He tells us where Wielding has been suspected, and we follow up accordingly." He continued, unaffected, as though he wasn't chipping away at me with every word, "He may not use a blade, but your father is as much a Hunter as the rest of us."

I felt the fracture in my chest as a physical pain.

"You wanted to know why I'm telling you this?" Garret moved closer. "Why, after seven years, I'm telling you *anything*? Because I finally can."

My eyes dropped to his bare wrist. To the hand he should've had to cut off if he'd removed the oath band himself. Briar was away tonight; she couldn't have unlocked it. Which meant she'd never had the key.

And Garret's oath band—the emblem of his betrayal—had been locked by someone else.

"No." The protest felt dry on my tongue. Landed empty in the silence.

Garret's expression hardened. "I vowed to help him maintain your safety. I vowed to keep you out of this world—to never reveal the work he did or why he'd had to do it. I promised to say whatever it took to keep you away, and I regretted it the moment he locked the clasp."

The floor seemed to tip, the cruel memory replaying. *Put your dirty specter on me again, and I'll cut through it, Wielder.*

He'd said the words with so much hatred. But his hatred had been for my father.

Because my *father* had forced those words out of his mouth—had put that oath band around his wrist.

My father had stolen Garret out of my life.

"Tonight gave me an opportunity." Garret spoke faster now, the dam broken. "I told your father I wouldn't retrieve those prisoners until he unlocked the band."

Oh, gods—the Wielders in that wagon . . . Had Father caused their imprisonment?

Had he caused Marge's death?

"I was at your estate this morning," Garret ploughed on, heedless of my unraveling, "because I was begging him to free me from my oath. To let me tell you everything before it was too late—"

"*Enough.*" I went to stride around him, but he blocked my path.

"Alissa, you have to hear this—"

My specter whipped out before I'd consciously released it.

Garret thwacked sideways into the bookcase, then hit the floor. A glass ornament shattered beside him. He was climbing to his knees when I stormed away.

"Don't you want to know what happened to Marge?"

The words landed like a punch, and I spun. "I know what happened to her." My voice hitched. "I know what Briar did."

"Not Briar." Garret's open shirt flared in and out with his heavy breathing. He took a parchment from the shelf behind him and tossed it across the floor. "Check for yourself."

One glance at the page, and my stomach dropped. This was the list Garret had mentioned. The list of confirmed Wielders in Daradon.

Each name had been penned in Father's handwriting.

"Your father didn't give us Marge's name," Garret said. "He wouldn't have. He doesn't want you to know the faces of the people he's killed."

The people he's killed.

I forced the words aside, fists trembling. "Then, how—?"

"Your kidnappers wanted your father to empty the hold. To release the dozen or so Wielders we should've amassed over the last two months. I wasn't lying when I said we didn't have them. But I lied about why." Garret grimaced and hoisted himself up, his palm pecked with bloody glass. Terror seized me as he captured my stare and said, "Alissa . . . The person who stole the compass is *using it.*"

10

"It started in Parrey ten months ago," Garret said. "A name your father hadn't provided. A Hunting Briar hadn't approved." He picked the glass out of his skin, shards falling at his feet. "Then another, in Avanford. Two more in Henthorn. Again and again, we found our mark painted on houses we hadn't targeted, each mysteriously filled with dullroot ash. We're equipped to burn dullroot inside our wagons," he explained, "but not inside our targets' houses.

"At a Creakish site, we discovered the trick." He extracted a small steel canister from his pocket, blood trickling down his wrist. "Their devices produce a concentration of burnt dullroot to incapacitate Wielders without even touching them."

Horror held me still. It was how Marge's lounge was coated in ash, and how Tari had still smelled its bitter burn a week later. It was why Marge hadn't been able to fight back.

"Briar's been reproducing the devices," he said. "This is one of her more successful prototypes."

My specter writhed as he returned the canister to his pocket. He could have deployed it at any time. Could have stopped me from striking him. Instead, he was bleeding into his sleeves.

"We reduced our own Huntings to keep the pattern unchanged," he continued. "A Hunting every month or so. We didn't want the king, or the citizens, to notice anything amiss. And that worked..."

"Until two months ago," I finished quietly. When the Huntings had increased inexplicably. "*Why?*"

"We suspect they're Wholeborn purists. Extremists who wish to eradicate Wielders entirely." Garret drew a handkerchief from his other pocket and wrapped it around his palm. He winced, and I almost felt guilty. "When their activity became impossible to hide, King Erik grew suspicious. Fearing his wrath, Briar confessed everything. The theft of the compass seven years ago. The new activity of these copycats." His voice dropped meaningfully. "Your father's involvement in hiding the truth."

My arms skittered with greater stirrings of dread.

"Erik ordered us to reclaim the compass before this new keeper—whoever they are—incites chaos. So, Briar dispatched Capewells around the kingdom to track the copycats, hoping they'll lead us to its whereabouts." He procured a length of silver from the bookcase, then paused, inhaling deeply. "I want to strike at the source."

He tossed the silver something toward me. I jumped as a key clattered at my feet.

"That was found near Wray's body," Garret said. "Briar disregarded it back then, too enraged at her brother's death and the loss of the compass. Recognize it?"

I toed the key toward the fire glow. Its head gleamed with an emblem that churned my stomach. A rose.

"It's from the palace," I said. Roses were engraved on the keys of the highest ranking nobles. My father had one just like it. Every ruling noble did.

"In the days before his murder, Wray had been acting furtive. He didn't divulge his comings and goings. He burned his journals. The night he was killed—the night of Erik's coronation ball—he traveled into Henthorn for reasons unknown. I think he was meeting someone he wasn't supposed to. Someone who ambushed him, stole the compass"—Garret nodded toward my feet—"and accidentally left that key behind."

"These keys unlock private chambers at the palace," I said. "They're only given to ruling nobles."

His scarred eyebrow arched.

I blinked. "You think a *noble* murdered Wray?"

"It wouldn't be the court's first hidden scandal, or the most shocking." Garret tilted his head, bruises reddening in the light. "But you know that, don't you? You're one of them."

I inhaled a shaky breath.

You've always thrived here, Garret had said at the ball. *It's your craft.* This was why he'd been pushing me to join court for my eighteenth season. He believed I could find the compass's keeper among the nobles.

And return the compass to where it belonged.

"*No,*" I said.

"You'll have free rein of the palace for your eighteenth season. You can find out who that key belonged to, and whether they were meeting Wray the night he died. If they didn't kill him, they may have information about the person who did." He looked me over, eyes bright and fervent. "You alone possess the advantage of Erik's favor. The nobles have already noticed. Apply enough pressure, and they'll give you anything you want."

"Anything *you* want," I corrected. "Why would I return the compass to the Hunters who killed my mother?"

"Because that's where Erik wants it. We don't know why this keeper is imitating us, but as long as they possess the compass, they risk destabilizing the equilibrium we've created. Over the last two months, the activity of Wielder sympathizers has risen across the provinces. Even the Ansorans have taken notice."

I pulled up short, my indignation guttering. "That's why they requested an invitation for Rose Season."

Garret nodded. "Their branches of surveillance extend to our continent. They claim to want to improve international relations, but Briar suspects they know more than they're letting on. If they investigate these Huntings, they could discover the compass is missing."

"Why would they care?"

"The compass was forged by Ansoran Spellmakers and belonged to their empire long before it landed here. The Ansorans might consider this the perfect time to repossess what they believe is rightfully theirs. And the compass will become one more item which the empress of Ansora can either barter away or exploit for her own gain."

It explained Briar's restlessness at the ball; she'd believed the ambassador would interfere with her search. And I shared her unease.

All of Daradon knew the tale of the empress of Ansora, the most politically powerful Wielder this side of the world. Born into the lower echelons of nobility, she'd won the former emperor's favor and had been named heir—superseding the emperor's own sons. When those overlooked sons had tried rising against her, she'd slaughtered them . . . and had imprisoned their innocent children to barter away in marriage alliances.

I didn't know what the empress might do with the only device that could separate Wielders from Wholeborns. Whether she would indeed keep it or sell it off to a Wielder-hating nation, not caring about Wielders outside her own empire. But I knew that such a coveted, powerful object should never belong to someone so ruthless.

"Erik only agreed to host them," Garret said, drawing me back, "because they would've construed his denial as fear—as *weakness*. And the king refuses to look weak." He massaged the back of his neck, his shirt shifting with the movement. Baring the fine sweat of anxiety now glistening over his tattoo. "Erik exercised mercy after Briar's confession. But if we continue to fail him—" Garret cut himself off as though fearing he'd said too much, then inhaled through his teeth. "He won't spare us again."

At his odd air of caginess, I narrowed my gaze. "You think I care what he does to any of you?"

A twitch—almost a flinch—at the corner of his swollen eye. Then he said, with cool intent, "I'm sure you care what he'll do to your father."

My chest twinged, bruised from what I'd learned about Father. But I said tightly, "My father is the ruling lord of Vereen."

"And in aiding Briar's deception for seven years, the lord of Vereen committed treason. If we don't recover the compass and fix the mess we've made, what's to stop Erik from punishing your father with the rest of us? You saw what happened at the Opal."

My specter jerked as the four-year-old memory slammed into me, stealing my breath: *the beating sun and the baking cobblestones, roses shedding into the blood.*

"You know nothing about the Opal," I said weakly, struggling to bury the image.

"I know Erik's guards tortured a sympathizer to death in the city streets," Garret said, with enough harsh certainty that I recoiled. "I know you stayed in your chambers for months and made yourself ill from not eating. I know you still won't let them plant roses at your estate. Now imagine," he pressed, "if Erik got his hands on your father. Can you be sure his title will save him?"

The scene shifted in my mind's eye: my father's face superimposed onto that man's bleeding body. Shrinking from Erik's cruel laughter. Shrieking under the blade.

My vision narrowed, the *throb-throb-throb* of my heart slamming between my breasts.

In finally agreeing to do business with the Hunters, had Father signed his own death warrant?

"These copycats aren't like us," Garret said, more gently. He approached cautiously, glass crunching beneath him. "With them, there is no balance. They leave behind blood. Fingernails. *Teeth.*" I squeezed my eyes shut against the bloodied memory of Marge's tooth. "They take pleasure from their kills," Garret continued. "And I don't think they'll stop until they find every last Wielder in Daradon."

I opened glassy eyes to find Garret standing before me, his brows drawn. "You've been safe for a long time," he said. "You're not safe anymore. You won't be safe until we take the compass out of their hands."

"And put it in *Briar's?*" I whispered.

Garret shook his head. "Wray was the last keeper. As his heir, I'm meant to be the next. If I find it, I'll keep it." He swallowed, then said quietly, "I'll keep it safe."

I heard the unspoken promise beneath his words: *I'll keep you safe.*

Garret slipped one hand into his pocket. With the slowness of a huntsman trying not to spook a rabbit, he stretched his other hand toward mine. "I meant what I said," he murmured. Our fingers met, our bandages grazing. "You don't have to end up like her."

Carefully, he withdrew my mother's coin and set it in my palm.

A hot tear slid down my cheek.

I'd left the coin in the parlor tonight, not wanting to bring it with me to death. But already, I sensed my time spilling like sand between my fingers. I felt myself hurtling toward the bottom of my own hourglass to join the mother I'd never met.

Because my safety had been an illusion, my greatest enemies no longer composed of the people I'd known from birth—the Hunters whose negligence had first turned their eyes away from me, and whose trust in Garret had apparently *kept* their eyes away.

With these copycats targeting Wielders indiscriminately, picking us off at a faster rate than ever . . . my days were truly running out.

My specter curled itself tight as I acknowledged, for the second time tonight, the truth I hadn't wanted to admit:

That I wasn't ready to die.

And if I found the compass . . . maybe I didn't have to.

I looked to Garret's hand—still holding mine, his thumb stamping a blood-print onto my bandage. In this very room, he'd leaped upon Briar to stop her from hitting me. At thirteen, he'd shackled himself to the task of ensuring she never touched me again. The burden had calcified him into someone hard and unfamiliar; I'd lost that boy long ago.

But perhaps he hadn't completely lost himself.

So, it was to that boy I spoke now, slow and even, ignoring the ache in my chest. "You won't tell Briar we're working together. We'll find the compass before she does." I hesitated, then added, because it was for the best, "And then you'll stay away from me. Forever."

Pain flashed across Garret's face, but I refused to interpret it. I slammed familiar walls against him and held his stare with cool contempt.

He released my hand, stepped back, and said, "You have my word."

 # 11

Stale air rushed past me as I barreled into Father's study.

Amarie shot from the sofa with a cry of relief; Father staggered around his desk, his bloodshot eyes widening to take me in.

"My girl." His voice broke; his mouth trembled. "Are you—?"

"Did you kill my mother?"

Father froze. The color drained from his face.

He was dressed in rumpled ballroom attire, his hair disheveled, sleepless shadows curving under his eyes. He'd waited all night for my return, surely fearing the worst.

And yet he suddenly looked more fearful now than I'd ever seen him.

"Please leave us, Amarie," he said quietly.

A sniffling shuffle marked her exit. The door clicked shut.

He began, "How could you ask me tha—?"

I slapped Keil's ransom note onto the floor, slicing through Father's last word. Garret had salvaged the note from the hold before I'd left Capewell Manor, and the sight of it seemed to puncture a hole in my father, air rushing from his chest.

"You've killed so many others." The acknowledgment blistered my throat. "It's a fair question."

With my kidnapping, Keil had rescued five Wielders from the Capewells' hold. I didn't know if Father had handed their names to Briar. But judging from his tortured expression, they wouldn't have been the first.

Father wetted his parched lips. "I loved your mother," he rasped. "I never hurt her."

"Did she know what you are?"

"It—it wasn't like that then. Alissa—" He started forward again.

I staggered back. *"Don't come near me."*

Father stopped. His face crumpled with devastation.

My father was the person I used to call for in my nightmares; the person whose arms I'd launched into after waking, whose chest I'd nuzzled against for shelter. Now here I was, lurching away from him. As though he were one of the monsters he used to shield me from.

I saw the moment it broke his heart.

He slumped onto his claw-foot desk, rattling an empty brandy glass. Dawn was breaking beyond the one domed window, washing the mahogany study in bruised shades of yellow. "When Briar told me the compass had been stolen, I felt only relief. For the first time, they couldn't Hunt. They wouldn't discover your specter." His hand quivered down his face. "But months passed without a Hunting, and it drew King Erik's notice. Briar needed an informant. If I had refused, she would've chosen another."

"You should have let her."

Father's head snapped up. "You were a stubborn, reckless child, and became more reckless as you grew. You believe nobody notices when you trip people, or twirl coins, or unlock doors." He gave a bark of pained laughter. "Or scrub away Hunters' Marks at dawn."

I flinched; Lidia must have told him I'd been to Marge's house.

He'd known, and he'd buried it with the rest of his fear.

"I could never influence you." He gulped, then said stiffly, "At least this way . . . I could influence *them*."

I curled my hands to stop them shaking. "Like you influenced Garret?"

Father swallowed again. "Garret was hand-selected as an infant during the Starling Rebellion. Briar believed nobody could make a better Hunter than a boy orphaned by Wielders, and she convinced Wray to take him in. Wray delayed Garret's training, but after he died, Briar wanted to initiate the boy at last." A long, wobbling breath. "But Garret was not what he should have been. He never feared your specter. He was in awe of it—of *you*. I knew, as long as Briar trusted him, he could help keep you safe."

"You made him keep your secret," I whispered, disgusted. "You locked an oath band around his wrist. How did Briar never question it?"

"I told her I'd made him promise to stay away from you, and she approved. Your friendship was a distraction Garret couldn't indulge in if he were to reach his full potential."

My specter shuddered to the surface, rising faster than bile. "He was thirteen. And you let her turn him into—" My sentence fractured, branching out in horrific variations. *A Hunter. A monster. A murderer.*

Father hung his head. "She turns us all eventually."

He pulled the neck of his shirt, and a deep horror seized me.

His skin was raw, aflame in its own rebellion, crisscrossed with welts from where he never stopped scratching.

Because inking the space above my father's heart, like a stamp declaring ownership, was the Hunters' Mark.

"I couldn't bear for you to know." His face webbed out with agony lines. "For you to look at me as you are looking at me now." He whispered, with so much sorrow that I felt the words branding my memory, "I cannot lose you, too."

My specter slackened, the pain weighing me down. After a lifetime of toe-dipping into the acid of my guilt, I finally felt myself tip fully into its depths.

I hadn't survived this long because of the blind fortune of my lineage. I'd survived on the time stolen from other Wielders—on the minutes of their lives, trickling into mine.

Because every life Father had taken, he'd given to me.

I could never repay the debt he'd amassed in my name. But I could keep it from growing.

"I'm joining court for Rose Season," I said. Father shot up but I continued, "I will retrieve the compass from these copycats—"

"*Alissa—*"

"—and I will finally be safe."

The finality of my tone made Father flinch.

"It's too dangerous." He dared a step closer. "Please. I can't protect you there."

A vicious coldness crept over me as I met my father's eyes. "You can't protect me anywhere," I said. "You couldn't even protect her."

The sun crested, and in the glittering morning light, roses arrived alongside a silver card. Boldly inscribed were the words:

We didn't finish our conversation.

Soon.

—E

I bundled King Erik's roses for disposal with last night's gown. I touched the corseted waist, which Erik had gripped in his cold hand.

The now-filthy hem, which had glided across the marble untrampled—because the other nobles hadn't dared to encroach upon our privacy.

Garret was right; I'd always thrived at court. But now the courtiers would pay me a new degree of respect. Would *gratify* me, more than they even gratified my father. Erik's interest—however unwanted—had made me the perfect choice for Garret's mission. If a noble *had* stolen the Hunters' compass, if they *were* at court this season . . . nobody was better equipped to root them out than me.

Yet an anxious sweat broke over me at the thought. I'd been wary of joining court as one of the faceless horde of nobles. But to be actively mining for information about the compass while all eyes were already fixed upon me . . .

I'd spent eighteen years painfully concealing my specter. And now I would be putting myself in more danger of exposure than ever before.

But to protect Daradon's Wielders—and truly protect my future—I had to find the compass before anyone else.

Including Garret.

So, as I'd done all my life, I smothered the hum of my fear. I forced my trembling fingers to steady as I burned the king's note above a candle flame. *What's to stop Erik from punishing your father with the rest of us?* Garret had asked.

I believed I knew the answer.

As my world fought desperately to fall apart, I held the pieces together. And two days later, I left Vereen without looking back.

 # 12

I ran shaky hands down my gown, then cursed myself for the mistake. Showing nerves was to show weakness.

And standing atop this staircase—alone for the first time—I couldn't afford to look weak.

A confectionery shop had spilled its bounty across the ballroom today. Caramel-spun towers bursting with cream puffs. Candy pearls dripping from chandeliers. Glacé fruits and syrupy sunlight and powdered sugar in the air. Servers weaved between partygoers, carrying potted desserts that would've made Father anxious. *What do we do with the pots when we finish?* I imagined him saying. *Put them in our pockets?*

My heart wrenched at the thought of him. But I made myself ignore the pain.

"Heron disappoints me," Garret drawled, his near presence startling me. "I thought he would've tried confining you to your chambers. Or at least elbowed his way into that carriage with you."

Surprisingly, Father had done neither. While Amarie had pleaded with me tirelessly—for she'd known about Father's business with the Capewells all these years—Father had locked himself in his study, and even my departure hadn't roused him to face me.

But every night since our argument, a shadow had pooled under my door. I'd heard the floorboards creaking, and I'd imagined him raising a fist to knock.

And every night, he'd lost his nerve, leaving me feeling hollow and slightly ashamed.

"Why are you here?" I asked. Like all the Capewells, Garret's alias as a merchant afforded him entry into every event of the season. But I hadn't expected him here today, defiant of his purpling bruises, cutting a dapper figure with his freshly pressed trousers and freshly trimmed hair. Only his blazer appeared less crisp, slightly limp from overuse.

As he offered his elbow, I caught its stale citrus-and-lavender scent and realized this was the blazer he'd draped around me when I'd been unconscious at Capewell Manor.

The blazer that must have absorbed the scent of my perfume . . . and had apparently been spared from the washboard.

"I'm here," Garret said, quieter now, "so you wouldn't be alone."

The words sent a needle through me—acute and startling—and it struck me anew that I hadn't known who Garret truly was for the last seven years. My perception had centered around our divide when I'd seen his oath band and believed he'd chosen the Hunters over me.

Now, unshackled from the task of protecting me, he was still offering an arm.

My defenses shuddered. Softened.

I remembered how painful it had been when Garret had stopped feeling like my home. But what had Garret been feeling back then, alone? Having been forced to walk away, how difficult had it been to stop looking at me as *his* home?

As I studied the memory from a new angle, I suddenly ached to think of the path we might have taken without my father's interference.

Because I knew, deep down, that if we'd kept growing up *toward* each other, we would have inevitably intertwined.

And now I couldn't help wondering, as Garret patiently awaited my hand, if he also resented the loss of a future neither of us would ever see.

Feeling strangely mournful, I reached up to accept Garret's arm. His eyes flickered in surprise; he stood straighter, holding his breath. My fingers were just skimming him when I noticed the slight ridge in his blazer. The crease of a weapon, sheathed under the front seam.

I paused. And as my specter hardened with the memory of his double-edged knife, so, too, did my defenses.

Garret appeared quietly defeated—but unsurprised—as I descended into the crowd without anyone on my arm.

In their most recent Hunting, the copycats had targeted the Jacombs' household, slaughtering their two dozen employees. On my last visit here, news of the mass Hunting had shaken me—had driven me home early. Today, it fueled me.

I'd planned my ensemble like a general designing battle armor: a plunging crystal-beaded bodice; A-line tulle skirts, sparkling with penny-blossom dye; diamond earrings peeking through my loosely waved hair. I'd always wanted to stand apart from the satin and brocade of Henthornian fashion, but as a Wielder-in-hiding, standing apart had its own sinister consequences. The outfit had never been worth the risk.

Now the risk was worth the outfit.

Wray Capewell had supposedly been lured to his death by a ruling noble—a noble who'd accidentally left their palace chamber key at the scene. My first task here would be to test the key along the nobles' halls; if the locks hadn't changed, I could discover whose chambers it opened. Until then, I'd planned to learn as much as possible about my suspects.

Five families presided over Daradon's provinces: the Brogues of Creak, the Jacombs of Dawning, the Byrds of Avanford, the Kaulters of Parrey, and the Paines of Vereen. Excluding my own, that left four families to investigate.

This ballroom swelled with enough information about those families to sink a ship.

If one of them was using the compass to direct the copycats, I would employ every tool in my arsenal to stop them.

As fresh trays flooded the crowd, I glimpsed a long-legged server with a thick braid swishing beyond her waist. The light caught her copper-brown skin and high cheekbones. Her straight nose and clever eyes.

My confidence curdled into horror as I hauled Tari into a dim alcove. "*What are you doing here?*"

The custard tarts wobbled on her tray. My best friend righted them with a scowl. "Do you mind? I'm working."

"You don't work here," I said, gaping at her servant's garb: black pinafore trousers over a billowing white blouse. The silver-plated lotus pin—her eternal tribute to Bormia—winked at her collar.

"I do now." She flicked her braid. "My friend recruits palace staff, and—"

"Your friend?"

"I do have other friends, you know." At the look I gave her, Tari sighed. "Fine. She's one of Mama's patients. I asked about Rose Season openings, and she said a servant had fallen ill after some . . . bad soup." She averted her eyes.

"You *poisoned* someone?" I hissed.

"Just a little wayleaf for gastric relief," she said quickly. "She'll be fine by morning... or in a week." She screwed her face. "Or three."

My mouth flopped open.

"All right, so I was *unintentionally* heavy-handed with the wayleaf. But getting the right dosage is harder than you'd think!"

"I wouldn't know," I said. "I've never poisoned anyone."

Tari put a hand on her hip. "This is your fault. You can't tease me with an espionage scheme and expect me not to come. Besides, I thought you'd be happy to see me."

"Do I look happy?"

"You look like you're about to pop a vein. Does that count?"

I folded my arms. "Go home."

"You don't have the authority to dismiss me."

"I'm the lady of Vereen."

Tari snorted. "And I'm the queen of Daradon." She swooped her tray under my nose, turned, and said over her shoulder, "Now that I'm here, I can sneak you extra desserts. Though I doubt you'd find room, with that pole stuck so far up your—"

She squeaked, her tarts almost toppling as a figure appeared at the alcove's threshold.

I saw the distinctive crimson ringlets first, bouncing above glitter-dusted shoulders. Then canary-yellow satin, slinking off a generous hourglass figure—a sleek twist on Henthornian fashion nobody else had dared to emulate. But it was the jewelry that stole my breath. Huge yellow diamonds dripped down her wrists, her neck, her fingers— loudly declaring her status at court.

Princess Carmen of Daradon. King Erik's first cousin. And next in line to the throne.

The princess angled her head around Tari and looked me over.

"*That's* the ensemble they're all fainting over?" A crooning, toffee-sweet voice. "Our last queen threw women in the dungeons for upstaging the royals. I can think of ten more creative ways to make you suffer."

Tari stiffened. But I put myself between her and the princess, and matched that treacly tone. "Like forcing me to wear that instead?"

Carmen arched a perfectly groomed eyebrow.

Then she cackled and crushed me in a vanilla-scented embrace.

Tari relaxed, and I shot her a glance that said, *We're not finished talking about this*, before she could stride away.

"Just a moment, peach." Carmen halted her with a light touch to her wrist, then plucked a tart off Tari's tray and popped it into her scarlet mouth.

Tari flushed, either at the casual term of endearment or the way Carmen licked the crumbs off her fingers one by one.

I rolled my eyes.

With an eruption of sunshine fabrics and a constellation of golden freckles, Carmen Vard possessed an uncanny magnetism that drew people into orbit around her. On her first visit to Vereen—aged seven—she'd charmed Father out of his garnet-inlaid pocket watch and had the cooks whipping up her favorite desserts, all within an hour.

I'd decided then that she was the brightest girl I'd ever met.

Carmen threw Tari a parting wink that only deepened my friend's blush; then the princess linked our arms and drew me back into the roaring party.

"You're a wretch," she declared, mock-frowning. "You told me you weren't joining court this year."

"I wanted to surprise you."

"Bah! What if I'd worn silver today? We'd have clashed, and I really would have thrown you in the dungeons!"

I chuckled, shaking my head. "Have I missed much?"

"Well, Rupert drank a case of spoiled rum and couldn't leave his chambers for two days. That gave the gentry a good laugh."

"That's awful."

"Oh, I know. You'd think the Kaulters' own distillery would churn out finer products."

I didn't bother telling her I was referring to the gentry. Having grown up at court, Carmen was too accustomed to their cruel humor.

"And of course," Carmen said, more serious, "there was the Jacombs' trial."

I startled. Though the last Hunting had exposed the Jacombs' staff as Wielders, I hadn't yet heard news of the family themselves. "They stood trial?"

Carmen nodded. "They were accused of knowingly housing those employees. The lady of Dawning pleaded ignorance and stripped her jewelry at Erik's feet."

To strip one's jewelry was the ultimate act of submission at court—as degrading and damaging as a brand.

"Erik pardoned her?" I asked.

"Of course he did. She *submitted*." Carmen's voice soured, and I understood why.

Carmen's mother, Lady Nelle—afterward dubbed "the Mantis"— had allegedly poisoned her husband, the late queen's younger brother, five years ago. No courtiers had defended her at the trial. And when she'd refused to submit to Erik's judgment—to strip her jewelry before his throne—Erik had exiled her for her insolence.

On the other hand, the lady of Dawning had submitted . . . and Erik had been lenient.

It was unnerving—how many lives could be destroyed or salvaged according to the seesaw temperament of one man.

"But really," Carmen said with renewed vigor, "all anyone can talk about is the Ansoran ambassador, though they do so out of Erik's earshot. Nobody knows how he wants them to react, and gods forbid they think for themselves."

I asked, carefully casual, "Is the ambassador . . . ?"

"A Wielder?" Carmen managed to say the word without it sounding like an insult. "We can't very well ask outright. It might be like asking a woman's age or her shoe size. But between us, I don't think Erik would host a Wielder regardless of diplomacy."

My specter twinged, but it was for the best. Though my kidnappers had only wanted to rescue Wielder prisoners from the Capewells' hold, the bitter aftertaste of that night still lingered. If I hoped to find the compass before the copycats struck again, I couldn't afford more Wielder-shaped distractions—especially in the form of the ambassador, who may try to retrieve the compass for his ruthless empress if he discovered it was missing. We already stood on opposite sides of the gameboard.

And truthfully, I didn't want to be disappointed again.

Carmen suddenly yanked me across the dance floor. She nodded toward an alcove, where a petite young woman watched the revelry, her untouched wine flute glinting from the shadows. Possessing the porcelain features of a doll, complete with large brown eyes and a mass of raven-black hair, Lady Perla Byrd of Avanford had always seemed more breakable than beautiful.

"It's uncanny," Carmen whispered. "Every event—the same alcove. She'll stand for hours—on those rickety heels, too, mind you—then retreat to her chambers without having spoken a word."

"Perhaps she's grieving," I said. "I heard her older sister passed last year. Petra, wasn't it?"

"Yes, and gods rest the poor darling! Where Petra was quite an enchantress, Perla is mild, obedient, and tepid as a cup of old soup. When her father heard that Erik was considering marriage this year, he bribed Erik's advisors into campaigning for her."

"He's so eager to marry off his only remaining daughter?"

"His grandchildren would rule Daradon. He'd be a fool to dally." Carmen gave me an appraising look. "Especially since His Majesty has eyes for another."

My cheeks heated, but I kept my face neutral. "You've done your research."

"I have a duty to my kingdom."

"To be a gossip?"

She lightly smacked my arm. "To learn everything I can about Erik's future consort." She added in a singsong voice, "Whoever that may be."

I drew my attention back to Perla. Her family, the Byrds, ruled Avanford, a coastal province renowned for their naval forces and fishing economy. Of all the ruling families, I knew the least about them. But any information I gathered could aid my search for the compass.

So, I said, "Introduce us."

Carmen's eyes sparkled. Then she prowled forward.

"Lady Perla!" she called, startling the poor girl. "Meet Lady Alissa Paine. It's her eighteenth season too."

I smiled, nodding in greeting. "It's a pleasure, Lady Perla. We met once as children, but I wanted to officially make your acquaintance."

"I remember it well," Perla murmured, though we'd had an unmemorable meeting at Erik's coronation, both eleven years old and mere shadows behind our ruling fathers. Now drowning in a bruised-plum gown and clinging to the gloom of her alcove, Perla didn't look much changed. "The pleasure is mine, Lady Alissa."

She didn't smile, but inclined her head lower than I had. As she drew up, her gaze snagged on my plunging neckline, which revealed the faded edge of my blueneck fever scar—a faint bluish splotch creeping up between my breasts. Perla must've mistaken it for a bruise because she glanced away, her mouth pinched tight as if by a drawstring.

"You girls have much to look forward to," said Carmen, oblivious. She'd secured a pot of chocolate mousse and now spoke around a heaping mouthful. "We Henthornians pride ourselves on Rose Season entertainment. Oh, and the fealty ceremony, of course," she added as an afterthought. "But take my advice, and don't challenge Lady Sabira to a game of Aces if you want to keep your gold. She's been working the Games Hall like a shark this year."

Before I could reply, a fanfare trumpeted through the room. Perla flinched, wine sloshing over her flute. Not just timid. Jumpy, too.

Despite the mass of people, it wasn't hard to spot the king. Erik never weaved through a room; he walked straight across it, expecting the crowd to scatter for him like birds in the way of an oncoming carriage. Because unlike the rest of us, he didn't need jewels to announce his power. His power announced itself.

The gentry bowed, servile and reverent—all except Carmen, who went for another bite mid-curtsy, her spoon clacking inside the pot.

As the music resumed, Erik strode toward Lord Rupert Brogue of Creak. The older man's walrus mustache twitched in delight at the king's attention. With their teeming fields of grain and dullroot, the agricultural province of Creak had always experienced preferential treatment from the Crown—and Rupert, its retired ruling lord, had made himself a particular favorite.

True to form, he now guffawed at something the king had said, the sound so exaggerated that it sent him into a coughing fit.

Carmen muttered, "If Rupert stoops any lower to lick Erik's boots, he'll need a back brace." Then she glanced at Perla and froze, as if she'd forgotten the girl was there. "Tell me, dearest Perla"—with a new, dazzling smile—"did Rupert really purchase a house on the Avanish coast?"

Perla gulped. "I'm afraid I don't—"

"Oh, if the news reached us here in Henthorn, you must have some idea!"

Perla squirmed like she wanted her gown to swallow her, rickety shoes and all. "I've heard rumors—"

"Aha!" Carmen jutted her spoon at me. "That's his third summer home this year, each one worth a treasury. Is he growing gold alongside the grain?"

I shrugged. "Maybe's he's taking pointers from Lady Sabira at the cards table."

"That oaf wouldn't know a winning hand if it sat on his lap and sang him a sea shanty." Carmen scraped up her last spoonful and dropped the pot with a passing server. "Well, ladies? Shall we relieve my cousin of Rupert's company?"

Perla tensed, color rising to her ivory cheeks.

"Lady Perla," I interjected before Carmen dragged her away by her sleeves. "The Verenian jewelers have been eyeing your rings." I nodded to the white pearls adorning her fingers. "Perhaps you could indulge them with a closer look?"

Perla looked pitifully grateful as she scurried off—in the opposite direction of the king.

Carmen was watching me, her azure eyes keen and bright. "Clearing away the competition, I see."

"What competition?" I said sweetly, then weaved between the spun-sugar towers. Carmen hurried after me, not one to be excluded.

At our approach, Erik sent Rupert off with a good-natured pat on the back—a clever little gesture that had Rupert beaming, even as he was being dismissed.

Then the king turned to me with a knowing half smile. I'd left him searching for me in this very ballroom after his almost-proposal, and his roses had arrived with an almost-threat.

We didn't finish our conversation. Soon.

Now here I was, curtsying before him, a present glittering in silver wrapping. *Is this soon enough?* I wanted to bite out.

"Lady Alissa." He took my hand to draw me up from my curtsy, then dropped a kiss to my knuckles. "I see the princess beat me in welcoming you to our home."

"If I'd known it was a race, Your Majesty, I would have let you win."

Erik's eyes flared—with surprise, perhaps, but certainly satisfaction; I'd never returned his flirtations before. I ignored every instinct that told me it was a mistake to start now. That told me to run, like Perla, away from the king. This had to be done.

"Look at you two." Carmen cackled. "Shall I have the wedding bed prepared already?"

Erik sighed. "Forgive my cousin's crude humor. She has no suitors of her own to occupy her."

"I won't settle for less than I deserve." Carmen swooped red-painted nails down her curves. "The gods themselves would worship these hips."

"As would an Orrenish royal," Erik countered.

"You would marry me off to Orren? After that trunk of Rose Season gifts?" Carmen swiveled to me and exclaimed, "The Orrenish sent daggers and jewelry and cutlery sets—all doused in dullroot essence!"

My stomach bottomed out. "How—how did you know it was dullroot?"

"The note, of course! 'May these protect you from foul guests this season.'"

I cringed. Though the kingdom of Orren had eradicated its Wielders centuries ago, Orrenish royals still bathed in dullroot so specters couldn't touch their skin. To extend that extremism to Erik . . .

"They've heard about the Ansoran ambassador," I said.

Erik laughed, low and unconcerned. "The Orrenish have always wanted our backing in the Western War. They're bound to be disgruntled."

That was one way to put it. Orren had been launching attacks on Ansora for two decades, claiming that the Wielders would extend their rule to our continent if given the chance. The Orrenish military camps were situated so near our borders that our forces had had several skirmishes with them over the years—skirmishes that, according to the Orrenish, would cease upon a formal alliance. But Daradon had always remained neutral.

Now the Ansorans had come knocking on our door. And Erik had let them in.

The Orrenish were probably a step or two beyond *disgruntled*.

"Speaking of our political endeavors . . ." Carmen looked over my shoulder and excitedly ruffled her curls.

Erik was suddenly beside me—too close, too unexpected—and I went rigid as his hand settled on the small of my back. "I'll be here," he whispered, intimate and reassuring. "The creature wouldn't dare to harm you."

He drew away, and I was too tense from his nearness to fully understand. He said, "Lady Alissa, meet Ambassador Arcus of Ansora," and I turned, heart hammering—

Then stopped dead.

And met Keil's golden eyes.

 # 13

My ears were ringing.

Keil stood apart from the crowd, a gilded monument to contradiction—his strong shoulders set in an easy posture, the hard line of his jaw countered by a soft, full smile. Dressed in tailored trousers and a simple white shirt with the sleeves rolled up around his forearms, he could've been just another courtier.

But he was the Ansoran ambassador. The Wielder who'd journeyed here to improve international relations.

And the man who had held me for ransom.

Carmen's laughter cracked through my shock. "My goodness—rendered speechless! What an accomplishment, Ambassador. Our Alissa rarely gives so much away." Her words tinkled with mischief, but she slightly tilted her head—a warning.

Because Erik's gaze had narrowed on my throat. On the throb of my racing pulse.

I snapped my focus back to Keil and noticed the quiet appeal in his eyes. *I pray that you can accept my apology,* he'd said on the field, with a heaviness I hadn't understood.

Suddenly Goren's warning—*she's a noble*—made sense. I was never meant to see Keil's face because I was likely to encounter him again at court. And now my knowledge could ruin him.

Was that what I wanted?

I drew a deep breath and Keil tensed, preparing for the strike.

"You must excuse me, Ambassador." My voice held steady. "I'd imagined someone rather different."

Keil blinked. Then his chest sank with relief.

"Oh, we'd all expected a gnarled-looking fellow in robes!" Carmen said with a flourish. "Aren't we lucky to have gotten him instead?"

"Very lucky," Erik said dryly.

I straightened, regaining my composure. "Arcus, was it?"

"Keil Arcus, my lady." He flashed a charming smile, the chandelier glow threading highlights through his gold-brown hair. "I must admit, you also differ from my imaginings."

"Oh?"

His fingers brushed mine, and he raised my hand for a kiss. "You're even lovelier than the whispers claim."

The words were smooth, the performance flawless. He had nerve, I'd give him that.

"Careful, Ambassador," Carmen teased while Keil was still lifting my hand. "My cousin loathes to share. But I'll happily bear the burden of those compliments."

Keil paused, gaze sliding to Erik. Though the two were similar in age and height, with Keil being slightly broader, a unique power steeled Erik's spine—a power greater than any Wielder's. The power of a king.

And the force of that power was currently directed toward my hand, cradled in Keil's.

Whether from protectiveness or something more territorial, Erik offered the Wielder a bland smile. Almost daring him.

Keil's mouth quirked up. "I see." He lowered my hand without finishing the distance to his lips. But he subtly angled my palm before he released it—to check the thin line of my cut, I realized. Finding the wound almost healed, he stepped back, content. "And which area do you preside over, Lady Alissa?"

"Alissa's father is the ruling lord of Vereen," Carmen answered.

"Ah, the gem of Daradon. The most affluent province in the kingdom, I've heard." Keil slipped his hands into his pockets, grinning now. "Although I suspect the person who told me was biased."

I cocked my head, giving him a pointed look. *You want to play this game?* I asked silently. *Then we'll play.*

"Have you visited?" I asked.

"I can't say I have."

"No, I suppose you can't. I'd invite you to tour my estate, but I'm afraid someone's been taking an axe to it."

Keil went rod-still. Erik and Carmen shifted in interest.

"Refurbishment," I clarified, and the group relaxed.

"That's unfortunate," Keil said, more careful now.

"Indeed." I gave a sharp smile. "I much preferred my parlor the way it was."

His eyes tightened at the corners. With satisfaction fueling me, I made one last stab.

"Are the others in your party here?" I glanced around, brows high. "I'd love to make an official introduction."

My words strung a rope around the group, drawing everyone up taut. Keil looked at me like I'd pulled a mace from under my skirts and thwacked it around his head.

"Ambassador Arcus made passage alone." Erik's voice held a low, questioning edge. "Those were our terms, were they not, Ambassador?"

"They were, Your Majesty." Keil held my stare, waiting.

But I'd made my point.

"My mistake," I said lightly. "I assumed a man of your standing would've traveled with an entourage." I swept my eyes over Keil and winced, as if I'd found the span of him awkwardly lacking. "But I must have overestimated."

The silence dragged.

Then Carmen laughed a little too loudly, breaking the spell. Erik glanced between me and Keil, a dark glimmer in his eyes. Keil looked like he needed a strong drink.

Fortunately, Erik then snapped his fingers to summon a young server. The girl's tray held four faceted glasses, fizzling with champagne.

"Let us toast," Erik said, his smile not quite reaching his narrowed gaze. "To new unions."

"Well put, Cousin!" Carmen grabbed a flute and took a swallow, bubbles sputtering up her nose.

Keil and I reached for opposite glasses, our eyes catching above the tray. "New unions," he repeated, and I faltered, my heartbeat skipping at the soft meaning in his voice.

So I saw the second his eyes widened. And his hand flinched violently from the glass.

His flute toppled, and the tray with it. Erik thrust an arm in front of me, forcing me back a step before all three glasses shattered where my feet had been. Carmen yelped, lifting her train as champagne effervesced against the marble. Young, shaky hands reached for the shards, and I automatically dived to help the server.

"Leave it." Erik gripped my elbow, and my stomach clenched. His voice rumbled with dark amusement. "A lady shouldn't cut her fingers because of one ambassador's clumsiness."

I looked toward Keil, and a chill skittered down my back. Because gone was his easy charm, his glow of good humor. Now he looked exactly as he had at the ransom exchange—posture hard, fists tight, his gaze bearing down fiercely on the king.

Then Carmen gasped softly. She held her unbroken glass aloft, and sunlight shone through the facets. Illuminating the crown-and-anchor emblem—the *Orrenish* emblem—engraved on one side.

Erik had toasted using the glasses from Orren.

Glasses doused in dullroot.

My specter lurched, rocking me backward out of Erik's grip. Had he heard my breath catching? Had he felt the goose bumps rising on my skin? All arrogance flooded out of me as the moment looped frantically in my mind.

I'd been *inches* away from being the first to touch those glasses—and Erik had unwittingly saved me seconds later when he'd held me back from the shards. One breath of difference, and I would've flinched as Keil had, exposing myself as vulnerable to the specter poison.

Exposing myself as a Wielder.

And Erik wouldn't have smirked at me as he now smirked at Keil, with barbed satisfaction.

He would've made me tonight's entertainment.

My specter heaved backward again, and my eyes pricked with the strain of keeping still—of fighting my own instinct to run. Father was right; court was too dangerous, the king too volatile.

My heart galloped as the pressure built between the two men, the nobles looking nervously toward us. But just as Erik's smile grew full and sharp with victory, Keil released a long breath.

And he returned the king's smile.

"Quite right, Your Majesty," he said. I gaped, specter shuddering, as he fetched a handkerchief from his pocket and laid it across his palm. "Nobody should injure themselves on my account."

Keil crouched and murmured a kind dismissal to the young server. Erik's jaw tightened.

Then, using his handkerchief as a buffer, Keil gathered the shards of Orrenish glassware and set them on the tray. As if the poison didn't bother him one bit.

As if Erik had been a fool for thinking it would.

It wasn't until later, when Carmen left my side, that a spectral thread curled around my hand. I twitched, still shaken from my close encounter with dullroot. But the moment I recognized the contours of Keil's power—the warm ripples, the steady thrum of strength—my specter flared, bright and tingling, aching to pour free.

I leashed it, wincing at the sudden effort. If the threat of dullroot buried my power, then skin contact with another specter—especially a *familiar* specter—seemed to rouse it dangerously to the surface.

I would have to be more careful.

I was still exhaling through the strain when Keil's specter laced between my fingers. A silent, secret request.

I moved before I could second-guess myself.

The din of the ballroom faded as I drifted around marble bends and up staircases, not sure if I was following the tug of Keil's specter or my own internal pull. As I landed inside an ivory-furnished drawing room, his power receded, leaving the barest tingle on my hand.

Birdsong filtered from an open balcony, gauzy curtains billowing with the rhythm of steady breathing. I waited for my heart to stop pattering, for my specter to stop flurrying from his touch. Then I glided between the curtains, an apple-blossom breeze tousling my hair.

Keil was leaning back against the stone railing, hands in his pockets, eyes gleaming with amusement. Dipped in the light of a caramel sunset and dripping with casual power, he seemed the living embodiment of Ansora—the Sun Empire—where the days were long and lazy, and the summers said to be spun of gold.

I warmed as his gaze trailed over me—a similarly languid appraisal he couldn't have gotten away with in the ballroom. All twinkling in crystals, I must have appeared different today, too. If he personified Ansora, then I was Vereen—the gem of Daradon.

I straightened, letting the knowledge reinforce me.

"That was quite the performance," Keil said, smiling softly. "I was going to ask why you didn't reveal me, but now I see you had a far more entertaining torment in mind."

I kept my expression hard. If he wanted to believe I'd known about the dullroot glasses, I wouldn't correct him.

"So, you're an ambassador as well as a kidnapper," I said.

"Actually, just an ambassador. That was my first kidnapping."

"Mine too."

I waited for him to squirm under my glare. It took longer than expected.

"I have no further dealings with the Capewells," he said. "My business in Daradon is now strictly political."

"I should take your word for it?"

"Not if you don't want to. But . . . I doubt you would've ventured here alone if you feared for your safety."

"Perhaps I'm carrying a weapon."

Keil looked me over again, wind rippling his shirt. Without the leather armor, I could make out every hard, streamlined muscle of his torso, and I suddenly wondered which version of him I liked best—

I jolted, flushing at the direction of my thoughts.

This Wielder had brought me nothing but chaos. The best version of him was the version that existed far away from me.

Then he said, quietly, "After our first encounter, I wouldn't blame you."

And the memory surfaced—Keil's hands, trembling toward that wagon. My question slipped out: "Who was it?"

His brow furrowed.

I clarified more gently, "Who did they steal from you?"

He drew upright. His lips parted, but no words emerged. No witty reply or flippant comment.

Though I couldn't lament my kidnapping, for the Capewells would've slaughtered those prisoners without Keil's intervention, I couldn't help myself from lamenting my first encounter with Wielders. Or from harboring a knot of resentment toward the people who should've been my allies.

But now, seeing the deep pain alongside Keil's remorse . . . that knot loosened.

Then he murmured, "My sister." And the knot unraveled entirely.

This was why Keil hadn't risked targeting Capewell Manor himself. Not because he was a coward. But because he would've been risking her life alongside his own.

"Is she—?"

"Alive, yes. But . . . they'd had her for a month."

I caught his dark meaning, and clasped my quivering hands. Before I'd known what he'd traded for my freedom—before I'd understood Father's share of the blame—I'd said Keil had deserved whatever the Capewells had done.

I now regretted those words.

Because the Capewells had tortured Keil's sister for a month.

He cleared his throat, returning from the depth of his emotion, and I forced myself to return with him. To file down this shard of guilt and lay it beside the rest.

"My empress," he said, "was already looking to improve Daradonian relations when news arrived of my sister's capture. We extended a request to your king so I could journey here under diplomatic immunity."

I pieced the information into the story Garret had told me—and noted, too, Keil's tone when speaking about the notoriously callous empress: strangely easy and familiar, without a drop of fear or unease.

"And Erik knowingly allowed a Wielder into his home?" I asked.

"It was my empress's request. Knowing Daradon's treatment of Wielders, she considered it a test of good faith. Your king agreed under the condition that I wouldn't Wield within his walls."

I lifted an eyebrow. "And did you not understand the demand, or do you simply lack self-restraint?"

Keil's lips twitched, that mischief returning. "If your king understood Wielders, he wouldn't have made such a request. To Wield is to breathe. Locking a specter away would be like going through life holding your breath."

The words reminded me of an account I'd sneakily read in one of Father's textbooks. Owing to a specter's natural tendency to stretch into the open, there was allegedly a time in history when specters constantly ebbed like tidal water across the surface of a Wielder's skin—moving as freely and unobtrusively as air flowing in and out of the lungs.

While I'd always experienced the internal, ever-present strain for release, I'd become... *familiar* with the discomfort. I'd even convinced myself that this idealized history possessed an air of myth.

But hearing that Keil's experience of Wielding truly resembled the necessary act of *breathing*, my insides twisted with a bitter yearning I begrudgingly identified as jealousy.

At least I finally understood my kidnappers' carelessness with their specters. Not all Wielders were born afraid. Because not all Wielders were born criminals.

Then, like the delayed heat of a spice, another question crept over me. "Your sister," I said, tentative. "She was dwelling in this kingdom?"

Keil must have gathered my true question—*Why would any Wielder relocate to Daradon?*—because he hesitated. Then he said, smiling, "Ansoran humidity is murder on her hair."

I narrowed my eyes at the nonanswer. Garret believed that the Ansorans would try to find the compass themselves if they discovered it was missing—that their ruthless empress would want to exploit it in her own bid for power...

But how much did the Ansorans already know?

Pocketing a theory, I slanted my head. "If the king discovered your ulterior motive in coming here, it would put your diplomatic immunity at risk."

"It would," Keil said slowly. "But I hadn't anticipated discovery."

"Yet here we are."

"Here we are indeed."

We assessed each other as the sun sank, its last rays flaring in my eyes. Despite Keil's easy posture, I knew he could feel the balance of power shifting between us, as invisible but tangible as a specter changing form. Back in the ballroom, I'd given him that taste of exposure for a reason.

To show him we were on my battleground now.

I stepped forward, a dangerous smile pulling my lips. "Go ahead, then. Ask me."

Keil's eyes ran over me, faintly wary.

I breathed a little laugh. "Ask me if I'll reveal that the Ansoran ambassador and his cronies kidnapped the lady Erik plans on marrying."

Keil's eyes widened slightly at that last declaration, but he otherwise kept his composure.

"Of course," he ventured, "I wouldn't expect something for nothing."

"My silence"—I adopted a lilting, weighing tone—"in exchange for what? I don't desire riches."

"I can't imagine you would, Lady of the Most Affluent Province in the Kingdom." He smiled wryly around the faux title, but I wouldn't coax the words from his mouth. I would wait until he offered them freely.

After a beat, he ambled forward. "A favor, then. That's the currency at court, isn't it?"

"A *favor*," I echoed.

"Any favor that is within my power to grant." He held out his hand, an offer and request, his muscled forearm bridging the gap between us.

I bit my lip as if considering his suggestion. Let him stew for five glorious seconds. Then I spread my serpent smile wide. "Very well, Ambassador. You've convinced me."

I reached out and his hand swallowed mine, as warm as the cocoon of his specter that night in Vereen.

"I hope you're better at keeping to *this* agreement," I said, the breeze ruffling my skirts. "You wouldn't like making an enemy of me."

I went to pull away when Keil's grasp shifted, became that of a gentleman. My power tingled to the surface again, spreading soft heat within me, as he lifted my hand and paused just shy of his mouth. "Oh, I think I'd enjoy making an enemy of you, Lady Alissa." His voice was low and tempting, his breath tickling my skin. "What an interesting dance that would be."

Then he smiled—slow, satisfied—and held my gaze as he pressed a defiant kiss to my knuckles.

As I journeyed back through the palace, my specter humming and my face strangely hot, I wondered if perhaps we'd both won that round.

14

"Blackmailing an ambassador is the most foolish thing you've ever done," Tari said. Though I hadn't exactly agreed to her staying, she'd swept in with a pot of drinking chocolate, sprawled beside my luggage case, and refused to get up. I was torn; though I didn't want her involved in my mission, she presented an invaluable comfort in this harsh, foreign place.

Previously occupied by generations of Paines, my chambers glistened with marble and polished silver, each cushion on the canopy bed perfectly plumped, each curtain pleated in crisp white lines. I'd been so nervous about spilling the drinking chocolate that I'd gulped it still scalding.

Now I transferred my garments into the dresser drawers, throat fuzzy from the burn. "Don't be absurd. I've done far more foolish things. Besides, it's not blackmail. It's an agreement."

"Agreements don't have threats attached."

"I have no desire to reveal Keil's secrets, but it can't hurt to have him in my debt—especially if he's after the compass."

Tari propped up on her elbows. "You really think his sister came here to investigate the increase in Huntings?"

"I don't think she came for the lemon cakes," I muttered.

"She could've been fleeing her country."

"A Wielder fleeing from Ansora to Daradon?"

"It's possible." A grim smile. "Even Wielder-tolerant nations have their drawbacks."

Tari would know. Bormia, a small, peaceful nation on the other side of Orren, had mounted little defense when the Orrenish began sending scouts across the border, seeking mercenaries for their war on Wielders. Tari's father had been a renowned blacksmith, famed for his artistry with eurium, a rare, iridescent metal notoriously difficult to forge—and also the most damaging to specters. Eurium pierced so deep into the spectral muscle that Wielders were left incapacitated as their specters struggled to heal, making the blades invaluable in Wielder warfare.

Knowing his talent would attract Orrenish attention, Tari's father had painstakingly acquired passage to Daradon, where he and his family may be labeled as sympathizers, but at least wouldn't be targeted by Orrenish scouts.

I'd been deteriorating from blueneck fever at the time, so delirious that my specter had pulsed freely around me; when Father had heard of a Bormian physician who'd entered Daradon, he'd ridden through a snowstorm to beg her aid.

Having treated Wielders in Bormia, Tari's mother, Jala Dehrin, hardly acknowledged my specter. And when I woke to the sharp attention of her willowy daughter, Tari had grinned and said, *That's nothing. I once saw a Wielder juggle shoes in his sleep.*

"It's not the same," I said now, folding away a nightdress. "The seas around Ansora are rife with warfare. Keil's sister couldn't have journeyed here without a vessel equipped to withstand conflict. A vessel perhaps issued by the Ansoran empress herself."

Tari's mouth bunched to the side. "Isn't this the empress who imprisoned her predecessor's grandchildren so they wouldn't threaten her rule? Would Keil really hand the compass to someone so... *cruel?*"

"I don't know anything about Keil," I said, even as I remembered the feel of his specter around my hand today. The confident, thrumming power contrasted with the gentleness of his pull. "But if the empress really sanctioned the mission to save his sister, I'm guessing his sense of duty toward her outweighs his knowledge of her cruelty."

Tari was frowning, seemingly unconvinced, just as a knock sounded. Her expression brightened, and she darted to the lounge. "Maybe that's the princess!"

The outer door whined open to silence. I was smiling at the memory of Tari blushing after Carmen had called her "peach" when I noticed two hematite stones tucked into my case.

Emotion thickened my throat. Amarie must've stowed these in my luggage, a tribute to the gods of protection.

Daradonian religion revolved around duality, with each pair of gods balancing the weight of power like two pillars supporting a roof. Ever since that miserable tutor had frightened me with the idea that Wielder spirits were shackled to this realm, I'd felt ambivalent toward religion. But Amarie, who lit two protection candles in the foyer every night, taught me that even a single set of beliefs could be widely interpreted.

Some might believe that Wielders have no place in the next realm, she'd said. *But don't the gods have power too? How, then, are they different from Wielders?*

The gods carry power in pairs, I'd said.

And you carry it alone. She'd cupped my cheek with a proud, maternal smile. *Perhaps, then, Wielders have the strength to bear more than the gods themselves.*

Now I remembered how she'd sobbed to the gods of protection during my kidnapping. How she'd darted between me and Goren, trembling yet determined. And I suddenly regretted my coldness before leaving home—refusing her help with my wounded palm, taking my dinners alone. All because Amarie was the only person Father had trusted with his secret.

So in her honor, I set one hematite stone on the dresser and turned to place the other at the opposite end of my bedchamber.

Then my door whooshed open, and I stumbled. The stone clattered under my bed.

"What is she doing here?" Garret sliced a path inside, bladelike, his expression livid. "If she's discovered as an imposter—"

Tari gasped, storming after him with hands on her hips. "I got this job legitimately." I cast her a look, and she added, "Well, mostly legitimately."

"This isn't a game," Garret snapped. "If you draw attention—"

"*Attention?* You're the one who traipsed in like a bruised potato." She gestured to his face. "How did you explain those?"

"A mugging gone wrong."

"What did they steal? Your self-respect? Oh, wait," she deadpanned. "You don't have any."

His nostrils flared, his composure unraveling in a rare return to his childhood self.

Tari and Garret had always coexisted on the precipice of conflict, even during that window of youth when I'd been the chain binding them together.

He cheats at every game, she'd said.

So do you, I'd replied.

Yes, but I always confess. He *won't admit it until someone catches him out.*

Now Tari surveyed him with unflinching disgust. He may have been a Hunter—but to her, he would always be the slippery little boy who never played fair.

The problem was: That boy now carried weapons. And from his dark expression, he was considering how best to use them.

"Sit down, Garret," I said, drawing his glare off Tari. "Your tantrum can wait."

His eyes narrowed with a hint of betrayal—the same look he used to give me whenever I'd taken Tari's side in a fight.

Tari scoffed, plonking back onto the bed. My luggage case bounced with the movement.

Garret glanced at the open case, and color rushed up his neck. He looked quickly away from my undergarments, his scowl deepening. "Don't they send people to unpack for you?"

I buried the undergarments, more for his sensitivities than for mine, then I retrieved the silver key from a side pocket and tossed it onto the bed. "I didn't want anyone going through my things."

He looked toward the rose-engraved key I'd taken with me from Capewell Manor. The key that had been found near Wray's body, linking his death to a courtier.

This hallway still bustled with too much activity to attempt testing the key. For now, I'd have to settle for gory details.

"How, exactly, was Wray killed?" I asked as the last red bloom faded from Garret's skin.

"Two knife wounds." He sat rigidly on the vanity stool. "One in the stomach, one across the throat. The killer took the weapon and left

Wray's body atop a drainage gutter so the blood wouldn't seep into the street. He wasn't found until hours later."

Though I hadn't been fond of Wray, I shuddered at his gruesome end.

"The person must have been strong," Tari offered, "to have bested a Hunter in combat."

Garret looked scornfully toward her. "You think my father was taken down by one person? It would've been an ambush. The killer must have had others working for them, even then."

I paused, hand in the dresser. I'd never heard Garret call Wray his *father*; they'd always seemed so indifferent toward each other. But Wray *had* been Garret's main guardian from infancy.

Perhaps Garret wanted to find Wray's murderer for more reason than one.

"You said Wray was acting strangely," I said, "like he'd traveled to Henthorn that night for a secret meeting. Did he have any court connections?"

"None he'd mentioned, even to Briar."

Tari said acidly, "So, the keeper of the compass could be sleeping next door to Alissa and we wouldn't even know. Doesn't that bother you?"

"Quite a few things are bothering me right now." Garret spoke between his teeth. "Would you like to know where you rank?" He looked her over, lip curling. "What are you even doing here? You couldn't play sidekick for anyone else, so you had to follow Alissa to court?"

Tari's cheeks darkened with anger and a tinge of humiliation. Though he'd jabbed blindly, Garret had happened to strike a raw nerve.

Tari was proud of the life her parents had carved out for her in Vereen, where she spent mornings learning at her mother's clinic and evenings cooking dinner with her father. But she sometimes felt like she'd been swept away by the tide of their routine, into a life she'd had no hand in shaping.

Recently, she'd suffered a self-inflicted pressure to find her calling. Had harbored doubt that she would stamp her mark on this kingdom the way she wanted to.

Hearing her purpose reduced to *sidekick* must have burned like a wasp sting.

But although I wanted to eviscerate Garret for the remark, I bit my tongue. If I revealed her vulnerabilities, he would learn to use them as ammunition.

It was Tari who sneered back at him, holding her own, "After that stunt Erik pulled with dullroot, you should be glad someone's looking out for Alissa."

Garret faltered. He looked toward me. "What happened?"

"Erik's idea of a good time." I began folding away a pair of short silk gloves, then, on second thought, left them atop the dresser. "Dullroot on the glasses."

Garret sat up, startled. "Did you touch—?"

"Would I be alive right now if I had?"

His forehead puckered, forming a little crease of concern.

Even Erik must have doubted the Ansorans' good intentions. If they truly sensed something amiss in our kingdom—if they were gauging Daradon's strength—then those dullroot glasses had been Erik's answer. No—they'd been his *warning*.

Perhaps the first of many.

"You still think court is the safest place for me?" I asked tartly.

Garret's face hardened again, and I was glad to have sealed that crack of worry. It was easier to hate him when he looked like this.

"Yes," he maintained. "I don't think the keeper would bring the compass within Erik's reach. Besides, the copycats have never Hunted at the palace."

"Maybe no Wielders are stupid enough to live here," Tari muttered.

Garret acted as though she hadn't spoken—a habit he'd carried over from childhood—and turned to me. "You still need to move fast. With every Hunting—" He broke off. Inhaled through his nose. "You become more at risk," he finished.

But he'd seemed close to saying something else.

I was about to press him when he added, inexpressive, "They struck again last night, in Creak."

A chill gripped me.

After almost touching those dullroot glasses, I'd questioned whether staying at court was worth the danger. But even in the ear-ringing aftermath, I hadn't come close to leaving. Because with the way these Huntings were accumulating, it wasn't just my own life at risk.

"This is their shortest interval yet," Tari said, alarmed. "The Hunting on the Jacomb estate only happened a few days ago."

Garret wavered. Then he said, with reluctance, "The copycats didn't target the Jacomb estate."

At first, I didn't understand. Then Garret's words from Capewell Manor drifted back to me. *Briar was called away on business tonight.*

The night two dozen Wielders had been Hunted on the Jacomb estate.

My stomach churned.

I'd foolishly assumed—no, I'd wanted to *think*—the copycats had orchestrated that mass Hunting. Because if the Capewells had targeted those Wielders *without* the compass...

"Your father didn't turn them in," Garret said, yanking me from sinister thoughts. And though it was still awful—*heinous*—I felt impossibly relieved that Father hadn't sentenced those two dozen staff members to death.

"A citizen had started talking," Garret continued, speaking low. "He used to work at the Jacomb estate. He saw plates arrange themselves in the kitchens, wheelbarrows drifting uphill with nobody to push them. The stories reached court. Erik couldn't let the rumors fester without taking action, especially with the ambassador arriving. So, he ordered us to deal with it. There may have been twenty Wielders among the group, or two..."

"But you didn't have the compass to separate Wielders from Wholeborns," I finished darkly. "So, you killed them all."

"I wasn't part of that Hunting group, but yes. The employees were rounded up that night and executed the next day. Their deaths were quick," he added, as if that made it better. As if the Capewells hadn't tortured Keil's sister for a month.

Garret had claimed that the Capewells were the kinder of two evils, and I'd selfishly wanted to believe him. I'd wanted to believe that Father's actions had yielded death without violence. That Garret, in his twisted way, had been merciful with his blade.

But now, realizing that if Keil had kidnapped me one day later, he could've saved *two dozen* Wielders from the Capewells' hold... I felt myself buckling under the terrible weight of grief.

I wondered if this was how Father felt all the time.

"This is Daradon," Garret said, devoid of feeling. "Wielders will always have to die. Find the compass first, and you won't have to be one of them."

Then he stood, grimacing at whatever injury must have still been plaguing him. I hoped it hurt like hell.

"We'll schedule a date to review your progress." With a glare at Tari, he added, "Don't get her caught."

Tari made a rude gesture at his back. As he slammed my door, I did the same.

 # 15

When I was seven, Father had spread a card deck face down on his desk and said, "Pick one, but don't turn it over. Now—do you want to see the card?"

I nodded. Then Father took the card and shuffled despite my protests.

"Does it bother you, my girl? That you'll never know which card you chose?"

I paused and, for the first time, wondered about myself. It *had* bothered me.

"I know how you like to Wield your specter," Father said. "Unlocking doors, sneaking biscuits when the cooks aren't looking."

"I don't mean to be bad."

"I'm not angry." Father patted my little hands. "All children make mischief, but not all children are like you. You can't expect to get everything by Wielding." I pouted, and Father spread the cards again. "We'll do this until you no longer want to turn the card over."

"But why?"

"Because you must learn the art of control. Though you *can* turn the card, it doesn't mean you *should*. You must think before you act, or you could get hurt."

"They're only cards," I grumbled.

Father smiled sadly before bidding me to pick again.

The memory chased me from sleep, leaving me aching. That had been the first time I'd seen fear in Father's face. And, honestly? He'd been right to worry. I *had* been a stubborn, reckless child, emboldened by our relation to the Hunters. As I'd grown, the strain of my power had only roused me to Wield more.

I used to think, upon finding texts in Father's study about specters and Spellmaking, that he was trying to understand my discomfort through research. Yet I sometimes craved what only my mother could've given: the shared experience of having to confine a specter.

I yearned to ask about her—about her power—but Father couldn't even bear to say her name. He'd had to mourn her as secretly as he'd loved her, and now his grief was a festering wound, still unhealed. To some degree, that wound had driven him into the Hunters' service. Into choices he loathed but didn't regret. And could I blame him for choosing *me*, his only daughter, over the faceless *them*? Wouldn't any good father have done the same?

Good father.

Those words didn't seem congruous with the image I had of him, handing the Hunters that list of Wielders. I wanted to hate him for it.

But when I'd woken to that memory, I'd unapologetically longed for my father. My heart wasn't built for hating the person I loved more than anything. And that somehow felt like a betrayal to my people.

So, I had to help my people now.

From the start, I'd known I couldn't return the compass to the Hunters, but last night had hardened my resolve. As the compass's keeper, Garret wouldn't hesitate to expose Daradonian Wielders; even during our childhood mission to steal it, he'd apparently only cared about protecting *me*. He may continue to keep my secret. But Hunting under Erik's orders and Briar's tutelage, how long until he became as brutal as the copycats themselves?

This is Daradon. Wielders will always have to die. And maybe he was right. While the Execution Decree existed, only the king could stanch the bloodshed completely. But even as a child, I'd known that Daradon would be safer for all Wielders if the compass belonged to someone who would never use it as a weapon . . . someone like me.

Erik would punish the Capewells for failing, including Garret—a thought that curdled my stomach. But only the prospect of Father's punishment had terrified me—had almost convinced me that relinquishing the compass was my only option.

But deep down, I'd known it wasn't.

If Father's title couldn't save him from Erik's wrath . . . there was something else that could.

My bleak conviction was still resounding when I noticed a silver card under my lounge door, penned in a familiar script. And though my specter writhed in anxious rebellion, I knew this was the right choice. No matter what he'd done, Father always came first.

I dressed quickly, putting on the short silk gloves I'd set aside last night. The nobles were enjoying tea and buttered crumpets in the courtyard this morning, so I'd hoped to follow the lead of the silver key. But this task was just as important.

So I hid the key inside a riding boot, where even the maids wouldn't look. And ten minutes later, I stepped into a sun-flushed morning, a lilac chiffon day dress rippling around my legs.

The gardens were exquisite—an eruption of texture and color flourishing half-wild, with wisterias dripping from pergolas and buttercups frothing around water fountains. I might've spent afternoons here, drowsing under a parasol, if not for the rose shrubs teeming from every corner. Even muddled in the floral haze, their scent carried on the breeze. But it was always easier to manage when I expected it.

I was lifting my wrist, inhaling my citrus-and-lavender perfume, when a deep, velvety voice rumbled from behind me: "Do you know why Daradon's symbol is the rose?"

I quickly dropped my wrist as King Erik emerged between the shrubs, glistening as though he'd just stepped out of a young girl's daydream.

"It's because they despise competing for space and nourishment. They must fight to monopolize the sunlight, to climb over every competitor. And they're spiteful to those who dare to stop them." He bowed the stem of a plum-colored rose, revealing the thorns. "I can't help wondering," he murmured, "if your sudden attendance for the season derives from a desire to climb over the competition."

I held his stare. "You made it clear that I wouldn't have far to climb."

Erik smirked. I'd said the right thing. The king didn't want me brawling over him with the other ladies, like magpies over a jewel. He wanted a chase—a *hunt*. So I would give him one.

He offered his arm, and I caught the flash of a sapphire ring I'd never seen him wear before. My specter recoiled, Carmen's words blaring like a warning in my head. *The Orrenish sent daggers and jewelry and cutlery sets—all doused in dullroot essence!* I didn't know how many more dullroot-doused items might be lingering around court.

But this was why I'd worn the gloves.

So despite my quivering specter, I took his arm and forced my body to loosen against him. He led me through the gardens, the swaying leaves and trickling fountains murmuring softly around us.

"Well?" he asked at last, looking down beneath thick blond lashes. "Is that an acceptance?"

I gave an airy laugh. "You don't mince your words, Your Majesty."

"Erik," he corrected. "And candor is underrated. Though I admit, I quite chastised myself for my last display of candor. I'd considered riding to Vereen myself if you didn't respond to my note, so I could apologize."

I blinked. "Apologize?"

"For springing my intent upon you so brutishly that first night of the season, in view of the whole court." He lowered his voice, angling closer. "I was crowned at fifteen. But I learned even earlier that I would never rise among those older and more experienced without first showing my thorns. I therefore acted that night from habit, with the barbed, proprietorial nature of a king... when I should have acted as a gentleman."

He drew back, and I was stunned into silence. Jarred by his demonstration of tact, along with that soft, repentant smile that made his face so beautiful that I wondered if he'd practiced it in the mirror.

"Do you think," he asked, "you might forgive my indelicacy?"

I reoriented myself. Then I said, with just enough seriousness that he could be sure of my teasing, "I'm afraid that shall depend."

His brows rose. "On?"

"Your efforts to win my forgiveness."

My words sparked like a match between us, forming the first flame of this new dynamic. His lips curved with approval—and then his laughter was shaking his shoulders, shifting my grip on his arm.

"Very well," he said. "Tell me how I should begin."

I allowed a coy smile. "I can't yet accept your offer," I said slowly. "But perhaps we might start with a trial of compatibility."

"A courtship, you mean." His cheek flickered with amusement. "Are my kingdom and countrymen not enough for you?"

"A kingdom is tempting... but I'd have no use for countrymen." I made my voice dangerously intimate. "I'd only need one."

Again, I hit the mark. His eyes dipped hungrily over me, his bicep fluttering under my fingers. *The longer he cannot have you*, Amarie had said, *the more he will want you.*

Gods, I hoped that was true.

"Well?" I echoed him. "Is that an acceptance?"

As if in response, Erik dropped to one knee before a patch of cloud-puff dandelions, his indigo cape puddling around him. He pinched a stem and pulled. "My mother taught me to wish upon the seeds. When the final seed sprouts a new flower, the wish sprouts with it." He stood, offering me the dandelion head. "Make a wish. Make several, if you like."

I met his gaze and blew.

I wish monsters like you never hurt Wielders again. I wish you get everything you deserve. I wish I could take back the things you've made me do.

The seeds dispersed on the wind.

Erik took my hand; as his ring brushed against my glove, my specter flinched with expectation, coiling tight in my gut. He must have thought I'd worn the gloves to be demure because he raised a brow at my covered fingers, laughter glimmering in his eyes.

His thumb dipped over the hills of my knuckles, teasing, teasing, as if he were about to rip the glove right off—

Then he pressed a kiss to the silk and I exhaled, my specter turning liquid inside me.

"I'll see that your wishes all come true," he said, lowering my hand.

Heart still racing, I replied sincerely, "I hope you do."

Early the next evening, once the downstairs celebrations had drawn the courtiers from their chambers, I donned another plunging tulle-and-crystal ball gown—this one in shimmering violet—and crept into the nobles' halls. The nobles had protested against guards here several years ago, demanding the same privacy enjoyed by the royals. I was grateful for their persistence as I withdrew the silver key and set to work.

I tried the chambers of the ruling families first: the Brogues of Creak, the Kaulters of Parrey, the Byrds of Avanford, and the Jacombs of Dawning, who—according to gossip—hadn't returned to court since their trial. Then, although the rose-engraved keys were only given to the highest ranking nobles, I continued to the rooms of the wider gentry, including Erik's advisors—weathered aristocrats whose combined efforts swayed Erik no more than a bothersome gust of wind.

But it was useless. The key fit in no door.

The occupant must've changed the locks after all, and I was back where I started—with no way of knowing who Wray had been meeting the night of his murder, and no idea who'd stolen the compass.

Instead of heading straight downstairs, I trudged to the royal wing, weighed down by my failure. Perhaps I could indulge in Carmen's renowned fudge collection before another night of fruitless socializing.

Angry voices rang against the marble, and I slowed.

"I—I resigned my seat three years ago," Lord Rupert Brogue was spluttering. "Take your problems up with my son."

"Your son is denying my province a quarter of the grain we paid for," said the second voice. Lord Junius Jacomb.

Had the Jacombs returned to court after all?

"*Denied* is a strong word," Rupert said.

"Have the other provinces received their grain?"

"Well, how should I—?" Rupert broke off as I stepped into view, his monocle fogged.

"Excuse the interruption," I said.

Rupert scrubbed the monocle over his brocade jacket. "Not at all, dear girl."

I turned to Junius, and my smile went taut. For all the years I'd known him, Junius had looked the same: slender, immaculately dressed, a dark bun of braids artfully arranged atop his head. But now his embroidered waistcoat crinkled in all the wrong places, flyaway hairs straggled around his bun, and a fine stubble crept beyond the edges of his manicured shave, like the unkempt lines of a child's coloring book.

The trial must have taken a devastating toll on him.

"Shall we ask Lady Alissa if Vereen has received its grain?" Junius asked.

Rupert went red. "I don't—"

"Well?" Junius rounded on me. "Have you received your shipment?"

I bristled at his tone. "You'll have to ask my father," I replied curtly. "I'm not privy to matters of inter-province trade."

"Of course you're not," Junius drawled. "Why worry your pretty head?"

Rupert puffed up again. "Now, hold on—"

"It's all right." I gave a serene smile. "Do we have a problem, Lord Junius?"

As Father's closest acquaintances at court, the Jacombs had always shown me kindness. Now Junius looked me over scornfully, with eyes significantly older than his thirty-something years, creases gathering in his warm brown skin. "I forget myself, Lady Alissa. I now see that the blind adoration usually reserved for the king must also be spent on the lady he favors."

Dangerous words. Spoken by someone with nothing left to lose.

Junius sketched a mocking bow, lantern-light slicking off his white stud earring—his only piece of jewelry. Then he strode away.

"He's paranoid," Rupert blustered. "He's been like this with everyone. But to address *you* like that . . . His Majesty will have a thing or two to say—"

"Why trouble our king with such pettiness?" I interrupted smoothly.

Rupert nodded and turned away, muttering about the *state of court these days*.

I took a moment to compose myself before moving again.

Junius wasn't paranoid; Vereen had received its grain from the agricultural province three days ago. Which meant the Creakish had purposely withheld Dawning's share.

It explained why Junius had come to court after all. The nobles were turning against the Jacombs because of the Hunting on their estate. It didn't matter that Junius's mother, the ruling lady of Dawning, had pleaded ignorant of housing Wielders and stripped her jewelry at Erik's feet. It didn't even matter that he'd pardoned her. The damage was done, the label of *sympathizer* stitched across their name as surely as the Hunters' Mark had been painted upon their door.

The gentry were fools. Dawning was the kingdom's most respectable province, famed for nurturing scholars and architects. Their ruling family wouldn't have knowingly committed treason. Especially not for Wielders.

I arrived at Carmen's door, knocked, then waited one minute before I sighed and turned away, adjusting my skirts.

The extra weight in my pocket halted me.

Slowly, I reached for the silver key. A spark of hope quickened my heartbeat as I realized my error. Rose-engraved keys didn't only belong to the ruling nobles . . . They also belonged to the royals.

Carmen had been twelve when the compass was stolen. But this suite had once belonged to her mother—Lady Nelle, the Mantis herself.

Surely it was worth trying.

I tried to control my expectations—steady my shallow breathing—as I pushed the key into the lock and twisted. My specter flared as a cheerful *click* sounded.

Then Carmen's door whispered open.

16

Carmen's sweet vanilla scent poured over me, reminding me of her embrace. And despite the excited flutter of my victory, this suddenly felt wrong.

But this key had been found near Wray's body the night the compass was stolen; I needed to know why. And I wouldn't find answers on this side of the threshold.

So, I drew a wobbly breath, stepped inside, and shut the door behind me.

Carmen's lounge succeeded in the impossible task of clashing with itself: deep-auburn furnishings and maroon walls buried under bright, blushing fabrics; vases of dried autumnal flowers filled with glossy bonbon-pearls. Carmen layered over Nelle in a palimpsest of styles, as though she'd refused to erase her mother from the suite entirely.

The thought bolstered me. Seven years had passed since Wray's murder and five years since Nelle had even occupied these rooms. But perhaps she'd left something behind—journals, records, *anything* that might link her to Wray.

I swept toward the bedchamber, my specter flurrying.

I examined the closet and foraged through the vanity drawers, their bottoms encrusted with spilled lotion. I found books and garters and even the fudge collection, stacked in multitiered tins.

Losing patience, I knelt before the black-lacquered dresser—another of Nelle's acquisitions, no doubt—and unlocked the bottom drawer with a tendril of my specter. The shallow space overflowed with silks and loose jewelry. I went to relock it but halted.

The drawer looked bigger from outside.

Using thin spectral wisps, I eased up the bottom panel. The contents sloped to the back, and I smiled. There was something worth finding after all.

A thin stack of shipping documents sat beneath the false bottom. Though the destination wasn't specified, the date puzzled me. The ship was set to sail two weeks after Rose Season—*this* year. How had Nelle possessed shipping documents so far in advance?

Flipping the page, I had my answer. I'd received enough birthday cards to recognize the handwriting in these margins.

These documents didn't belong to Nelle. They belonged to Carmen.

"Let me guess. You picked the lock."

I jumped, slamming the drawer shut. Keil was leaning against the wall behind me, arms crossed and eyebrows raised.

I shot to my feet. "What are you doing here?"

"Witnessing a robbery, apparently."

"I'm not—" I stopped, checking myself. "I'm not explaining myself to you. Were you following me?"

"Why would I be following you? Perhaps the princess invited me to her chambers." His lips spread with a slow smile. "Could you really blame her?"

A lock click sounded from the lounge. My stomach swooped.

I grabbed Keil, and he didn't resist as I dragged him into the closet, tumbled in after him, and yanked the door shut.

Keil's deep chuckle rumbled across the darkness. "If you wanted to put your hands all over me, you only had to ask."

"Be quiet." I backed up as far as the tight space allowed, cool satin gliding over my arms. I breathed so heavily that a musty-clothes smell tickled my throat, threatening a cough. "This wouldn't be happening if you hadn't sneaked up on me."

"Ah, so you *were* engaged in illicit activities. Should I be concerned that you've made me an accessory to your crime?"

"There was no crime," I hissed.

"Is that so?" Keil splayed a hand against the closet door. "Then, I suppose she won't mind if we—"

I screwed my fists around his shirt, tugging so hard that he had to brace his hand on the wall above my head to keep from toppling over me.

"Trying to rip my clothes off now?" Another low roll of laughter blew across my flushed face, heat on heat. "Though you may be impatient, my lady, I suggest you start with the buttons."

I tightened my grip, knuckles pressed against his chest. "Take one step into that chamber and I swear by all the gracious gods—"

Distant movement rustled and I inhaled sharply, a feather boa ruffling up my nose. I batted it off in a panic, mortified when my fingers caught between the buttons of Keil's shirt.

"Almost," he whispered, clearly entertained. He was still leaning over me, one bicep blocking my view of the door. "But next time"—he raised his free hand, latched a finger under his top button—"you actually have to unhook—"

"Your head from your shoulders?" I interrupted. "What a lovely thought."

"I expect murdering me would be quite loud."

"Not the way I would do it."

"Oh?" His voice deepened, rich with teasing. "And how would you do it?"

Heeled shoes pattered on the marble and I jolted back, catching the white flash of Keil's grin. I was considering smothering him with one of Carmen's petticoats when I heard a clatter of drawers, then the tap of wood on wood.

My heart shot up into my throat. I'd left the dresser drawer unlocked. Had Carmen already opened it and discovered that someone had rummaged beneath the false bottom?

Holding my breath, I ducked under Keil's bicep and peered through the gap between the closet doors. Carmen wasn't near the dresser. If I eased my specter toward it—

Keil's arms folded around me, pulling me flush against him. I jerked automatically, but those solid arms tightened, one hand cradling the back of my head.

"Wait," he whispered.

A second later, darkness fell across that slice of light. A mirror stood beside the closet, I remembered. And Carmen had stopped before it. Three steps away.

One misplaced foot, one creak of wood, and she'd find us buried among her gowns.

I didn't dare move from where Keil had tucked me against his chest, his soap-and-linen scent overwhelming Carmen's vanilla and that odd musty-clothes smell. His heartbeat raced beneath my ear, twin to my own. And as Carmen's train whispered over the marble, snaking closer, I squeezed my eyes shut. Pressed nearer to Keil until my crystal bodice dug into my skin.

"Easy." He whispered the reassurance into my hair, the warmth of his breath licking down my bare shoulder.

His hand slipped absently to the nape of my neck.

And then my heart was slamming for all the wrong reasons.

I was suddenly too aware of my hands, trapped between our crushing bodies. Of the shared *heat* rushing off us, feeding itself on our heavy breaths. My cheek pressed the ridges of those wicked shirt buttons, and now I couldn't shatter the mental image of Keil teasing them open, revealing the muscled planes of honeyed skin beneath—

Carmen's footsteps shifted, and we tensed against each other. Keil gathered me impossibly closer, as though he could shield me from view.

A rustle as Carmen adjusted her gown. An appreciative hum at her reflection. Then, after an unbearable eternity, her footsteps receded.

The thudding in my head quieted as the lounge door clicked shut.

"She's gone," Keil murmured, his voice rumbling through me.

His muscles shifted, and he slowly peeled back, one arm unfolding from around me, the other hand drifting from my nape to my spine as he eased away. Then he paused, his palm spread across the center of my back, as if unable to detach fully.

With a spike of horror, I realized my fingers were bunched in his shirt again.

He glanced toward my hands, his own tenseness melting with a slow curve of his mouth. "But we can stay a while longer, if you like."

My cheeks blazed.

I swatted him away and crashed through the doors, stumbling around my skirts. Keil's exit was far more composed. I turned to hide my blush—unreasonably angry at myself—and my eyes snagged on Carmen's vanity.

The top drawer wasn't shut all the way.

I bolted forward and slid it open, finding a new addition: a palm-size wooden box, engraved with a crisscross pattern. Before I could grab it, the box flew up past my head.

Keil plucked it from the air—from his *specter*—with smug satisfaction.

I stormed toward him, and he lifted the box above my reach. "Are you serious?" I snapped.

"I'll make you another deal," Keil said, mischief bubbling over. "Tell me what it is, and you can have it."

I stared, agape. I'd have kicked him in the shins if it would lower his arm, but I knew he'd keep the box aloft to be contrary. So I said, evenly, "It's a jewelry box."

Laughter played around his mouth. "I don't know what's more impressive. The lie or the conviction with which you said it. But for the attempt—" He tossed me the box and I fumbled, catching it awkwardly against my chest.

Brassy numbers lined the opening—a combination lock, like those the Parrian military used to secure their armories.

I thumbed the first number just as Keil said, "I wouldn't do that. That's a Bolting Box. Spies use them to organize meetings and avoid speaking among listening ears." He sauntered closer, and I craned my neck to hold his stare. "The sender enters a time and location using the mechanism, they close the box, and it locks in place. Only those with the code can reopen it. Entering the wrong numbers will destroy the information inside."

I squinted at the box, doubtful.

"Try your luck if you don't believe me. I'm certainly curious as to why the princess has a Bolting Box in her possession."

I was too. But from the way Keil quirked his head in challenge, he *wanted* me to attempt it. Either to watch me fail spectacularly or to land me in a greater heap of trouble.

I wouldn't take the bait.

"Then ask her." I smacked the box against his chest, forcing him back a step. "And while you're at it, you can explain what you were doing in her chambers." I went to let the box fall when Keil's hand snapped over mine.

"Tumbling around in the closet with you?" His thumb grazed my knuckles. "I'd hate to make her jealous."

The words curled in my core, molten, making me forget my retort. It took me a second to rip my hand away.

Keil caught the box and chuckled, all heat and honey. "Picking locks, rifling through the princess's belongings..." He brushed around me, circling with slow, predatory steps. "I'm beginning to think you aren't as clean-cut as I'd believed."

I swung around, skirts twisting at the waist. "And I'm glad to confirm that you are precisely the man I thought you were."

"Charming and indecently handsome?"

"Conceited and inappropriate."

His eyes sparkled. "You have a lovely way of making compliments sound like insults."

"Or perhaps, with your head so far up your own backside, you can no longer tell the difference."

Keil's eyebrows snapped up. Then he tipped his head to the ceiling and laughed so wholeheartedly that the sound must have traveled into the hall.

I crossed my arms. Tapped my foot as his laughter pattered out. "Have you finished?"

"With you?" he asked, lightly flushed from humor. "Certainly not, my lady." He took a single step closer, golden eyes heavy. "I have a feeling we're just beginning."

Again, warmth crawled up my skin—and not just from anger. Keil must have known it, too, because his roguish smile was broad. A little dimple creased his left cheek, and my hand twitched with the desire to smack it off his face.

Still grinning, he returned the Bolting Box to the vanity and swept an arm toward the door. "After you."

Just like that, suspicion turned me cold.

I'd thought Keil had been following me . . . but maybe he was similarly searching Carmen's suite. I'd theorized that Keil's sister had come to Daradon to investigate the Huntings, and what if I was right? What if Keil already knew the compass was missing, had stationed himself at court to find it, and, like me, possessed evidence leading to these chambers?

Though I wouldn't return the compass to the Capewells, I couldn't let Keil reclaim it, either. Before my kidnapping, I'd never imagined fellow Wielders as a threat to me in *any* capacity. Now I knew better. As long as Wielders were being executed—in any part of the world— that compass could only be a weapon.

A weapon I couldn't let anyone use against me.

But as Keil waited placidly, arm still outstretched, I glimpsed a shrewd flicker in his eyes. And I knew I couldn't let him realize what I'd been doing in this room.

So, although my instincts rebelled at leaving the Bolting Box, I stormed out across the lounge. Then I tugged the doorknob and cursed.

Carmen had locked the door behind her.

Keil strolled to my side, glanced at the keyhole, and turned to me expectantly. Waiting for me to produce my imaginary lockpicks. "Stage fright?" he teased.

I opened my mouth, grasping for an excuse, when the lock clicked free on its own.

Keil winked. "You're welcome."

Scowling, I wrenched the door open and stomped away.

 # 17

Keil's soap-and-linen scent still lingered in my hair as I entered the Games Hall, where tonight's celebrations were in full swing. Nobles laughed around games tables and lounged beside the open doors to the courtyard, chilled glasses of pink lemonade sweating under the starlight.

I returned every smile distractedly. If Garret's theory proved correct, the night Wray had been murdered, he'd journeyed to Henthorn to meet Lady Nelle. And Nelle had accidentally left her chamber key behind.

But what had happened in the interim?

Nelle had been married to the queen's younger brother at the time, and Wray had been acting strangely—taking secret outings, burning his journals. Had they been having an affair? Had Nelle seduced Wray into lowering his guard, then orchestrated an ambush in the city because she'd wished to be the keeper of the compass all along?

It wouldn't be the first time the Mantis had murdered a partner.

Despite the lack of proof at her trial, there existed little doubt in any courtier's mind—including mine—that Nelle had poisoned her husband; with his death, Carmen had been made next in line to the throne—and Nelle, mother to the heir presumptive. Though Nelle had been exiled before reaping the benefits, her beloved daughter had become the court's darling, flourishing as a blossom among thorns when the world had expected her to wilt.

Now Carmen possessed a Bolting Box—a device used for secret communication. And I could think of no better person with whom she would secretly communicate than her own exiled mother.

"*Wretch.*"

I jumped at Carmen's voice, hissing beside me. Though she glittered in tangerine satin, I hadn't noticed her approach, and it took me a moment to arrange my expression into one of innocence.

"Excuse me?" I asked, pulse fluttering.

Carmen crossed her arms over the swell of her chest. "She's been rinsing the gentry like a maid with a dishcloth."

I followed Carmen's gaze to a middle-aged woman with creamy brown skin, tumbling dark curls, and a green velvet dress paneled with glossy leather armor. While coins piled her side of the table, her Aces opponent fumbled with his scarce handful.

Lady Sabira Kaulter of Parrey, the shark of the Games Hall. Carmen's *wretch*.

I exhaled silently. Carmen had no idea I'd been rummaging through her chambers.

"She looks dressed for a fight," I said, aiming for lightness.

"She'll incite one, at this rate." Carmen added, deliberately loud, "Cheating is not condoned within the king's palace."

Sabira's jaw ticked; she'd obviously heard.

"She really cheats?" I asked.

"No, of course not." Carmen's voice returned to its normal volume. "She likes to think she's better than everyone else, and that wouldn't work if she's playing pretend."

"She's already playing pretend." I nodded to the quartz stones on Sabira's bracelets, shining dully in place of diamonds. "I've seen better costume jewelry at the local theatre."

"They're fake?" Carmen perked up, bouncing on her feet. "This is brilliant—the snootiest courtier in Daradon, skimping on her jewelry! I expect all her gold goes toward those mercenaries she surrounds herself with."

"I don't see any mercenaries."

"Well, Erik would never allow them *here*; he hates mercenaries. But she's been acquiring them for years, building a little private army. Last week, the Kaulters intercepted a report that sympathizers were gathering in Parrey's abandoned smithies, trying to organize shelter for Wielders. At her sister's behest, Sabira's been sending her mercenaries to sweep through every site."

I startled. Even before the Execution Decree, specters had garnered mistrust—and the people of Parrey had been the least tolerant. When Wielders began joining the Parrian military, their specters had demonstrated an advantage in combat. So the Wholeborn soldiers—resentful and frightened—had killed their Wielder comrades while they slept.

When the monarchy turned a blind eye, similar conflicts arose across the provinces, until Wielders were seen as the enemy—a danger to civilization.

Now—in Parrey, of all places—the extent of sympathizer activity had warranted *intervention?* Garret had said the rise in Huntings had produced some upheaval, but sympathizer units hadn't needed to be quashed since the Starling Rebellion.

Was that the new keeper's aim? To provoke a rebellion?

The Capewells believed the copycats were Wholeborn purists,

intent on eradicating Wielders. I didn't know to what degree Lady Nelle fit that description, but she certainly possessed motive to incite chaos across Daradon. After all, an unstable kingdom made for an unstable king . . . and a clear path for the next person in line to the throne.

I side-gazed toward Carmen, who now stirred a glass of pink lemonade with her little finger. Though Nelle presented a shrewd, flinty contrast to her daughter's effervescence, the pair had always been close.

If Nelle was truly orchestrating these brutal Huntings to secure her daughter's future . . . how much did Carmen know about it?

A clatter returned me to where Sabira's opponent tossed his last coins across the table.

Inspired, I said to Carmen, "I used to watch your mother play Aces. She would've drained even Sabira's pockets."

"Oh, she did." Carmen raised her dimpled chin. "On many occasions."

"Does she still play?"

"It's hard to play a court game when you're no longer allowed at court." Her voice turned a little sour around the edges, like I'd touched a nerve.

Perfect.

"Of course; I wasn't thinking." I dipped my head—the picture of embarrassment. "I heard she'd taken up residence in Creak."

I'd named the province at random and Carmen chuckled.

"Goodness, I hope not! A little Creakish farm would bore her to an early grave. She likes to keep busy—flitting around Daradon, never staying long in one place."

"That's no way to live."

"It's an exceptional way to live when the alternative is death." The words came out fast and unfiltered. Carmen paled, abruptly aware of what she'd said. "Don't misunderstand, Alissa, darling." She gave a smile that didn't suit her—too tight, and dull at the eyes. "Erik spared my mother's life by exiling her from court. I'll never forget his mercy."

I returned her smile with more sincerity, having gotten what I wanted. Then I strode forward, shucking off the tension. "Come teach me to play Silvers."

"You don't know how to play Silvers?" Carmen gasped. "What do they teach you in Vereen?"

My heart panged as I remembered all the games of Double Decks with Marge. But I rallied my energy and grinned. "How to spot fake jewels."

Carmen cackled as we wended between the tables, all talk of her mother forgotten.

I rounded a marble pillar and startled. Perla was backed in the shadows like a trapped mouse. "Lady Perla!"

She flinched, her eyes darting around before landing on me.

"Lady Alissa," she said on an exhale, then curtsied to Carmen. "Your Highness."

Carmen sashayed ahead of me, eyes twinkling. "Dearest Perla, aren't you a vision!"

Perla cringed, glancing down at her flouncy sand-colored dress.

"Lucky we caught you." Carmen threw me an obvious wink. "Alissa was looking for an Aces opponent."

"Oh, I—I'm only watching, Your Highness."

"Nonsense! Be a doll and fetch a table."

Perla stammered before dashing off like an anxious little bird.

"Now you're being mean," I said, fixing a look on Carmen.

But the princess's eyes had lowered, trained on a spot just behind my waist.

I frowned, about to turn, when she caught my eyes and smiled. "*I'm not the one taking garden strolls with Perla's intended*," she said. I stiffened, and her face lit with devious amusement. "Oh, I know everything that goes on in this palace."

I swore I heard an edge to her voice. And as she left me at Perla's table, she seemed oddly glad to be rid of me.

"I didn't bring gold." Perla tugged a loose thread on her bodice and nervously balled it between two fingers. Her pearl rings gleamed with the movement.

Perhaps Carmen had unintentionally done me a favor. When else would I get Perla alone?

"I didn't, either." I unfastened my earrings and placed them between us. "These should do."

Perla had the good sense to hesitate. I'd paired my earrings with matching bracelets tonight, the amethyst still glinting at my wrists. But Perla only had her rings. In handing them over, she would be stripping herself bare of jewelry. The ultimate submission.

After a moment, she slid the pearls off her fingers, her pink mouth downturned.

I played half-heartedly at first, my mind on Carmen. But soon, Perla was winning against my best efforts.

"You're very good," I said.

Color flowered across her cheeks. "My mother taught me."

As she shuffled for the next hand, I slipped a hairsbreadth of my specter around the ace. The tendril rippled on the card like a tag, avoiding her quick fingers.

You must learn the art of control, Father had said. And the next time I'd chosen a face down card on his desk, I'd curled my specter around it. Father had noticed immediately, feeling the thick ripple of my power.

So the next day, I pilfered one of Amarie's sewing needles, and, holding the majority of power inside me with gritted teeth, I tried to feed my specter through the needle's eye.

It was a tedious affair. I'd always Wielded with the boisterousness of youth, and forcing my specter into a thread produced a dull ache behind my eyes. But again and again, I thinned the power out. And soon, I knew how to cling to a card's edges—to spread my specter finely in the places Father wouldn't touch. Once he left his desk, I would slide the card from the deck to see its face, satisfying my curiosity.

And so I'd taught myself the art of control. Though, not how Father had intended.

"How are you finding Henthorn?" I asked, breaking Perla's concentration.

"It's... *busy*," she ventured.

"Any place must seem stifling compared to Avanford."

She sat up straighter. "You've been?"

I nodded, remembering the chalky cliffs and the frothing sea. "My father taught me to swim at Claren Cove."

"I go there every summer." Her expression brightened. "It's the best place in Daradon to find shrimp."

"Honestly, I've never been fond of shrimp."

"Seasoned with garlic and parsley, you might change your mind."

"You should ask the palace chefs to re-create the recipe," I said, leading the conversation where I wanted it to go. "Since you won't be returning to Avanford for a while."

Perla suddenly deflated, looking a little betrayed at the turn in topic. "Only five more weeks of Rose Season," she mumbled.

"Oh? You're not staying longer?"

Her slender throat bobbed. She knew what I was asking: *Won't the palace be your permanent home? Aren't your sights set on the king?*

With all the charm of a paper napkin, Perla wasn't exactly competition. But right now, I needed Erik's attention solely on me. I couldn't have her getting in the way.

"I'd be honored to stay," she said shakily. "But the decision isn't mine alone."

A vague, careful answer. She was certainly harder to crack than Carmen. And from her tight-lipped expression, I gathered she wouldn't say more.

Withdrawing my specter, I peeled the ace from the lineup. Perla slumped as I turned it over.

"It seems I've won the game." I refastened my earrings and nodded toward Perla's rings. "You can keep those."

"You won them fairly."

I hadn't, of course. But I stood with a beneficent smile. "Consider them a gift."

I glimpsed Carmen's twinkling figure in the courtyard and deemed it safe to sneak out.

Halfway across the Games Hall, I noticed Lady Sabira watching me, her gaze as sharp as Parrian steel.

I nodded as I approached. "Lady Sabira."

"Alissa," she replied, so informally that I bristled. She looked pointedly behind me, her armored bodice gleaming. "Well played."

I glanced around to see Perla shoving the rings onto her fingers and frowning at the cards.

"I remember your mother," Sabira said, making me whirl back toward her. She drifted close enough that I could smell the old-fabric musk wafting off her, see the pinprick beauty marks nestling like vanilla seeds around her eyes.

"Lady Fiona came from a good family," she murmured, referring to Father's late wife. "You don't look a thing like them."

The back of my neck prickled. Did Sabira suspect something amiss in my supposed heritage?

"I favor my father's side," I said, wary.

Sabira adjusted an emerald ring—the one real jewel she wore—and glanced toward Perla again. "Hm." Her scornful gaze ran over me. "I've noticed."

And she stalked away, robbing me of the opportunity to turn from her first.

But I had a greater opportunity to seize tonight.

Carmen had all but admitted that she and Nelle still corresponded. But from her unguarded comment regarding Nelle's residence in Creak—*Goodness, I hope not!*—it seemed she truly couldn't predict her mother's movements. Without a permanent address, Nelle would have to initiate contact—and I believed she already had. I believed the Bolting Box would contain the time and location of their next meeting.

If I could somehow open the box, I could find Nelle. And then I would learn exactly what had happened the night of Wray's murder.

I was clacking through the dimly lit grand foyer, heading toward the arched stairwell that would take me to the royal wing, when Keil's deep voice reverberated against the marble.

"Early night?"

I clomped to a halt.

He was standing under the arch of the second stairwell, hands in his pockets, one shoulder propped against the side.

I smoothed my skirts—calm, unaffected. "It's been a long day."

"I can imagine." He glanced at the stairwell I'd been walking toward—the stairwell that would lead me back to Carmen's suite. His mouth turned up in a wicked, knowing smile. "Don't let me keep you awake," he said, pushing off his own arch. Because behind him stretched the stairwell leading to my own chambers.

If I were really heading up early, I should've been walking in *that* direction.

I ground my teeth, caught between the two arches. But there wasn't really a choice. Though my specter strained inside me, as if to pull me toward that first stairwell, I couldn't risk Keil following me tonight. If I wanted that Bolting Box . . . I would have to wait until morning.

So I smothered my specter and, with it, my desires. Releasing a long, hissing exhale, I walked in Keil's direction.

He remained in the center of the threshold, deliberately leaving little space on either side as my approaching shadow stretched over him.

Did he know I was searching for the compass? Could I even be sure *he* was? Right now, I couldn't be sure of anything. But I knew, as his eyes glimmered with victory and soft chandelier light, that he believed he'd won this battle. And my specter tingled to meet the challenge.

So instead of squeezing gracelessly around him like he wanted me to, I stopped squarely before him. We faced each other under the arch, shadows lapping around us, music from the Games Hall tinkling far away.

Keil raised a brow.

Then I leaned forward—shoulders high, chin angled up—drawing almost as close we'd been in Carmen's closet. Certainly close enough to get a fresh lungful of the soap-and-linen scent that had rubbed off into my hair.

And from the way Keil's breath snagged, I would've bet that my perfume had rubbed off on him, too.

"Sleep well, Ambassador." I slipped sideways around him, tilting my neck, giving him a second drink of my scent. His body turned with me, as if pulled by a magnet. I smiled the moment his gaze touched my lips. Then I turned up the stairs, brushing against his chest—relishing that his body shifted automatically with mine again. Without a backward glance, I echoed, "Don't let me keep you awake."

The Bolting Box was gone the next morning. Worse—I'd forgotten to relock Carmen's dresser drawer, and now those shipping documents were missing, too. Carmen must have realized someone had rifled through her chambers, and she'd known exactly what to hide. I was thankful for one small mercy: She couldn't possibly link me to the break-in.

Then, as I was hanging up last night's outfit, I noticed what had snagged Carmen's sharp attention in the Games Hall. And a slow, icy horror trickled down my spine.

Because caught in the crystal bodice of my gown, swaying with every stir of movement, was a little pink feather. A feather I must have accidentally torn from the boa in Carmen's closet.

A feather she must have recognized as hers.

 # 18

Garret should have been here by now.

My foot *tap-tap-tap*ped on the pebble path, the gardens rustling in the chilly night air. I shivered, still dressed in a sheer turquoise gown. Though today was Grayday, the day we halted Rose Season celebrations to remember our past monarchs, Erik had insisted on hosting me for a first dinner together.

I'd been so focused on my mask of effortless charm that I'd hardly touched the hot, crispy potatoes or chestnut-stuffed quail. Similarly occupied during the fruit course, I'd only remembered to eat when Erik had handed me segments of his clementine between his own bites—a seemingly unconscious generosity, and one I hadn't understood until he'd asked what dish I would prefer next time, since I'd barely eaten tonight's.

I'd faltered, surprised by his notice. By his concern that I might not feel content or comfortable—and his desire to do something about it.

Then I'd laughed, brushing off his patient attention. *I suppose it takes a special man to distract me from my meal.*

Erik hadn't seemed convinced.

Only as I'd left his private chambers, feeling oddly liquid-full, had I realized he'd strategically fed me half the fruit off his own plate.

Frowning at the memory, I tore off my short silk gloves—now constant accessories around Erik—and mentally recapped everything to tell Garret.

I believed Nelle and Carmen had arranged a meeting via the Bolting Box. But with the box now lost, Tari had eagerly offered to monitor Carmen's movements. Garret wouldn't like that, but I was more concerned about the pink feather that had undoubtedly alerted Carmen to my presence in her suite.

She'd seemed distant these past few days, and it had produced an acidy guilt in my stomach. I wasn't yet certain that Nelle had the compass—or that Carmen was involved with the copycats at all—but even in a best-case scenario, I'd potentially ruined our friendship.

Movement whispered between the hedges, and I peered ahead. The pergola lanterns were unlit for Grayday, and black organza draped the windows above, blocking the light from the palace. With the grounds steeped in soupy darkness, it was the ideal night for a meeting.

But no footsteps followed. No cold drift of Garret's voice.

My specter thrummed, unsettled. Everyone should've been indoors for the Grayday tradition of solitary reflection. Even the staff ran on a bare-bones crew, the guards included; it was one of the reasons we'd chosen tonight, when Garret could enter via the hidden servants' gate and sneak through to the gardens unobserved. I ventured forward, skirts snagging on the shrubs.

A *crunch*, louder this time.

I halted, breaths quickening. I felt eyes on me, closing in like the heat of a flame.

Goose bumps erupted over my skin, and I scrambled into the palace.

My footsteps clapped across marble, candlelight trembling in my wake. I slowed at a wide hall that split off into different corridors. Then—to my left—black organza, rippling.

I shot in the opposite direction, then paused inside a dark alcove to catch my breath.

After three long, quivering minutes, I peeked out.

The halls were empty. The organza hung limp across the windows.

My panic drained, and I began to feel rather stupid. This was the palace, for pity's sake. The worst thing lurking in these halls was Rupert with a full glass of wine and a long story to tell.

I straightened my skirts, chiding myself, and continued to my chambers at a more reasonable pace. I would have to send Garret a report tomorrow, because I certainly couldn't return to those gardens. Though I'd likely been driven to nervous tatters by nothing more than loud lovemaking nobles, we didn't need those nobles overhearing our conversation.

I sagged into my chambers, leaning back against the door. I blinked, adjusting to the dimness, then crossed into the bedchamber.

A wave of nausea hit me.

Thorned roses overflowed from a vase on the vanity, filling the room with their fresh scent. Erik must have sent them up after our dinner. I brought my wrist to my nose, but the night air had blown off my perfume.

My head began to throb. I'd rather sleep in the lounge than handle the roses tonight.

I was plodding out when shadows stirred beside the dresser, and I snapped my head around. A silver-tipped boot peeked from the darkness. The boot of a palace guard.

I frowned, voice sharpening. "You shouldn't be here—"

My words hitched as that boot stepped forward to reveal strong, leather-clad legs and a heavy torso. Black hair fell around the man's snarling face.

"Stop your search," he said.

I gulped, pulse pounding in my throat. "How did you get in here?" But I already knew. This man must have stolen those boots—a whole uniform, probably—to walk these halls unnoticed.

Because he was certainly not a guard.

"Stop your search." His hands rested on twin knives, one sheathed at each hip. "We won't warn you again."

"*We?*" I echoed. "Who are you?"

He smiled viciously, shifting between his feet. Metal glinted below my eyeline, and I felt the floor tip as I looked slowly down. Toward the steel canister sheathed at his thigh.

With bright, blazing horror, I realized I hadn't been followed through those halls. I'd been *steered* through them.

So I would end up back here.

"You killed Marge," I whispered, my specter trembling. "Didn't you?"

He unsheathed a knife, its handle glaring bone-white. He pointed the blade at me. "You'll stop your search, or you will join her. Do you understand?"

I could hardly hear him over the roaring in my head, over my own harsh breathing. The blood-spatter on Marge's floor, her abandoned mug, her *tooth*—

The man started toward me. "*Do you understand?*"

I whipped around, ready to bolt, when his rough hand fisted in my hair.

I cried out, eyes watering. I staggered back against him.

"I asked you," he growled with another sharp tug on my hair, "a question."

My specter nettled at the pain, but I leashed it tight. That canister would produce enough dullroot to choke my specter. If he hadn't deployed it, he didn't know I was a Wielder.

I couldn't let him find out.

In a rush of panic, I scrambled behind me to where his second knife was still sheathed. I drew the weapon and thrust back—blindly.

The blade met resistance.

The man bellowed, tossing me aside so hard that my neck whipped *up-down*. I lost the knife and side-smacked the vanity, biting my tongue. The vase wobbled—then tipped and shattered, roses showering my arms, my gown, the floor. Their scent lifted and mixed with the coppery taste of blood.

Nausea threatened to buckle my knees.

The man straightened, leather trousers blood-slicked from where the blade had skimmed his thigh. His eyes leveled on me, and I knew I had to move—to *run*. But I could only gasp for air against the vanity, the wood digging into my ribs.

"Highborn scum." He spat on the floor and prowled forward. "Someone needs to teach you a lesson."

My specter grew frantic, lashing me from the inside out. I tried to scramble upright. If I exposed myself now, the copycats would know what I was. I would never be safe again.

Unless he never got a chance to tell the others.

It would be so easy to wrap my specter around his throat and squeeze. To let my secret die with this brute who'd murdered Marge. His pulse would throb under my hold, quickening then dying out. His lips would turn blue, his eyes white from rolling back.

My breaths rushed out in wet puffs, and I felt myself swaying. Plummeting back toward that day at the Opal, with the crowd and the heat and the roses everywhere—strung and potted and crushed under wooden staffs. Petals tumbling under sunlight, carrying the reek of blood and sweat.

I knew how it would feel to watch a life slip away. I knew it would tear open the wound inside me.

The man's fist reared back, and I couldn't do it. Couldn't end his life before his knuckles landed.

I shrank back just as silver spun in my periphery.

The man roared and pitched forward. We toppled together, limbs tangled. A knife hilt stuck out from his arm.

I whipped my head around, heart hammering—confused, until I saw the sharp outline of a blazer in the dark.

Garret wrenched the man's weight off me, yanking out the knife in the same movement. The man spun, swinging his fist, and his knuckles whooshed through empty air. Another swing. Another miss. He blinked, as though seeing Garret for the first time.

Garret smiled. Then he attacked.

Where the man was slow and solid, Garret moved like a blade—each dodge precise, each strike deliberate. Boots scuffed the marble; ornaments rattled and smashed.

The man was losing. He knew it. And maybe that was why he hurled himself at Garret in a clumsy, desperate tackle, slamming them both against the wall.

Garret made a pained sound, and I knew it was over.

The man whipped toward me, and I prepared for the blow of his fist. The smash of his boot into my ribs. But he just sneered and staggered out, wounds gushing.

Three seconds later, the lounge door slammed shut.

In the spluttering silence, I vaguely registered Garret struggling to stand.

"Grayday vigils were clogging the streets," he panted, supporting himself against the dresser. "I was late, and you weren't in the gardens." His voice sounded far away, muffled through the ringing in my ears. "We could've questioned him. Why didn't you do anything? Did he use dullroot?"

I blinked numbly.

Garret looked at me then, and he paused at what he saw. I'd landed in the mess of sopping roses and vase shards. Warmth oozed down my lip from where I'd bitten my tongue.

He pushed off the dresser, crystal clinking. His knees bent; his eyes wavered before me. He reached for my face. "You're bleeding."

His thumb grazed my mouth, and I flinched. He stilled, palm hovering above my cheek. A smear of my blood darkened the pad of his thumb.

"He's gone," Garret said, as if that should stop my trembling. As if an equal threat wasn't still in the room, breathing hot streams against my face.

I knew the moment he saw the change in me.

His brows drew in tight and his hand lowered, catching the strands of my hair on the way down. He rocked back on his heels, mouth pressed thin. "I won't hurt you, Alissa."

"Why not?" I whispered. "You could kill me right now. Just another name crossed off your list."

His features flickered with hurt and then hardened, his own defenses slamming down. "I'm not Briar."

"Aren't you?" I searched his face for the boy I knew. Only the man stared back. "A quick death. That's what you offer, isn't it? Or is that just for the ones who don't fight back? I'll bet the ones in that wagon fought. Did you torture them yourself before you were forced to free them? Would you have killed them if—?" I hiccupped on the words. "How many have you killed?"

A bloated silence passed. Dimly, I knew I should've felt grateful; Garret had just saved me from a battering. But instead I felt eggshell-hollow and just as breakable, and all I wanted was to heave until the rose stench emptied out of me. And here was Garret—the ally who should've been my enemy—trying to comfort me. I thought I'd resigned myself long ago to his role as a Hunter, but watching him battle that man, watching him *relish* it . . . the full magnitude hit me.

The person who'd once reached for my specter with awe in his eyes had become this murderer, crouched before me. He was right *here*.

Yet I would never reach him again.

Garret drew a slow breath, then said flatly, "I was fourteen for my first kill. Briar took me into a cell with a Parrian man, handed me a knife, and locked the door behind me. Do you know what the man said? 'It's all right, son. Do what you must.' Would you believe that? I was holding a blade to his throat, and he spent his last words reassuring *me*. Briar heard me crying. She wouldn't open the door until his blood cooled on my hands."

"Stop," I breathed.

"Why? You wanted to hear it, didn't you? The tale of how the Big Bad Hunter began slaughtering your people. A child, with a life in his hands."

"You're not a child anymore. Who's forcing you now? Who's locking you in that cell?"

He shook his head with bitter laughter. "You will never know what this is like."

"Then explain."

"Explain what?" he snapped. "That I look into the eyes of every Wielder and see *you* looking back at me? That I lie awake, replaying each Hunting, because I don't deserve to sleep? Don't you understand?" His voice cracked; his eyes shone tear-bright in the dark. "This wasn't supposed to be my life. But if I run from it now, Briar would mark me a traitor. And she wouldn't just hurt me. She would hurt everyone I—" The words choked him, and he looked at me with so much spite that it stole my breath. "Everyone I've ever loved," he finished, harsh, without feeling.

And I understood. A part of me would always hate Garret, but a part of him would hate me, too. Not just for what my father had done in my name—sending him to Briar, putting that first weapon in his hands. Garret hated me because he still loved me, and Briar could use that love against him.

She wasn't the one locking him in that cell anymore. *I* was.

"You know better than anyone," he said, "that we don't always get to choose what we are." He sniffed, then went to stand.

My specter shuddered out. And despite the threat he'd once given me, despite the more recent memory of his blade, I touched my power to Garret's brow.

He inhaled sharply, halting in his crouch. His wide gaze locked onto mine. My specter rippled gently against his eyebrow scar, as faint as fingertips, and I held my breath—waiting for him to cut through it again.

But his throat only bobbed once, twice. He closed his eyes. And slowly, he raised his hand.

Tears scalded my throat as Garret's fingers brushed my power, the touch strange and new—and yet as ancient as the pained lines across his forehead.

My specter flickered faster, fraying thin with my desperate hope, and I stretched it across Garret's jaw in an embrace.

"I believe that you are good," I whispered.

His eyes shut tighter, lashes swallowed by the squeeze. He turned his face into my touch until the shimmering edges lapped against his mouth. For three delicate seconds, his breath trembled across my power.

Then his eyes quivered open. Fixed distantly away.

"One of us should," he said.

He left my specter curled in the air as he withdrew from its touch, stood, and left.

19

"You should be watching Carmen," I said, sweeping crystal onto a metal slat—the remnants of last night's battle. Tari had found me on the floor this morning, sweaty and exhausted from replaying the attack. She'd cleaned my face, fetched me tea, then held my hair as I'd emptied the liquid straight into the washbasin. She'd refused to leave my side ever since.

"Don't worry," she said now, wiping dried blood off the dresser. "When I went down for the tea, I told one of the girls to serve cocktails in the Games Hall."

"Why?"

"Because then Lord Rupert will spend the day there, Lady Sabira will abandon the room because she can't stand him, and without the pleasure of gossiping about Sabira's winning streak, Carmen will grow bored and retire for an afternoon nap."

I frowned. "Sabira can't stand Rupert?"

"Well, she conveniently remains at least twenty paces from him at all times, so it's either that or a legal order."

I tipped the crystal into a waste bucket, wincing at the loud clatter. "You're brilliant."

Tari ignored the compliment. Because the moment she saw my

pained grimace, her own expression darkened. "I think it's time to leave court."

"All right, I'll call a carriage for you."

"*Alissa.*" She slapped her cloth onto the dresser. "You could've died last night."

"If they'd wanted me dead, they wouldn't have threatened me first. Garret must be right."

"A frightening start to any sentence," she said flatly.

I threw her a look. "I'm serious. Whether or not they have a larger end goal, these copycats must be Wholeborn purists. That man would've . . . hurt me." I shivered, remembering the pullback of his fist. "But as long as he believed I was a Wholeborn, I don't think he would've killed me." I added with bite, "They only kill Wielders."

Tari's mouth skewed with uncertainty, but it was easier to feign confidence when I hadn't shown her the bruising around my ribs—the bruising that would've brought my father to tears if he'd seen it.

I'd faced one of Marge's killers, and he'd been monstrous in his violence. So, yes, after last night's horror, I ached to huddle in bed while Amarie brought me broth and hummed a Verenian lullaby, like she had during my blueneck fever. But how long would that safety last?

I hadn't used my specter last night, which bought me more time before the copycats realized what I was. But if they really were scouring Daradon for every last Wielder—in every province and street and back alley—then the compass would find me eventually.

I had to find it first.

And I had to find it before another innocent took the brunt of those fists.

"I'm not leaving," I said, firmer now. "That man wouldn't have warned me off my search unless I was on the right track."

"So, you think Nelle is the keeper?" Tari's voice sank with a disappointment that matched my own.

Because the only way Nelle could have known about my search was through Carmen.

I hated imagining that my friend had any involvement with the copycats—or with my attack—but thanks to that incriminating pink feather, Carmen knew I'd been snooping around her suite. Had she gotten word to her mother, not realizing that Nelle would threaten me? Worse—had Carmen dispatched the attacker herself?

Or was there a third, kinder alternative I couldn't yet see?

"I don't know," I said honestly. "But the keeper now knows I'm searching, and they're clearly worried. The answers must be here at court. I just need to find them."

"And if that man returns?"

I looked away. Tari didn't know exactly what had paralyzed me last night. That it hadn't really been the man, but the memories of the Opal, roaring back from the grave on a tide of blood and roses.

It had been the idea of having to watch another man's life wink out from his eyes.

"Then I'll do what I have to," I mumbled, not even believing the words myself. But as I thought more seriously about my attacker returning, I added, "I really can call a carriage for you. I'll be all right."

"Oh? And who's going to hold your hair when you're heaving over the sink? Lord Rupert?"

I imagined Rupert fumbling with my hair—red-faced, awkward, slipping on the back of my skirts—and I actually cracked a slight smile. With a *hm* of vindication, Tari continued cleaning.

Despite Garret calling her my sidekick, Tari had never followed me into trouble blindly; she followed so I wouldn't bear the trouble alone. Of course she wouldn't let me face this new threat without her.

But also . . . she seemed oddly content at the palace. There was a new glow of purpose about her; a shrewd, hyperaware glint in her eyes—the same look her mother always wore when facing difficult cases at the clinic.

Tari had noticed Sabira's dislike of Rupert when I hadn't. She'd choreographed Carmen's movements for the day. She'd even orchestrated her own recruitment into the workforce—via poison, admittedly, but still . . .

I wondered if Tari realized she was engaging in court maneuvers herself. If she realized how seamlessly—and *skillfully*—she was navigating this world.

I was watching her, lost in thought, when a glimmer under the vanity caught my eye.

I reached toward it, then startled as I withdrew my attacker's knife—the knife I'd sliced across his thigh. A swirling, near-round symbol engraved the ashy white mineral of the handle. As I stood, the blade gleamed iridescent beneath dried blood.

Tari gasped softly. "Eurium."

My specter jolted. Eurium could gouge into spectral muscles with unparalleled force.

"These copycats can afford to commission eurium weapons?" Tari sounded slightly horrified. "And can afford to *lose* them?"

"How many smiths in Daradon work with eurium?" I asked, holding the knife at a distance though it couldn't harm my flesh more than any other blade.

"A handful, maybe. Eurium is rare on this side of the continent, and even scarcer since the king purchased all the eurium ore he could find at the beginning of his reign."

I shuddered. Of course Erik would hoard the metal most harmful to Wielders.

"Would these smiths work from Parrey?" I asked.

"Henthorn is more likely. They'd need a license to build the specific type of forge, and legislation is most lax in the capital."

I bit my lip, awaiting the offer.

Tari's face slackened. "No. I know what you're thinking, and the answer is no."

"I just need names," I pleaded. "Your father must have contacts. If I find the right bladesmith, I can obtain their client list, and I'd know exactly who commissioned this blade."

This could confirm my suspicions about Nelle, or at least point me toward the truth. I would get one step closer to the compass—and to stopping the copycats for good.

But Tari shook her head, braid swinging. "I won't help you dig yourself deeper into this hole!"

"Fine." I chucked the knife on the vanity with such disregard that Tari squeaked. "Then I'll question every bladesmith in Daradon. Approaching the wrong people might raise suspicion, but what choice do I—?"

"All right!" Tari threw her hands up, scowling. "I hope you're happy, using guilt as a weapon."

Glancing at the knife, I felt an impossible twinge of hope. "Very happy."

I sent Garret a report that afternoon, grateful that the halls had been empty last night and news of my attack wouldn't spread. The gentry would've feasted on every morsel of gossip with their teacakes and almond pastries. Worst of all, Father would have rushed over and begged me to leave.

And after receiving Garret's response, I wouldn't leave for anything. The copycats had struck again, in Avanford. A family of five.

The youngest had been fourteen years old.

Over the following days, I kept my specter on a tighter leash than usual. The sensation was stifling and uncomfortable, like trying to inhale through a blocked nose, but I couldn't risk exposure. The copycats hadn't yet brought the compass to the palace, or else they would've discovered my specter the night of the attack. But I didn't know how my attacker had stolen the silver-tipped boots of the palace guards—whether he'd been previously stationed here, or the keeper had somehow accessed those uniforms. Either way, it meant they could be watching me now.

And while they may have spared me as a Wholeborn, they would slaughter me as a Wielder.

I was about to retire from an early dinner with Erik when Tari tumbled into my lounge, cheeks flushed.

"Carmen's leaving the palace," she panted. "The stable master said she mentioned Backplace."

I rushed to my bedchamber for a cloak. "The stable master just told you this?"

"I may have borrowed some gold from your purse. For bribing purposes only!"

This was it. Carmen had to be meeting Nelle.

"One more thing." Tari thrust out a note. "Papa sent a list."

My eyes widened at the list of bladesmiths, each placed beside a Henthornian address.

Vincent Meade

Ada Zari

Constance Winters

Kevi Banday

Emile Chance

"He's a gem," I said, and left with the eurium knife wrapped in my cloak pocket.

I'd thought leaving the palace would feel like taking in a lungful of fresh air—the walls opening around me, the white spires fading into the distance, the heaviness melting off my limbs.

Instead, I felt exposed.

It was ridiculous; my attack proved that the palace was no safer than anywhere else. Yet every shoulder-brush made me flinch, every shout made me turn, and every up-and-down glance made my specter shiver with dread.

Where Henthorn had once been a vibrant hub of the kingdom's varied people, the winding streets had since congealed into a melting pot of sweaty crowds, offensive smells, and raucous laughter, all hazed over with the acrid smoke of grill fires. Vendors urged me to sample their charred corn or seared beef, and I wished I'd changed out of my day dress. The champagne chiffon sang of wealth, and amid the aged buildings, stacked and slanted and spilling laundry from the windows, it made me a target.

Tugging my hood low, I weaved toward the distinct sea of sound.

Wielders had once integrated into the bustling city of Henthorn more comfortably than anywhere else in Daradon. In the first years after the Execution Decree, Henthorn had therefore been hit the hardest, with the Hunters' Mark glaring on every street. On the twentieth anniversary, when a new generation had ushered in a fresh threat of rebellion, the masked Hunters—my ancestors—had dragged twenty Wielder families to the platform of Backplace and cut their throats one by one. Since specters were dominant in the bloodline, always passing from parent to child, not even the youngest were spared.

Amarie once told me the gods of justice had imbued the stones with their blood, so the Henthornians would never forget the atrocities they'd allowed to happen to their neighbors.

I stopped beside a dress stall to observe Backplace in its entirety. Before the slaughter, it had been a stage for street performers. Now the red sandstone platform overflowed with sympathizers, clanking wooden staffs and calling for justice. City guards wandered nearby—checking on suspicious carriages, keeping watchers from loitering. To others, they must've looked rather important: frontline forces ensuring the sympathizers didn't get too rowdy.

But I knew the sympathizers rarely did anything besides clanking and shouting and clanking some more.

I clenched my jaw and refocused, scanning for Nelle's wine-dark hair. I expected that she and Carmen would slink off for a private conversation, and I planned to trail them and eavesdrop. If they'd truly orchestrated my attack, they would undoubtedly speak about it—and Nelle would be confirmed as the compass's keeper. My plan hadn't developed much further than that—even if Nelle *did* possess the compass, I couldn't exactly saunter over and stick my hand in her pocket—but it was a start.

Minutes later, Carmen's crimson head bobbed through the crowd. Her lips were pale without their signature red, her freckled cheeks uncolored by rouge. But even dressed in plain hemp, she drew the eye—all swishing hips and high shoulders, a queen without her crown. Grinning, she bounded for the westernmost corner of the platform.

And threw her arms around a man.

He was lean but muscled, with close-cropped black hair, a deep brown complexion, and a jagged scar across his chin. He returned her embrace stiffly, his expression alert. Carmen whispered in his ear, and his posture loosened. Then Carmen drew back and, with deliberate slowness, kissed his full mouth.

She took one last glance around before drawing him into the streets.

I remained frozen, slack-jawed, my insides churning with wasted anticipation.

I'd been wrong. Nelle hadn't sent that Bolting Box. Carmen's lover had.

Carmen had no preference in gender when it came to partners; she only favored beauty—and that man had certainly been beautiful. But why sneak out to meet him when courtiers could take lovers as they pleased?

Unless he wasn't just a lover.

Carmen had bickered with Erik about rejecting suitors, but perhaps he truly wouldn't let her pursue an unbeneficial match. And perhaps she already had someone in mind.

With new understanding, I remembered the shipping documents I'd found in her chambers. I'd believed the Avanish navy patrols made it impossible to secure secret passage out of Daradon, but Carmen was a royal with powerful connections . . .

Had she found a way out from under the bell jar of this kingdom? Was she fleeing for the sake of a romance?

Dragging my attention from Backplace, I stifled my disappointment. I wouldn't encounter Nelle tonight. But perhaps I could draw closer to her through another route.

I retrieved Tari's list of bladesmiths from my pocket and began my hunt around the city.

The first two bladesmiths on the list produced immediate failure; both flatly denied their ability to forge eurium blades and even refused my offered coin.

The third admitted her talent after I bribed her with half the contents of my purse—but my rising spirits sank once more when she didn't recognize the knife. "Look again," I kept insisting, thrusting the blade under her nose until she gave three coins back just to get me to leave.

With only two names left on the list and no other leads, I was already preparing for defeat as I trudged toward an ancient-looking smithy tucked into a narrow street. Heat and soot blew from the open doors with the sounds of crackling and ringing metal.

I removed my hood, and the oven-hot air dried my eyes. "I'm looking for Kevi Banday."

A powerfully built woman in soot-stained overalls looked me up and down. "Kevi's not here." She gestured to another smith, whose arms shuddered with each thwack of his hammer. "But Owan does fine work."

"Can Owan forge eurium?"

She sized me up again. "What's a girl like you want with eurium?"

"Not much." I withdrew the bundle from my pocket and uncovered the cleaned eurium knife. "I already have a specimen."

She eyed the blade with far less interest than I'd expected. "That's Kevi's work, all right."

My pulse skipped. "How can you tell?"

"Bonestone. Dawni architects build their towers from it. Kevi liked to bring it over from Dawning to make into handles."

The memory flashed: spiraling white towers, dripping like candles across a breathtaking skyline. Though I hadn't visited Dawning in years, I should've recognized the mineral.

"And this symbol?" I asked, newly animated. "Was it Kevi's?"

"Never seen it before. But some buyers want motifs on their weapons—a fish for Avanford, a family crest for the highborns. If you want the meaning, you should ask whoever commissioned it." A wry grin. "I'm guessing that wasn't you."

I bundled the knife back into my cloak. "I need to talk to Kevi."

"Kevi left on a delivery two months ago. Haven't heard from him since."

"You didn't find that unusual?"

She shrugged. "He came and went as he pleased, found work where he could. He traveled with his equipment, so I figured he went home to Dawning."

"Did he leave his client list?"

"Client list? This isn't a tearoom, love."

"Do you know his address?"

She shook her head, laughing. "Didn't even know his last name until you said it."

I frowned, thanked her with a few gold pieces, and returned to the streets.

The sky now resembled a xerylite gemstone, black-blue and flecked with stars, and I entered an alley decorated with tattered hanging baskets.

Kevi had left Henthorn two months ago—which was when the copycats' Huntings had increased. As though an influx of eurium weaponry had enabled them to pick up speed. Was the timing coincidental? Or was Kevi working for the copycats now, forging eurium blades to aid their butchery of Wielders?

And what about the roundish, swirling symbol he'd etched into the knife handle? The Hunters had their own mark: the two-tined crown. This symbol could be something new, an emblem specific to the copycats. Maybe it was crucial to finding the compass . . . or maybe it was meaningless, a pretty pattern Kevi had chosen on a whim.

I wouldn't know until I found him. If Kevi wasn't currently working for the copycats, he could at least tell me who'd commissioned my attacker's blade—and perhaps give me a location, if he'd delivered the weapon himself.

But my specter squirmed with my growing uncertainty. If Tari's father couldn't rustle up more than a name, and that woman hadn't known Kevi's address . . . I didn't know how I would locate the bladesmith, especially before the copycats slaughtered another Wielder.

Or before they realized I hadn't heeded their warning . . . and they came to finish what they'd started.

I wrapped my cloak tight, a chill nipping my chest. With my eyes on the cobblestones, I didn't notice the man staggering toward me until he seized my arm.

My blood spiked in warning, and I tried to pull free. "Get your hand off me."

"You look highborn," he slurred. "Got any gold?"

I shoved him off, but he moved to block my path.

I fumbled into my pocket, shook off the cloth, and drew out the eurium blade. "Stay back."

The man laughed at my awkward hold on the knife. He swayed forward, and I loosed a tendril of my specter at the hanging baskets above. Their chains snapped; they crashed over him. He bellowed, and I ran.

The bricks of the alley walls sped past me, wind rushing to the back of my throat. I slowed when I knew he wasn't following, my breaths thin and uneven.

Kneading the stitch in my side, I squinted around the unfamiliar alley; the stench of sweat and ale curled up my nostrils.

A hand fell on my shoulder and I spun, raising the knife high. A firm grip caught my wrist.

For the first time, I was glad to see Keil.

20

My breath shuddered out, my knife clattering to the cobblestones. Keil released my wrist, smirking. "I suspected you weren't fond of me, but I didn't think you were serious about murder."

"Were you following me?" I asked, heart still racing.

"Must we go through this every time?"

"How many more times do you plan on following me?"

Keil chuckled and stooped for the knife. But it was too coincidental. First, Carmen's suite—and now the city? I'd assumed Carmen had hidden the Bolting Box after my break-in, but had Keil returned to steal it himself? Of course, he couldn't have known the code for the combination lock. But he was the one who'd *told* me about that lock. He might've tricked me out of following this lead so he could find the compass first and take it to his empress.

Keil straightened, surveying the symbol on the knife handle with an interest that raised my hackles. Then he threw me an easy smile. "I haven't seen eurium in a while." He flipped the knife, offering me the handle. "Yours?"

I studied him with narrowed eyes.

If he'd trailed Carmen to Backplace, he must've similarly realized the Bolting Box was a dead end. But I had to remain one step ahead from here on out. If he believed I was also searching for the compass—which I now suspected he did—he would quicken his pace.

I snatched the knife without answering.

"You'd think a Hunter's daughter would know how to wield a weapon."

I paused. "Excuse me?"

"You'd do little damage with that grip." Keil reached for me. "May I?"

I started to refuse, then remembered how I'd lost the knife during my attack. How the man's fist had reared back, and I hadn't known how to fend him off. Even tonight in the city, I'd felt unusually vulnerable, expecting the copycats to rush from the shadows.

Whether or not Keil was racing me for the compass, he now offered something I needed: the knowledge to defend myself *without* my specter.

So I nodded.

Keil's brows quirked in surprise before he took my knife-wielding hand. His skin was warm, the calluses on his palm scraping my knuckles.

"Everyone," he said with an air of instruction, "no matter how physically strong, holds some kind of power. The power to run. To fight. To scream."

My skin tingled at the new authority in his voice, low but firm.

"An attacker's first job," Keil continued, "is to identify where your main power lies . . . so they can take it away." He drew my arm to its previous position; my cloak slipped off my shoulder, cool air kissing my skin. "Strike at me."

I hesitated, then thrust the knife down.

He snapped forward—hands on my arm, my wrist. I stumbled,

cloak twisting around me—

My back thumped hard against his torso. His left arm had encircled my waist, trapping my arms down and pinning me to him, while his right hand encased mine around the knife handle.

"*This*," he murmured against my ear, "is not a position you want to be in."

I breathed fast, growing steadily warmer, though I couldn't tell if it was from Keil's body heat or my own rushing blood. I'd out-flustered him in the grand foyer, with our bodies pressed almost as close. But now we were on Keil's turf—playing *his* game—and I was acutely aware of his self-assurance.

And even more aware of my overactive specter, now flittering like a second heartbeat beneath my breast.

Then Keil said with deep command, "Reclaim your power."

And I blinked back into the moment. I twisted, trying to free myself from under his arm, but it had turned solid around me. My shoulders writhed against the wall of his chest, but with my elbows locked flat against him, I had no leverage to thrust him back.

"You see why it's more difficult now?" His voice vibrated along my spine.

I kept struggling, determined. It was like trying to fight against iron. "Because you won't let go?" I said, winded.

"No. My victory isn't *here*." His left arm contracted in emphasis, the movement bringing me closer. His contoured muscles shifted against my back. "It's *here*." He lightly squeezed my right hand, still wrapped around the knife handle.

"When you attack from up high," he explained, "you're showing me your weapon before you use it. I know exactly where you've placed the majority of your power. And now"—he freed my right arm to raise my hand, turning my own weapon against me—"I only have to do *this*." I froze as the blade flashed under my chin. "And you go still. That quickly, your power becomes mine."

I swallowed, less focused on the knife than on his strong arm across my waist, his warm breath stirring my hair. His left hand remained closed at the side of my torso rather than spreading across it, and I knew he was being careful not to touch me with that degree of intimacy while I was at a disadvantage, locked against him like this.

And maybe that was one of the reasons why I didn't fear the blade as I would have if someone other than Keil had been holding it. Why I felt curiously safe with the man who, three minutes ago, I'd accused of following me into the city.

The realization produced a little swoop inside me. I could feel the blush rising up my throat, crawling to the tips of my ears, as Keil unlocked his body from around mine, and the knife clanged to the ground.

I turned to watch him retrieve it, my skin impossibly hot from where we'd made contact. He pressed the handle back to my palm. My hand drooped with the weight.

"It's a weapon, not a quill." He carefully adjusted my grip, positioning my thumb on the handle's spine and tightening my knuckles. "Keep a firm hold, or it'll slip." Then he nudged my feet apart with the toe of his shoe, murmuring deep encouragement. "Good; a little to the left; that's it," he said as I landed in the proper stance.

I would've expected that teaching a member of the Capewell family how best to wield a weapon would feel counterintuitive to him. So I was surprised to find sincerity in his guidance—an air of *wanting* to impart this knowledge, so I would know how to defend myself.

But then, watching him patiently retighten the grasp I'd accidentally let slacken, I wondered why I'd been surprised. From the start,

Keil had treated me with kindness, even when he'd had every reason to hate me. Even when he'd probably believed I was no better than the Hunters, and had still chosen to bandage my hand with the same gentleness he used now.

It was more than I would've offered if our positions were reversed. And though I didn't know what kind of person that made me ... I was starting to understand what kind of person that made *him*.

Now Keil took my waist from above my cloak, leaving an extra layer of fabric between his bare palm and my dress. Yet as he angled my body toward his, as if leading me in a dance, my awareness narrowed on the broad shape of that hand. On the way it molded around the curve of my waist, with the slightest hint of pressure to aid his instruction.

A new, hazier warmth stole over me, the blood pounding so palpably in my lips that I knew if he glanced toward them, he would find them full and strawberry-ripe.

"Aiming low gives you more control," he said, so close now that the breath of his words grazed the side of my face. "And you can better conceal the weapon until you're ready to use it. Deliver a good blow and you're more likely to get away." With a soft press on my elbow, he added, "Keep this tight to your body."

Then, with one hand still enclosing my side, he guided my grip forward, poising the knife tip against his abdomen. "The knife is an extension of your arm. Point your thumb where you want the blade to go ... and *push*." He applied enough pressure that his white shirt wrinkled under the blade.

At this angle, his soap-and-linen scent enveloped me. Each steady rise of his chest grazed my hair, and the heat of his hand was finally radiating through my layers of fabric, warming my waist.

The air thickened and his grip shifted, losing the pressure of instruction. Softening instead with a splay of his fingers—a slight, almost unconscious, brush of his thumb against my ribs.

For a moment, my posture loosened. I felt myself relaxing into the touch.

Then I blinked, catching myself. I started to pull back, but Keil didn't let go.

I looked up to find him smiling faintly, his mouth rich with its own little blood rush of color. As though he'd been absorbing the feel of me with the same vivid detail.

"Always yank out the blade," he said, a shade hoarsely, that sultry mouth still holding my attention. "They'll lose blood faster."

He hesitated, his hand twitching against me. He inhaled. Then he took a step back.

I drew a rushing breath, the stab of cool air scattering the steam of my thoughts. Keil's mouth was none of my business. I would be a prize fool to *make* it my business.

And even more of a fool to lower my defenses for a man who could only ever be my competition.

So, ignoring the skin-prickle of my fading heat, I weighed the knife in my palm. "Should you really be telling me the best ways to hurt you?"

Keil's smile grew, that little dimple winking in his cheek. "Go ahead." He spread his arms as if to embrace me. "I suppose you've been fantasizing about this from the moment we met."

I laughed, astonished. "You're inviting me to stab you?"

"I'm inviting you to *try*."

I couldn't resist the challenge in his voice. So, I lunged, knife aimed at his stomach.

He shot forward so fast I couldn't register the maneuver. I yelped as the knife twisted from my grasp and clattered at my feet once more.

Keil chuckled at the look on my face, then bent to recover the knife. I had half a mind to kick him in the head.

"So, was there a point to your little lesson?" I crossed my arms. "Or was it an excuse to show me up?"

"Of course not, my lady. That wouldn't be gentlemanly."

"A gentleman would've let me stab him," I muttered.

Laughter danced in his eyes. "You're welcome to try again. I'll even teach you more moves." The knife suddenly hovered above his palm, held by the specter I couldn't see. "Well," he drawled. "Perhaps not all the moves."

I startled, astounded both by his public Wielding and that he'd released his specter so near to eurium. Keil didn't share my concern on either front; his posture was relaxed, his expression lazy with harmless mischief.

Envy burned a sudden hole through me, my specter bristling. I'd been leashing my power more forcefully over the last few days, and yet Keil's indifference—his casual freedom—threatened to erode my self-control.

I drew a sharp breath through my teeth. Resentfully tightened those internal restraints.

"As much as I'd like to gut you"—I captured the knife, jolting when my fingers skimmed his specter—"I'll have to decline."

I rebundled the knife, shoved it into my pocket, and marched away.

Keil's footsteps clipped behind me. "I can walk you back to the palace."

"Because I'm incapable of walking there myself?"

"I doubt you're incapable of anything," he said, a grin in his voice. "But you *did* look rather distressed when I found you. Does the king know you're roaming these streets without a guard?"

"The king is not my keeper."

"Not yet."

I spun on him. "We're not at court now, Ambassador. Say what you mean."

"I merely speak from observation. Your king strikes me as a territorial man. I doubt his bride will be able to wander farther than he allows."

"He allows *you* to wander freely."

"He has no desire to keep me close."

"Because you would exasperate him to death?"

Keil smiled bleakly, then said with a note of warning, "Because kings only lock up treasures."

Dread coiled my insides. I didn't want him to be right, and the force of my denial loosened my tongue. "Perhaps not all rulers are like yours—locking people up like possessions, and taking them out to play when it suits them."

He slanted his head, deliberating something. Then he said, his tone unreadable, "You're referring to my empress's reputation, I assume, in imprisoning the would-be heirs who might threaten her rule."

"I hear she's almost as vicious as King Hoyt," I said, naming the most tyrannical ruler in Daradon's history—the creator of the Execution Decree.

"Then you've been misinformed." Keil's grim smile took on a wry twist. "I'm fairly certain she would fillet King Hoyt and feed him to her dogs as a morning snack."

His brows were slightly raised, as though he expected me to prod him for more. As though he'd posed a riddle, and wanted to drip-feed me the answers just to watch me lap them up.

But his chilling statement had given me all I needed to know about the ruler he served.

So I stomped away. His footsteps followed mine a second later.

The alleys were forking off now; he could've branched away at any point.

"I don't know how it works in your empire, but men who stalk women in Daradon end up with their heads on spikes."

"What a waste of a perfectly good spike." Keil overtook my stride and faced me, walking backward as he said, "As lovely as you are, my lady, I didn't come here for you. I came for them."

He turned, and I followed him into the busy street. With a start, I realized I'd circled round again to Backplace.

Keil leaned against a brick building to watch the sympathizers. I joined him, trying to see the scene from his perspective: Wholeborns clanking their staffs on the platform, voices high and condemning.

"Sympathizers don't exist in Ansora," said Keil, enraptured.

Unable to bear his wistful expression, I asked sourly, "Do you think even half of them truly care about Wielders?"

"They seem angry."

"Of course they're angry. Two centuries ago, the mayor of Henthorn tried to incite a rebellion against the Execution Decree and failed. After King Hoyt executed her for treason, he permanently forbade the appointment of a new leader here and let the city fall into disrepair. Now the citizens see the palace spires from their windows while their own roofs are leaking. They smell roses from the royal gardens while their streets are soaked with urine. Hoyt's one act of vengeance became a generational punishment."

Just like the Execution Decree, I added silently.

I tugged my cloak tighter around me. "These people don't care about Wielders. They just need a place to spend their anger."

Keil turned back to the platform in disbelief.

I huffed a bitter laugh. "You look at them and see people willing to fight for you. My perception is not distorted by such biases."

"Do you only ever look for the worst in people?"

"I don't usually have to look very hard."

We remained there a while, listening to the sympathizers' chants, the street lanterns casting a warm halo around us.

Finally, Keil sighed. "You're biased, too. Daradon is all you know."

"And all *you* know is the happy, golden center of your Sun Empire."

Because apparently, Orrenish troops used the islands of the Ansoran archipelago to launch attacks on the mainland, creating a gradient of destruction—and leaving the inner districts still untouched by war.

"Hardly," Keil said, and I raised my brows. He explained, "I did two tours around the archipelago."

"Of duty?"

"No, of the vineyards."

I rolled my eyes, then shifted against the bricks. "Were you drafted?"

Keil shook his head. "There is no draft."

"So, every Ansoran fighting in the Western War . . . has chosen to fight?"

"Is that so hard to believe?"

I bit my lip, considering. Even in Daradon, we'd heard of the Ansoran soldier—the Wielder war hero—who'd single-handedly defended a narrow pass on one of those islands, saving a Wholeborn town from massacre.

To learn that it wasn't from obligation, but *choice* . . .

"I spent nearly two years there," Keil said, faraway with memory. "I saw Wielders fight for Wholeborns, and Wholeborns fight for Wielders. There are no distinctions when the bodies bleed the same."

No distinctions. It was a foreign concept to me.

I looked to the sympathizers again, their eyes flaring with righteous anger—burning brightly for now. But too easily snuffed.

"You won't find such kinship here. The Wholeborns of Daradon don't even fight for each other. They would never fight for people like—" I stopped, shocked at how easily the words had nearly slipped out: *people like us.* "People like you," I finished, keeping my face blank.

Keil was silent for several seconds. I turned to find him studying me with that same knitted-brow expression I'd seen in the tunnels. Like he wanted to take me apart and hold the pieces to the light.

"Stop that," I snapped.

His frown deepened. "Stop what?"

I pushed off the wall and strode from Backplace, the knife thumping against my thigh. The ale-soaked citizens gave me a wider berth than usual, so Keil must have been close on my heels, shooting daggers at those who swayed too near.

"I should add that to my list of talents," he called as the crowds thinned. "The ability to irritate you without saying a word."

"Don't flatter yourself. My irritation is reserved for people who actually matter."

"And what about that wonderful sneer on your lips?" His voice became heavy, teasing. "Is that reserved just for me?"

I scoffed, ignoring the traitorous swoop of my stomach. "Do you have nothing better to do than goad a reaction out of me?"

"I'm doing you a service. I know you relish every opportunity to impale me on your words."

"You don't know a thing about me."

"Oh, you're not so hard to decipher."

I whirled, eyes wide. "Is that so?"

Keil prowled closer. "Lady Alissa Paine." He drew out my name as if to savor the taste. "Intelligent, beautiful, sharp-tongued. It's no wonder the king wants your hand . . . A shame, then, that you don't want his."

I blinked, then forced a bark of laughter. "That's what you think you know about me?"

"I told you: I speak from observation." Keil leaned forward, his honeyed breath tickling my face. "When you mention the king, you clench your jaw. And I see the tiniest flutter right *here*." He brushed a fingertip along my temple. Goose bumps rushed up my arms, and I batted him away.

"You're rather fixated on my prospects," I said, glad that the cool night air stole the hotness from my cheeks. "Do you spend a lot of time imagining me in a crown?"

His grin was maddening. "Do you want me to?"

I scowled, and his deep laughter sent another spike of heat along my bones.

"And what about you?" I asked. "You think I can't read you just as easily?"

He canted his head and said, for the second time tonight, "Go ahead."

Very well, then. I angled back and looked at him—really *looked*—past the loose stance, the twinkling eyes, the easy confidence. Had he been like this even as a soldier, fighting for people who couldn't fight for themselves?

No . . . I'd seen a crack in that light, down in the tunnels—and again, on the palace balcony. A facet of him that contained something deeper than sorrow. Something more like *guilt*.

"You blame yourself for what happened to your sister," I said in soft realization, "though the blame isn't yours to bear."

Like the slow dying of a flame, Keil's smile faded. That same shadow crept over his face. He stood silent, strands of gold-brown hair sweeping in the breeze.

When he finally spoke, his voice was pained. "The empress wouldn't let me travel here without the shield of diplomatic immunity. The others made passage first, hoping to stage a rescue. But I waited until your king approved our request for entry. I waited those weeks while they—" He stopped, released a juddering breath. "I don't know what would've happened if I'd arrived sooner, against the empress's orders. But if it had made one day of difference . . . one hour . . ."

He held my gaze with a frankness that made me feel ashamed. Like I was stripping him bare. Or, rather, that he was baring *himself*—offering a vulnerability I couldn't reciprocate even if I wanted to.

And despite our silent competition for the compass, despite the fact that he would hand such a valuable device to the empress who'd kept him from his sister . . . a part of me *did* want to.

So, I offered in quiet confession, "I didn't know about the dullroot on those glasses."

Keil surprised me with a faint, tender smile. "I know."

My specter fluttered—an echo of my churning emotions—and I had to look away. My gaze landed on a charred patch of cobblestones, and all feeling went out of me.

I hadn't realized how quiet it had become. How we were the only ones around. Had I known where I was going when I'd stormed from Backplace?

I turned to take it in, a chill creeping down my spine.

The Opal had been modeled after Vereen, set to burst with color and craftwork—the first new capital district in two hundred years. That made it worse, seeing it like this: dim and grimy, with paint peeling around the shop fronts and rotten wood boarding the windows. It was how Vereen would look in the wake of disaster.

And the scorch marks beneath that lantern pole, where Erik's guards had tied the man . . . Four winters hadn't washed them away. I could still taste the rancid smoke, still hear the screaming.

Or maybe the screaming had never stopped. Maybe I was still in that crowd, roses grazing my feet, a piece of me tearing away and dissipating like heat rising off the cobblestones—

A touch on my arm—and I jerked, my specter surging. But Keil's eyes anchored me, his steady warmth blooming across my skin.

"Are you all right?" he asked, brows drawn with concern.

I gulped, waiting for the terror to wash over me. Being here so soon after my attack was like digging a scalpel into a reopened wound.

I nodded and drew back, leaving the Opal on weak legs.

Keil's solid presence behind me forced me to keep myself together—to focus through my hazy tunnel vision. In the bustling city center, I finally twisted toward him.

His face quickly slackened, and in that moment he didn't look like a powerful Wielder here to reclaim a coveted Spellmade object for his empress. He looked like a man trying to hide the bemused frown he'd been aiming at my back.

"Good night, Ambassador." I spoke firmly, so he would understand the dismissal. Then, after a brief hesitation, I added, "Thank you. For your help tonight."

He blinked, his expression softening in a way that flipped my stomach again—left me feeling too exposed before him.

So, I walked away. And this time, Keil didn't follow.

 # 21

The nightmilk was easy to find in the royal kitchens, shelved openly in glass vials for use in evening teas. I hadn't needed to take the sedative since my fourteenth summer, when the horrors of the Opal had roused me sobbing from so many nightmares that Father had arranged his blankets at my window seat so he could watch over me.

But tonight, with the peeled-and-faded corpse of the Opal bloating in my mind, I would need *something* to help me sleep.

I was tucking a milky-white vial into my pocket when the light shifted behind me, casting a shadow across the shelves.

"I know why you're here."

I spun and thrust myself back against the wall, whacking my elbow.

Perla stood like a wraith in her nightgown, kitchen blades gleaming around her, the lantern glow outlining her inky shroud of hair.

"Gracious gods!" I clutched my chest, a surge of anger drowning my alarm. "Are you barefoot? I didn't even hear you approach!"

"I know why you're here."

"Yes, I heard the first time." I grabbed an apple from a fruit basket and waved it around. "A late-night snack. Well done."

Perla slowly took me in. Then her dark eyes lifted, round and clear. "You want to see if you can catch him. This is all a game to you."

The apple drooped in my hand. *I know why you're here.* Not here in the kitchens. Here at court. Perla thought I'd come to toy with the king—a cat with a full belly, tormenting a mouse for fun.

And when I'd chosen my prey, I'd deprived Perla of a meal.

I lifted my chin, head clearing. Perla's sister, Petra, had died last year; according to Carmen, she'd been *quite an enchantress*. Perla must have felt she was falling short of her sister's talents, and she needed someone to blame.

It was better to feed her theories than hint at the truth.

So, I would let her think me the cat.

"Everything's a game here," I crooned. Then I added, half-serious, "Don't worry. You can have him back when I'm done."

Perla's eyes flickered with irritation. I set down the apple and went to brush past her.

Then she said, "You were with him tonight, weren't you?"

And I halted, my specter lurching. The city stink clung all over me—sour ale and grill-fire smoke. But beneath the harsher smells lingered the softer notes of soap and linen.

The distinctive scent of Keil.

No. Perla couldn't have possibly known—

"You think Erik won't notice?" she asked, eerie with calm.

I held her stare, pulse thrumming wildly. She must've been watching me more closely than I'd realized. How much had she seen?

"I don't know what you mean," I said.

"I mean you should leave while you still can."

My specter reared at the threat. "What is that supposed to—?"

I gasped as she grabbed my arm, her nails digging into my flesh.

"It will be your own fault," she said, hissing. "You know that, don't you?"

I wrenched away, heaving backward into the counter. Trays crashed behind me, turning my head.

When I whipped around again, Perla was gone.

My nerves were in shreds as I hurried to my chambers. Even if Perla took her claims to Erik, she possessed no proof of my association with Keil. Yet I feared she wouldn't need proof. I feared that Erik's loathing of the Ansorans would be quite enough to kindle his rage.

So I didn't drink the nightmilk. I stared at the ceiling—heart racing, ready to run at any moment. Because if Erik believed I was sneaking off with the ambassador during our courtship . . . I knew exactly what he would do to me.

Judging from the artisanal bonbons Erik sent up with my breakfast tray, Perla hadn't made good on her threat. The miserable girl had probably just intended to unnerve me.

Yet I was still restless as I found a weary-looking Junius playing a solitary card game, his dark bun of braids glistening under a triangle of sunlight. He didn't look up as I slid opposite him.

"I wouldn't sit there," he said flatly. "I'm contagious, apparently."

Indeed, though Junius occupied the best table—positioned beside the open doors to the courtyard—the chattering nobles had miraculously filled every seat in the Games Hall except these seven empty chairs. Across the room, two noblewomen were bunching their skirts to squeeze onto the same ottoman.

Since their two dozen staff members had been Hunted, the Jacombs' status within the gentry had dangerously declined. And courtiers embodied Daradon's symbol better than anyone; why wield knives when thorns cut deeper?

"Don't take it to heart." I toyed with the gilded edge of a playing card. "Nobles hang off each other like accessories. You're simply not fashionable anymore."

Junius snatched the card, nearly nicking my fingers. "What do you want?"

"To be friends."

"I have enough friends."

"Oh?" I glanced at the empty seats. "Are they hiding under the table?" Junius continued playing, and I sighed. "I know you don't like me."

"Do you?" he purred. "How clever."

"*But*," I said, sharpening, "you're spiting the wrong person. I don't choose my friends based on popular fashions."

"No, you choose them based on what *you* gain from the friendship. I've been a courtier far longer than you, Lady Alissa. So I ask again: What do you want?"

I breathed deeply, trying not to bristle at his tone.

After my failure with the Bolting Box, Kevi Banday was my best lead. If he was forging the copycats' weapons, he might steer me directly toward the keeper of the compass. But the fastest way to find him was through records I couldn't obtain.

Junius could.

So I said, with practiced calm, "As a lord of Dawning, you can access the records of every Dawni citizen. I have a name. I need an address."

A breeze wafted from the courtyard, fluttering the cards. Junius laid a palm over them, then said, "No."

I laughed under my breath. "Whoever taught you to haggle did a poor job. You're meant to hear my offer before you refuse."

"I know you overheard my disagreement with Rupert. In return for the address, you'll convince the Creakish to deliver our grain." Junius ran his dark gaze over me before returning to his cards. "A loaf of bread isn't worth the trouble of your friendship."

"Do you think someone smart enough to keep the king's attention would tempt you with something as trivial as grain?"

"Oh, I doubt it was your smarts that grabbed his attention."

I gritted my teeth. Garret had assumed the nobles would be tripping over themselves to earn my favor, but Erik's interest worked against me when it came to Junius.

Luckily, I'd never needed the king's interest to get what I wanted.

I lounged back, nails drumming on the table. "First, the Creakish grain; next, the fish from Avanford. Where courtiers are fickle in their admiration, they're steadfast in their scorn. How far will they go to injure your once-great province?"

"Do you have a point, Lady Alissa, or has aimless cruelty become your nature?"

"I only lament that one allegation can cause such ruin. I'll bet the person who accused your family of knowingly housing Wielders is laughing in their cell as we speak."

I waited for Junius's eyes to narrow. Then I grimaced in a weak imitation of embarrassment. "Excuse me," I said breathily. "I assumed they'd been brought to justice. To besmirch the Jacomb name without consequence . . ." I shook my head. "Have you even identified the accuser?"

Silence.

Then: "Are you a Spellmaker?" Junius snarled. "Because only Spellmakers can bring back the dead. Is that what you're offering?"

I blinked, suddenly rattled. "You know what I'm offering."

"Vengeance?"

"Justice."

"Justice would mean two dozen innocents returned to this world. If you can't offer me that, we're done." He gathered his cards, chair scraping back.

I grasped his hand. He cast me a flesh-searing look, but I didn't let go. Because I finally understood.

The trial hadn't taken this toll on Junius. The *Hunting* had.

"I can't bring them back," I said quietly. "But maybe I can do something else."

22

"I looked into Nelle's whereabouts," Garret said, the revelry outside drowning his voice. Beyond our ivy-covered alcove, the fresh air was abuzz with laughter and the rhythmic *whoosh-thud* as arrows sent apples into troughs.

This afternoon, every noble would pay tribute to the gods of harvest by firing two arrows into two apples—the first for good produce, the second for good appetite. All pierced apples would be stewed, spiced, and folded into sugar-dusted pies.

"And?" I asked, stomach growling as the scent of caramel sauce drifted from the kitchens.

"And Carmen wasn't lying. Nelle moves around often and covers her tracks. She was last seen in Avanford one year ago."

I grimaced. Nelle was still my lead suspect, but since visiting Backplace, my threads of information crisscrossed like cobweb silk. I'd considered that Nelle's strongest motive for these Huntings was to produce an unstable kingdom, ripe with tension and ready to fall.

But fall to whom, if Carmen was truly fleeing Daradon with her lover?

Perhaps Garret had been right and we *were* dealing with Wholeborn extremists, motivated only by their hatred of Wielders. But if so, was Nelle still best-placed at the top of my list? Other figures at court displayed a more obvious Wielder intolerance—like Sabira, who was already scouring her province's abandoned smithies for sympathizer units.

But it had been *Nelle's* chamber key beside Wray's body—and that fact looped me back to the beginning of my theory cycle.

Clearly missing a piece of the picture, I'd thought to access Nelle directly.

Now I could only hope Kevi Banday knew enough about the copycats to make my next request worthwhile.

"I need information," I said stiltedly, "about the Hunting on the Jacomb estate." I lowered my voice to explain exactly what I'd offered Junius yesterday.

Garret's forehead puckered. "You shouldn't have promised that."

"Can you get it or not?"

A sigh whistled through his nose. This was the first we'd spoken since Grayday, when, after having touched my specter for the first time in seven years, he'd left me staring after him. I'd believed he'd drawn all the way back into himself then, unreachable.

And yet our interaction today felt . . . *fragile*. Like the pain we'd both laid bare that night had truly paved a new ground beneath us—but that one wrong step would send us falling through the cracks.

Finally, he said, "I'll try." Then, stiffly, unused to showing concern: "Remember they might be watching you now. You're being careful?"

Actually, I replied internally, *I've been traipsing around the city, not-so-subtly asking for information about my attacker's weapon.*

But before I could think of a more palatable answer, applause erupted from Erik's group of nobles; the king had just struck his first apple off its stand. He milked the attention before aiming again, his second arrow zipping straight and true. The group cheered louder, like the juice spray of an apple was the most entertaining thing they'd ever seen.

My gaze drifted to a nearby group, where, in contrast to Erik's silver-blue grandeur, Keil stood as a figure of sun-soaked gold, all easy composure and rolling muscles. He was chatting, laughing, demonstrating the proper archery stance to a cohort of giggling noblewomen. Defying tradition, he'd nocked both arrows at once, and now he angled diagonally before the two stands.

He drew the bowstring taut—his white shirt straining around his biceps, his back muscles bunching with the pull—and I warmed with the memory of his body locked around mine. I was wondering how those muscles might feel in a softer embrace, going loose against me, when Keil released the bowstring—and his arrows whooshed free, hitting the apples in a successive *splat-splat*. The resulting applause of Keil's little group rivaled that of the king's.

I bit my lip around a smile.

"That's the ambassador?" Garret murmured, reclaiming my attention. He'd been watching me watch Keil. Now his gaze narrowed on the Wielder, and I tensed, awaiting that spark of recognition. But Garret's expression flickered instead with something like rivalry as he said, "He's young."

I exhaled. I didn't want Garret knowing where to find the Wielder who'd disarmed him on the Verenian fields, and whose accomplices had beaten him bloody. Though, truthfully, I didn't know which of the two men I was trying to protect.

Garret turned toward me again, adjusting his cufflink. "I should get back before Briar notices I'm gone. She's no closer to locating the compass, and growing more anxious by the day."

"Good," I muttered.

"*You* don't have to live with her." He quirked a brow, smirking. "She nearly disemboweled one of your cousins last night for breathing too hard near her dinner plate."

I huffed in amusement—then blinked, surprised. It was the first time in years that Garret had drawn from me anything resembling laughter.

He must have realized it, too, because his smirk fell. He watched me closely now, brows pinched—unease bordering on panic. As if the sound of my humor would pull him somewhere he didn't want to go.

Then he cleared his throat, all sharp edges and brutal business. "She'll calm down once the compass is in my hands."

Once the compass is in my hands.

I averted my eyes at the sudden twist of guilt. Then I paused, noticing redness around Garret's tanned wrist.

"What's that?" I grabbed his sleeve, and he actually startled.

"Nothing." He tried to extricate my searching fingers, but I'd already bared his raw skin—slightly raised and shiny, as if from a slow-healing rope burn.

"Garret—"

"It's nothing," he repeated firmly, pulling away. But I'd seen that look on him before—proud and resigned, with a shadow of humiliation.

It was how he'd looked after Briar had beaten him as a boy.

My specter bristled.

"Did she do that?" I asked, dangerously low. Garret looked away—a silent admission. "Let me see." I grabbed for him again.

"No." He drew his arms back. "You still fuss like a nursemaid."

"And you still grouse like a child." I reached all the way around him, my cheek skimming his blazer.

"Alissa." The way he said my name—soft and unguarded—made me look up. My arms encircled him in a near-embrace, our bodies brushing close, but he didn't pull away. In fact, an uncertain smile was testing itself around his mouth. He gently took my wrists from behind him, unwound me, and returned my arms to my sides. "I'm fine," he promised.

My chest twinged as his touch slipped down, grazing my hands before withdrawing.

I swallowed, taking a long backstep.

I'd always known it would hurt to stitch the tear between Garret and me; the needle would have to skewer us both before dragging us back together. But it wasn't until Grayday, when his shuddering breaths had kissed across my specter with enough vulnerability to crack me down the middle, that I realized how deeply he'd always cared for me. How he'd never really stopped.

But while I'd forever taken the same form in Garret's mind—never changing, because I hadn't been the one who'd walked away—*I* had to relearn him. And I didn't yet know how to feel about this new openness in his eyes. I didn't know how much of myself I wanted to trust him with again—or whether, after all these years, whatever I *could* give would be enough for him, considering he'd never quite let me go.

But maybe having Garret in my life again—in any capacity—might be worth the pain of finding out.

So I smothered my pride. Decided to take the next skewering. "You could stay," I offered quietly. "Make your tribute to the gods."

Garret squinted across the field, dark lashes tipped with sunlight. His barely there smile disappeared. "I haven't had an appetite for seven years. An arrow won't change that."

I considered trying again. But it felt like we kept reaching toward one another at different moments, missing each other every time. So, I donned my silk gloves and let him be.

We split in opposite directions without a second glance.

I was climbing the field, still troubling over Garret's rope burns, when Erik blocked my path with an outstretched bow.

His eyes sparkled. "Care to make your tribute?"

I grasped the bow, pulling up a smile. "I'd be honored."

As I joined the king's group—heavily composed of eighteenth-season girls—I glanced coldly at Perla, having lost all sympathy for her since she'd practically threatened to expose my association with Keil. Though as I watched her shrink from the king now, I realized I shouldn't have worried. She couldn't stand to look Erik in the eyes long enough to make her claim against me.

I nocked my first arrow as the attendant placed an apple atop each stand. Then he moved so far aside that I glared. Though I wasn't exactly a talented archer, I was unlikely to veer *that* far off target.

Erik drifted over, chuckling, his embroidered jacket scratching my arms. "Allow me."

I tried not to clench up as his body curved behind me. He commandeered my hold on the bow, fingers closing over mine, his cool breath tickling my bare nape. I shivered, wishing I'd worn my hair down. Of course trapping a girl had to be Erik's idea of courtship.

"They're good shots." His words grazed against me. "The Parrians."

I took the opportunity to shift away slightly, looking toward the nobles from the military province and their trough of conquered apples. Sabira seemed the anomaly of the group, having just about hit her second apple after widely missing the first—a combination foretelling no produce, all appetite.

For a woman who always appeared battle-ready in her armored gown, I'd expected better aim.

"Did you know," said Erik, lifting my bow into my eyeline, "that Parrians have a way of identifying Wielders?"

My body tensed. My specter curled into a knot. "Oh?" I breathed.

"In fact"—he drew the bowstring for me, forcing my elbow back—"Sabira's mercenaries employed the method a few days ago, on sixty-three sympathizers."

These must have been the mercenaries who were scouring Parrey's abandoned smithies. My palms slickened inside my gloves.

"The trick," Erik said, "is to tie a person down . . ." His lips brushed my ear. "Take aim between their eyes . . ." His grip tightened until it hurt. "And fire."

He released the bowstring, and I jumped as my arrow thwacked the apple.

I tried to control my breathing while Erik nocked the second arrow. But my pulse was pounding in my throat as he folded himself around me again, taking my fingers under his. Keil had held me in a comparable position only recently, his embrace more confining than Erik's. And yet the heat flooding me now wasn't similarly slow and molten. It was a blotchy fever-heat. The sickly sweat of a body in danger.

"If you strike true," Erik continued, "you've offered a Wholeborn a quick death. But if the arrow veers off course?" He swiveled abruptly. Cocooned in his hold, I was forced to swivel with him.

As he directed my next arrow squarely at Perla.

"Well." Erik's voice betrayed a cruel smile. "Then you've caught yourself a Wielder."

Perla froze. Her eyes went round; her white-washed lips trembled. A more violent tremble rose up my limbs.

"It's very clever," I said, voice wispy with panic, my fingers trying to strain away. Though Perla wasn't my favorite person, I didn't want her *dead*.

"Shall we test the method, you and I?" Erik angled the bow toward Perla's foot. "Perhaps someplace she won't miss?"

"I believe most people would miss their toes."

His laughter juddered against my back, and I fought the impulse to arch away. "Did I misread that look you gave her?" His voice took on a twist of teasing. "Wouldn't you like to make her bow to you—right here, in front of everyone?"

I flicked my eyes around to the alarmed faces of the gentry, trained in our direction. About to watch the king of Daradon fire an arrow into a young woman's foot. About to watch *us* fire the arrow, together.

"Not like this," I panted, my specter writhing with indecision. Because to redirect the arrow would be to expose myself—or implicate Perla. But to *release* the arrow, to hear her screaming, to have her blood on my hands because of Erik—

No.

My specter roared forward, frantically coiling around the arrow shaft, ready to swing it aside.

Then Erik—just as suddenly—swerved me back toward the apple. My specter swung with the movement, the breath hitching up my throat.

"Very well," he said placidly. "Imagine, then, a Wielder tied to your stand. Perhaps our Ansoran friend." I felt his face shifting behind me, and I followed his stare.

Unlike the open-mouthed nobles, Keil was watching us from against his own apple stand, his expression calm and unreadable—so at odds with my own anxious jittering.

"Picture the arrowhead burying deep," Erik whispered. "And then"—his fingers slid off mine, leaving them quivering around the bowstring—"*fire*."

The bowstring slipped from my hold.

My specter rushed out like the line of a fishing rod, guiding the arrow straight toward the apple. Too straight.

With a painful tug, I forced its release. The arrow lost momentum.

And plummeted into the grass.

I released a wobbling exhale as a collective sigh rushed across the fields. Too overwrought to lift my specter, I dragged it back through the prickly grass.

It was pouring thickly into me when Keil's power slid inside my glove.

I twitched, peeking toward him. But while his specter thrummed against my fingertips with that soft, familiar strength, Keil was looking behind me—toward Erik, whom I assumed was holding his steady gaze. A bitter anger worsened my trembling. Had this display been for Keil's benefit? Just one more hideous example of Erik showing his thorns—a habit he'd adopted as a young king and now couldn't relinquish?

I was still shaking when Keil's specter flared, reminding me of his warm touch at the Opal when he'd asked, *Are you all right?*

I turned before Erik noticed the trail of my attention. Then I curled my fingers slightly. Answering Keil's question with my own silent *yes*.

Erik squeezed my shoulder, and I jolted. Keil's specter glided up my arm in retreat, leaving a trail of goose bumps in its path.

"An unfortunate fate," Erik declared as the gentry bustled up again. "All produce, no appetite." The exact of opposite of Sabira's result.

I struggled to uphold a smile. "I don't possess your skill in archery."

"No matter." His expression softened with understanding. "There's still time to learn." His tone made me uneasy; it was the indulgent tone one used toward a child who wasn't yet daring enough to dive into the deep end of a lake.

Before I could analyze it, he repossessed the bow and swept it wide. "Lady Perla. Take your turn."

Perla gulped, looking as ill as I felt. "Oh, no, Your Majesty, please—"

"Quickly, now. Don't make the other ladies wait."

Perla stumbled forward. And despite the jelly looseness of her limbs, she took the bow with a steady hand, her knuckles slightly clenched.

I went to excuse myself just as Erik said to me, his voice rich and sweet, "I ordered a gift from Vereen to be sent to your chambers. Tell me how you like it."

With another fraught smile, I darted off.

All the way through the palace, one scene saturated my mind: Sabira's mercenaries tying down those sixty-three Parrian sympathizers, shooting arrows into their foreheads one by one.

This show of violence would surely deter more potential sympathizers. Where other nations may have mutinied, Daradonians would recoil. I'd witnessed it myself at the Opal; for every step forward this kingdom took, those in power would shove us back.

And yet . . . for the first time in four years, I felt a kernel of hope opening up. I'd told Keil that Wholeborns wouldn't fight for Wielders. But the recent increase in Huntings must have fostered enough sympathy that for one brief, shining moment, *sixty-three* Wholeborns had actually tried to organize shelter for Wielders.

The knowledge was bittersweet. After all, it had cost them their lives.

I was pulling off my gloves, silk clinging to my palms, when I approached my chambers and slowed.

My door was ajar. Even if Erik had sent a gift, why would anyone leave the door open?

My specter stirred as I inched over the threshold, door hinges whining.

Sunlight blanched the empty lounge. A shuffle sounded and I backtracked, reaching behind me for the doorknob.

And from my bedchamber, Father stepped into view.

23

Father's face had just begun to sink with uncertainty when I crashed into him, wrapping my arms tight. He went rigid for a moment. Then he exhaled long and warm into the crook of my neck, his arms enveloping me.

Maybe I'd known how fast I would melt for my father. Maybe that was why I hadn't tried to see him before leaving home—because I couldn't hold on to my anger while I was holding on to him.

We pulled apart and he looked me over, eyes glassy.

"You look like a courtier," he whispered. Regret tinged the words. With a weak sniff, he drifted to the window and stared across the gardens. An aura of sunlight bronzed his face.

"I promised your mother I'd bring her here one day." His words were fragile, as if he feared they might shatter upon release. "She hated the luxury, but she longed for the views. The white palace spires. The famous gardens. She wanted to swing her legs over the highest balcony and watch the sunset. And all I ever wanted was to make her happy."

It had always pained Father to speak of my birth mother. I didn't know exactly how she'd died, or even how she'd lived; I only had her lucky coin, an inherited specter, and the empty space inside me where her story should have been.

Now I drifted beside Father, heart pattering, desperate for more but afraid to push.

He closed his eyes and sighed. The xerylites on his brooch glimmered, containing a thousand bursting stars. "I was enchanted by your mother from the moment we met. She was charming and brazen and everything I wished I could be. And the way she looked at the world . . ." He opened his eyes, smiling. "You're like her in many ways, but I fear you've inherited my cynicism."

I laughed as the first tear tracked a warm path down my cheek. Already, I was committing these words to memory, to hoard inside me like jewels.

"She knew the truth about the Capewells from early on. When she discovered she was pregnant, she didn't want you to have to hide your specter as she did. She . . . also struggled with confinement."

I swallowed hard, throat burning. My mother had known the pain of self-restraint. Though we'd shared so little time together, we shared that pain.

"Even then," Father continued, "Bormia didn't accept refugees. But she found someone who could forge Bormian citizenships. We'd planned to sneak across the border through Orren—a long, dangerous journey that would have put us in the heart of Orrenish territory. I didn't sleep for weeks in preparation—burning all evidence of my connection to your mother so nobody could link our disappearances.

"Then my wife, Fiona, became ill again. The physicians said this bout would be her last." Father dropped his gaze. "Lady Fiona knew my heart belonged to another even before our arranged marriage, and she knew of my affair afterward. She was kind to me, though I didn't deserve it. I'd been ready to abandon my province, my title . . . but I couldn't abandon Fiona in her sickness."

Father looked up at me, eyes shining. "Then you were born," he whispered. "And it was as if you'd brought my life into the world with you. As if there had been nothing before you, and all that mattered was everything after. Once Fiona passed, we would journey to Bormia as planned."

His hand shook, scrubbing over his mouth. He turned back to the window. "But your mother was discovered. She knew the Capewells were tracking her, and she kept it from me." His voice cracked. "She made sure you weren't with her when they came."

My cheeks were hot with tears, but I didn't wipe them away. Father and I cried together—silent tears for a silent mourning.

"When I found out," he said, "I wanted to take you and run. But I knew I couldn't protect you on our journey through Orren as she would have. And I"—he exhaled tightly—"I was too afraid to try. You must have sensed my anguish because you wouldn't stop crying. Fiona heard you from her deathbed. I told her then about the child I'd sired, and she requested to see you. The moment she held you, she somehow knew what you were. I told myself it was the delirium—she couldn't have possibly known about your specter. But I remember the awe in her eyes . . . as if she were gazing into a light so radiant she couldn't stand to look away." Father shook his head, lost to the memory.

"Fiona insisted I put her name on your birthing papers, so you would be my legitimate heir. She'd been out of society long enough that nobody would question a pregnancy. She signed the papers herself, her hand shaking."

I pressed a palm to my chest, feeling an eighteen-year-old weight lift off me. I'd always carried a secret guilt for sewing Fiona's name onto mine. But now I knew . . . she'd taken up the thread by choice—had lovingly rewoven her past to allow me a future.

I sent up a thought of gratitude to my mothers, one of birth and one of name, both of whom had protected me in their final acts.

Father unfolded a parchment from his jacket, and fresh tears filled my eyes. "I burned the others," he said, "but I couldn't part with this. I drew it the day you were born. It was the happiest I'd ever seen her."

Looking into my mother's face was like coming home. Joy marked every brushstroke, from the laughing eyes to the crinkle at the bridge of her nose. And her smile—wide and crescent-shaped, with dimples pinching each cheek . . . that was my smile. Beneath the corkscrew curls of her hair, Father had written, *Darcy Calloway, my only love.*

My specter wound around the coin in my pocket. As I set it rotating between us, Father's face lit with a wonder I'd never known him to possess. Slowly, his hand lifted to brush my specter. My mother's coin faltered and I reshaped the power, threading it through Father's fingers like the flow of water around rocks in a lake.

"It feels like hers." He smiled fondly. "It always has."

The moment stretched between us, silent and shimmering.

Then Father cleared his throat and folded the drawing back into his pocket. "When Erik summoned me this morning, I'd feared it was for another reason."

My smile wavered; the coin dropped to my palm.

Father's expression turned pained. "Tell me you're not entertaining him, my girl."

I refrained from looking at the floor. *I can't let the Capewells reclaim the compass*, I wanted to explain. *Erik will punish them for their failure. And I can't risk him punishing you alongside them.*

So I'd formed a backup plan. I'd been toeing a precarious line these last weeks, making Erik believe I was interested enough to consider his proposal, yet challenging enough that he would do anything to possess me. But clearly, my methods were working: having remembered my reluctance to leave home for my eighteenth season, Erik had gifted me with Father's presence this afternoon.

Now I had to hope he would gift me with Father's safety if I begged.

Of course, it would be that much harder to refuse him the next time he proposed. But that was a dilemma for another day—a dilemma far favorable to its alternative.

"Of course I'm not," I lied. "Besides, his advisors are pushing for Lady Perla."

Father looked unconvinced.

"Did Briar find out you released her prisoners?" I asked, swerving off topic.

Father winced. "Garret took sole blame. Briar gave him twenty lashes for insubordination. She came to the manor to taunt me about it."

Twenty lashes. I recoiled at the mental image of Garret's shredded back—and those rope burns, probably caused by sagging against restraints. Then I realized . . . Garret had fought my attacker with those wounds.

Father said, regretful again, "You care for the boy."

I couldn't deny it. I didn't know what would become of the Capewells after Erik finished with them—if he would choose others to take their place, or force them into service again, broken and blue. But I would use all my influence to liberate Father from the Hunters' Mark tattooed over his heart. To detach him permanently from Briar's claws.

And I'd known, for some time now, that I would detach Garret, too.

I wasn't sure what Father had read in my expression—whether he suspected more about my plans than he let on—but he grasped my hands then, his ink-stained fingers brushing my knuckles. "Your mother would be so very proud of you," he said. "Just as I am."

I sank into his grip. There were still so many lies to untangle, so much pain to process; trying to protect him had distracted me from the greater agony of trying to forgive him. But . . . I was beginning to *understand* him in a way I never had. I was prepared to sell myself to a king in the hopes that he would spare my father. Would it be so different to sell the lives of others? To damn them if it meant saving the person I loved most?

I didn't yet know how to heal this fresh wound between us. I knew that one day, I would have to try.

But for this moment, I let my father fold his arms around me. And I breathed him in with the scent of home.

24

The ballroom sparkled in cherry red.

Tonight was Budding Ball, one of the most anticipated events of Rose Season, famous for how many courtships it kindled each year—especially among the eighteenth-season nobles. Indeed, this evening's festivities had swept like a cake knife across the tiers of the gentry to skim off the youngest, sweetest frosting layer of courtiers and whip them up into a state of romance.

Silk sheets flowed from ceiling to floor like spilled wine, creating a maze of screens—some falling close enough to form hidden pockets of space, meant for shared touches and stolen kisses. The servers, dressed in burgundy trousers and bowties, sprayed partygoers with blood orange essence, and the mist coasted like a heady syrup through the air. I stifled a laugh as I glimpsed Tari spritzing the essence straight onto her tongue, a ruby moon of rouge at each angular cheek.

Even Carmen, who I'd been avoiding since my attack, had insisted I sport proper Budding Ball attire, and had barreled into my chambers this evening with the most beautiful gown I'd ever seen. Whorls of scarlet lace comprised the sweetheart bodice and gave way to tulle skirts, layered like unfurling petals and dotted with garnets. I'd donned matching chandelier earrings, and Carmen had made me up with kohl flicks around my eyes, gold-flecked rouge, and a deep red lip.

I'd felt uneasy and strangely vulnerable with my eyes closed in the beauty chair, Carmen's breaths whispering across my face. At one point, when I'd peeked through my lashes, I'd found her looking toward my closet—and I'd stiffened, wondering if she was thinking about her own closet, and the pink feather I'd accidentally snagged when I'd hidden inside it. The feather I still suspected had led to my attack.

Now she shimmied between the silks, a vision of red diamonds on slinky satin, and I pasted on my performer's smile. There was something deeply sad about having to use it with the only friend I'd ever made at court.

"Your face matches your hair," I said.

She mussed her crimson curls. "A burden I must bear."

Tonight, the ballroom was split into kissers and receivers, with kissers sporting painted mouths in every luscious shade of red, and receivers sporting lipstick kisses across their cheeks, giving the appearance of blooming rosebuds. Carmen, in typical defiance, occupied both roles—her scarlet mouth smudged from kissing, her cheeks boasting more "rosebuds" than anyone else's.

I leaned over to plant my own. "Another rose for your garden?"

"On the cheekbone, darling. I'm working up a blush."

I could've sworn she tensed when my mouth met her cheek.

As I withdrew, my gaze fell on Perla's alcove. Swamped in maroon skirts, she watched the party with a cheerlessness more suited to a wake. I had to pity her. When Erik had aimed that arrow at her on the fields, my fear had been red-hot and quaking—but hers had been pale and still. The freeze-up of a creature feigning death.

"Remarkable, isn't it?" Carmen said. But her azure eyes were on

Keil, currently being devoured—peck after peck—by a group of noblewomen.

My stomach made a strange *flip* at the sight.

"What do you think makes him so alluring?" Carmen patted her lips in appraisal. "I think it's the mystery. *Is* he a Wielder? *Isn't* he a Wielder?"

"You know what he is," I said, referring to his telltale flinch from the dullroot glasses.

"Well, all right. But would his diplomatic immunity then allow for our romance?"

I barked a laugh. "Your romance?"

"Hypothetical, of course. There's something tragically beautiful about the forbidden."

"Public urination is forbidden. Is that tragically beautiful?"

"Oh, you take the fun out of everything. Some of us don't have monarchs lusting after us like puppies in heat. We must make do with our fantasies." She sighed wistfully, and I couldn't tell if she was thinking of the man she'd secretly met at Backplace, or—oddly—if she wasn't thinking of him at all.

"Maybe a foreign ruler will sweep you off your feet," I said, watching for her reaction.

Carmen just swigged her wine, smearing red across the rim. "Why play a king's bride when I could play king? Now if you'll excuse me, I must go and charm the breeches off Rupert. His new scotch collection is in desperate need of pillaging."

I waved her off and plucked up a wine flute. Keil's eyes landed on me instantly, like he'd been waiting for Carmen to leave. He peeled away from the noblewomen and swaggered to my side, a red cummerbund adorning his white shirt this evening.

"Someone's popular." I nodded toward the lipstick marks crowding his face.

"Don't worry." He pulled at his collar, exposing the bare neck beneath. "I can find an exclusive place for you."

"Is that place *in your dreams?*"

He grinned. "Not even for tradition?"

"Not even if you paid me in lemon cakes."

"Ouch." He laughed around a sip of wine. "I heard some of the noblemen competing for the most kisses, and I like a challenge. A few ladies are offering dances to the victor." He glanced down at me, eyes bright. "Care to add yourself to the prize pot? I'd try twice as hard to win."

"You seem to be trying hard enough already," I crooned. "I wouldn't want you to overexert yourself."

He laughed again—a deep, sultry sound that curled my toes. "Do you know," he said, swirling the bubbles in his flute, "I still haven't heard an explanation for tonight's peculiar customs."

I gave him a scathing once-over. "Yet you're enduring them like a hero."

His smile widened until that dimple flickered in his left cheek. And with sudden conviction, I knew I would've placed my first kiss right there. Right over that wicked little crease.

But my second kiss, I would've savored along the column of his throat . . . trailing low enough that he really would need to pull down his collar.

If only to distract myself from the abrupt flutter behind my ribs, I said, "The tradition started with King Emory, the most irresistible ruler of Daradon, whose cheekbones could cut glass. The noblewomen constantly squabbled over him."

"With cheekbones that sharp, who could blame them?"

I smothered a smile. "One night during Rose Season, the ladies decided to end their bickering. They each donned a different lip color and declared that whoever marked the king with a kiss could have him. One by one, King Emory took the ladies strolling under a sky so dark they had to remove their heels to keep from falling. When the ladies congregated at dawn, they each claimed they'd seduced him. Of course, Emory's face would reveal the truth. But when they located him, his cheeks and lips were spotted with every shade of red. 'Why pick one,' he asked, 'when I could have you all?'"

"What a dreadful king," said Keil.

"The women weren't any better. They thought to own him with a single kiss."

"Are all the characters in Daradon's stories so unpleasant?"

I peered up at him. "I suppose Ansoran tales are brimming with do-gooders?"

"Far from it. Our most famous tale is that of the First Emperor Saxon, who conquered every kingdom on the continent with his sword, the Unbreakable Blade. Legend says Saxon imbued the sword with an unknown power—a power so great that his enemies trembled in fear when they beheld it."

I chuckled into my flute.

"You think it's far-fetched?" Keil asked.

"Not at all. For a children's tale, I think it's perfectly proportioned."

"In that case"—he deposited his flute on a passing tray and offered me his hand—"would you do me the honor of celebrating such *believable* immorality with a dance?"

My specter tingled at my fingertips, as if to carry my hand into his.

I shifted toward him with a sweet smile. Pulled my specter back. "Win the game," I said. "Then we'll see."

I slipped my flute into Keil's hand and left him staring after me.

As it turned out, the theatrics of Budding Ball left little opportunity for dancing. Once the ballroom heaved with enough music and wine, those who sought amusement assembled on the dance floor, where red ribbons hung from the ceiling amid the silks. The kissers tied a ribbon around one wrist and weaved between the silk screens; the receivers followed the trail of these ribbons toward the promise of a kiss. It was a tangled, boisterous affair, made all the more chaotic by Carmen wrapping every kisser in their own ribbon and twirling them back out into the crowd.

I was kissing the cheek of an Avanish nobleman when the princess caught me. She spun me round and round inside my ribbon so fast that even my eye roll lost its trajectory. Then, with a devious twinkle and a little more force than necessary, Carmen thrust me away again.

I unraveled—skirts twisting, head spinning, silk gliding against my skin. My ribbon reached its end and I landed with a huff against a hard body.

I knew before looking that it belonged to Keil.

We stood in a crevice, red silks rippling as the game raged unseen around us. I was breathing heavily, flustered from the twirling, and when Keil's eyes dipped over me, I grew doubly flustered.

Someone jostled against me and I winced, feeling a sharp tug on my earlobe. My hair had tangled around my chandelier earring. I lifted my hand—and jerked as the ribbon held me back.

Keil shifted closer. And he slowly reached for my ear.

The surrounding noise seemed to muffle, voices bleeding away, as Keil disentangled my earring. He worked with gentle care, freeing strand by strand, leaving patches of warmth wherever his fingers grazed—my earlobe, my neck, my jaw. The little space grew heavy with our shared breaths, and he must have noticed my flush because he met my gaze as he finished, wicked amusement lighting his eyes.

"You're free," he whispered.

Then another tug—on my *wrist*—and the world rushed back to me as I was yanked by my ribbon into the crowd.

I followed the pull to Erik.

The king half smiled, pleased at his conquest, and, with another playful tug, asked me for a kiss—his first and only of the night. My instincts must have numbed since that day on the fields, because I leaned toward him without flinching. And as I pressed my lips to his cheek, I found Keil's eyes in the crowd of red.

Keil's throat bobbed under my stare, his honey-gold skin flaming with a shade I wanted to paint on a victory flag.

I didn't know why I journeyed to the drawing room after the game ended. I only knew that I felt hot all over and a little lightheaded, and I needed the fresh air to cool off.

Coming up behind Keil on the balcony, I realized he'd needed to cool off, too.

He must have sensed my presence because he chuckled without turning. "If you were too shy to kiss me in front of the gentry, you could have said so."

"How have you not already tripped on the train of your ego?"

"I pin it to my belt to keep it out of the way."

I rolled my eyes, turning to leave... But the sky was an open geode tonight, clear and clustered with stars. A string of red paper lanterns encircled the railing, casting a rosy vignette on the stones. I told myself I was staying for this little pocket of enchantment. For the lush view of the gardens, twinkling below.

But as I joined Keil at the railing and glimpsed his growing smile, I knew that wasn't true.

Still, I stood far enough away that I wouldn't be tempted to lean toward his body heat. More lipstick splotches covered his face, some layered as if the poor girls had run out of room. His mouth was noticeably unmarked, which gave me a pang of relief.

Then Keil said, slow and soft, "He's rather taken with you."

And I knew I wasn't the only one thinking about the unwelcome lips of others.

"Yes." I sighed, lifting my face to the cool night air. "Apparently, I'm quite the catch."

"Hmm," Keil agreed.

I peered over my shoulder and found his gaze trailing the stretch of my neck, the sweep of my collarbone. He blinked, and his eyes landed on my face again, alight with new heat.

My cheeks tingled. So much for cooling off.

Then, for the first time, nervousness wriggled at the back of my mind. Because although we'd been alone in the palace before, our seclusion now felt different—*heavy*, with more secrets than one. And if anyone saw the look passing between us, they would realize what I hadn't wanted to admit. What even Perla must have known but hadn't possessed enough gumption to reveal.

That in whatever space existed between me and Keil, the air was charging to ignite.

So, I looked away. Then I paused, detecting a gleam in Keil's hand. Over the railing, he fiddled with a small, diamond-shaped slat of glass—sometimes twirling it between his fingers, sometimes taking it up with his specter, making it appear as though floating.

It reminded me of how I twirled my mother's coin—though

perhaps a sharper, more dangerous version.

"Dayglass," Keil said, noticing my attention. "Ansoran lands are rich with it."

"Your lands are rich with broken glass?" I asked dryly. "How painful that must be for your feet."

"Not glass." He smiled. "*Dayglass*." Then he drew back, raised the shard, and whacked it against the railing.

I gasped, instinctively recoiling from the shatter.

But there was no shatter. The glass remained whole and glossy, without even a scratch.

At my expression, Keil's smile turned mischievous. He offered me the shard. "It's as strong as diamond. Under sunlight, it glows as if a rainbow has been captured within."

I couldn't resist pushing off the railing and taking the dayglass for a closer look.

The shard was warm from Keil's touch, the edges softer than I'd realized—filed for safe handling—but it otherwise felt like any other glass fragment.

"Keep it," said Keil. "View it in sunlight for yourself. Though I ask that you don't show it to your king."

I quirked a brow. "Erik's interested in dayglass?"

"Most kingdoms are. But my empress doesn't desire a trade deal yet."

Yet.

She might then use this valuable material as a bargaining tool—just as she would likely use the compass. For her *own* benefit, rather than for the protection of fellow Wielders.

Keil slipped his hands into his pockets, head tilting. "It would be best if Erik remained unaware of this sample. One taste of pleasure usually begets an appetite."

I glanced back at the dayglass, now frowning slightly. "You would trust me with this?"

Keil laughed under his breath. "You sound surprised, my lady. Do you forget that every minute I spend at court is a product of my trust in you?"

My frown deepened. I could've exposed Keil as a kidnapper several times over by now. But my silence had nothing to do with trust.

"You still owe me a favor, Ambassador. I'm unlikely to reveal your secrets until I recover the debt."

"*Until?*" Keil ambled closer, amusement teasing around his mouth. "And after my debt is settled, would you go back on your word? Reveal me after all?"

I could, I wanted to say. *Because you're here for the compass, just like I am. We both know we're waging a silent battle. And neither of us is going to let the other win.*

Instead, I placed the dayglass on the railing. This game of flirtation was one thing, but I didn't want the burden of Keil's trust. Not when I might have to break it.

"Court is filled with charming vipers," I said, chin lifted. "But we are vipers all the same."

Keil stopped two paces away. The playful light in his eyes softened. "I saw your face at the exchange," he said quietly. "When you realized what was inside that wagon."

I winced at the memory of my kidnapping—the horror in realizing Keil had traded my freedom for the Capewells' Wielder prisoners.

"I know vipers," he said, still earnest. "You, Lady Alissa, are no viper."

The dayglass lifted from the railing, glistering with a sheen of starlight, and slid into my pocket.

As the pressure of Keil's specter trailed against me, withdrawing, I raised my hand to find it—grasping, as I had that night on the Verenian fields.

Keil froze. And though I couldn't feel it anymore, I knew his specter had paused, too.

All my life, I'd wanted to meet another Wielder. Now Keil was in front of me, and there was a distance between us—one I hadn't allowed myself to cross because we were competing on opposite sides.

But for one night, I wanted to indulge the tenderest part of myself—the part I'd always had to secure with thorned defenses. The part that never could've thrived in a kingdom that wanted my blood.

Tonight, I didn't want Keil to be my rival.

So I stepped closer, my layered skirts brushing his knees. And despite how exposed we were atop this balcony, despite my own better judgment, I whispered, "Show me."

The world stilled again, only our quiet breaths and the bobbing lanterns filling the silence.

Then Keil's specter coiled between my fingers. I didn't twitch; the rippling pressure was familiar now, akin to the warm feel of his skin. He guided my hand upward, then lifted his palm to face mine. His power flowed through the inch of space between us, twining our fingers and wrists, thrumming with the pace of Keil's quickening heartbeat.

Locking a specter away would be like going through life holding your breath, he'd once said. He was right. My specter strained inside me, yearning to exhale—to comb through his power like fingers through sand.

"How does it feel?" I breathed, aware of the moment's fragility.

Keil said, just as quiet, "That's like asking how it feels to move an arm. There's no separation. The specter *is* me."

Was that how I felt? After years of leashing my specter—of bending it to my will—I'd come to think of it as an entity separate from myself. The specter was mine, but it was not *me*.

It felt like something I should've been sad about.

Keil studied my face. "Would you choose to have it if you could?"

I faltered, an odd sense of guilt creeping over me. Because, once again, Keil was baring himself. And once again, I couldn't bring myself fully to do the same.

So, coming as close as I dared to honesty, I mentally rephrased his question: Would I give up my specter? I didn't think so, and yet . . . "I would always be afraid," I said. "Always Hunted for the crime of being born." I swallowed, dislodging the admission from my throat. "I could never be happy as a Wielder. Not in the ways that mattered. It would . . . *hurt* to keep a part of myself inside."

As I spoke, I realized I'd never verbalized my experience so openly. That these words to Keil—even wrapped in a half-truth—might be more than I'd given anyone.

Keil slowly shook his head, unaware of my confession, yet still somehow enraptured. "It's never been that way for me. Where I'm from, there is no crime in existing. A specter isn't something to be ashamed of. It's a gift. And gifts should never hurt."

My specter squirmed for release—a near-cruel contradiction to the tender resonance of his words. Because if I ever explored the depths of my power as Keil did, if I ever learned to love it . . . I feared I would lose the will to confine it.

Embracing my specter was the most dangerous thing I could ever do.

And so I never would.

"That's beautiful," I whispered with an aching smile, drawing my power painfully back.

Keil's head slanted, his specter lapping further across my hand. A warm, questioning touch that brought out a breath of my laughter, turned my smile into something truer.

"I love those," he said, and I paused. I was about to ask what he meant when Keil's specter suddenly spiraled up my arm and lifted off, knocking the hanging baskets on the balcony above. Powder-pink apple blossoms rained over us, tickling my nose, and I laughed again—truly *laughed*—the sound carrying on the breeze.

When I turned back to Keil, my pulse stuttered. Because his gaze drew between my cheeks, his expression soft and starved all at once.

I love those. He'd been talking about my dimples, pinching deep whenever I smiled.

"I wonder," he murmured, still looking me over with an intensity that warmed my skin, "if it's your Hunter's blood that makes you unafraid."

I glanced across his lipstick-spattered face. "You want me to fear you, looking like that?"

"Never," he said quickly, then continued, more gently, "I never want you to fear me."

My heartbeat skipped again, my traitorous body leaning toward his. Keil's eyes swooped down me, noticing the incline, which only made my breaths come out faster. "Why not?" I asked.

He hesitated, seeming at war with himself. Probably realizing, like me, just how dangerous this was.

Then he said, voice low and hoarse, "Because if you did . . . I couldn't do this." Slowly, he reached for my hair. His fingers drifted through the strands, and he lingered a moment before withdrawing, a blossom pressed between his thumb and forefinger. The flower swirled on the breeze, and his hand lifted again, gently brushing a wayward strand from my brow. "Or this," he whispered.

My body hummed as a tendril of his specter echoed his movement—grazing my temple before it glided down with his trailing fingers. Painting lines of fire down the curve of my face, my jaw, my fluttering throat.

"Or this," he breathed, pouring that spectral thread down the back of my neck while his fingers drew inward, across my collarbone.

My specter coiled inside me, hot and trembling, as Keil's power thrummed along my spine, pausing at the top edge of my gown. His fingers similarly stilled at the dip of my collarbone—barely making contact, like he was touching something sacred.

I swallowed, and his touch bobbed against my skin. "Well," I said on an exhale. "It takes more than a party-trick power to rattle me."

His pupils swallowed the gold in his eyes.

Then Keil's specter swept fully around me. *Wreathed* me—hands and arms and shoulders—in tingling, mischievous vines. My right hand landed in his palm, while the left dropped onto his shoulder. His spare hand curved around my waist, his skin feverish against the lacy fabric.

His power glided off me, and his heated gaze fell to my mouth. "How's that for a party trick?"

Because he'd positioned us as if to dance.

My chest rose and fell rapidly, his breaths spilling hot between full, parted lips. And I realized how much I wanted those lips on me. Not just crushing against my own, soft and open and tasting of Keil. I wanted them on *me*—mapping my skin with that near-reverence, following the path his specter had taken. I wanted to breathe him in and lose myself in the rich, head-emptying scent.

With that image singing in my mind, I lifted on tiptoe. Keil leaned down to meet me, pulling me closer from the waist.

It took all my self-control to turn at the last second—to brush my lips against his ear and whisper, "Impressive. But I'm still not going to dance with you."

I pulled back to watch a smile gather around Keil's eyes—the smile of a competitor who'd met his match.

He released me slowly, his shoulder muscles shifting under my fingers, his thumb making one last sweep over my knuckles before he freed my hand. I stepped back and the night felt colder.

"Good night, Ambassador," I said, breathless.

Keil cleared the hoarseness from his throat. "You don't have to call me that, you know."

I looked him over and raised a brow. "You wouldn't like the other names I have for you."

Keil's laughter chased me through the drawing room as I tried, and failed, to cool down from the inside out.

25

By the time I returned to my chambers, cheeks ablaze, I'd mentally run through thirty different scenarios that would have ended with my lips on Keil's.

Perhaps Father had been right to keep me from other Wielders. Perhaps I was too easily entranced, too likely to let my guard down, because of what Keil was.

But . . . it didn't seem that way. There had certainly been a thrill in exploring his specter, but once the specter had receded, I'd wanted to explore *him*—his conflicting softness and solidity, his unwavering faith in the world.

I'd wanted to explore the full sweep of his mouth.

And that kind of exploration had nothing to do with Wielding.

A knock pounded my door, and I shook myself. This was a dangerous slope of thought. But not as dangerous as the dayglass in my pocket. I shoved the shard under my mattress, hiding the evidence of my evening.

I was still a little flushed opening the door.

Junius's dispassionate gaze doused me in cold clarity. "Finally." He swept inside, his white-stud earring—bonestone, I now realized—peeking above a stiff collar. "Do you know how many times I've come knocking?"

I shut the door, sighing. "I'm sure you're going to tell me."

"You didn't answer my note."

"You didn't send a note."

He huffed with vindication, like my five-word response confirmed every ugly thought he held of me. "I thought to make the exchange in person since you're clearly too busy to respond, but I see you're just as immature as I'd—"

"You have the information?" I stopped short.

Scowling, Junius handed me a folded note from his jacket.

As a member of Dawning's ruling family, Junius could access the records of the Dawni bladesmith who'd forged my attacker's knife. The bladesmith who I suspected was now working for the copycats.

"His address?" I asked.

"No."

My eyes snapped up. "I asked for his address."

"And it would've gotten you nowhere." He released a long-suffering sigh that implied I was the most incompetent person in the kingdom, then he unfolded the note to reveal written coordinates. "Kevi Banday was due to make a weapons delivery to this location. The client had refused to give their name, and since the blades were of a rare, expensive metal, Kevi had been wary of the transaction. He sent the coordinates to his wife as a precaution. She said he never returned home."

I read the coordinates. Read them again. "This is in Vereen."

Junius nodded. "Kevi's wife traveled there after he didn't show, and found nothing but 'a slat of grassland.' It seems Kevi should have trusted his instincts regarding this client."

My heart sank. Kevi must have possessed useful information after all—information that could have led to the copycats. Because rather than commission him for more weapons . . . they'd *silenced* him.

And my final lead ended at a slat of damned grassland.

"This is more than I asked for," I mumbled, deflated. "Thank you."

Junius's eyes widened, like my thanks had shocked him. "You asked me to find Kevi," he said slowly. "I wanted to ensure you'd fulfill your end. Speaking of which . . ."

I nodded, shuffling to my bedchamber. Garret had sent the information late last night.

Junius's attention was pinned on the parchment when I returned, but I didn't relinquish it.

"Who did you send to question the wife?"

"Loyal acquaintances," he said absently.

"They obtained this information humanely?"

His gaze flicked up, alert once more. "She received three purses of gold for her trouble. I am not a monster."

"No." I handed him the parchment. "I don't believe you are."

Junius's eyes misted as he scanned the coordinates of a Dawni forest.

Despite the Jacombs' growing alienation, Junius hadn't wanted to know who'd accused their staff of Wielding. I could almost understand. I'd forever known that the Hunters had executed my mother, yet it hadn't brought her back. Even knowing which of them had dealt the killing blow wouldn't mitigate the loss.

Vengeance was an empty meal. What the Jacombs really wanted was the chance to say goodbye.

"The graves are unmarked," I said softly. "You'll have to search a while."

"We will be honored to serve them now as they served us all our lives." His voice cracked, and he cleared his throat. "How did you get this information?"

"I take care of my friends."

Satisfied with my answer, he tucked away the parchment with great care. "Thank you," he said sincerely, and turned.

"Can I ask . . . ?" I started, uncertain. Junius paused. "You would—would do all this"—I wrung my hands—"for *Wielders?*"

Junius faced me fully, and I braced for his scathing reply. Instead, the corner of his mouth turned up with a sad smile. "You are young," he said gently. "One day, you might find that there is no difference."

He shut the door softly behind him.

As the silence took on the weight of his words, I realized the gentry had been right. The Jacombs had known they were housing Wielders . . . and they hadn't cared. Now, they would dig through a Dawni forest to exhume the bodies of their staff. To offer them the funeral they deserved.

That kernel of hope glimmered inside me again, almost within reach. It was a foolish hope. A desperate hope. But as the memory of Keil's specter rose, free and warm and rippling with unchained strength, I wondered if it was a hope worth nursing.

Finding the compass and stopping the copycats would offer me safety, but never happiness . . . because I would still have to confine my specter.

And I didn't want to die before I'd gotten the chance to breathe.

Slowly, with a tentative, searching touch, I reached within myself.

My specter resided dormant and shapeless inside me, vaguely uncomfortable as ever, producing the straining background ache I'd learned to live with. But upon deeper inspection, I realized that its regular thrum had taken on a slight squirming quality—a manifestation of my worry and frustration since Junius's information about Kevi.

I drove further into the power, and it was like peeling back a tulip petal to reach the dense, pollen-rich center. There seemed to be folds here. All constantly feeding off my energy and emotion, gently pulsating with my heartbeat . . . all ineffably, undeniably, *me*.

I swallowed and withdrew my touch, somehow afraid to keep unfurling. Caught instead with the urge to wind an internal rope around those petal layers to hold them together.

Had my mother died with restraints around her own power, not realizing that her daughter would suffer the same fear of exposure? Was she buried in another forest, her grave unmarked? I might've walked over it during my autumn strolls, unaware of the atrocities under my feet—

The air rushed into me. As a Dawni woman, Kevi's wife might not have known about the xerylite mines under Vereen, whose locations were supposedly lost. So, she'd looked in the wrong place: above the earth.

She should have looked beneath.

I grabbed my cloak and ran for the stables; the night was ripening but I couldn't delay. Father held all those mining records, including how to enter the tunnels.

Happiness would have to wait.

My search wasn't over yet.

The midnight journey to Vereen blurred with frenzied thoughts and thunderous wheels over cobblestones. Then I was tumbling from the carriage, telling the coachman to return to Henthorn without me.

The sight of home was a balm to my agitation. I ran up the front steps and burst through the doors. The hinges squealed, and a chill seized me.

I squinted into darkness. Amarie usually left the protection candles burning in the foyer all night.

I hung up my cloak. "Father?" My voice bounced off the polished walls. "Amarie?"

Silence. *Emptiness.*

I drifted through the lower level, the *thump-thump-thump* of my heartbeat rising for no tangible reason. Everything was in its place . . . and yet the air skittered with dread.

Something wasn't right.

A squeaking sound halted me outside a linen closet. I rattled the doorknob, my specter winding between my fingers. The squeaking intensified.

No—not squeaking. *Whimpering.*

I plunged my specter through the keyhole and yanked the door open.

Amarie shook under the linens, arms shielding her bruised head. I dropped and grabbed her wrists. She tugged against me; a sob tore up her throat.

"Amarie, it's me!"

She looked up, eyes bloodshot. "Alissa?" Her voice croaked with another sob.

"What happened?"

"Y–your father."

"Where is he? Amarie, *where is he?*"

I didn't wait for her reply.

I bolted for the staircase, taking the steps two at a time. I tripped on the third floor, but scrambled up and kept climbing.

He wouldn't be there. Somehow I knew it—I couldn't feel his presence.

Someone had taken my father.

His study doors were open. I stumbled in, grasping the doorframe.

I saw the blood first. I'd almost anticipated it, but I hadn't expected its volume. And I hadn't expected the inky halo of hair spilling around my father's vacant face.

The wound in his chest gaped like the mouth of a beast.

Then screaming. In my head, in my bones. Screaming and screaming and *screaming and*—

The room blurred, and I fell to my knees.

I hadn't been here to protect him.

A hand closed around my arm. I didn't care who it belonged to. I didn't care if they plunged a knife into me right now.

I was already hemorrhaging. Emptying out, waves choking over themselves—hot and thick and rippling. Layers upon layers I hadn't known existed, hazing like steam in the air. Convulsing in their own shriek of agony.

Glasses rattled in the liquor cabinet. Books ripped from their bindings. Wood groaned and splintered.

Screaming and screaming and screaming.

Someone was shaking me. *Stop, Alissa, stop!*

Their touch receded. The doors slammed shut.

The dam inside me fractured and exploded in a shower of glass and wood and blood.

The world was ending, and I was grateful.

26

To cleave a person's heart was the greatest crime against nature.

The heart became forever ruined; the gods could not weigh it to determine its goodness, and the victim was left to wander the empty halls of limbo, never reaching the next realm but unable to return to the living world.

It meant dishonor after death.

It meant the killing was personal.

27

The hours were long and empty yet impossibly full. Black roses arrived from the palace, and I turned my stomach out into the malachite bathtub.

The Verenian nobles knew of my position at court and pushed for a lavish funeral. *To honor Heron*, they said, faces drawn. They only wanted to spend the king's gold. But I was the ruling lady of Vereen now. I vetoed their ideas and they obliged me, though whether it was from pity or genuine respect, I couldn't tell.

Tari had been granted bereavement leave, and she coaxed the meals down me each day. She stirred nightmilk into my tea when the world became too heavy and sat beside me while I slept. I caught her weeping in the parlor one morning and wished she would return to Henthorn.

Stop your search, the attacker had said.

I hadn't listened.

I found Father's birthday slippers wrapped in my closet, and I vomited again.

Amarie hadn't seen the killer's face. She'd been knocked unconscious and locked in the closet, too afraid to scream for help once she'd woken. Neither of us talked about what happened after I'd discovered

Father's body, when Garret had arrived with the rising sun.

"She's been like this for hours," Amarie had said to him outside the study. "You have to do something."

Garret had paused at the doorway before approaching. He'd said words I hadn't understood and then he was pulling me up. I'd thrashed against him, slipping on my blood-soaked dress. But he'd held on to me, even when I'd clawed his hands. He'd held on, collapsing with me into the dark red puddle and stroking my hair until my screams had dried out.

I went back the next day and realized what I'd done.

Stuffing spilled from the peacock-blue sofas; ripped documents and crystal shards scattered the floor. The domed window had blown apart, and wind whistled between its jagged glass teeth. The balusters stood cracked along the balcony railing like so many broken legs. Father's beloved claw-foot desk had fractured clean down the middle.

I didn't want to know how I'd managed such a thing.

"I'll handle it," Amarie had said. "Nobody will know."

But the state of the room didn't matter as much as that discolored spot on the hardwood where the blood had pooled. So much blood that, in my state of shock, I'd imagined mopping it up with a dish towel and wringing it back into my father's body.

On the day of the funeral, Amarie laid a black velvet dress on my bed. It had no pockets for my mother's coin, but I couldn't bring myself to care. My only piece of jewelry was Father's xerylite-studded brooch, weighing against my breast with each jolt of the carriage.

The day was stark and clear, the penny blossom trees' shimmering near-blinding across the Verenian fields. I blinked away the sun-dazzle, and the two connected spires of the Paine mausoleum—meant to represent the two gods of passing—created a Hunters' Mark afterimage inside my eyelids.

Verenian nobles gathered around the stone building, wiping their noses with pristine handkerchiefs. Then came the ruling nobles from the other provinces. Sabira's older sister, the ruling lady of Parrey, stood in a black armored gown beside Rupert's son. Perla's handsome father had a muscled arm around his thin-boned wife. Junius's mother stood apart from them all, a netted veil dappling her lovely features. Rupert headed the congregation from court, a red-nosed Carmen close behind.

A string of Verenian citizens rimmed the fields, clutching yellow carnations. Tari's parents would have been rammed among them—Father's *real* friends, and they wouldn't even hear the ceremony.

I climbed from the carriage to find Erik waiting for me, his hand outstretched. I pressed my bare palm to his without thinking.

"You have my deepest condolences." He lowered his brow to my knuckles—a gesture of sorrow and respect. "Lord Heron was a good ruler and a kind man. He was taken too soon."

Erik led me to the gray-stoned walkway, and I caught a glimmer of displeasure from Perla's mother.

I turned from the king and started on the path alone.

The congregation dipped their heads as I passed, my velvet dress rasping over the stones. It was a Verenian tradition reserved for the next of kin: a final journey to meet the deceased before sending them off to the higher realm. Halfway through, I spotted the Capewells gathered behind the Verenian nobles, a stony Briar at their helm. Garret stood beside her, his blazer crumpled, his shoulders hunched. He didn't meet my eyes.

I climbed the mausoleum steps and faced the crowd: the Hunters and the nobles. A small voice told me to unleash my specter on them all, to let them taste the pain they'd caused me.

But my specter barely stirred.

"Welcome," I called, my voice strong and assured—belonging to someone else entirely. "We congregate today to celebrate the life of Heron Paine, ruling lord of Vereen. He was best known as the generous ruler of these lands, but he was more than that. He was a loyal friend, a passionate artist, and a wonderful father.

"My mother died shortly after I was born. Though I never knew her, I know the love she and my father shared was a love that inspires poetry. A love that stirs the beating heart of this world. My father will be dearly missed, but he is no longer alone, as he had been in life. He has been reunited with his love in the higher realm. May you all find in that the comfort it has given me." I paused like Amarie had told me to, taking in their dour faces. "It is with a heavy heart that I inherit my father's title, and it is my honor to rule Vereen in his memory."

I didn't wait for a reaction before I descended the steps. The high minister took my place to speak, but I'd already stopped listening.

A Verenian noblewoman turned to me, dabbing her eyes. "Such a moving speech," she whispered. "Lord Heron would be proud."

I nodded my thanks. Amarie had written the speech. I hadn't felt a word of it when I'd first read it, and I didn't now.

The ceremony proceeded in a blur. Erik gave a somber address, and then I stepped into the mausoleum to bid my father farewell. My footfalls rang hollow, cold air radiating off the stones. Father was musk and ink smudges and floppy dark hair. He belonged in the creaking spine of a book or the crystal facets of a brandy glass. He did not—*could* not—belong here.

I turned back out only because I had to. It wasn't until the doors thudded shut that I realized I wanted to curl up in the tomb beside him.

Amarie guided me to a copse of trees to receive condolences. My role should have been shared among the immediate family, but I was the only one left. The last of the Paines.

Rupert approached first, a blubbering mess. He cupped my face and told me I would always have a place in Creak.

The Jacombs paid their respects together, but Junius lingered to give my hand a little squeeze. "You will get through this," he whispered.

Perla came to me alone, her large eyes brimming with sympathy. "I'm very sorry for your loss, my lady." She opened her hand and offered a single black pearl. "In Avanford, we string them along our windows for mourning. I know it's different in Vereen, but—"

"It was a lovely thought," I said. "Thank you for your kindness."

I dropped the pearl to the dirt as soon as she walked away.

The journey home was swollen with foggy sunlight and silence. Jewel-toned houses smearing past my unseeing eyes. *Pat-pat-pat*, Amarie's clammy hand atop mine.

I'd always been tortured by the idea of dying before my father—of having to leave him behind. Why then, as the distance from the mausoleum stretched out like a fraying thread, did it still feel like I was the one abandoning him?

The Verenian nobles were assembled in the gardens when I returned. My stomach plunged as I saw the Capewells among them—the monsters I'd feared for eighteen years, crawling around my lands like locusts and drinking my father's brandy. Some were fair like Briar, others darker-skinned or blue-eyed, with hair straight or braided or shaved close to the scalp. I'd always known they were a vast family, with branches that stretched across Daradon, but I hadn't realized how vast until today.

"I couldn't say no," Amarie whispered. "They were your father's only family."

"I'm my father's only family," I replied, and drifted into their midst.

Garret was nowhere to be found but many Capewells approached me, their words dripping with compassion. A particularly beautiful young woman with glossy blond hair, who introduced herself to me as Mara, toasted to my father and downed her brandy with such enthusiasm that I considered smashing the glass against her forehead.

After an hour, I escaped to a jasmine-adorned gazebo and leaned against one of the poles. Capewells and nobles milled around me, their voices droning like bloated flies.

Then one voice bit out above the rest. "He was a good man."

"Everyone keeps telling me that," I said blankly.

"It's true." Briar stepped into the gazebo—a shark rising from the churning black sea of mourners, the wind teasing straw-yellow wisps from her braid. Her neckline swooped to catch the tips of her Hunters' Mark tattoo. The same tattoo she'd inked over my father's heart. "He never enjoyed the more... *challenging* aspects of the family business."

"Family business." A sharp huff escaped me—the closest I'd been to laughter in days. "That's a quaint way to describe murder."

"Careful where you point your finger. I hear you're growing close to the man who sanctions those murders."

A spark of feeling—of *rage*—crackled inside me. I grabbed on to it before it slipped away. "Why are you here? To use me as you used my father? Don't waste your breath. I won't be so easily persuaded to join your service."

"You might not have suffered captivity if you'd joined our service earlier. Garret told me about that ordeal."

"You flogged him."

"I disciplined him. If we released prisoners whenever an innocent was threatened, there would be chaos."

"Maybe if you didn't take prisoners, innocents wouldn't be threatened."

A condescending smile—the same smile she'd given after slapping me as a child. "Innocents will always be threatened. Our job ensures that those threats come from the natural world alone."

"You think what you do is natural?" I spat. "That executing an entire household is natural? That tearing a mother from her child is *natural*?"

"We don't tear mothers from their children," Briar said calmly. "We eradicate the bloodline in its entirety."

Not always.

"And how is business lately?" I asked. "I'm sure Erik would love to know that you're no closer to finding the compass than you were seven years ago."

Briar looked me over, unblinking. "You're very much like your father, aren't you?"

I flinched. When I'd pictured Father working for Briar, I'd never imagined him challenging her authority. My chest split at the thought, but I shoved the pain far down.

"Take your Hunter filth," I said, "and get off my lands."

"Is that any way to address your elders?"

"I'm your ruling lady as long as you reside in Vereen. If you don't like how I speak to you, relocate."

"With Heron gone and the compass lost, there's still a space to fill in our ranks."

"You don't want my service. You want to exploit my sway with the king."

"Could you blame me if I did? This secondary group is unpredictable. Dangerous. They cut my brother's throat seven years ago, and now they threaten to topple the system our ancestors have upheld for two centuries—all while using our name. There were two more Huntings in the time you've been mourning. Valuable lives wasted."

I nearly flinched again. Too preoccupied with the slow rot hollowing me out, I'd lost track of the Huntings.

I asked, sneering, "You approve of Wielder slaughter only when you're the one holding the knife?"

Briar's eyes narrowed. "I refer to the valuable lives of *Capewells*. The people with whom you share blood." At my blinking silence, she raised her brows. Then she canted her head in thought. "How very unlike Garret. What with his oath band removed, I assumed he would once again be yapping at your feet like a lovesick pup, telling you everything."

"Telling me what?" I snapped, my mind already returning to Garret's odd moments of caginess. Moments when he'd halted midsentence, as if cutting off the most crucial part.

"The Capewells failed the king in losing the compass," Briar said. "Each time these copycats Hunt in his kingdom, we fail him again." A strained, hissing breath. "And he executes one of our own as punishment."

I startled, blood chilling.

I knew Erik would punish the Capewells . . . But to pluck individuals like splinters from their group—to have them looking over their shoulders, unable to predict the next slaughter. The next *Hunting*.

He was kindling in them the dread they'd always brought to the Wielders of Daradon.

It was cruelty poeticized. Exquisitely vicious, just like him.

"Many more Capewells will die at his hands if nobody steps in." Briar's mouth tightened—an expression I'd first seen when she'd talked about the Ansoran ambassador. *Fear*. But not fear of the Ansorans, I now realized.

Fear of the king.

I truly laughed now—a tattered, ugly sound. "What a great loss that shall be."

Briar glanced over me. "Highborns are rarely so bloodthirsty. Perhaps you'd fit better on our front lines. Then you and Garret could spill Wielder blood together."

My specter uncoiled from where it had been struck numb these last few days. It took more effort than I'd anticipated to rein it back in.

"You're a demon," I said through gritted teeth.

"And you are blind. Didn't you ever wonder who facilitated your kidnapping? Daradonians know the Capewells as merchants. How did those Wielders discover what we really were? How did they know you weren't one of us—a weak link in an otherwise unbreakable chain? Somebody fed them information. Somebody close to you, most likely." Her face twisted with contempt. "Perhaps your busybody house manager. If I were you, I'd subject her to interrogation."

My hands curled at my sides. "Get out."

"Join my service, keep Erik at bay, and you and I will find the betrayer together." Briar ambled forward, coaxing. "You're the ruling lady of Vereen now. You must defend yourself from those who would harm you. I mean only to protect you. To teach you. Heron refused to train with us and look what happened to him. Maybe if he hadn't been so weak he'd still be alive."

My hand whipped out. The slap of skin against skin cut through the roaring in my head.

The surrounding nobles gasped. The Capewells snapped to attention, some sliding their hands under their jackets, others into their sleeves. The young woman, Mara, saluted me with her brandy, grinning wickedly.

Briar's face slowly realigned. Even as I prepared for the retaliative blow, I knew it had been worth it—if only to watch that red splotch flowering across her cheek as it had once flowered across mine.

Then Briar looked to her Hunters, one hand lifting in an order to halt. "The poor girl has lost her father. She's not in her right mind."

After a tense pause, the Capewells returned to their conversations. Only Mara seemed disappointed.

I stepped closer to Briar, palm stinging, my body humming from a strike repaid. "I don't care what you are," I said roughly. "I don't care what you do. Speak ill of my father again, and I'll show you exactly how bloodthirsty a highborn can be."

An eager look crept over her. "I was told you hadn't the stomach for this business, but I've always believed differently. Thank you for proving me right."

28

The mourners were trickling out on a cloud of brandy fumes. I fled upstairs before the last of them could ambush me in the foyer.

Somehow, I ended up in Father's study. Though laborers had worked here for days under Amarie's instruction, I hadn't yet seen the results.

The floors gleamed, sofas restitched along the seams. They'd rebuilt the balcony railing and fit a cleaner glass into the window frame. Even the old-parchment smell had given way to the bite of surface polish.

But nothing was worse than the sleek new desk sitting in place of its predecessor. It reminded me that this was *my* study now, as ruling lady of Vereen. The title didn't sit right on my shoulders.

A seating ceremony would take place in the coming months, upon which the Verenian nobles would officially pledge their loyalties to me. The day would spill out with parades and merriment, craftwork and good food, culminating in a rite that should have seen Father handing me the seat of his power, as Rupert had done for his son.

Now I'd have to endure the ceremony alone.

How could the rest of my life seem so small and so gaping all at once?

I ran my fingers over the desk's shiny surface, on which Amarie had placed two unlit candles—one at each end, to be lit in supplication to the gods of passing. Though she wouldn't admit it, Amarie truly feared for Father's place in the next realm. She wanted me to fear for him, to pray for him, too. To believe in the gods who would take pity on his spirit.

I flicked the candles down, one after the other. The gods hadn't been here when Father had needed them. They had no right to claim this space now.

I turned to the liquor cabinet—another glossy replacement—and poured a measure of brandy. I drained it in one.

A pile of parchments sat in an open box on the floor. The survivors of my eruption. I grabbed a handful and smacked it onto the desk.

Most of the pages belonged to the books I'd ripped apart—texts about specters and the lost art of Spellmaking—but some bore Father's sketches. One sheet depicted the hilt of a sword—unfinished, I knew, because the pommel was still empty and the drawing stopped a little way down the blade. As though Father had halted suddenly.

I touched the smudges where his hand had grazed the charcoal. Was this the last thing he'd ever drawn? Prematurely abandoned, like the crack we'd only started to seal between us?

I didn't know what to do with that fracture, still unhealed. How to repair it alone when my grief now oozed into the wound, putrefying it against any chance of closure.

But I knew I didn't want to deal with it today.

I returned to the paper stack, flipping blindly. The task of finding the mining tunnel records seemed so distant now, as foreign as this bare, polished room that Father had always kept in disarray. He'd never taken care to hide anything of importance; it would've been easy for someone to locate those records.

Especially when Father kept letting the wrong people inside.

I poured more brandy, sloshing it over my fingers.

Footsteps shuffled behind me. The doors clicked shut.

I brought the glass to my lips and said to Amarie, without turning, "Why refill the bottle if you're going to reprimand me for enjoying it?"

"Go ahead," a deep voice answered. "This will be easier if you're drunk."

The air slowly hissed out of me, fogging the inside of the glass. I turned.

My attacker was an inflamed version of himself—smudged with watercolor bruises, breaths whistling between clenched teeth. Garret's assault couldn't have produced that volume of injury; it must have been a Wielder victim, flaring out in defense before they'd died.

The idea hardened my spine. "I thought you wouldn't warn me again."

"Who says this is a warning?" The man took a long, creaking step across the hardwood. No silver-tipped boots today. "I was told to offer my condolences. Leave you a parting gift." He drew a eurium knife from his right side—he'd replaced the one on his left—and angled his head. "You never learned your lesson, did you, girl? To stop sticking your nose where it doesn't belong."

"Apparently not," I said flatly.

He bared his teeth. "You got what was coming to you."

I set my glass on the desk and met his stare. "So will you."

My specter roared forward.

The man slammed into the wall; his head thwacked backward. He spluttered, blinking out the shock. His hand darted down, but I was faster. I whipped the dullroot canister from his belt and sent it skidding across the hardwood.

I'd avoided fighting him the first time, fearing exposure. I wasn't worried anymore. This man had killed my father.

He wasn't leaving this room alive.

My lips twitched up as I sent another wave toward him. But this time he was prepared. His arm heaved back—

And he lobbed the knife toward me.

My specter rushed aside with my sharp inhale, parting like a river fork to avoid the eurium. The air zipped past my head, and warmth bloomed at my ear. I turned to see the knife jammed in the wall behind me and realized too late that I shouldn't have turned.

Because now the man barreled for me, swinging his second knife in wide, vicious arcs. I scrambled aside, heart pounding in my throat, my specter retreating from the blade.

Then his rough hand grabbed my neck. I heard the wheezing before I realized it came from me.

My arms flailed. I couldn't take in a breath. Couldn't gather my frantic specter, my sudden panic thinning it out.

His laughter blew across my face. "*Stupid little—*" I didn't hear the rest.

My hand connected with something hard. I raised the brandy glass and smashed it against his head.

He roared as blood and crystal showered us. His grip slipped off my neck.

I wrenched back all the way, half sliding onto the desk. My foot swung out. He grunted as my pointed heel caught his thigh. A sloppy defense, but it gave me the time I needed to build a spectral wave—to build it up, up, *up*—

And launch it between his legs.

He collapsed, moaning. His knife clattered beside his knees. One last smack from my specter—and he sprawled across the floor.

I dropped from the desk, panting. I circled him on shaky legs. "This was how I found my father. An undignified way to die, isn't it?" He reached for my ankle, but I secured his wrist with a throbbing tendril of power. "How should I leave you? Bleeding out the same way?"

"*Wielder scum.*" He sucked in ragged breaths, his face contorting. "Keep pushing and you'll see what happens. You won't win this fight."

"This doesn't feel much like a fight." I wrung his wrist until he howled, and I lapped up the sound. I'd thought vengeance was an empty meal—but watching my father's killer squirm beneath me, I knew I could devour this feeling until I choked on it.

"Who sent you here?" I demanded. "Where can I find them?"

He laughed wetly, his hand turning crimson. "What's it worth?"

"Your life."

He turned his head and spat. I cringed, not seeing the flash of the fallen knife until agony exploded through me.

My body convulsed. Fire ran along my specter—through my blood—into my bones, and I didn't know if I was screaming or blacking out until my knees hit the hardwood and I knew I was doing both.

If regular metals cut through specters like blades on skin, eurium shattered them like shrapnel.

I was dangling on the edge of consciousness, trying to scrape up the pieces of myself, when the man's body whacked against mine, stealing the last of my air. He crushed me to the floor.

Then he found my throat and squeezed.

I thrashed automatically, trying to shove him off, trying to breathe. But the pain through my specter was all-consuming, making me sob between my teeth. My legs writhed, tangled in velvet. I bucked my hips. Dug my nails into his wrists.

He tightened his hold.

My specter shuddered, fighting to convalesce. Fighting to *live*.

"Wielder scum," the man growled again, eyes hovering close above me. "You are nothing to us. You are nothing."

Nothing.

Creature.

Vermin.

Something inside me was screaming again—making acid of my blood, claws of my specter. And as the man's neck swam out of focus, I knew—with painful clarity—I would not yet lie in the tomb beside my father.

I pulled my nails from his wrists, slick with blood, and scrabbled for the base of his throat. Then I burrowed my nails deep.

He bellowed, and his grip loosened. My specter heaved through me with my gasping breath. I thrust it forward—a rush of solid power.

The *crack* echoed through my bones.

A pause.

Then he slumped on top of me, arms collapsing around my head. My brooch bit into my breast under the weight.

For several muzzy seconds, I could only lie there, inhaling his hair, my vision crisscrossing on the ceiling's painted beams. At last, I forced him off using both my arms and my quivering specter. The dark spots blinked out, and air streamed into my burning lungs. Warmth trickled down my neck from where his knife had clipped my ear. My face felt tacky with blood, but I didn't know if it was mine or his.

I labored up, grasping the knife he'd plunged through my specter.

With a wisp of power, I drew the dullroot canister toward me, steel screeching across the floor.

The canister bit cold inside my clammy palm, slightly larger than Briar's prototype yet much lighter than I'd expected. I was lucky he'd only brought one. He'd returned here to cut up a Wholeborn girl—to leave me with a "parting gift" after I'd dared to interfere with the copycats.

He would've been better prepared against a Wielder.

I staggered toward the knife in the wall, locked all his weapons inside the desk, and leaned against it. Then I took the brandy decanter by the neck and tipped back a swallow. My raw throat burned. I drank deeper.

A knock. A door whispering open.

"Alissa, everybody's gone—"

Garret froze. He paled as he took it all in: my red-smeared face; the decanter in my steady hand; the man's neck, bent stiff at a gruesome angle.

I wanted to immortalize the look on his face—to trap it between glass like a pressed penny blossom.

"Don't look so disturbed," I croaked. "I'm sure you've seen worse."

"You killed him," he whispered, more stunned than accusatory.

"He killed my father," I said. "I didn't heed his warning, and he killed my father."

Garret's sunken eyes lifted to mine. "You can't blame yourself."

"I don't. There's only one person responsible for the role I've been playing at court."

I set the decanter down with a *thunk*, and Garret blinked at me, still dazed. As though I wasn't capable of murder. As though he couldn't believe the blood under my nails.

And I realized, for all these years, I'd represented the last glimmer of Garret Shaw's morality. The lifeline to his conscience, keeping him from dropping into the storm of himself.

Because now, I was watching him fall.

"You didn't tell me Erik was targeting Capewells," I said. "Did you think I might like what he was doing? That I would stop pushing so hard to find the compass?" I tilted my head, looked him over. "Or did you worry I would realize your own time was running out?" My voice darkened. "And that you always played the riskiest hands when you felt cornered."

Garret's expression shifted. Cleared.

The irony struck me: I'd been trying to unearth the boy in him, and now here he was—that boy. Wearing the same expression he'd worn whenever he'd been caught cheating at a game.

But this wasn't a game.

"Briar was called into Dawning on the first night of Rose Season," I said, eerily calm. "The Capewells targeted the Jacombs' employees, and she went to help round them up. You brought me home early from court, remember? You made sure to be here when the Wielders came."

I remembered how he'd grabbed my arm in the carriage. How he'd looked toward the house, hesitant. How he'd let me go anyway.

"Alissa, let me explain—"

"I can explain well enough. Erik began targeting the Capewells upon each Hunting, and you didn't want to be next. You needed me stationed at court to find the keeper, but your oath band bound you to silence. So you arranged my kidnapping for a night when Capewell Manor would be empty. And, knowing my father would need you to access the hold, you finally had enough leverage to put him in your debt."

Tonight gave me an opportunity, Garret had said that night. *I told your father I wouldn't retrieve those prisoners until he unlocked the band.*

"You pretended to fight for me." The words soured on my tongue. "After all, it wasn't just the Wielders you needed to convince."

Garret raised his palms, breathing heavily. "I did what was best for *all* of us. I'd caught rumors that a group of Wielders were attempting to rescue our prisoners. They would've died trying to break them out. But if I anonymously leaked the information, a peaceful exchange would—"

"A *peaceful exchange?*" I laughed roughly. "You gave them the means to kidnap me. You stole the mining records from my father's study and told them which tunnel to hide me in."

"I had to influence where they kept you," he said desperately, "to make sure you were safe. They didn't know about your specter. I knew you could escape if you had to."

"I was *unconscious!*"

He faltered. "Th-they weren't supposed to give you nightmilk. I said you were untrained, could be easily bound and subdued. When I realized—I knew it was too dangerous—I swear, I tried to stop them—"

"Father wanted me to stay home," I murmured, eyes glazing over. "For my eighteenth season. I should've stayed home."

Instead, I'd buckled under Garret's manipulations. I'd let him convince me to join court—to wage war with these copycats.

And now Father was a casualty of that war.

Garret slowly approached, his movement blurring in my eyeline. "You know why we had to do this. You know the copycats could've discovered you with the compass just as easily as they found the rest. Alissa, please understand." He stood before me now, one hand reaching toward my cheek. "I was afraid for you—"

My specter smacked his hand away before he could make contact. He gasped, stumbling back.

"You were afraid for *yourself*." My gaze refocused on his eyebrow scar, pulling taut with the pained gathering of his forehead. I met his stare with fierce loathing.

Because if it weren't for Garret's deception, my father would still be alive.

"You were right," I said quietly. "You're not like Briar. You are a far greater demon, Garret Capewell."

He recoiled. It was the first time I'd tagged their name onto his. Because, for the first time, I believed it belonged there.

I pushed off from the desk, and he tried to reach for me again. At the look I gave him, he instantly dropped his hand.

"A person changes after their first kill," he said. "Believe me, I know. When the remorse fades, you'll remember that whoever ordered this is still out there—using the compass to Hunt countless Wielders. We have to finish this for them."

I glanced numbly at my attacker's body. *A person changes after their first kill.* Garret didn't know how right he was. Somewhere along the way, I must have changed.

Because I felt no remorse at this man's death. Only satisfaction.

"Is that what you've been telling yourself?" I asked. "That you're doing it for them? How many of *them* would you kill if Briar told you to? How many would die before you grew the backbone to turn the knife on her instead?"

Garret's nostrils flared with the pressure of unspent emotion. "That's not fair."

"The truth rarely is." I scanned him up and down, sneering. "Look at yourself. Did you really think I was going to hand the compass to someone like *you*?"

I must have appeared as wild as I felt, coated in the blood of the man I'd killed. And yet my harsh words—*look at yourself*—made Garret's shoulders bow inward. Made him appear just as small as he'd always been.

"You lied to me," he rasped, his deep-rooted shame warring with anger. "The king—"

"What the king does to the Capewells is irrelevant." I gave him another scornful once-over. "I have nobody left for him to hurt."

Garret's neck reddened, anger winning out. "You can't keep the compass, Alissa."

"I wouldn't recommend trying to stop me." With a bitter, hateful smile, I said, "I'm not in my right mind."

I climbed over my attacker's legs and stalked away.

But I halted at the door, looking over my shoulder. I spoke softly, as if with the slow twist of a knife. "I would have begged the king to spare you," I said, holding his stare. "You would've been free."

Garret's face sank with regret. He inhaled to speak when I wrenched the door open, silencing his wet apology.

"If Erik asks me," I said, turning away, "I'll tell him to kill you all."

29

It was strange, being bereaved. The courtiers who'd gossiped with me ten days ago were now grave-faced and formal, heads dipping as they passed me in the palace gardens.

Only Carmen treated me the same. She still wore black in solidarity, though all manner of brilliant jewels adorned her wrists and fingers. The wretched girl couldn't last an hour without a splash of color.

"Nobody would blame you for withdrawing from the rest of Rose Season," she said for the third time today. Though she'd embraced me as soon as I'd returned to the palace—and I'd wanted to crawl out of my skin at her touch—she'd been encouraging me to leave ever since.

"It's too painful to be home right now," I said. "I need space to heal."

It was the same dismal excuse I'd fed Amarie when she'd begged me, teary and trembling, to remain with her in Vereen. As if the days after the funeral hadn't been excruciating enough, having to watch her weep into her tea, or wander aimlessly about the parlor, or dissolve into a guilt-ridden mess whenever she walked past that linen closet. The closet from which she hadn't tried to escape while her oldest, dearest friend had bled out several floors above.

You couldn't have done anything to save him, I'd told her without feeling, too depleted to ease anyone's pain but my own. Then, for the second time in a month, I'd ignored her pleas to stay. And I'd left my home—left her alone inside it—without turning back.

Carmen nodded now, curls bouncing. "After my father died, I couldn't set foot in the dining hall. That was where he choked, you know."

Choked.

I almost laughed.

"I heard they caught the man," she went on. "That must offer some comfort, at least."

The circulating story was that a Verenian citizen had attacked Father for raising the tax; the town guards had caught him breaking into the house again after the funeral, and they'd executed him on sight. Though a hideous little tale, it would give the copycats a reason as to why my attacker hadn't returned to them—hopefully without implicating *me* as the one who'd broken his neck.

Maybe I'd offer Carmen's mother the same fate if I found the compass in her hands. Or maybe I'd poison her and blame it on choking, in echo of how she'd killed her own husband.

Maybe I'd make Carmen watch.

"Yes," I said, nails biting into my palms. "It gives me great comfort."

We were rounding a hedge of blue hydrangeas when footsteps clacked toward us.

"Lady Alissa," Tari said, panting, her braid swinging. "A delivery arrived for you." Her gaze flicked to Carmen, then back to me. "From Vereen."

Carmen turned toward me, smiling tightly. "You should tend to that."

I walked back through the palace alone.

Every part of me ached, from my bruised throat to the constant pull of my specter. My loose hair kept catching the shell of my ear where my cut was scabbing over. The most alive I'd felt since discovering my father's body was the night I'd killed his murderer. I didn't know what that said about me, but I didn't really care.

Keil was leaning against my door when I arrived, looking more solemn than I'd ever seen him. I'd almost forgotten he existed. The rosy memory of Budding Ball didn't seem to belong with this version of me.

"My lady." He bowed low. "I haven't seen you since . . ." He swallowed, wincing. "I wanted to—I mean, I came to offer my condolences."

I'd never seen him stumble over his words. It was a rather pathetic look on him.

"Thank you," I said dully.

"I wanted to attend the funeral. But I thought, considering my past with your father, it wouldn't have been appropriate."

Because their only interaction had been through a ransom note.

"No, it wouldn't have," I said.

Hurt flashed in his eyes. And I realized I wanted to hurt him—this man who, by always remaining half a step behind me in his hunt for the compass, had conveniently hidden himself from the keeper's notice. The copycats had warned *me* to stop searching. They'd killed *my* father when I'd continued anyway. And Keil was still standing here, golden and glowing and *alive*.

Hadn't he been handed enough at birth, in the form of his freedom? Did he have to win in this, too?

"Was that all?" My specter writhed as I retrieved my key and shifted toward the door. "I have business to attend to."

But Keil wasn't finished.

"I know what it's like to lose parents," he said quietly. "It's one of the hardest things a person can face. If you ever need to talk . . . I would listen."

I paused, craning my neck toward him. He stood close enough now that I could smell his soap-and-linen aroma, deepened with a note of leather.

I wanted to wring the scent from my lungs.

"Why would I go to you, of all people?" I asked. "Wasn't I your captive less than a month ago?"

Keil balked. "I thought—"

"Thought what? That I'd forgotten? Or that you mean anything more to me than an unspent favor? Allow me to unburden you of your delusion." My eyes narrowed, and I went for the kill. "You were only worth toying with when it was entertaining. I'm no longer entertained."

I savored every moment of watching Keil's face fall, so much raw pain there that it overflowed, feeding the pit inside me.

I was about to turn when I noticed the dark change in his expression. His attention had caught on the high neck of my dress. The fabric had rumpled when I'd twisted toward him, baring the bruises beneath.

Keil slowly raised his fingers, dazed, but stopped short of the tender skin. His eyes met mine, and fury rippled across his face. "Who?"

I tugged at my neckline and unlocked the door.

He lashed an arm across the threshold, barring my way. His knuckles whitened on the doorframe. "*Who?*"

A long breath hissed between my teeth. I dragged my focus back to him and asked, low and vicious, "What would you do about it, *Wielder?* Hit them with a party trick?"

A muscle flickered in his jaw.

Then he lowered his arm, chest heaving, eyes burning a hole through the fabric around my throat.

I didn't spare him a second glance before I slammed the door between us.

Before leaving home, I'd instructed Amarie—during one of her drier-eyed moments—to locate a copy of the mining records from what remained of Father's files. It would be difficult, she'd said, and not just because she didn't know if multiple copies existed. But because she was still struggling to organize Father's belongings after my specter had destroyed the study. *Heron kept journals. I should have at least found the pieces of them by now.*

Hadn't she realized she'd already erased away every trace of him in that study? Why bother salvaging a few journals only to burn those, too?

But a few days after I'd set her to the task, Amarie found a map of the xerylite mines, unscathed on one of Father's bookshelves.

Tari and I unrolled the parchment across my bed, weighing the edges with silver candlesticks.

"The coordinates Junius gave me sit closest to this complex." I tapped the location, tracing my finger to the tunnel's access point. "The fields above stretch for a mile."

Tari coiled her braid around her wrist, unusually quiet.

"What?" I asked.

"It's just . . ." She sighed, sounding both pitying and exasperated. "You can't honestly think this is a good idea. Kevi Banday delivered eurium weapons to these tunnels and never returned. Those same weapons were used to attack you and—"

"And kill my father," I finished. "What of it?"

Tari grimaced. "You believed these copycats wouldn't kill Wholeborns, but they'll kill anyone who gets in their way. They could've gone after you first, but they went for your father. They wanted to *hurt* you. And if you continue down this road, they will do to you what they did to him." She took my hand, squeezing gently. "It's not your job to stop them."

I held her gaze, unmoved. "So I should let the Capewells find the compass first? Garret is finally desperate enough to tell Briar everything I've learned at court, and he'll no longer be inclined to keep it from her hands—to keep her from consulting it around *me*."

It should have devastated me to lose him like this, when I'd been so close to having him in my life again. But right now, I hated him too much to feel the loss.

Tari shook her head. "Garret wouldn't—"

"Garret is a coward and a traitor," I snapped, pulling away. After years of hostility between them, she chose to defend him *now*—after learning he'd orchestrated my kidnapping?

Tari looked down, guilty. "I just want to make sure you're thinking this through."

Didn't she understand that this was all I *could* think about? All that roused me into waking each morning?

"Do you know what today is?" I asked. "It's the fifth of the month. We should've been in Vereen this morning, playing Double Decks with Marge and Lidia, drinking hot lemonade. But Marge was killed, remember? These copycats found her and poisoned her and hit her until she bled." I rolled up the map and turned. "I won't let them slaughter anyone else."

Tari's gentle question halted me. "Is that the only reason you're doing this? For Wielders like Marge?"

My specter swelled—an internal admission of what I wouldn't say aloud. That although I was hunting the compass for all the Wielders of Daradon, I was hunting the keeper for myself.

"It doesn't matter," I said. "Kevi Banday was murdered on Verenian soil. So, yes, this is my job." I strode away. "You don't have to do it with me."

The next evening, Tari and I rode from the hidden servants' gate, the eurium knife smacking at my belt. Inky darkness spilled all the way to the Verenian grasslands, the humid air rustling my blouse collar. We tied the horses to the trees and continued on foot, my limbs pumping with energy and purpose as we drew closer to Kevi Banday's last location.

If the copycats had chosen this xerylite mine as a delivery point, they might be storing their weapons here. At the very least, I could relieve them of their armory.

But in an even better scenario, I would find here a piece of evidence that would lead me right to the keeper.

"Here." I stopped at a boulder propped against a dip in the field, where the grass had been stamped out. "It's been moved recently."

I heaved the boulder away with my specter. Just like the tunnels where Keil's Wielders had taken me, a mesh of foliage concealed the dark entry.

I crouched, and Tari grasped my shoulder.

"We're only looking," she said. "If we find anything, we'll come back with reinforcements."

I nodded, though I hadn't a clue what reinforcements Tari was depending on. Vereen was hardly known for its military, and our meager forces were spent guarding the square.

Whatever we found tonight, I would deal with myself.

We descended via a string ladder and landed in a cocoon of warm, damp earth. The ground spread unevenly, soil grinding under my boots. A crackle—then Tari's face flickered with torchlight. She tossed her match aside as I lifted the torch from its rusty holder.

This complex appeared cruder than the last, the air staler, with open entryways gutting the walls.

"It looks empty," Tari said.

"Maybe it is." I couldn't hide my disappointment.

We slunk forward, our shadows wavering.

"If anyone's here," said Tari, "that torch will draw them like a beacon."

"And if they don't see us, they'll hear us," I retorted.

Her mouth snapped shut.

We continued for several minutes, our breaths heavy in the stillness. With each turning that produced another stretch of unlit torches, my heart sank lower into my stomach. This couldn't be where my search ended.

Then Tari nudged me, nodding to her left.

A wooden door stood between the earth-packed walls, its hooped handle glinting under our torchlight. I inched forward and pulled the handle. The door squealed open.

So much for quiet, I was about to say. The words dried on my tongue.

"Gracious gods," Tari whispered.

I couldn't respond.

Dark and hellish, with grime-encrusted metal bars and loose shackles snaking in the dirt, these prisons were unsuited to housing anyone remotely human.

Yet the vestiges of human life were everywhere.

Bare footmarks dimpled the floor of the empty cells, while

boot-treads pitted deeper grooves in the open space. A hunk of gray bread lay discarded, a crescent-shaped bite taken out of it. The tang of urine and feces mixed with the coppery stench of blood.

If Garret had described Hunting as a business, then this . . . this was *savagery*.

Tari made a low sound of warning as I stepped into an empty cell. One corner of the tunnel had caved in, and its earth-spray had scattered outward, leaving the ground sharp and craggy underfoot. Something glimmered, and I squatted, tilting the light.

A sleek wooden cylinder sat on the dirt, half the size of my little finger and painted with a black stripe. A length of metal spiked one end, shorter and thinner than a dressmaker's pin.

The memories flooded me: a cool cloth on my forehead; a prick behind my neck; Tari's mother, Jala, telling her young daughter to make more ginger tea.

I lifted the instrument by its wooden end and held it to the light.

"A dispenser," Tari said. Her mother had used them during my bout of blueneck fever. The cylinders contained medicines—or nightmilk, for sedation—and pressure on the needle head emptied their contents into the bloodstream.

I twitched my finger toward the metal. My specter lurched, twisting from the residue on the needle. *"Dullroot."*

I flung the dispenser aside and stood. Xerylite mines had been used as strongholds during the Starling Rebellion, emblematic of Wielder resistance.

This site had been transformed into a Wielder slaughter ground.

"It's like the Capewells' hold," I said. "The copycats must be bringing the Wielders here before killing them. Or"—I looked toward the disintegrating wall—"they *were* bringing them here." The collapse must have driven them to abandon this location.

"Why?" Tari's voice trembled. "Why would anyone do this to innocent Wielders?"

My specter squirmed, my own rising horror mixed with outrage. I said bitterly, "There is no such thing as an innocent Wielder."

Then I grabbed an unlit torch, touched it to my flames, and plonked it in Tari's hand.

She startled. "Where are you going?"

"To look around."

Her expression darkened. "You said—"

"That we'd leave once we found something."

"I think *this*"—she threw her arm wide—"qualifies as *finding something*."

"There might be a clue here as to where they went. We need to find them before they Hunt again."

"Alissa, it's too dangerous."

"Then stay here if you're afraid." I turned. "I'll be back."

"*Alissa—*"

I stormed away.

I had slim odds of discovering anything else here. But how could I leave without trying when, all this time, the Hunted Wielders were being slaughtered under my province? Marge would've been among them, unaware that she was just a few miles from home when they'd run a final blade through her.

My bruised neck smarted as I imagined my lifeblood spilling by that same blade. Because the keeper would do this to me, too, the moment the compass's needle pointed in my direction. The eighteen years of my life—every moment of love and pain and longing—would be reduced to a bare footprint inside a cell.

A bolt of fear hastened my steps.

Then I stopped before a mound of crumbled earth, riddled with rock and debris. This section had caved in, too. Perhaps the entire structure was unstable.

But what if answers stood on the other side, just five feet away?

Squaring my shoulders, I poured my specter toward the mound. Powdered earth trickled at the disturbance, pattering my boots. I wriggled deeper, teeth gritted against the weight.

Voices rumbled on the stagnant air, coming from behind.

My specter jolted, walls shuddering around the mound. But my blood hummed with new promise.

I carefully withdrew the tendril and set the torch in a spare holder. Tari was right; it would be a beacon.

I followed the voices back the way I'd come, hugging the walls and breathing raggedly. I stopped outside an open chamber where light bled through the darkness.

"It's definitely Ansoran?" The voice was deep, authoritative.

"It's the ancient language, for sure."

"How can you tell?" A third voice, female and husky.

"Because it's the only language I *can't* read."

"Is now the time for bragging?" the woman asked.

"It's not bragging if it's the truth."

"Enough, both of you." The first voice again. His timbre tickled my memory, but I couldn't pinpoint its owner. "Do you know anyone who could read it?"

A hesitation. Then the other man replied stiltedly, "You'd be lucky to find a living being who can read the old language." Not quite an answer, I noticed.

"Then what are you even good for?" A fourth, gravelly voice sent a shard of ice through me.

Drink, that voice had ordered during my kidnapping, gloved fingers handing me a nightmilk vial. I hadn't realized my fear had seared the moment into my memory. Yet I knew now, with certainty and fresh alarm, that this voice belonged to Goren.

And these were Keil's Wielders.

My fists clenched. I'd assumed Keil was working alone to recover the compass for his empress. Clearly, his cronies had lingered in Daradon to help. But I'd acquired these coordinates from Junius—who'd obtained them from Kevi Banday's wife. How had they beaten me here?

"Nobody's here, Dash," said the woman, Osana. "Maybe her information was wrong."

Dashiel sighed in reluctant agreement. "This isn't exactly what we were expecting."

I poked my head around the threshold. Four figures occupied the rugged room, black masks again concealing the lower halves of their faces. All wore hoods apart from Lye, whose blond hair fell loose to his shoulders. He shifted, and in the flickering light of the torch he carried, I saw what they'd been looking at:

A swirling, rounded symbol—the same symbol etched into the weapon at my belt—glaring red on the earthen wall.

I almost heaved. This wasn't like the Hunters' Mark I'd scrubbed from Marge's door. Somehow I knew from the dark color, from the macabre drippage that had gathered and dried into the ground . . . this wasn't paint. It was blood.

Wielder blood.

A shuffle sounded, and I ducked from view.

"Who's there?" Dashiel called. "Show yourself."

I crept away, heart pounding.

Then Tari's shriek tore into the silence.

30

My specter roared toward the surface but I tugged it back. I had to breathe. I had to think.

"You said it was empty!" Goren yelled.

"It was," Osana replied in disbelief. "She must have come in after us."

Another bout of scrambling, and Tari released a cry of struggle. I reached for the knife at my hip.

"What's your name?" Dashiel coaxed.

Tari cursed in Bormian.

"What did she say?" asked Osana.

Lye grumbled, "I shouldn't repeat it." Then his voice curled out softly in Tari's native language.

"I speak the common tongue, fool," she snapped.

"Then answer the question," Goren said.

Tari didn't get the chance to.

I stepped from the shadows and stood behind the smallest figure. I gripped the knife steadily, my thumb on the handle's spine as Keil had taught me. And I pressed the blade to Osana's back.

She stiffened. The whole *room* stiffened, the three men training their attention on me.

"Lockpicker," Lye breathed.

Goren's eyes flashed. He had Tari's arms pinned behind her—the tallest girl I knew, and she looked impossibly fragile in his hold.

Dashiel straightened. "Lady Alissa."

Tari's eyes went saucer-wide. "You know them?"

"Release her," I said to Dashiel. "Now."

"And if I don't?" Goren answered instead.

I pushed the knife as far as I dared, and Osana hissed.

"Release her," I repeated.

Lye glanced between us, one hand hovering over his bandolier. Then Dashiel let out a relenting breath, and I automatically reduced pressure on the knife.

Osana spun. She twisted the knife from my grip and slammed me against the curved wall so hard that my teeth rattled. She barred my throat with a forearm, and pain lanced across my bruised skin.

"Let her go," Dashiel boomed.

"Do you know what your family did to the Wielders in that wagon?" Osana growled. "Maybe I should demonstrate."

My eyes watered as she increased pressure on my neck. I kicked at her, but she knocked my knee down with a slam of her specter. Tari screamed my name.

Then the pressure lifted.

I gasped, hands flying to my throat.

Lye hauled Osana off me, his torch juddering. "She's not our enemy!"

Osana whacked his hand away and squared up to him. "Tell me that again when her knife is pointed at *your* back."

The knife.

I lunged toward it too late, cursing as Osana grabbed my arm.

The knife lifted off the ground and landed in Dashiel's palm.

Tari's mouth flopped open. I saw the moment she realized: these were the Ansoran Wielders who'd kidnapped me. The Wielders who were hunting for the compass.

And who now knew, without a doubt, that I was hunting for it, too.

Dashiel looked between the bonestone knife handle and the symbol on the wall. His voice betrayed nothing as he asked, "Where did you get this?"

Tari pulled against Goren's hold. "She doesn't answer to you."

Goren yanked her back. "Shut up."

"She's right," I said, pulse thumping. "You're trespassing through *my* province. How did you even find this place?"

Osana squeezed my arm. "How did *you* find it?"

"It's a Wielder prison," Goren said. "Her ancestors probably built it."

I whipped my head toward him. "You really are exceptionally stupid."

Lye barked a laugh. "I knew I liked her."

Goren glared at him. "Find some rope," he said. "We're taking them both."

"Is that your solution to everything?" I demanded. "Kidnap?"

"Get a gag, too," he added flatly.

Lye shifted on his feet. "I don't like this. And neither will Keil."

"Keil will have to deal with it," Goren snapped. "There are more important things at stake here than his little sweetheart."

"*Excuse me*—?" I began, seething, but Lye talked over me.

"So, we keep them for weeks?" he said. "Until it's done? Call me unreasonable, but I think people might notice they're missing."

I felt a prickle of uncertainty at Lye's odd phrasing. *Until it's done.*

"Goren's right," Osana said. "She'll run straight to the palace with this, and it will all have been for nothing."

"She won't do that," Lye insisted. "Keil said—"

"Look at her!" Osana shoved me toward him. I stumbled, and Lye had to whip the torch flames away from my face before catching me awkwardly with one arm. "Has Keil been thinking clearly? Or has she been batting those lashes at him?"

Lye glanced down at me and winced, as if he didn't want to admit she was right.

"That's enough," Dashiel said. I was inclined to agree. So I aimed a tendril of my specter toward the low ceiling and corkscrewed through the earth. These tunnels were unstable; a minor displacement would offer enough distraction to grab Tari and run.

Dashiel stepped closer, and Lye's warm hand settled on my shoulder—in defense, rather than restraint. Dashiel noted the gesture and frowned at Lye before looking back to me. "If we could only talk, my lady."

"We're not talking." My specter burrowed deeper into the ceiling. "You're going to leave my province *now*, and I will allow you to keep your lives."

"Generous of you." Goren jostled Tari's arms. "But I think you'll tell us anything we want to know."

My specter flared, about to redirect toward him. I painfully tugged it back.

"Alissa," Tari said, voice strained.

"And *I* think"—my specter juddered with my growing agitation—"that if you don't release my friend, you'll be sorry you ever set foot inside this kingdom."

"Alissa—"

"We handled the other Capewell just fine. I'm sure we can fend off a pretty noble girl who doesn't want to scuff her boots."

"Goren," Dashiel warned.

My specter shook inside the earth and I couldn't subdue it. A *pitter-patter* drummed over the floor.

"*Alissa!*"

All heads snapped to a wide-eyed Tari, whose attention was fixed above—on something that made her legs tremble.

For one stunned second, I thought she could see my specter as I did—a vein of power feeding upward, frantic wavelets running along its length.

Then thunder growled through the tunnels. *Not thunder*, I realized, looking higher. To where the earthen ceiling had cracked from the pressure.

Lye's hand slipped off my shoulder. "It's collapsing," he whispered.

I hadn't just destabilized this portion of the tunnels. I'd destabilized the entire complex.

My specter flinched out of the earth. A mistake. Because, like yanking a blade from a wound, soil hemorrhaged from the opening.

Urgency whip-snapped through the group. Goren discarded Tari and ran toward the noise, Dashiel close behind him.

"Get them out of here!" Dashiel called over his shoulder.

Osana pushed us forward, Lye leading the way. The rumble chased us through the tunnels as our boots pounded the earth, our breaths rasping. I tripped, and Osana grasped my elbow to steady me.

Lye halted, and Tari slammed into his back. Another earthen mound blocked the path ahead. He ran his torch over the area. Then the mound shuddered—*shifted*—as an invisible force threaded through it.

He rounded on Osana. "You'll bring the whole thing collapsing around us!"

"There's no other way out," she said, the rigid set of her shoulders marking her exertion.

"It's true," I said, panting, remembering the map. "There's only one exit."

Earth spurted from the mound, and we shielded our faces. The walls shook around us.

"Help her," I said to Lye. "She can't hold it alone."

"I don't need help," Osana said.

Tari threw her hands up. "We're about to be buried alive, and you're being proud?"

"*I don't need help*," Osana repeated tightly, straining against the weight.

I swiveled to Lye, about to throttle him into Wielding his specter, when I noticed the strange mix of helplessness and acceptance shadowing his green eyes.

I staggered back. "You're a Wholeborn," I whispered. "Aren't you?"

His eyes crinkled, suggesting a grim smile beneath the mask. "You can't tell right now, but it wouldn't be fair for someone so handsome to also possess the power of a specter."

I swallowed and turned to Osana. "Can you bear it alone?"

"I have no choice."

As if reading my thoughts, Tari groaned. I loosened the internal grip on my specter, and it rushed up, rushed *out*—

Too fast.

I panicked, yanking it back before it reached the Ansorans. My breath snagged sharply, and Tari shot me a questioning look.

I squeezed my eyes shut, blocking the distractions. But my specter rioted along my bones now, swelling under my skin; I couldn't get a grip on it.

A low grumble sounded, and I opened my eyes to find a hole forming through the mound. Osana was panting between her teeth, and guilt stabbed at me. I'd caused this. But I didn't dare add my wild power to her efforts now.

Once the gap widened enough, Lye nodded toward me. "Go."

I pushed Tari forward first, then scrambled after her. As my hand brushed Osana's power, my specter churned toward the surface again. I swallowed it thickly, a sharp pain splitting behind my brow.

The Ansorans clambered after us and the wall caved in, spraying earth in every direction. I blinked grit from my eyes.

"It's this way." Tari strode forward when another roar shook the walls.

"Move!" Lye dropped his torch and sprang.

They crashed to the ground before the ceiling collapsed between us. Powdered earth flurried, washing everything in foggy brown.

"Tari!" I lurched forward.

Osana's strong hand held me back. "Get in my way and I'll leave you here to rot."

The earth parted again under her power, but slowly—*so painfully slowly*.

"Can't you go faster?" I said.

"You're welcome to get your nails dirty, *my lady*."

I glimpsed Tari through the growing gap, tangled around Lye and struggling for purchase. I labored through, then dragged her close to my side, feeling her long limbs for injuries. She looked dazed but unhurt.

Osana breathed heavily behind me, holding the torch. "Let's go."

We staggered ahead until the exit appeared, and I could've sobbed with relief.

Lye grabbed my waist with both hands, ready to hoist me upon the ladder. I shoved him away and pushed Tari forward instead. She climbed with wobbling legs, and I didn't exhale until she'd hiked over the lip.

Lye gave me a leg up, and I was halfway to the top when another rumble sounded.

A crack in the ceiling barreled toward us. Osana trembled—sending another wave of power out to meet it.

I paused, foot dangling.

"Keep moving, lockpicker," Lye called, arms outstretched beneath me.

"She can't hold it."

"Neither of us can help her. Just go!"

I hurried through the climb and hauled myself up, grass scratching my palms. Tari was on her knees, hacking up bile and grit. I had no strength to go to her.

Lye and Osana collapsed after us, wheezing under their masks. Osana's hood had fallen back, revealing a loose bun of dark braids.

Lye rushed to Tari. He thumped her back, eliciting a barking cough. "That's it." He rubbed a circle between her shoulder blades. "Get it out."

Tari spat onto the grass as her breathing evened.

Lye looked to me, eyes wide with concern. "You all right?"

I gulped, shaking. I was not all right. Not as my specter settled inside me with an unfamiliar heaviness. The heaviness of gas-rich air before a spark set it alight.

An axe shot up from the hole, and gloved hands clawed after it.

Goren's immense muscles shuddered as he hefted himself out. Dashiel emerged a moment later, and the entry collapsed with a *boom*, soil gushing from the sunken hole. As if they'd been the last force keeping it open.

Dashiel ripped away his mask and sucked in the clean air.

I stilled.

It took me a second to fit the face to memory. The deep brown skin, the broad jaw and full lips, the rough scar etching his chin.

"It was you," I breathed. "Carmen met *you* at Backplace."

Goren looked toward Dashiel and growled. *"Fool."*

I stood, ready to wring him for answers, when Tari touched my shoulder.

"We need to go," she said. Her face was dirt-stained, her eyes still watery from heaving.

A more powerful guilt twisted my stomach. Tari had never let me face trouble alone. And tonight, it had nearly gotten her killed.

She was right; we had to go.

But Dashiel staggered upright and stood before us, one palm raised as it had been the day he'd cornered me in the parlor. "Please, my lady. Can we talk?"

"Don't let them leave," Goren said.

But they were all exhausted, their specters frayed from carrying the walls of a collapsing mine. My power was unspent. Even in its current state—bloated and unsteady—I could take them all.

"Get out of our way," I said slowly.

"Please." Dashiel went to step closer. I slipped a thread of my specter under his boot before it met the ground. He lost his balance, stumbling.

I shoved Tari forward and ran.

We made it twenty yards before a fierce tendril snatched my ankle. I hit the ground, palms scraping, arms reverberating as they caught my fall. I knew instinctively that the thick, undulating power belonged to Goren. He wrenched me back, and I dug my nails into the dirt.

Teeth gritted, I reached for my specter. I would not let him drag me through this field.

But then Tari was at my feet, a blade glinting in her grip.

"Hold still." She thrust her hand out blindly, jolting when she met with Goren's specter. She kept her palm there for guidance, then swung the blade down.

The phantom grip released me. A roar sounded, and I glanced around to see Goren collapse in agony.

Tari lifted the eurium knife and smirked. "You didn't think I'd leave without it?"

We were riding before their voices could reach us, the ropes we'd used to tie the horses snapping in the wind.

31

The door ricocheted off the wall before slamming shut behind me. Keil had been pacing his ambassadorial chambers, arms crossed over his chest. His face slackened as he looked between me and the door. The door he'd locked. "How did you—?"

"Your cronies nearly got my friend killed last night," I said, storming forward.

Keil blinked. Shifted. Then his face became guarded in a way I'd never seen it. "From what I heard," he said slowly, "they saved your lives."

"Was that before or after they tried to interrogate us?"

He assessed me with a gaze void of his characteristic charm. "What were you doing in those tunnels?"

"Vereen is *my* province. I could've been hosting a tea party in those tunnels and you still wouldn't have the right to ask me that. So, unless you plan on kidnapping me again, *I'm* asking the questions. How long have you been plotting a secret alliance with Carmen?"

Keil went rigid, and I knew I'd struck truth.

The realization had emerged only after the night's chaos. The meeting between Carmen and Dashiel at Backplace; the deliberate kiss she'd planted, as if she'd known someone would be watching.

Keil had been in the city that night—but not because he'd stolen her Bolting Box. He hadn't needed to.

He'd been the one to deliver it.

He'd likely left it in Carmen's lounge before catching me in the bedchamber. When Carmen had deposited the box in her vanity drawer, he'd played along, offering enough information that I wouldn't suspect him.

But that meeting had made us wary of each other; while I'd believed he was after the compass, he'd believed I was after their secret—to use against them, perhaps, as another piece of leverage. Crossing paths again near Backplace had solidified our respective theories. I'd never considered that *he'd* entered the time and location into that Bolting Box. That *he'd* been a part of Carmen's secret meeting.

And there could only be one reason for the secrecy.

Why play a king's bride when I could play king? Carmen had said. Because she wanted Erik's crown. And she would use Ansoran support to get it.

Keil had never been searching for the compass at all.

"I understand why she would need you," I said. "But what does Ansora get out of it?"

Keil's jaw ticked for three long breaths.

"Fine." I turned. "I'll ask her myself."

"Wait."

I faced him, eyebrows raised.

"If this gets out," he said quietly, "Wielders could get hurt."

"*Your* Wielders?" I scoffed. "After last night, I think I can reconcile myself to that event."

I swiveled again, only to crash into Keil's specter.

My own specter blazed to life with a force that shook me. And in that white-hot second, I knew I was the stronger Wielder between us. I knew I could tear Keil's specter apart if I wanted to—could splinter it out like a eurium blade, until he felt the pain deep in his bones.

I forced myself to rebalance, to bury the strength.

"Not just them," Keil said, oblivious to my internal battle. He stepped closer and lowered his voice. "My sister journeyed here before me as an envoy of a different kind. With the Huntings rising so rapidly, she and Carmen were working to find vulnerable Wielders and offer them safe passage out of Daradon. That's when the Hunters found her. That's why they *kept* her. They realized she was reaching out to other Wielders, but they didn't know why."

I straightened, taking it all in.

So we keep them for weeks? Lye had said last night. *Until it's done?*

He'd been referring to the date on the shipping documents I'd found in Carmen's chambers. Not a means for her own escape . . . but for the escape of Wielders.

This was why the empress had sanctioned Keil's rescue mission but hadn't let him travel to Daradon without diplomatic immunity. Because if the Hunters had discovered Carmen's plans with Ansora—if they'd managed to torture the information from Keil's sister—it would have been enough to start a war.

"Carmen was helping to locate these Wielders?" I asked.

"Yes. And in return for aiding our people, my empress will support her claim to the throne if and when she chooses to make it."

"The Wielders—how did Carmen find them?"

Keil went silent. He couldn't come up with an answer.

But I could.

Was Nelle the keeper after all? After months of brutality, was she now using the compass to "help" Wielders and put her daughter on the throne?

I laughed in disbelief, lightheaded. "And your cronies think *I'm* fooling you."

Keil remained stone-faced. "Carmen is not fooling me."

"You're so sure about that? You've known her for less time than it takes milk to turn rancid."

"And in that time," he said firmly, "she's given me no reason to question her motives or her sources. Every connection she possesses, she's used for our aid. She disclosed safe, secret naval routes for our Ansoran vessels, and now she's helping Wielders find refuge—innocent people who would otherwise be slaughtered."

"Yet she fed you false information. She sent your Wielders to those prison tunnels, didn't she? And they were conveniently empty. Aren't you curious as to how she knew about them?"

"I'm more curious as to how *you* knew about them. You're the one who rifled through Carmen's belongings and followed her to Backplace. You're the one who possesses a eurium knife bearing the same symbol as the one in those tunnels."

"Yes, I suspected they would tell you as much." I reached into my pocket for the parchment on which I'd drawn the symbol.

I'd overlooked it before. But to have been etched into their weapons and blood-painted in that Wielder prison, this symbol had to hold significance to the copycats—a name or location or something else entirely.

It could lead me straight to the keeper who'd ordered my father's murder.

My specter throbbed in vicious anticipation. Because whether or not the symbol led to Nelle, I would be ready.

Keil's face was unreadable as I tossed the parchment on the lounge table.

"They said the symbol is ancient Ansoran. Read it."

"I can't," he said.

My voice darkened. "You owe me a favor, Ambassador."

"And the terms were specific: *Any favor that is within my power to grant.* This is a dead language. Even if any living being could read this symbol, I wouldn't know how to find them." He shook his head and said carefully, "You can't demand this of me."

"As long as I know what I know, I can demand anything of you."

He flinched as if I'd struck him. He looked me over, aghast. "Where is your honor?"

"You would lecture me about honor? You came to Daradon on the pretext of friendship while planning to support a coup for Erik's throne."

"You're defending him now? He is—"

"He is *what*, Ambassador?" I stepped up to him, holding his stare. "What do you have to say about the king who holds your life in his hands?"

Keil's eyes sailed over me again, disbelief mingling with pain.

My conscience tugged at me. Whatever other cruelties the empress of Ansora had committed, Garret had misread her intentions in sending her ambassador to court. Keil had never wanted the compass; he'd only wanted to help the Wielders of Daradon—the people he considered his own. He wanted to save them from these Huntings, just as I did.

But he was working with Carmen to do it. He believed he was doing the right thing by trusting her—and that was precisely the problem. Keil gave his trust too freely, and to the wrong people. Even when he'd believed I was after his secret, he'd trusted *me*.

Carmen and her mother might very well be responsible for the rise in Huntings; Carmen might now be leading these Daradonian Wielders into a *trap*. But Keil wouldn't believe it until their bodies lay scattered around him.

And he certainly wouldn't believe that she had anything to do with my father's murder.

Even if I did.

The irony was crushing: For the first time since we'd met, I was sure Keil wasn't my enemy. But as long as he remained blind to Carmen's manipulations, as long as she and her mother remained the most likely suspects in my search for the keeper . . . I would have to make him one.

We seemed to harden in the same moment, each resigned to our positions on the battleground—on opposite ends, as we had been all along.

"I'm sorry, Lady Alissa." He drew a deep breath and squared his shoulders. "I cannot help you. And I do not believe your threats."

It could've been the words or the severity of his tone, but I knew this was no longer the man who'd trailed his specter down my spine atop the balcony. Nor was this the ambassador who'd handled those dullroot glass shards with a feigned smile.

This was the soldier who'd fought in the Western War. The commander of the Wielders who'd attacked my estate.

This was the man who saw me as a Hunter's daughter.

So I would give him a Hunter's daughter.

"You're not only gambling with your life now," I said, dangerously soft. "What do you think Erik will do to Carmen when he discovers she's trying to steal his crown?"

"You wouldn't throw her to the wolves," Keil said. He sounded uncertain.

"No?" I lifted my chin, my smile dripping poison. *"Dare me."*

Keil swallowed, and I knew he saw the truth in my eyes. Saw that, for the first time, I wasn't bluffing.

"Carmen is a good person," he bit out.

I choked on a laugh. "You still don't understand? There are *no good people*. Your Wielders aren't good, and the princess isn't good, and the sympathizers you watch in awe aren't good. Shall I tell you how I know that? It's because I watched them, too. I watched them drop their staffs and fall silent as one of their own was dragged forward. I watched as the king's guards tied the man to a lantern pole and the king ordered them to—" I gasped, my specter surging.

After four years, that day at the Opal still had so much power over me.

"The sympathizers just *stood there*," I said through my teeth. "The guards didn't need to hold them back. Because nobody tried to stop it."

Keil's face had lost its color, stunned and bewildered. But he recovered quickly. "They were afraid," he said.

"They were *cowards*. Erik tested them that day, and they failed."

"And what of you?" Keil narrowed his eyes. "If your beloved husband-to-be delivered the same sentence to another, what would you do?"

"It doesn't matter what I'd do. I don't profess my beliefs and then back down when those beliefs are challenged."

"How could you, when you have no beliefs to profess? You have faith in nothing but futility and hopelessness. I pity the way you must live."

"Of course you do. Because despite your honor and your faith and your untested beliefs, you can always return to your empire. And it won't matter how many Wielders you save along the way or how many battlefields you return from. You will always be free to Wield as easily as you breathe." A sneer curled my lips. "Look around you," I said. "Everyone else is suffocating."

My heart was slamming, fire rushing to my cheeks; my fists shook at my sides. Keil saw it all—my violent pain and resentment—and his own anger guttered, as if my unraveling had brought him back to himself.

His brows gathered, his gaze searching, searching, like I'd sparked something in his awareness, and he could almost see me clearly—

Dangerous. Too dangerous. I turned before his understanding took root.

"Alissa." Keil's hand closed around mine, and I ripped away.

"Don't."

Don't speak my name with that familiarity. Don't look at me with that wretched affection in your eyes.

Keil must have read the words in my expression because his face took on that pained look again.

"You have no right," I snarled.

He retreated, his almost-discovery evaporating with the movement. "I'm sorry."

Keil had only been half-right that night in the city. I always looked for the worst in people, but I hadn't in him. I'd gotten swept away in the current of him, so quick and unexpected that even now, something deep within me panged at having extinguished the light in his eyes.

I steeled myself against the feeling. I'd already risked losing my secret to him.

I wouldn't risk my heart.

"You have one week to get me that translation," I said, leaving. "Or you can all hang together."

32

After that long-ago day at the Opal, I'd expected a new fog of terror to settle over Daradon as it had settled over me. There were whisperings, of course. Pieces of the tale that had stowed out of Henthorn with vendors and travelers to worm across the provinces. But soon, the stories changed. They said a sympathizer had attacked the courtiers—or attacked the city folk—or a helpless elderly woman—and our great ruler had fearlessly taken action. In some stories, Erik had run the man through with a sword. In others, he'd defeated him in hand-to-hand combat. But in every story, one thread remained the same: Erik had emerged a hero.

Then the autumn winds had blown across the kingdom as if in a unified sigh of relief. If anyone wondered why the locals had let the Opal fall into disrepair, they knew better than to ask. The world forgot; people moved on. And months later, when I was still jolting awake every night, washed in tears and sweat, I realized it was a torture of its own—having to hold on to what everyone else had let go of.

Again, the world was moving forward. And I didn't know how to move with it.

Since my father's death, a slow rage had started simmering in my blood, and it was feeding the force of my specter. The power constantly pulled at my bones now, swollen with my pent-up emotion, until the Lady Alissa who performed the motions of day-to-day activity felt like a wooden shell around me, directed by the puppet-strings of obligation. And my specter, for the first time in my life, felt like the true core of myself rather than an extension: writhing and agonized and volatile to the touch.

Each night, I had to let the power ripple around my bedchamber to ease the ever-growing ache. By day, I clenched it tight like a fist and gathered up a smile; it was the only way to get the nobles talking to me again. Apparently, my grief was more palatable when tempered with a positive outlook.

Maybe that was why I accepted Erik's next invitation to dinner: because he was the only person who demanded my candor. "You mustn't pretend with me," he'd said, low and sweet. "The others, I understand. But not me. I shall never balk at your sorrow."

So, I let my smile drop. I let myself be authentic with the first man I'd ever feared. And in the comfort of my misery, my restless power began to settle.

On his balcony, Erik poured my wine and fed me sugar-dusted cranberries. When the night cooled, he took my gloved hand and said, "I want to show you something."

He led me through the palace and into a perfumed gallery, where each past ruler of Daradon stared down from their own wide arch. The two-tined crown was painted everywhere, spiking from foreheads like straight, silver horns, its sapphire embellishments rendered with exact detail over the generations.

I spotted King Hoyt, the creator of the Execution Decree, beside his blushing consort, whose murder at the hands of her former Wielder lover had roused Hoyt into spiting every Wielder in Daradon. With intolerance already rising at the time—along with more and more stories depicting specters as uncontrollable—many believed that King Hoyt's tale illustrated the highest act of romance.

I'd always thought it was a horrifying indication of what powerful men could get away with in the name of love.

Erik's portrait hung inside the largest silver frame. The rendering was handsome—strong-jawed and sultry, with the crown elongating his bone structure—but inaccurate. The artist hadn't captured the cruel light in his ice-blue eyes.

"It doesn't feel like you," I said.

"No?" He smoothed his jacket, the silver embroidery kissed with lantern light. "I think it captures me rather nicely."

"Your face, maybe, but not your essence."

He gave a heavy-lidded smirk. "What do you know of my essence?"

"I know enough."

Chuckling, he strolled toward his mother's portrait. I'd met Queen Wilhelmina once during childhood, when she'd scrutinized me with beady eyes and pinched my cheeks until they'd hurt. *You should use rouge, little petal. Brighten up that pretty face.*

I shivered at the memory and glided beside Erik, whose expression had turned cold.

"Do you miss her?" I asked.

"Not particularly. She was . . . *difficult*."

And she must not have valued her own consort, Erik's father, as his image was nowhere to be found.

Erik sighed. "We're not here to discuss my mother. I said I wanted to show you something, didn't I?"

He reached toward her arch, his hand seeming to disappear behind the trim. Then he tugged and the arch creaked open, emitting a breath of fusty air.

Erik smiled at my expression. "The palace is rich with concealed rooms and passageways. How do you think the previous monarchs hid their affairs?"

I lifted an eyebrow. "Have you appointed me your mistress already?"

He laughed softly. "Never you."

I followed him into the concave room. It was unfurnished, with crumbling stones, cracked flooring, and a heavy sheet covering one portion of the wall. Dust whirled in the cool air, furring my tongue with each inhale.

"You've been lying to me," Erik murmured. My specter jolted, but he continued evenly, "You consider my proposal with a fine lady's restraint, but I see your eagerness. I see you aching for the power you know you deserve . . . and I'm the only person in this world who can quell the ache."

A sense of foreboding crept over me as he drifted toward the sheet. He clenched up a handful. Then he whooshed it down.

Dust billowed and fogged the room, gritting my eyes. I was clearing my throat from the musty stench when the gray haze parted.

And I locked eyes with my own painted stare.

The artist had depicted me with a generous hand—reddening my lips, darkening my lashes, setting my cheekbones aglow. A crystal bodice dived knifelike down my chest—a severe rendering of my usual style—and my hair was twined back, lone tendrils curling toward my collarbone.

Mounted on my head was the two-tined crown, encrusted with diamonds and sapphires.

The dual spikes shot skyward and the center plunged low against my brow, mimicking my neckline and evoking the helmeted look of a warrior. I looked glorious and forbidding—iced with jewels and bronzed with fire.

I looked more powerful than I'd ever felt in reality.

"I don't understand," I whispered, alarm now swelling inside me.

Because only blood-royals wore the two-tined crown. Never consorts. Never *me*.

Erik's profile cut a sharp shadow across the portrait, like a cloud blotting the sun. "Immense power cannot be held by a single entity. The weight must be split—balanced between two—or else it can crush its bearer." He trailed reverent fingers over the crown's painted tines, the movement forming a long V. "It's why my predecessors left mediocre legacies, remembered for their failures and their tragedies, their vanities and vengeances. They failed to consider that even our deities must rule in pairs. But I've always known that to have more—to *be* more—I must choose for myself a worthy partner."

His fingers stilled on the brow of my portrait. His eyes glimmered across my painted lips. "I ache, just as you do," he said quietly. "For gods cannot stand alone."

Then he turned to me, taking my gloved hands, standing so close that my short breaths fogged the silver buttons of his jacket.

"You would not be my consort," he said tenderly. "You would be my finest conquest. I would make you a queen."

My specter heaved; I clenched my muscles to hold it down. This was more than I'd ever expected from him—more than I'd *wanted*—and my body was responding with the panic of an animal who'd just had a cage dropped over them.

But I forced myself to ask, breathless, "I'd rule by your side? As your equal?"

"You'd be my equal in all things if you would let me make you mine."

Mine. The word rang hollow in my ears.

"And you'd be mine?" I asked.

"Until my dying day."

My specter pulsed faster, straining now. This little room was too stagnant, too suffocating. I pulled away and stumbled for the door.

The gallery's perfumed air hit me, and I gasped in a lungful.

Erik followed, obscenely calm. The arch clicked back into the wall behind him. "Most women wouldn't run from a declaration like that."

"Why not Lady Perla or the others?" I asked, almost accusingly. "You could take your pick."

Erik slunk closer. He grasped my chin and turned my head toward his portrait. "It doesn't feel like me, you said." He whipped my face back toward him. "You're the only one of them who sees me. The only one who ever could."

He was right. I knew the monster he was because I'd witnessed it for myself.

My eyes flicked to the portrait again, and I gulped, imagining my own beside it. And suddenly, I knew I wouldn't have feared that crowned image of me—I might have even embraced it—if not for what it implied. That Erik's intentions weren't built on temporary attraction. That he'd found within me something he truly desired.

And he would relinquish half his crown—half his *power*—if I would let him take it.

Slowly, I drew my gaze back to his. Maybe this *was* more than I'd wanted from him. Maybe the intensity of this gift frightened me more than anything he'd ever done.

Yet maybe this was exactly what I needed. Because now, as I absorbed the enormity of his offer, as I saw the yearning in his eyes . . . I suspected this monster would give me anything I asked for.

But if I was going to do this, I had to be *sure* he would.

So I smothered my specter and steeled my spine. Then I turned for the opposite wall, needing the breathing space to summon my next words. "You ordered the Capewells to reclaim their compass, and you are selecting individuals for execution until they do. At what point shall you punish them all?"

Erik's brows rose. Then he half smiled, crossing the distance between us. "Is Briar sending you to do business with me now?"

"She'd slaughter me if she knew I was asking."

His eyes flashed. "She could try." He stopped close, backing me flat against the wall. His body blocked the light. "The Capewells failed me in losing the compass, and covered it up with seven years' worth of lies. They don't deserve the mercy of a mass sentence nor a mass execution. Unless they recover what they lost, they shall each feel the consequence of their choices. And then I will appoint others to take their place."

Others to fulfill the Execution Decree, he didn't have to say. *To ensure the continued slaughter of Wielders.* Though I'd expected nothing less, I was glad for the confirmation. I needed it to fuel me.

"You'd kill every person with a Hunters' Mark?" I asked.

Erik tilted his head, taking me in. "Would their deaths displease you?"

"Would my answer matter?"

He paused, considering. I held my breath. Then he said, with his own faint air of surprise, "Yes."

I exhaled, somehow knowing it was true. And though my victory over the king tasted bittersweet, arriving too late to save my father, I knew I couldn't waste it.

Especially for the Capewells.

So, I laid my palms on his jacket, my silk gloves snagging on the embroidery. "No," I whispered. My specter writhed as Garret crossed my mind. But I chained it tight, reminded myself of all he'd done, and tried with more conviction, "Their deaths would not displease me."

I heard the waver in my voice.

But Erik must not have, because his laughter rumbled against me. "Then why pose such a question? You're not a Hunter."

"No?" I angled closer. Wetted my lips. "What if I told you I've been hunting here this entire time?"

His pupils flared, eyes darkening. He braced his palms on the wall, caging my head. "And?" he asked gruffly. "Have you captured your prey?"

It was the reaction I'd wanted: a slip of his decorum, this undressing of his desire. Yet my specter squirmed with dread—an instinctual rebellion against what I was about to do.

Still, I craned my neck, my breaths coming out sharp and shallow. "You tell me."

Erik's gaze sank from my parted lips to the length of my fluttering throat. To the space I'd offered, just under my jaw. His heartbeat kicked up against my palms, slamming in time with my own—though for a different reason. Then, with leisurely care, as if savoring the meal I'd laid out for him, the king bowed his head.

The hair on my arms rose with the first touch of his mouth. I let him kiss a slow trail down my neck, his hot tongue sweeping like a brand. I shuddered as he approached my concealed bruises, but he fortunately pulled away before reaching them, skimming my lips instead.

"Tell me yes." His words grazed my mouth, leaving the taste of sugared cranberries.

"Yes," I exhaled. Because this—*he*—would be worth the outcome.

Erik whispered my name like a claiming.

Then he was kissing me, rough and fast and fervent. His hands were everywhere, one tangled at the nape of my neck, the other searching the small of my back.

I made myself open for him, tugging him closer even as he held me flush between his body and the wall. I was drowning in him, grasping for dry land each time we broke away for breath but falling short every time.

Somebody gasped.

I jolted; my head smacked the wall. A group of servants stood open-mouthed in the doorway.

My stomach plummeted. Because Tari's features were screwed in disgust.

"Your Majesty!" One of the girls curtsied. "Forgive us. We didn't—"

"No need to apologize." Erik drew back, breathing heavily, his fist still twisted in my hair. "We should have retreated to somewhere private."

A few girls blushed and turned their heads. Tari's gaze remained locked on mine.

"I trust you'll keep this among yourselves," Erik said.

The girls giggled their agreement and scampered away. *It's not what you think!* I wanted to scream after Tari. Instead, I grasped Erik's shoulders and dragged him back to face me. "This will spread to the gentry like wildfire," I said, panting.

"Good." He extricated my hands. "I hope they stew in it."

Then his eyes slid to my gloves. He wore no ring today—there was no chance of encountering dullroot—and yet sweat slicked my palms as he pinched the empty fingertip of my right glove and dragged it off my skin. He repeated the motion with the other, baring both my hands, then he planted an open kiss inside each wrist, inhaling deeply the skin I'd always denied him.

"Don't wear these again," he murmured, tucking my gloves into his pocket.

He leaned down to taste my mouth once more, nipping my bottom lip between his teeth. Then he pulled back and smiled, like he knew this was just the appetizer.

Like he would gladly wait to devour me whole.

33

An impatient *tap-tap-tap* awaited me in the lounge. I glanced at the mirror on my way in. My lips were swollen and raw with color, my hair a tangled mess. Only my eyes remained vacant, empty of all the passion that had blazed in Erik's.

At last, I turned to Tari. "That wasn't what it looked like."

She paused her foot-tapping. "So, it was a trick of the light? If I'd looked from another angle, I *wouldn't* have seen you kissing Erik's face off?" She crossed her arms. "You only pursued him to secure protection for your father. But now . . ." She trailed off, too kind even in her temper to finish the sentence.

"Now my father's gone," I said. "I know."

"Then what were you doing with him?"

"What I had to!" I pushed a hand through my hair, wincing as I snagged in the knots. "Even if I find the compass before Briar, and Erik kills every Capewell in Daradon, he'll assign others to take their place. As long as he rules, Wielders will be slaughtered. But if I ruled at his side . . ."

Tari dropped her arms, eyes whitening with horror. "You're serious," she breathed. "You really think your kisses can save a kingdom."

My hackles rose. "I could have swayed him tonight—about the

Capewells. I can sway him again when it matters."

"To abolish the Execution Decree? To reverse two hundred years of prejudice against Wielders?"

"Daradon's rot began with the monarchy," I said firmly. "That's where it has to end. It won't happen overnight, but as long as Erik wants me—"

"He doesn't want you!" Tari shouted. "He wants the Wholeborn girl he thinks you are! Gracious gods, do you hear yourself? What happens when Erik wants an heir, and a Wielder baby pops out of you? How long do you expect a child to contain their specter?"

"I've controlled mine for eighteen years without instruction."

"Have you?" Her face hardened. "Then what happened in those tunnels, Alissa? You couldn't control your specter, and it nearly got us killed."

I smothered my guilt as soon as it rose. I had no place left inside me to hold it.

"The keeper won't target you again if they don't see you as a threat," Tari continued. "Go back to Vereen and lie low, and let that be enough."

My fists trembled. "So, I get to live, but only if I'm a good girl and keep my specter hidden? I get to breathe, but only by sucking the air from other Wielders' mouths to sustain myself? How is that fair? How is that *enough*?" My words cracked around the mental image of Father. To spare him from the pain of my death, it *had* been enough. But not anymore. "They stole my rights and choose what I can buy back with a thank-you. They didn't create me. I shouldn't have to thank them for letting me exist."

My specter was lashing inside me again, and I turned to hide my pained expression. I breathed deeply, winding the power down thread by thread.

Tari's steps clicked toward me. Her voice gentled. "You're right. It'll never be fair. But right now you're angry and hurting. You can't see any other way out. And maybe..."

"Maybe what?" I whirled, and she hesitated. "Say it."

"Maybe this is what the keeper wants. For you to be alone. Without allies."

I spoke through my teeth. "Which *allies* did you have in mind?"

"You've put so much focus on Nelle and Carmen, but what if you're wrong about them? Why would they have built a prison in those tunnels only to reveal them to the Ansorans? Why kill Wielders like Marge only to help others find refuge? If they intended to stage a rescue in front of the Ansorans, then those prisons would've been full." She sighed. "I don't know Nelle. But I don't think Carmen had anything to do with your father's death."

"And why not?"

"Because," Tari said, her voice full of resolve, "I monitored her after you found the Bolting Box, remember? I saw her treating the staff with respect and generosity. I saw her kindness to Lord Junius while the gentry shunned him. And I saw her crying at your father's funeral. It didn't look like guilt. It looked like grief."

"Carmen is the daughter of the Mantis," I said, seething. "You spend a few weeks at court, and you think you understand it? You think tears can't be manipulated as easily as words?" Then, because I realized this went deeper than a fleeting infatuation, because I knew it would hurt her, I said, "Carmen has you fooled without even trying. Imagine the damage she could do if she knew you existed."

Tari flinched; my blade had found its target. It wasn't even a little bit satisfying.

"I know where my loyalties lie," she said, face flushed.

"Then you should know that Carmen will do anything to get the crown."

Tari looked me over with an expression I'd never seen on her—an expression of giving up. "She's not the only one," she said sadly, and I knew I deserved it when she left me standing there, alone.

I couldn't sleep. Each time I drifted off, I would see myself in an ivory gown, vowing to bind my life to Erik's. I imagined the horror of waking up beside him, bathed in dusty morning sunlight. His pale lashes tickling my cheek as he blinked the sleep from his eyes. My name on his lips, his lips on my skin . . .

My specter surged out, rippling the bedsheets. I righted them with clammy hands.

Tari had been right about one thing: My control was slipping.

It had always ached to confine my specter, but never like this—with the intense sensation of choking over my own breath. I could barely focus from the need to expel the power inside me. To let it ravage the world as wholly as it had ravaged my father's study.

It was almost laughable: In Erik's loathing of Wielders, he was missing out on the most vicious side of me—the side he would most enjoy. Though he seemed to enjoy the rest of me well enough.

You would be my finest conquest. I would make you a queen.

The sheets shot off the bed this time. I didn't bother retrieving them. I squeezed my eyes shut, willing my skin to cool. I'd lost Father and Garret; I'd distanced myself from Amarie; I'd made an enemy of Keil. Now even Tari was retreating. But tonight, I needed only to forget the taste of Erik's rose-sweet tongue in my mouth.

I drew a shuddering breath; let it out. Then another.

But the musty air of that hidden room still clung in my hair, taunting me with each inhale. I ground my teeth against the smell—earthy and familiar, akin to moth-eaten fabrics. Yet it strangely evoked memories of Keil's fresh soap-and-linen scent, and something sweeter, like cake frosting, like—

Carmen's vanilla.

As if on the stale air itself, Erik's words drifted to me: *How do you think the previous monarchs hid their affairs?*

My eyes flew open.

I tumbled off the bed, slipping in the sheets, then grabbed my robe and hurtled from my chambers.

The halls blurred past, drizzled with moonlight and tinkling with music from the downstairs entertainment. I knocked at Carmen's suite several times, then let myself in.

I headed straight for the closet in which Keil and I had hidden weeks ago; it was the first time I'd smelled that musty-clothes odor, mixed then with Keil's scent and Carmen's perfume. I opened the doors and Carmen's vanilla washed over me again, mingling with that same stuffy smell.

Nelle's chamber key had been found at the scene of Wray Capewell's murder, his body left atop a drainage gutter nearby. I'd linked the key to Nelle's presence that night, and had attributed Wray's furtive behavior to their potential affair. But what if I'd been viewing it from the wrong angle all along? What if I never should have put so much importance on these chambers—or on Nelle—at all?

Because Nelle's key had always led beyond this suite.

I climbed into the closet and slid the gowns aside, exposing the back panel of wood. I ran a finger along the edges. *There*—a disruption in the seam. I hooked my finger behind the latch and pulled. The back of the closet gave way and with it went the last of my doubt.

Pulse thrumming, I stepped into the darkness.

34

My efforts to integrate back into the gentry were finally paying off. Nobles gathered around me once again, trading pieces of gossip like game tokens—eager to hand me more for free since my gallery tryst with the king. Sabira was one of the few who didn't grovel for my favor. She just watched me from a distance, her fake gems peeking dully beneath feathered sleeves.

Tonight marked Rose Season's annual tribute to a previous monarch, and this year, the ballroom had been styled as an aviary—a nod to Daradon's longest-reigning queen, who'd kept so many birds that the gentry had constantly carried parasols to protect themselves from the bird droppings. Now paper-crafted birds swayed from the ceiling and pink magnolias branched across the balcony. Plumes stuck out from every hat and pocket square, and silver ropes crisscrossed all entrances except the one leading into the grand foyer.

It felt less like an aviary than an overstuffed cage, but nobody else seemed to notice.

"Well?" Carmen dragged me from the Creakish bookkeepers, who were slurring over empty whiskey glasses. "Is it true?"

"Is what true?"

"Don't be coy, darling. The court is buzzing with it." She tickled my nose with her pink boa—the boa from which I'd once snagged that incriminating feather—and I had to stop myself from cinching it around her neck. Despite everything Tari had said, and the fresh theory I was still piecing together, I could no longer stand the sight of the princess. I couldn't stand the sight of any of them.

"Apparently," Carmen stage-whispered, "you and Erik were doing unspeakable things in the gallery."

"If they were so unspeakable, people wouldn't be talking."

She gasped. "So it is true! No wonder Perla confined herself to her chambers. She'll probably hide out here at court indefinitely."

"What do you mean?"

Carmen's sparkling eyes dimmed. "Her father will be furious at her for not seizing the opportunity he laid out."

I frowned. "He wouldn't . . . hurt her? She's his child."

"Some people are simply cruel," Carmen said gravely. "Fathering a child doesn't erase that cruelty."

The words left me uneasy as Rupert strutted over, brandishing his new ruby brooch. Carmen's face brightened as if by the strike of a match; that brooch would be hers by the night's end. Leaving her to her sport, I headed for a corner I'd been watching all evening.

Keil had glowered at the walls from the moment he'd arrived, ignoring the usual swarm of giggling noblewomen until they'd scattered to find another handsome plaything.

Now he stiffened at my approach, his face set in hard, formal lines. "Was that Carmen's arm around yours a moment ago? Tell me again how you would see her executed."

"I'll do whatever is necessary to get what I want," I said with equal frost.

"Judging from the rumors about you and the king, I have no doubt."

I tipped my head. "Jealous, Ambassador?"

A shock of red colored his cheeks. Though instantly remorseful, I forced a smirk.

There had been a double-Hunting the night before, the copycats killing four Wielders in total. While Erik would've ensured the Capewells suffered a double loss of their own, that was still four more Wielders I'd been too late to save.

And four fewer standing between the copycats and *me*.

While my discoveries behind Carmen's closet had pushed her down my suspect list, it had also created more uncertainties; understanding the copycats' symbol still seemed the best method of tracking them down. As long as I needed Keil's resources, this was the easiest way forward for us both.

We couldn't be barbed by flowers we'd never let bloom.

"Do you have the translation?" I asked in that same unruffled tone.

"No."

"And is that from failure or from a simple lack of trying? Not that it makes a difference, but I'm curious to know just how stupid you really are."

"I told you, it's a dead language. If you think I can miraculously summon a translation, you're overestimating my abilities."

"And you are underestimating mine."

His coldness thawed a fraction, eyebrows drawing together. "Yes," he said quietly. "I think I misjudged a great deal about you."

I couldn't allow his words to pierce me; they slid away like blood off steel.

"You have three days left," I said. "Or else I suggest running back to your ship. Once Erik fixes on a target, he rarely changes course."

I began turning when Keil's specter caught my elbow, faint as a shiver on my skin.

The effect was unexpected: My own specter rushed to the front of my body, as if to urge me further into his touch. I jerked, my breath hitching, betraying my discomfort. I leashed my specter resentfully, then recovered with a huff of laughter.

"Really?" I drawled. "Wielding in the ballroom? You're going to make it that easy for me?"

"Tell them, then. I won't deny it." Keil spoke firmly, but not unkindly—a challenge without the bite.

We were tucked into a dimmer corner of the ballroom, but the party thundered behind us, an ocean of bodies and sound. It reminded me of that moment at Budding Ball, when we'd stood between the silks. When he'd untangled my earring with a gentleness that had sent tingles across my skin.

"Don't test my patience within earshot of so many bystanders," I murmured, smothering the memory. "It won't end well."

Again, I went to turn. Again, his specter flared—with that same gentleness, easy to shrug off if I wanted to. But I held my ground as he stepped closer, my specter twisting painfully toward him. A manifestation of the deep yearning I was trying to pretend didn't exist.

"You wanted a dare," Keil said. "So here it is. Call for your king. Have them put me in chains." One step closer, and he towered over me. My breath caught again at the intensity of his stare. "If you're such a viper," he whispered, his specter grazing like fingertips down my arm, "then go ahead, my lady. *Strike.*"

The tension spilled out and hardened, cementing us in a deadlock. My pulse quickened; his rapid breaths washed across my face. I sensed the bluff between us, but couldn't tell if it was mine or his.

I didn't have to find out.

The fanfare sounded, and I shucked off his spectral touch, grateful for the excuse to look away. The room dipped with bows and curtsies as Erik sailed from the grand foyer, his cape billowing.

Then the music screeched to a stop. Laughter cut off in gasps and strangles as the crowd froze—some half-bent in their genuflections—a tableau of plumes and open mouths.

Because a group of guards charged behind the king.

They parted the herd on the dance floor, glaring at those who couldn't scamper fast enough. Then they opened their tight formation and tossed out a trembling figure. The man cried out as his knees hit the marble.

The sound had me tumbling forward before I realized what I was doing.

"Erik," I breathed, clutching the king's arm. "Who is this?"

His lashes dipped, eyes sweeping over me. His smile tightened my gut. "Why don't we ask our guests?" he called loudly. "Can any of our esteemed nobles identify this man?"

Silence crackled, heavy and scented with fear. The man whimpered into his shirt.

"Lady Sabira?" Erik asked. Sabira gave a haughty shake of her head, but I glimpsed her relief as Erik turned to another. "Lord Rupert? Can you identify him for us?"

"N-no, Your Majesty."

The man began to rock back and forth, arms curled around his knees.

"Erik," I pleaded.

But Erik ignored me, capturing the hand I'd hooked around his arm and threading our fingers together. I twitched, still unused to his bare skin against mine. Then I risked a glance at Keil, whose eyes were fixed on our twined hands—on Erik's firm grip versus my own limp, open hold.

Keil's jaw tightened.

"How about a clue?" Erik said, and I nearly stumbled as he pulled me closer to the man. To everyone else, it probably looked like we were meting out this man's fate together.

"It's Quincy, isn't it?" Erik asked kindly. "I hear you're a minister."

The man's throat worked with a loud swallow. "Y-yes."

"Yes, *what?*"

"Yes, Your Majesty."

"Very good. What kind of ceremonies do you preside over, Quincy?"

"All kinds, Your Majesty. Weddings, funerals—"

"Funerals!" Erik swung back to the gentry. "Does this summon any memories?"

The nobles fidgeted, a few shuffling toward the exits before they noticed the silver ropes barring their way. When they tried for the grand foyer, the guards blocked the threshold. Though many here might have heard the rumors—seen odd glimpses—most hadn't witnessed Erik at his worst. They didn't know what kind of beast lay beneath the dazzling facade.

They were about to find out.

"How about this?" Erik peered down at Quincy. "Three purses of gold for pointing out the face you recognize in the crowd."

Quincy shivered around his knees, unwilling to look up.

"Come now," Erik crooned. "For the right price, even a minister can be bought." He nudged Quincy with his polished boot, voice deepening. "Surely I needn't teach an educated man that people can only bend so far before they break."

My specter roiled, and I fought the urge to shake Quincy by the shoulders. *For your own sake—answer him!*

Then the crowd jostled. The nobles were parting again—*staggering out of the way*—as a sharp-shouldered figure sliced between them. Junius stepped forward, and dread sank like a stone inside me.

"Thank you for refreshing my memory, Your Majesty," Junius said steadily. "I do recognize this man."

Erik's face lit up. "Excellent, Lord Junius."

Upon hearing Junius's name, Quincy lifted his head and crawled for the Dawni lord. "Please, my lord—"

One of the guards raised his silver-tipped boot and kicked Quincy back to the floor. I gasped, and Erik's fingers tightened around mine. I was sure he could feel me shaking.

"Can you tell us how you recognize him?" Erik asked.

Junius shifted and, for the first time, looked nervous. "He recently presided over a funeral held for members of my family."

"*Members of your family,*" Erik intoned. "Is that what you're calling your staff nowadays?"

Ice flooded me, stilling my body. My hand solidified in Erik's.

No.

No.

Unbelievably, Junius straightened. "Many of our staff members raised me, Your Majesty. They fed me and clothed me and cared for me in my illnesses. One of them delivered me into this world. So yes, they were my family. And they deserved a proper burial in the presence of the gods."

I felt my head shaking. *No, no, no.*

I'd told Junius where to locate his buried staff, not thinking of the consequence. Not realizing the danger I would be putting him in.

Erik licked his lips, amused. "What a moving sentiment. There is one problem, however. Weren't those *family members* executed by my Hunters as Wielders?"

"They were, Your Majesty."

"And in accordance with our laws, do Wielders have the right to funerals? Or are they cut down and discarded like the animals they are?"

A gasp swept through the crowd, and then the guards were at our backs, swords crossed in defense as Keil stormed toward us.

Erik glanced languidly between the blades. "Is there a problem, Ambassador Arcus?"

Keil stood taut as a bowstring, fists clenched, a vein throbbing in his temple. "Shouldn't this be handled in private?"

"I don't recall asking for your advice, Ambassador. Why don't you settle in with the rest of the audience."

"*Audience?*" Keil hissed. "This is to be a show?"

"This shall be whatever I want it to be," Erik said softly. "Welcome to Daradon."

Keil's eyes darkened. "Think well on what you're about to do."

At that, Erik turned fully. "Careful, Ambassador. That almost sounded like a threat. Remember, your immunity only protects you so long as you remain passive."

"Erik," I said, dizzy with panic. "You have diplomatic relations to think about."

"Lady Alissa is right," Keil said, his stare fixed on the king. "My empress extended a hand of friendship toward you. I wouldn't recommend knocking it aside."

"Hmm." Erik looked him over blandly. "That would be quite the tragedy. Especially since you've been so very amiable with my court, Ambassador. Attempting to foster all manner of . . . *friendships.*"

The king increased pressure around my hand, and my breathing quickened. Keil must have heard the change, because he glanced at me for half a second—his only giveaway that Erik had touched upon a truth. But the brief locking of our eyes was worse than a continued stare; our gazes skimmed like flint and steel, with a spark-forming friction.

And I feared it had given away enough.

"Your empress knew our laws before sending you here," Erik said with a calmness that contradicted my thumping pulse against his palm. "If she's as smart as you say, she wouldn't risk future peace because her ambassador doesn't like how we handle lawbreakers."

Keil faltered, and I knew: The empress wouldn't back him in this.

He had obeyed her once before—had held back at her command—and his sister had suffered for it. What would it take for him to defy his empress now?

His eyes flickered, like he was trying to work out the answer himself.

With a cold smile, Erik turned back to Junius. "Well?" he drawled. "Nothing more to say?"

Junius held the king's gaze for longer than he should have. With pained reluctance, he unfastened his bonestone earring and sank to his knees.

"I submit to your judgment," he said quietly, mechanically. "On behalf of the Jacombs, I beg forgiveness, my king."

His mother must have said those same words at the Jacomb trial—must have set her jewelry on the marble floor just as Junius did now, in ultimate submission. She had pleaded ignorant of housing Wielders, and Erik had pardoned her.

But now, the Jacombs couldn't pretend. They had voluntarily

exhumed those Wielders. They had knowingly taken the risk.

And I'd given them the means to do it.

The room held its breath as Erik considered. Then he cocked his head and said, "I think I've had my fill of Jacomb jewelry."

My stomach dropped. Erik nodded to his guards, and Junius didn't struggle as they hauled him forward.

He would die because of me.

I tugged on Erik's hand. "Exile him from court," I said, desperate. "Let him endure the humiliation."

Before Erik could answer, Carmen's voice trilled out: "Be reasonable, Cousin." She elbowed to the front of the crowd, her face ashen. "Junius is one of us. Give him a slap on the wrist and let us enjoy the evening."

It was the wrong thing to say.

As the gentry murmured in agreement, and a hopeful smile pulled at Carmen's lips, Erik's expression sharpened.

"Does my court agree with the princess?" he called. "Do you all believe that treason should go unpunished?"

That quickly, the courtiers ducked their heads. Some whispered, while others cleared their throats as if preparing to speak up. But just like when Erik had aimed that arrow at Perla's foot, nobody spoke up.

Nobody ever did.

My specter writhed with violent memory. *Sunlight on steel and a wet, heaving torso. Erik's sharp laughter, shaving out into the air. And open, voiceless mouths—such resounding silence—*

But this wasn't the Opal. There were no cracked cobblestones to drink up the blood tonight. The blood would puddle on the marble and seep up my skirts, marring me. Damning me.

If your beloved husband-to-be delivered the same sentence to another, what would you do?

I thought I'd known the answer. But as Junius bowed his head and began praying, I knew I couldn't bear to watch the light drain from those shrewd, earnest eyes.

I grabbed Erik's jacket with my free hand, forcing him to face me. Someone in the crowd gasped.

"You can't execute your own nobles," I said with vicious finality.

Erik looked down at my fist, curled against his chest. His hand lifted, and I flinched without meaning to. But he didn't strike me; he stroked those shockingly cold knuckles down my cheek in a caress.

"You misunderstand, my love. Nobody is being executed tonight." Cruel anticipation glazed his eyes. "There is no suffering in death."

My specter lurched at the words.

Erik started to pull away, but I heaved him back. I'd told Tari I could sway the king—I'd *believed* I could. Now I had to prove it.

"Junius's mother is the ruling lady of Dawning," I said, voice low. "If you harm him, you will lose her allegiance forever. How will we ever achieve more than your predecessors if we can't keep our kingdom united?" And because Erik's gaze sparked hungrily at my phrasing—*our kingdom*—I dared to press closer. I made myself go loose against him in a last, desperate attempt, and whispered, "Gods cannot stand alone."

A pause. Erik's eyes narrowed, flicking doubtfully over my face. He raised the hand still holding mine and adjusted his grip to enclose both my wrists.

I tensed; he'd seen through me. And now he would toss me to my knees beside Junius. I heard the guards shifting behind us and knew that Keil had moved closer.

Then, branching one hand into my hair to angle my head back, Erik brought his mouth down on mine.

I gasped, and he swallowed the sound. My body went rigid. Far away, the crowd was rustling—growing louder—and my specter, *my specter*—

Erik released me as the first waves of power rolled across my skin. I began to tremble. If he touched me again, it would be over.

"Lady Alissa is a wise and compassionate woman," Erik declared. "She has counseled mercy for the lord. On this night, I am inclined to heed her counsel."

The congregation gave a unanimous sigh, and Erik was smiling at me like I was the most precious thing in the world. His figure wavered beyond the gauzy layers of my specter, now shimmering around me like heat off a blaze.

Erik turned to a still-kneeling Junius, whose eyes shone with tears.

"Of course," Erik murmured, "there remains the question of who will receive your punishment."

The crowd went silent. I couldn't process the words.

Then Erik gestured to his guards, and they yanked Quincy between them.

"No!" Junius thrashed against his jailors. "Please, Your Majesty. Punish me! It was my fault!"

Junius was wrong. This was my fault—all of it, *my fault*.

"The man is innocent!" Keil's voice boomed out. More guards had come to stand between us.

"Cease!" one of them barked. "Or we will restrain you."

Keil's eyes glinted, knife-sharp. "You can try."

My specter palpitated, fogging my vision. My ears popped from the strain of holding it back.

Junius was still pleading. Quincy had wriggled from the guards and was crawling to me. *"Please, my lady, don't let them hurt me. Please, my lady—"*

They wrenched him up again.

"Stop," I whispered.

One of the guards drew a knife from his belt. Carmen turned her head, shoulders shaking.

"*Stop*," I pleaded again.

Junius was sobbing now, and Erik was laughing. Just like last time, he was laughing.

Not again, not again, not again. My specter would gush from me in a flood and *I couldn't do this again.*

The guard sliced Quincy's tunic, baring his chest. Somebody screamed.

Erik said, with a terrible half-smile, "Begin."

"*No!*" A spasm jerked through me, and my control snapped like a breaking bone.

But my specter wasn't a flood as I'd imagined. It was a fist.

And its only target was the king of Daradon.

35

My specter connected with Erik's body and launched him into the crowd. I heard the low, gruesome *thud* as he hit the marble. Then my specter smacked back into me—violent as a punch—and I heard nothing. Just the roaring in my head. My own ragged breathing in my ears.

Distantly, I knew people were shouting, scrambling to tear through the exits as the guards tried to corral them. Quincy had crumpled in a heap, and Junius was stunned frozen in the guards' arms. Carmen's horrified gaze kept flicking from me to the space behind me.

I turned to see what she was looking at, and my knees nearly folded.

Keil was staring at me, eyes wide and mouth parted, a pained understanding finally settling on his face.

I could never be happy as a Wielder, I'd once told him. *Not in the ways that mattered.*

And here it was. The secret I'd been keeping. The root of every bitter thing inside me.

Keil shook his head, so much sorrow in his eyes. So much regret. No guards stood between us now. He took a step toward me.

Silence descended abruptly, and I whipped around to where Erik had landed. To where that coiffed blond head emerged from beneath the cape... and the king slowly rose.

Blood oozed down his temple. His left arm dangled uselessly at his side. He lifted his face, and the air went out of me. Because that was *rage*—raw, unbridled rage smoldering in his eyes.

And those eyes were fixed solely on me.

I staggered back just as Keil's broad shoulders appeared before me. Positioned squarely between me and the king.

Erik's fury sputtered—almost in *relief*—before it rekindled twofold. "*You*," he growled.

The voices started up again, now mixed with cries of outrage. Carmen covered her mouth in disbelief.

"Forgive me, Your Majesty," Keil said, calm and determined. "I couldn't sit back as you tortured that man."

What is he doing?

If Keil took the blame for this, Erik would slaughter him. He would do *worse* than slaughter him.

I stumbled forward, ready to shove him aside, when Keil's specter snapped around my waist. He squeezed tight, and my words broke on a gasp.

"Is this your empress's famed hand of friendship?" Erik said, seething. "To plant a wild creature at my court? To demonstrate the baseness of your kind?"

The gentry piled onto his sentiment, all aflame with indignation. As if Quincy wasn't still shuddering at the edge of the dance floor, his tunic gaping open.

Erik's lip curled, smeared red from the blood. "I should have expected nothing less from Wielders."

"Then I suppose this is on you," Keil answered smoothly.

I reached deep for any thread of power to rip through Keil's invisible hold. But after eighteen years of holding my breath, I'd exhaled against my wishes, with a rupturing force. Now my specter felt thin and quivering—a torn muscle still healing.

Erik straightened his jacket with his good arm and nodded to the guards. "Seize him."

The guards pounded toward Keil, swords whistling free. But they were inexperienced against Wielders. Too confident.

Two dropped instantly, swords clattering at their feet. Another charged at him sidelong, and I couldn't suck in the air to scream—

Keil's specter wrenched me aside. He grabbed a fallen sword, swinging to meet the attack. Steel clashed; the guard heaved backward. Keil's blade was still ringing as he twisted toward the onslaught—as more and more guards poured their efforts into the fight.

With a piece of his power still tethered to me—splitting his attention—I knew the blows from his specter came out stunted. Fell just short of driving the guards back.

But Keil wasn't just a Wielder. He was a trained fighter. Wherever his specter failed, his blade swiped with fierce precision—always going for the hurt, not the kill. A slash to one guard's knee. A wall of power to knock another back. Again, again, again—body and specter working in brutal balance—until the guards' blood splattered where Quincy's would have pooled.

The nobles looked on, in fear and awe. And with each guard that fell, the flames in Erik's eyes grew hungrier.

More guards rushed in from the grand foyer. One struck Keil from behind—a coward's move that sent Keil's blade skidding across the floor. His powerful body shuddered to block the next assault, and the power around my waist shuddered with it.

But he adapted quickly, striking with fists and elbows, ducking as steel whooshed past his face. He snatched a knife—the knife they would have used on Quincy—and his specter tugged me forward.

I'd barely taken a breath before his arm replaced that invisible hold. In one fluid movement, he pulled me in front of him and held the knife under my chin.

"Hold," Erik commanded, and the room went still.

The guards who panted on the floor tried to haul themselves up. Those standing seemed grateful for the reprieve. Only the newer guards widened their stances, prepared for their turn against the Wielder.

But Erik didn't give the order to attack. He said, his voice chillingly quiet, "Let the lady go."

Keil's breaths heaved hot and fast over my hair. His arm banded steel-hard around my waist. "Tell them to clear the way and I won't hurt her."

"I should have them kill you right now," Erik snarled.

I inhaled. "N—"

Keil's hand clamped over my mouth, cutting off my protest. I went to shove him off, but his pulsing specter curved around my arms, pinning me flush against him. He leaned toward my ear, muscles shifting against my back. "Please," he murmured. "Let me do this."

A whimper hitched in my throat. And with a stab of shock, I realized I would disregard everything my father had taught me. I would give Erik proof of my guilt—I would *confess*—if it meant saving Keil.

"You're playing a dangerous game, Ambassador," Erik said. His cold focus hadn't left the knife.

"Let's not pretend, Your Majesty. We both know I possess the winning piece." Keil brought the blade closer, and Erik actually winced.

I didn't bother blinking my tears away; they spilled over onto Keil's hand, and I let Erik see the truth in them. The truth of my begging.

For the second time tonight, the room hung off the king's silence, awaiting his verdict. But there was no delight in his words now—only vicious loathing—as he said through his teeth, "Let him pass."

The guards retreated.

Keil's specter untensed but remained curled around me, a fluid precaution. He whispered again, only for me, *"Please,"* before slowly removing his hand from my mouth. When I remained silent, his specter peeled away altogether. I quivered, hoping desperately that this would work, as he relocked his arm around my waist and pulled me backward toward the only open exit.

Erik began to follow but halted at whatever he saw in Keil's face.

"I'll release her at the gates," Keil said. "You have my word."

Erik barked a laugh that made the nobles flinch. "And what is your word worth, *Wielder?*"

Keil just kept guiding me backward—past the terror-stricken nobles, past the wary guards, past Carmen, whose incredulous eyes were shot through with red.

"If you pursue us," Keil said slowly, "her blood will be on your hands."

We backed out of the ballroom just as Erik growled, "Hurt her, and I'll have your head on a spike before the night is over!"

Keil towed me through the grand foyer and into the cool evening air. The arm around my waist tightened, and I gasped as he lifted me clean off the ground to thunder down the steps. As he set me back down for the walk toward the gates, reality hit me. I began resisting in his hold.

He lowered the knife to keep from accidentally nicking me. "What is it?" he whispered.

"You can't do this," I said, knowing it was far too late. But I had no other words. No thanks or apology could ever make it right.

Keil's arm became an embrace. His head nestled low, his breath flurrying against me as he whispered into my ear. I began twisting toward him but didn't get the chance to respond. Because the voices from behind grew louder, and Keil released me, shooting like a dart into the night.

36

They wouldn't leave me alone.

First the servants—steering me inside, fussing like nervous matrons. Then the gentry, converging in the grand foyer in a feeble show of solidarity.

"They're dangerous creatures. I've always said so!"

"Holding a knife to the lady of Vereen! Can you imagine—?"

"I thought His Majesty would execute us all just for being there."

"Fractured ribs, they suspect—"

"I saw him pop his own shoulder back into its socket. He was too enraged to feel the pain."

Their babbling went over my head. The only noble I cared about was Junius.

I pulled Carmen aside, but she whispered without my prompting, "Junius took Quincy from the palace. Once Keil—the ambassador—pulled you away, Erik wasn't interested in anything except getting you back."

A small victory, at least.

The voices around us suddenly became hushed and uneasy. Even Carmen took a clumsy step backward. Then the guards marched from the ballroom, rushing past me like a stream around an island, the movement stirring my hair. I turned to see them tumble out into the night. When I turned back, Erik was blazing toward me.

I tried not to recoil as he clasped my chin and tilted my face upward.

"Did he hurt you?" he asked roughly, eyes pale with fury. Blood matted his hair on the left side.

"I'm fine," I croaked, feeling every gaze upon us.

"My guards will find him. I will break every part of him that touched you."

"No," I blurted, then gulped and said, "I'm safe now. That's all that matters."

The muscles worked in his jaw. His expression softened as he looked me over. And with a tenderness I hadn't anticipated, he lowered a kiss to my brow.

I was speechless as he reeled out instructions to the servants: to see me to my chambers, prepare my hearth, bring up hot stew and stir some nightmilk into the broth. I didn't have time to think of Keil's whispered words until the maids ushered me upstairs and dressed me in silk nightclothes. The moment they left, I ripped the clothes straight off.

Tari scrambled into my chambers minutes later, a sodden dishcloth tucked into her pinafore trousers. She said between wheezing breaths, "You had to save the theatrics—for the one night I was on—*kitchen duty?!*"

I told the story as I dressed, then nodded to my untouched tray. "Erik told the servants to give me nightmilk. They should think I'm asleep. But if he thinks to check on me himself—"

"He won't get the chance." Tari's eyes flickered with a fast-forming plan. "I'll sneak some nightmilk into his favorite whiskey bottle—the one he doesn't let the courtiers touch. He'll blame the weariness on his injuries and go straight to his own chambers to avoid passing out in front of the gentry."

Reminded of how brilliant she was, how safe I felt in her hands, I faced her fully. The harsh words between us seemed so far away now, meaningless in the scope of tonight.

Still, I said, "I'm sorry. Everything I said before—"

"Was horrible, and spiteful, and you'll be paying me back in expensive gifts for the next decade, but you can start"—she grasped my hand—"by not getting caught."

I squeezed her fingers, nodded, and strode out.

The palace was in chaos. I needn't have bothered with my hooded cloak; nobody would've noticed me even dressed in one of Carmen's bright ensembles.

Servants and nobles skittered through every corridor, gossip issuing hot from their tongues like fresh blades from a forge. Reports of Keil's Wielding were already being spun into elaborate fiction, but I refused to listen as I raced toward the stables. If these Wholeborns knew anything about specters, they'd have noticed my raw, ragged exhaustion after Erik had been thrown. They'd have seen Keil's composure and realized he couldn't have produced an outburst of that kind.

For once, I was grateful of their ignorance. Unlike Keil, I wouldn't have made it out of the palace alive.

I now rode easily through the hidden servants' gate. And, recalling the location Keil had whispered in my ear, I snapped the reins and raced ahead.

A damp, briny smell suffused the air as I neared Emberly River, the moonlit strip separating my province from the capital. The rushing current covered all sound as I tied the horse amid the foliage where she wouldn't be seen.

Not that there was anyone here to hide from.

I inched toward the bridge, suddenly hesitant. Keil had whispered the location in a post-battle heat, when his decisions were still driven by impulse. Once his faculties had returned, had he remembered my cruelty toward him? Had he regretted saving me?

My hopes had just begun to fall when a shadow shifted under the bridge.

And Keil stepped onto the bank.

I halted. Even my specter stilled. A moment of uncertainty stretched between us, my own shallow breathing seemingly echoed in the quick up-and-down of his shoulders.

Then I felt a *shove* inside me—not from my specter, but from somewhere deeper—and I was in his arms, drinking his scent like a parched woman guzzling water. He held me tightly, head burrowed in the crook of my neck. His chest swelled against mine as he took a slow, deep inhale.

That was when I noticed his too-solid contours. I drew back enough to run my eyes down his matte leather armor—the same armor he'd worn the night we'd met. It was jarring to see him looking like a soldier again. How had so much changed since then?

I pulled back all the way, and Keil's arms slid off me slowly, unready to let go. We assessed each other for several seconds, the breeze rippling my cloak.

"You shouldn't have done that," I said at last, trying to sound firm. "You didn't owe me anything. Not really."

He gave a tentative smile. "If you think I did it because I owed you something, you haven't been paying attention."

"They would have killed you."

"They would've killed one of us. At least *I* had an escape plan. It was a convincing performance, don't you think?" He blinked, and his face grew serious. "Did I hurt you?"

I shook my head, and he exhaled.

"Your empress won't be happy," I said.

He winced. "No, she won't be. In one night, I single-handedly proved every terrible thing most people believe about Wielders."

I dropped my stare, not wanting to see if regret lined his expression.

But Keil dipped his head to catch my eye, forcing my gaze to rise with him. Showing me the sincerity in his face as he said, "I would do it again."

I swallowed hard, even as my shoulders relaxed. The events of the evening—of the entire season—were beginning to layer over me. I hadn't realized how tired I was.

Keil's palm settled against the curve of my cheek, achingly warm on my wind-bitten skin. He'd moved closer at some point, and I wanted nothing more than to sink into him again.

"You could have told me," he said, his voice as gentle as his touch. "All this time, you've been hiding. You've been fighting alone. And I never even . . ." He trailed off, shaking his head like he had in the ballroom.

I'd caught him trying to puzzle me out so many times, agonizing over the missing piece. Now here I was, whole and unguarded before him, and he couldn't seem to believe the final image.

"I saw your pain," he said quietly, thumb glancing over my cheek, "but I didn't know what it meant. I'm sorry."

"Don't be. I'm a good actress." A lump formed in my throat. "You have to know, I never meant—I wouldn't have—" *Wouldn't have betrayed your secrets. Wouldn't have let Erik hurt you.* Even in my darkest moments, I hadn't really considered it—and not because Keil was a Wielder, but because he was *Keil*. Because he'd coaxed something soft and intimate from inside me—something I couldn't quite destroy.

He must have read the truth in my silence because he sighed with a faint smile. An acknowledgment that he knew—he'd always known—I wasn't a viper.

I looked away again, but Keil cupped my face between both hands, lifting it until he was all I could see—shadows softening the strong lines of his features, moonlight silvering his lashes.

"Come with me," he said, and the whispered words flurried against my skin. "You can be free in Ansora. You can be *happy*."

I closed my hands around Keil's wrists but didn't push him away. Swathed in darkness, muffled by the rustling foliage, I could almost pretend that the world beyond this riverbank didn't exist. *Almost*.

"I can't leave. I have my province. My people. And . . ." I hesitated. "There are things I still need to do here."

Keil's pulse jumped beneath my fingers. "You can't marry him."

I blew out a hot breath, too pained to be laughter. "Is that jealousy again, Ambassador?"

His face remained sober as he repeated, "Come with me."

I opened my mouth just as whinnies sounded in the distance. Panic seized me.

But Keil burst into action. He swept me under the bridge and put us shoulder-to-shoulder, our backs pressed to the damp stones as the river current roared below.

Voices bellowed over hoofbeats—four, maybe five in total. Their timbres were rough and eager. Ready for a fight.

Erik must have armed them with dullroot.

Keil nudged me further into the shadows, one arm stretched defensively across me. His spare hand rested on the dagger at his belt.

The voices neared, crossing the bridge over our heads. I counted my thudding heartbeats as the river sprayed our boots. My specter still felt fragile, pulsating at the surface, but I fought to strengthen it. It would only take one guard to report my whereabouts to Erik, and this would all have been for nothing. The king would know the truth.

The voices rang clearer now, gathering on our side of the river. Keil shifted his body to cover mine.

A dull *thump*—so quiet I might've imagined it.

Then a horse's screech pierced the sky, and my skin bristled. Hooves clomped, and people yelled, and steel clanged with an ear-ringing force. Keil remained rigid throughout it all, feet angled toward the fray, neck craning for every sound.

There was a final thud. And silence.

Keil moved, and I grabbed his hand to hold him back.

"It's all right." He stroked his thumb along my knuckles before leading me onto the bank.

I saw the horses first—five brawny steeds racing away on a cloud of powdered dirt. I counted only three of their riders: two face down in the grass, another slung across the shoulder of a masked man with a topknot.

A double-headed axe glinted at his back.

As Goren stomped toward the foliage, another armored figure skidded across the grass after him, dragged by the invisible leash of Goren's specter. The guard's body made one long trail toward the tree line before the gloom swallowed him up.

The last guard stirred with a moan. I stiffened, gathering my specter. But a broad shape stepped from the darkness, and with one swift blow to the back of the head, the guard was down again. Lye tossed me a wink before hauling the guard away.

"They don't know it was you," Keil whispered just as Dashiel emerged, brushing off leaves and debris. Osana marched close behind, her braids swishing. Even with the mask, I knew she was giving me a sneering look.

"They're secured," Dashiel said, "but we shouldn't linger."

An axe *swoosh*ed through the greenery, hacking at branches. Goren trudged beside Dashiel and glowered at my hand, still wrapped in Keil's. I automatically dropped my grip.

"Are you two finished?" Goren barked. "The king's guards are crawling at every border."

Dashiel looked between me and Keil apologetically. "We have a long night ahead, Your Highness."

I jerked back. "*Highness?*"

Keil's laughter rumbled deep. "A decorative title only. A relic my cousins and I were allowed to retain upon the empress's ascension to the throne."

I blinked up at him, taking in his wry smile, his slightly raised brows—as if he awaited my understanding. The expression tickled my memory, bringing forth his words from that night in the city: *You're referring to my empress's reputation, I assume, in imprisoning the would-be heirs who might threaten her rule.*

Keil had always spoken of the empress with an easy familiarity, as though uncaring of her cruel treatment toward those innocents. But not because of blind loyalty or a rose-colored faith in people. Tonight had proved to me that he wouldn't thoughtlessly obey orders he didn't believe in. He wouldn't stand behind a cruel ruler.

So, perhaps the empress's reputation of cruelty had not been founded upon the truth.

"You're one of those heirs," I breathed. "A grandchild of the former emperor."

Keil's grin deepened, and the confirmation stunned me all over again.

The tales claimed that the empress had *killed* Keil's father. But as the glowing moonlight revealed his winking dimple, I realized there must have been more to the story. More than I would ever get the chance to know.

And yet I was unexpectedly grateful to know this much. To know that the empress of Ansora, the most politically powerful Wielder of my time, was not quite the monster people believed her to be.

Then Lye sauntered from the foliage, returning me fully to the present as he said, "That's right, lockpicker. Why did you think we let him boss us around? Because we like the pretty sound of his voice?"

"Wait," Keil said. "You don't like my voice?"

Lye arched a brow at me. "See what I mean? You should see him back home, making us bow to him in the corridors and shine his shoes with our dress shirts."

Keil rolled his eyes. "Do you *own* a dress shirt?"

Goren made a rough sound of impatience. "Impress your sweetheart another time. Those guards won't be the last." He turned his glare on me. "They'll make him pay for attacking your king. Is that what you want?"

"Maybe it is." Osana crossed her arms. "Maybe this was a trick to get us all in one place."

"Oh, because I've so enjoyed all our previous gatherings," I snapped.

"Isn't this the second time we've saved your life now?" she asked.

"I don't know. I lost count amid all the kidnapping attempts."

Lye raised his hand. "I was not in favor of that last one, if anyone cares."

"We don't," Goren said.

"Enough." Keil's voice had lost its humor. He was now all harsh authority as he met their stares, lingering on Goren and Osana. "Give us a moment."

They all deflated except Goren, who strode forward, flipping his axe. "We don't have a moment." The blade flashed. "We need to leave *now*."

I yelped as his specter knocked my side, thrusting me away from Keil and slamming a wall between us.

I didn't think before I struck. It was instinctual—the way my specter smacked against his, making him stumble. And with a brief, sweeping appraisal—

I shredded through Goren's specter as if with claws.

The force of it threw him backward. He grunted, landing hard on his rear.

The others whipped to attention—weapons out, feet apart, heads snapping around for the danger. My specter returned to me aching, but it was worth it as I sneered, "He told you to wait, *sweetheart*."

They all turned toward me and paused, the whites of their eyes shining wide in the dark. Goren's head lifted slowly off the green with an air of incredulity. For one long moment, there was only the river's burble to break the silence. Then Keil made a noise between a choke and a laugh, and they knew:

I was the one who'd attacked Erik. Keil had taken the blame for me.

Their weapons scraped back into their sheaths, but they didn't quite relax. Dashiel was watching me in awe; Osana, in something closer to discomfort, her hands twitching at her sides. Lye was the only one grinning—I could tell from the deep creases around his eyes. And as Goren labored to his feet, he looked me over with wariness and slight alarm. I imagined it was the same look others gave *him* when they crossed him in the street.

Satisfaction flared through me. If I were more like Carmen, I might have blown him a kiss.

"When you're ready, then," said Dashiel, still dazed. He gave me a last broad glance, then shook his head as if to clear it. I almost rolled my eyes. I wasn't the first Wielder they'd ever met.

But as they shuffled toward the trees, Lye leaned close to Dashiel and asked, "Did she just—?"

"Yes."

"And how many people can—?"

"Not many."

Lye whistled. "Well done, lockpicker."

"She can't really pick locks," Osana muttered.

Then they disappeared into the foliage, out of earshot. Before I could wonder what Lye had meant, Keil turned to me. That same strange awe glazed his face.

"Don't tell me," I said dryly. "Goren has a fancy title too, and now there's a price on my head."

Amusement cracked his odd expression, then his wicked grin stretched wide. "You'd look ravishing on a wanted poster."

"I bet you say that to all the Wielder girls."

He brought his hand to my face again, grazing the dimple that must have creased at my smile. "No," he murmured. "Only you."

The words twisted inside me, and my smile faded.

Keil's gaze became mournful. "I really can't steal you away?"

I wavered—because Keil was offering everything I'd always wanted. A chance to Wield uninhibited... a chance to be free.

But within my mind wriggled the image of those prison tunnels. Of Marge's tooth, and my attacker's swinging fist. Of all the Wielders who would buckle under similar blows.

And of the last clothes my father had ever worn, dyed with his own blood.

Father would've begged me to leave his death—*all* their deaths—unavenged. To leave this kingdom forever. The person I'd been one month ago might have begged, too.

Yet where my power would have once reared up at the idea of true safety... it now remained curled inside me. Hardened by my determination.

"Not this time," I replied sadly.

Keil nodded, throat bobbing. He went to pull back.

But before I could contain it, my specter reached out, lacing between his fingers. He stilled; his breath caught.

And slowly, Keil's specter poured against mine.

The sensation hummed over me, somehow more vibrant than skin on skin. We were hesitant at first, twining nervously like hands in their first clasp. But soon the tendrils were braiding together, thrumming at the contact, spilling warm and fast into the cool night air.

Then I was laughing, half crying, as my specter ran frantic—fluttering in the blaze of my joy. In its shimmering waves, I could see the indents where Keil's specter pressed close, and I wondered how the sight appeared to him—if, like me, he could see the shape I'd made against his power.

I tipped my face toward him and smiled wider at his expression: soft and joyful and amazed, all at once. He touched his forehead to mine, and I took a deep inhale. My sigh gusted across his lips. This was everything I'd always wanted.

And it was happening with Keil.

"I'm glad," I whispered, "that it was you." I meant it in every sense.

He shifted angle, and the barest brush of our mouths sent heat flaring across my skin. "I'm glad," he said, resting his hands at my waist, "that it was *you*."

His spectral touch flickered, its rhythm slowing as his heavy breathing tickled my lips. The waves went loose and tense in different places, like muscles shifting in an embrace.

My power heated, lapping out with its own tentative ripples. Each graze of contact—similar to the trace of searching fingertips—sent phantom tingles over my arms.

Keil was watching me, tender and uncertain. "Is this all right?" he whispered. Because this was a more vulnerable exploration. A mutual baring of ourselves.

I reached for his face, fingers trembling across the line of his jaw. "Yes," I breathed.

Though I'd never known true safety, I imagined it felt something like this: going soft and languid against someone who I knew would hold on to me, even as I melted.

Keil drew me closer from the waist, thumbs drawing faint circles over the thin fabric of my blouse. His power echoed the movement in a gentle caress across my specter.

"You're beautiful," he murmured, his mouth moving against mine. "Every part of you."

My power went fluid under his touch, a muscle rolled out from knots, and another sigh rushed out of me as the sensation soothed the tightness in my chest.

I swallowed, vision swimming. My specter had always represented the most uncomfortable piece of myself—a straining ache, weighing on my bones.

I'd never realized until this moment that it could bring me anything but pain.

Keil knew it. Which was why he brushed his power against my own again—with warm, intimate intent—and whispered the same words he'd spoken on the balcony, now with a deeper, softer meaning. "It's a gift," he said, turning his lips toward my hand. "And gifts should never hurt."

He pressed a kiss inside my palm. Smiled against my skin.

As our specters untangled and my power flowed back inside me—still flittering from his touch—my free hand climbed up his armor. I hooked the back of his neck.

And finally, *finally*, I drew him down to me.

Our mouths pressed hot and sweet and open, and Keil went loose as honey—one hand gathering me against him, the other cradling the nape of my neck. I buried my fingers in his hair, bringing him impossibly nearer until his groan rumbled through me. Until my back arched—my grip tightened—because I knew this was goodbye, and I could never bring him this near again.

Keil pulled away first, but only to run his lips down my neck, each kiss blossoming with new heat across my skin. His hand threaded through my hair, tilting me back, and my breaths rushed up into the night through parted lips.

He paused at my pulse point, and I felt myself unraveling as his mouth moved slowly against my throat. "Every part," he said deeply, his hair tickling my cheek. "So beautiful."

The words curled within me, as fragile and shimmering as a spectral thread.

Keil trailed those soft kisses back up my throat—across my jaw, my dimpled cheek—ending with one last brush upon my mouth. One last moment of shared breathing, lashes fluttering against skin.

As if we were both pressing into this silence all the time we should have had, because we had no time left.

Keil held my face between both hands again, calluses scraping softly where he brushed my hair away. "*Alissa,*" he whispered, and my name was a plea on his lips—a prayer. The sound of it turned me molten, almost had me saying yes to him—*yes, yes, yes*—because what did crowns and kingdoms matter when he'd already made me a god in his arms?

But as the river breeze cooled my skin, reality clawed back to me, sharp and insistent; an ache spread throughout my chest once more.

Because I knew I couldn't follow him down a path that wasn't mine.

Our parting was painful—arms drifting off each other, feet shuffling back as our bodies still leaned in. I'd never been a natural wish-maker, but I found myself wishing for a lot of things as Keil cleared his throat and straightened, that mixture of heat and sorrow still glassing over his eyes.

"Be careful," he said.

"I have to be. I owe you my life."

The ghost of that infuriating smile graced his lips. "I'll settle for a dance."

I waited until Keil's footsteps faded, until my chest stopped throbbing, before I slanted my head to the sky. I was as close to my estate as I was to the palace. I could ride home and never return to Henthorn again.

But I'd journeyed too far to turn back now.

So I rode into the city, the stars at my back. And, gathering the frayed seams of my aimless fury, I began to sew a plan.

37

This must have been how predators felt, waiting in darkness for their prey.

At the click of footsteps, I lazed back in the armchair, winding the string of imitation rubies between my fingers. Sabira shuffled into her bedchamber, her leather bodice gleaming from the shadows. She emptied her pockets, and coins clattered onto the vanity.

"A big haul tonight?" I asked.

Sabira jumped, cursing. Before she could flee, I angled my face toward the watery light.

She grasped her chest. "Alissa!"

I let her catch her breath before pursing my lips in appraisal. "I wonder . . . will you still address me so informally once I'm queen?"

Sabira stiffened. She looked over the scene, from the string of fake rubies to the little open jewelry box on the table beside me.

"How did you get in?" Her voice quivered. "You have no right—"

"Would you know a fine blade if you saw one, Lady Sabira?"

She blinked. "Excuse me?"

"You're a lady of Parrey, the military province, home to the finest bladesmiths in Daradon. Surely you can identify a high-quality blade?"

Her eyes narrowed. "I know fine blades."

"I thought so." I draped the fake rubies on the table. "It's the same for me and jewels. I grew up around craftspeople, you see, who gifted my father with all manner of bejeweled trinkets. He knew I was fascinated by them, and so he gave the gifts to me. *Little Magpie*, he used to call me." I lifted the jewelry box and lowered my voice. "I could identify real jewels by the time I was ten."

I brought the box down hard. Sabira flinched as the red gems smashed to pieces.

"If only people could be so easily judged," I said.

She swallowed. "What do you want?"

"I want to know why someone who rinses the gentry in the Games Hall every day can't afford real rubies."

"My winnings are my business."

"Rightly so. Too many nobles parade their fortunes these days. Take Rupert, for example. The scotch collections; the summer homes. It raises the question of how he's funding such purchases." I ran a finger down the velvet armrest. "Luckily, Rupert's not the only Creakish man with a low tolerance for drink. If you ply his bookkeepers with enough whiskey, their tongues grow embarrassingly loose."

Sabira's forehead glistened, her curls frizzling around her temples. I should've refilled the lanterns before she'd arrived, to better see every flutter of her panic.

"Apparently," I said, "Rupert has received a quarterly income from an anonymous benefactor for the last seven years." I looked toward the jewelry box. "Is that around the same time you started wearing these . . . baubles?"

I flicked a fake sapphire ring off the pile. It pinged against the dresser, and Sabira flinched again.

"That's enough," she said weakly. "Remove yourself from my chambers."

"Of course." I stood and brushed past her. "Which exit should I take? The one in the lounge, or the one in your closet?"

As Sabira staggered back, I noted the telltale scent coming off her—the one I hadn't recognized the first time.

Her leather-armored bodices, stored so close to a hidden passageway, had absorbed that distinctive musk.

"Surely you remember that door?" I asked, smiling. Then, trusting my intuition enough to take the risk, I said, "It's the one Wray Capewell employed to visit you during your stays at the palace."

Sabira's eyes went wide—the look of someone caught—and I tried not to show my triumph at the confirmation.

I'd suspected it when I'd realized the passage in Carmen's closet led to these chambers, but there had been too many gaps I'd needed to fill before confronting Sabira. And now I knew: While I'd been right about Wray's affair, I'd been wrong about his lover. He hadn't journeyed into Henthorn that night for Nelle.

All along, it had been Sabira.

"Tell me," I goaded, "was it difficult to kill your own lover?"

"How dare you," she said, breathing fast. "*Get out.*"

"This will be much easier if you answer my questions."

"I don't answer to children."

"Very well." I continued for the lounge. "Maybe you'll answer to Briar."

Her voice lashed out like a cane. "*Wait.*"

I turned slowly, head tilted.

"You know what Wray was," she said, her voice guttural. "How could one noblewoman have killed a Hunter?"

"During the throes of passion, I expect."

"For what possible reason?"

"Wray was a stern, diligent man. He must have been infatuated with you to have shirked his duties. I imagine he told you everything, from the number of Wielders he'd killed to the object he carried."

Sabira shook her head in disbelief. "The *compass*? You think I cared about that thing? I *loved him*."

"The worst things we do are often to those we love."

She opened her mouth but seemed to choke on her words. Her expression hollowed. Then she sank to the bed, her leather creaking. "Parrey is so far from Vereen that we could rarely sneak moments together. But we always met when I was in Henthorn. We arranged to see each other the night of Erik's coronation, when the festivities would make it easier to go unnoticed. But Junius ambushed me in the Games Hall. He was young and arrogant, and I relished the challenge. I came up half an hour late, pockets full of his gold. Wray was on the bed. The blood—" Her voice broke. She gulped. "The blood was everywhere. I tried to stanch it, but it was too late."

"You moved the body. Why?"

"For the same reason Wray and I hid the affair: Capewells don't allow love matches. Love makes Hunters weak. Briar would have blamed me for his death, and she would've slaughtered me." Sabira shuddered. "But Wray was too heavy. Rupert was the only one who knew of our affair. I trusted him, and I called on him to help move the body."

"Through the palace passages?" I asked, hoping I didn't sound too eager.

"Yes," she said, and I silently exhaled. "I knew the passages well by then. We smuggled him to a Henthornian alley, in an area well known for its sympathizers..."

"And you left his body atop a drainage gutter," I finished. Not to stop the blood from running into the street, as Garret had said. But to hide the *lack* of blood. To make it seem as though Wray had been killed in that alley.

And to erase any evidence linking him to Sabira's palace chambers that night.

Sabira nodded. "When news arrived of his death, I went on as if I'd hardly known him. As if"—she gave a ragged laugh—"I hadn't given my heart to a dead man." She fondled her emerald ring, the only real jewel she'd kept. Then her gaze hardened. "Weeks later, Rupert made his first request for payment. He knew about the Capewells—the Creakish supply their dullroot—and he knew I feared them. He threatened to expose where he'd found Wray's body."

"And reveal that he'd helped cover up the murder?"

"You know better than anyone where the king's favor can get you. Even then, Rupert was Erik's pet. He knew Erik would pardon his crimes before Briar discovered his involvement."

I nodded, unsurprised. When I'd first entered these chambers, I'd startled at the sheer abundance of fake jewelry along with the absence of personal luxuries. I'd fleetingly compared Sabira's style of living to Rupert's lavishness, and realized the imbalance was too large—too *strange*. Then I'd remembered Tari telling me about Sabira's dislike of Rupert, and I'd gone digging for more information with the Creakish bookkeepers.

Again, my theories were confirmed. Sabira had trusted Rupert. And the bumbling, liquor-pickled man I'd once seen trying to carve a turkey with a butter knife had been cunning enough to leverage that trust against her.

"I started accumulating mercenaries for protection," Sabira continued. "But between their fees and Rupert's blackmail, my gold was depleting. I couldn't dip into the family coffers without rousing suspicion, so I continued with the gold I won at Aces." She nodded to her jewelry box. "Then I sold the jewels."

"And that must have kept you afloat," I said, "until Rupert demanded more gold this season."

Sabira looked up, stunned.

I smiled bleakly. "The news of an Ansoran coming to court didn't sit well with Rupert, did it? He feared a change in the winds. Perhaps he worried that Erik's favor would shift to another. Either way, he demanded too much of you. So you tried to debilitate him."

"How do you—?"

"His spoiled rum," I said. "The case came from your own distillery. I heard your merchant eager to palm it off to Rupert on the first night of Rose Season. You spiked the drink with wayleaf, correct? But wayleaf is a tricky substance, and knowing more of cards than poisons, you made the dose too weak. Rupert was confined to his chambers for two days, but nothing more sinister came from your efforts. His resilience frightened you, and you surrendered to his demands once more." I made a flourish toward the coins on her vanity. "Hence your renewed ferocity at the Games Hall."

"It was the only way," she said tightly.

I didn't agree; I believed there were plenty of ways to get around Rupert's blackmail. But I wasn't here to counsel or judge her. I was here for one thing alone.

"Was the compass on Wray's body when you found him?" I asked.

Her brow creased. "I—I didn't search him."

I sighed. "I expected as much. Or else you would've recovered this."

I fished Nelle's chamber key from my skirts and dangled it before her.

This key hadn't belonged to the killer. It hadn't even belonged to Nelle. It was likely a servant's copy—one of many—which was why Nelle had never noticed its absence and had never changed her lock.

"I assume Wray stole it from the servants' quarters," I drawled. "It must've fallen from his pocket when you dumped his body in that alley."

Sabira's eyes glazed as she realized, after seven years, that she'd made a fatal mistake.

"The nobles' halls were guarded back then," she whispered. "The royals' halls were not. I found the passage in my closet, connecting my chambers to Nelle's. I told Wray to come through her suite . . . Nobody would know."

"Somebody did know." I returned the key to my pocket. "You never suspected who killed him?"

"The Hunters have many enemies: sympathizers, Wielders in hiding. It could've been anyone."

"This person must have been watching you. They had free rein of the palace, and they knew when Wray would be at his most vulnerable. Didn't you ever try to—?"

"*No,*" Sabira snapped. "Wray was already gone. I wouldn't make myself a target by playing detective." Absently, she rested a hand on her abdomen. "I couldn't afford the risk."

It took me several seconds to understand. Wray's anxious secrecy, the burning of his journals . . . Suddenly, his behavior sounded familiar. It sounded like Father's behavior in the weeks before I was born.

"You were pregnant," I breathed. "You were planning to run away together, with the child—"

"I lost the child at birth," Sabira said roughly, before my thoughts could travel further. I felt a twinge of pity as her head lowered in sorrow. And I realized why she'd started wearing armor over her stomach—why she'd *kept* wearing it seven years later. To honor the memory of what she'd been trying to protect. "Wray would have wanted to be there," she murmured, her gaze falling to the ring he must have given her all those years ago. "He was unlike the others. He was kinder than he showed."

Judging from my cold memories of Wray, I had to wonder whether Sabira's grief clouded her recollection, or if love simply went hand in hand with delusion.

At last, I smoothed my skirts and said, "I believe you." Sabira sagged in relief, and I almost felt guilty for the words that followed. "Let's see if Briar believes you, too."

She leaped up, ferocious. "You know I didn't kill Wray."

Of course I did. Even as I'd goaded her, I'd known that a woman who'd murdered a Hunter—and was now slaughtering Wielders—wouldn't have let Rupert blackmail her for seven years without taking more action than a feeble dose of wayleaf.

But I gave a small, commiserating smile. "I'll vouch for you. But I can't predict how Briar will react to the truth of her brother's death. I suspect you're about to discover whether your mercenaries truly match the strength of the Capewells."

Sabira seemed halfway between bursting into tears and clawing for my throat. It was an undignified look on someone with so much self-importance.

But the right words could bring anyone to their knees.

"Do you have any idea what it is to be afraid?" she rasped. "To live life looking over your shoulder?"

I didn't reply.

Sabira wheezed and slumped back onto the bed, all strength lost. "I watched you for a while. I was curious to see what fresh hell-spawn the Capewell line had produced. Even without your mother alive to raise you, I'd hoped her blood would cleanse you of their mark. But I suppose some stains can never be washed out."

Remembering that Sabira's mercenaries had fired arrows into the foreheads of sixty-three sympathizers, bile scalded my throat.

"You're not a good person, Lady Sabira. Don't embarrass either of us by pretending that you are."

She gave a wet, defeated chuckle. "Very well, then, little Hunter." She crossed trembling hands over her knees. "Tell me what you want."

A person could only bend so far before they broke.

From the start, it was my progress that had prompted the keeper into action against me. The first attack had come days after I'd tested the silver key along the nobles' halls. Then I'd searched Henthorn for the eurium bladesmith. And on the night of Father's murder, Junius had sent me a note with Kevi Banday's last known location. A note I'd never received.

Tari had been right. I'd put so much energy into Nelle and Carmen that I hadn't truly considered somebody else watching from the sidelines, directing the copycats. With each step forward, I'd been unwittingly bending them, forcing their hand.

My next action would break their restraint.

"But what encouraged this initiative?" Carmen asked one evening, her cheeks a stunned shade of pink.

"A Wielder holding a knife to my throat rather did the trick."

"Oh, it—it's understandable," she spluttered. "But using Sabira's mercenaries?"

"They did fine work in Parrey. They'll do just as well in Vereen."

"They're brutes! To sanction such carnage in your lands—"

"*Carnage?*" I kept my expression delicately critical. "You don't expect me to let them fester under my province, do you?"

Carmen blanched. "Of course not. I worry only that Erik won't approve. You know he loathes mercenaries."

"I already informed Erik. He thinks it's a splendid idea."

And it was true. Erik had shown overwhelming approval when I told him I'd employed Sabira's mercenaries to scour the Verenian mining tunnels for sympathizer units. After all, Sabira's family, the Kaulters of Parrey, had only thought to comb their abandoned smithies after intercepting a report. I was mimicking their actions in my province unprompted . . . It made me seem hungry for bloodshed. For *power*. Exactly the kind of woman Erik wanted.

He watched in satisfaction as the other nobles dipped their heads to me—not from respect, as they had after Father's death, but with new trepidation. I began to understand how Erik savored the taste of their terror; it fueled me, emboldened me, their cowardice dissolving like sugar on my tongue.

Only Junius had the courage to confront me outright.

He looked even more haggard since the night with Quincy, his bare earlobe drawing more attention than his earring ever had. But he'd remained here in defiance—a silent declaration that it would take more than relinquished jewelry to run the Jacombs from court.

"You told me where our employees were buried," he whispered in the ballroom. "You helped my family send them off. Why the change of heart?"

"Who said our arrangement had anything to do with my heart?" I responded coolly.

- 359 -

He looked me over in disappointment, and I pretended it didn't bother me. "You are the same as them," he said, and strode away.

Nobles scurried out of his path.

They'd been especially nervous since Keil's attack, expecting Erik to fly into a rage at any moment. Yet the king had emerged from that chaotic night almost *pleased*—a reaction that disturbed me more than his anger would have. But I was occupied by greater matters; with Keil gone, so too were my chances of translating the copycats' symbol.

I needed this plan to work.

So I fanned the flames of gossip. I discussed my initiative loudly with anyone who asked. I rubbed my throat during the balls, as if in bitter memory of Keil's blade pressed against it.

Revenge, the nobles whispered. *The lady wants revenge.*

The words spread like a disease through court, but only the keeper would make sense of them. They alone would understand the true intent behind my initiative.

I'd done my research: There were few complexes in Daradon both large and private enough to secretly imprison and execute Wielders. While the last tunnels had collapsed, over a hundred similar sites remained under Vereen. Scouring each location for the copycats might take months—time I couldn't lose if I wanted to find the compass before Briar and before the copycats Hunted again.

But I didn't have to search the tunnels. I just needed to convince the keeper that I was going to.

I needed to convince them I was a threat worth eliminating.

The words of my father's killer thumped like a drumbeat in my mind: *Keep pushing and you'll see what happens.*

That was exactly what I intended to do.

 # 38

"There," Tari said around a mouthful of hairpins, securing my last tresses. "Fit for a queen."

"Not funny," I mumbled.

"Not trying to be."

I tracked my eye roll in the long mirror, glad I'd iced my dark, tired circles before she'd noticed them. I'd hardly slept in ten days. Though my specter felt more solid, coursing through me with new purpose, my muscles were stiff and aching.

The gown didn't help. Though beautiful—strapless and shimmering in deepest indigo—the tulle skirts poured heavily from a tapered waist. A silver, crystal-embedded cape cascaded from the back, and hefty xerylite bracelets twinkled at my wrists.

I resembled the streaming flag of Daradon.

I felt more like a large, sparkly target.

Tari's face turned somber in the reflection. "They're baking lemon cakes and pouring the celebratory wine. The orchestra rehearsed the victory anthems. He'll wait until after the fealty ceremony so he can make a spectacle of it."

My palms grew slick, my anxiety overflowing. But I reminded myself that I'd chosen this. I *needed* this for the plan to work.

Erik would propose to me tonight—the last night of Rose Season, when the eighteenth-year nobles would assemble before him to swear fealty. The court would erupt in celebration, the crowds growing thick and unruly. It would be the perfect moment for a copycat to enter unnoticed—like on the night of Father's funeral, or the night of Wray's murder, when the palace had been bursting with coronation merriment. I would make a lone exit, seemingly drunk and exposed...

And they would strike. I was confident they would.

I held my own gaze in the mirror and drew a deep, trembling breath. There was so much to be afraid of tonight that each new fear had tangled with the previous one, creating a mess of nervous energy inside me.

But I couldn't let Tari see it.

So, I suppressed my rising dread and grabbed a letter from the vanity. My official seal waxed the envelope. "News of the initiative reached Vereen."

Tari cringed. "Amarie."

I nodded. Amarie's note had been a panicked scrawl of confusion. She couldn't understand why I would hunt sympathizers in my province; she seemed convinced I was dead and someone had given the order in my name.

"I need you to give her this." I handed Tari the letter. "It explains everything."

Tari tried to push the letter back. "Send a messenger."

"You're the only one she'll trust. You need to tell her about the underground prisons we found. Tell her the mercenaries have orders to *search*, not harm." I swallowed thickly. "Tell her I miss her, and I'm sorry I can't come home."

Tari frowned. "You say that like it's goodbye."

"Only for a while," I murmured. Then, unable to hold her gaze, I turned to the vanity and brushed rouge across my cheekbones.

Tari believed exactly what I wanted the keeper to believe—that I'd hired Sabira's mercenaries to search the tunnels for the copycats' new stronghold. I hated lying to her, but if she discovered the extent of my hazardous plan, she would want to help.

They'd already taken Father. I wouldn't let them take her, too.

"I know what you're doing," she said. I froze, following her approach in the vanity mirror. Beyond the window, the sun was bleeding into the horizon, and the red-washed light set her copper skin aglow. "You're trying to get rid of me before tonight. You don't want me to see you with him."

I tried not to look relieved, even as guilt curdled my stomach. It was better that she thought accepting Erik's proposal was the most dangerous thing I would do tonight.

"You know I don't agree with this," she went on. "Whatever good you think you're doing by saying yes to him . . . it's not worth it. You'll be unhappy for the rest of your life. And scared. And scrutinized." Her nose wrinkled. "And probably a little nauseous all the time."

I faced her, brows high. "Is this meant to be encouraging?"

"I'm not finished." Her cheeks puffed out with a long sigh. "I don't agree with the path you're choosing . . . But I'll walk beside you, every step. Even if that means watching you tie yourself to a ship on fire."

"Erik's the ship?"

A cheerless, lopsided smile. "Erik's the fire."

She deposited the letter on my vanity, and I grabbed her hand.

Tari sighed. "Alissa, I can't go. My contract doesn't end until tomorrow."

But I was already reaching toward the vanity again, handing her a second sheet of paper. "Actually," I said softly, "your new contract overrides that."

Tari's eyes slowly widened as she read.

I'd detailed everything in my letter—had planned on Amarie

telling her this last part—because I'd wanted Tari to know that this decision had nothing to do with my wanting her to leave. This was the one decision I would make again and again, regardless of circumstance, because it might be the best decision I'd ever made.

"The seat's counsel?" Tari asked, half-confused, half-disbelieving.

"It's an old title, created for the fusty aristocrats who would oversee the provinces when the ruling nobles were away at court, but..." I exhaled, smiling faintly. "I thought the role could use a revival."

She blinked. Gave a startled laugh. "Are you feverish? I can't—"

"Manage the Verenian nobles? Observe and navigate the social dynamics between them? Make quick, smart decisions under pressure? You've already been doing that here—and you're *good* at it."

For months, Tari had been agonizing over her calling, trying to map out the rest of her life. Yet I'd never seen her more content—more vibrant from the thrill of a challenge—than during these weeks at court.

"Don't you enjoy it?" I asked.

"Well... maybe. All right, *yes*, but—Alissa—managing a *province*? I'm not an aristocrat."

"No, you're not. You actually *care* about the people, no matter their background or bloodline. You want to make this kingdom better than it is. You deserve this role more than any aristocrat." I crossed my arms. "And if the lack of a noble lineage is the only reason you won't take it, then it's not a good enough reason."

Tari looked toward the contract again, concern etching her forehead. It was a concern I didn't share. Even in the best-case scenario—even if everything went to plan tonight—I would be engaged to Erik in the morning. I was about to tumble into a world of pomp and royalty, leaving the home I loved behind.

And there was nobody I trusted more than Tari to take care of it.

When she looked at me again, something soft and joyful gleamed behind her worry. Something akin to true fulfillment. "I don't know if I can do this," she breathed.

I looked at my best friend and hoped she couldn't see the sadness in my smile. Couldn't sense the twisting in my chest as I made another painful goodbye.

"That's all right," I said. "*I know you can.*"

Using myself as bait had been a last resort. But I had too many unanswered questions—about the compass's whereabouts, the keeper who'd ordered Father's murder—and I needed someone willing to give me answers. As Erik had told Quincy, anyone could be bought for the right price; Father's killer had even suggested it before he'd pinned me in the study. If the next brute sent to kill me wouldn't reveal his secrets for a generous amount of gold, I was prepared to incentivize him in other ways.

But like the last man, he would bring a dullroot canister—and his eurium weapons could incapacitate my specter. So I'd made my first demand of Sabira: *Map out the palace passageways for me.* And over the last ten days, I'd practiced running through every route.

Because to disarm my next attacker, to truly best him in battle, I would need to draw him onto a playing field I could control.

In hindsight, I shouldn't have worn heels.

I clopped into the grand foyer, where the first hum of festivity poured out with the scent of sweet wine. Fabric rustled and I jumped, whirling around.

Perla was watching me from behind a marble pillar, her fine features pressed thin. "You look lovely in indigo," she murmured.

"Thank you. You look lovely in . . ." I surveyed her gown: an awkward, watery color that couldn't decide if it wanted to be cream or salmon. "You look lovely," I finished. "Are you joining the celebrations before the ceremony?"

"I don't have much to celebrate."

"You're young and beautiful. Many can't boast the same."

Perla huffed a little breath that might have been laughter if not for her air of defeat.

I couldn't quite feel guilty about supplanting her, even after what Carmen had suggested about Perla's father. Marrying the king would've been torture for someone like her; Erik's bow-and-arrow stunt had proved it.

I was doing her a favor.

"I heard what happened with the Ansoran ambassador," Perla said now, watching me closely. "You must have been very frightened."

I maintained a blank expression. Whatever she'd once presumed about me and Keil, recent events must have proved her wrong.

"His Majesty straightened things out," I said.

"I heard he could have been killed."

"Thankfully, our king is stronger than one rogue Wielder."

"One rogue Wielder can do more damage than people think."

I blinked. I'd only ever heard Perla speak with such certainty the night she'd threatened me in the kitchens. Now that my suspect pool had widened to include everyone I'd previously overlooked . . . her threat seemed to hold a different weight.

"In that case," I said, smiling tightly, "I was extremely lucky."

I was walking away when she said, "I hear he's proposing tonight."

I stopped, eyes narrowing. "You hear a lot for someone who spends so much time in her chambers."

Perla shrank back, her conviction lost. "Pardon, my lady. The servants talk. I meant no offense."

"Oh, I'm not offended." I stepped closer, and she recoiled. "You should speak your mind more often, Lady Perla. I daresay it suits you."

I felt her eyes on me all the way into the ballroom.

 # 39

If I'd possessed any doubts about Erik's intentions, tonight's decorations would have swept them away. The ballroom glittered like a treasure trove—strung with diamonds and aquamarine and blushing rose quartz, with moonstones beading like dew drops on every surface.

A roaring celebration of my province, the gem of Daradon.

"My mercenaries are ready." Sabira's lofty voice coasted over the revelry. She'd dressed in funeral attire: black armored velvet, dark lipstick, fake onyx at her wrists. As if my rise to power tonight would mean a small death for court.

Gracious gods, she was dramatic.

"You understand what they are to do?" I asked.

She recited, in accordance with the second demand I'd made of her, "They will arrive at Vereen's borders at dawn tomorrow with orders to search the old xerylite mines for sympathizer factions. They shall wait there an hour before I call them off, saying you've had a change of heart. They shall return to Parrey"—her nostrils flared—"and I shall pay them anyway."

"Pinch some jewels tonight to cover the cost. I'm sure Erik won't mind a few missing pieces."

Sabira seethed in silence.

For the sake of appearances, my initiative had to be believable up until the last moment. But I couldn't allow Sabira's mercenaries to actually enter my province; I'd even given them a fake map of the underground tunnels. If my plan didn't draw out the copycats as expected—if something went wrong—at least Vereen would be safe.

"Why trick the gentry this way? To show them how cruel you can be, or how merciful?" Sabira stuck her nose in the air. "The game you wish to play requires more skill than you possess."

"You're boring me, Lady Sabira," I warned. "Ensure that your use to me outweighs the effort of hearing you talk."

"You make a mockery of your noble heritage." She looked over my shoulder and fear tightened her eyes, wrinkling her beauty marks. "I'm a woman of my word. I hope you are, too." Then she hurried into the crowd.

Someone seized my arm. I spun, yanking on my specter—

And paused.

Garret's tanned face was almost unrecognizable—gray-tinged and sickly, with dark stubble bristling down his neck, and eyes pink around the edges.

Still alive. Yet somehow, already a corpse.

"Do you have the compass?" he asked.

Relief drowned my shock, and I smacked his hand away. "Briar hasn't located it yet? What a shame. But don't fear; I'm sure she'll find some way to save her Hunters."

"She already has," he growled.

"Excellent. Then you have no use for me."

Garret's ears reddened. "I know you," he said darkly. "This initiative is a hoax. You would never wage war against Verenian sympathizers, which means you're doing this for another reason." He looked me over, air whistling through his nose. "You have a plan to get the compass."

"So, what if I do?"

"You need to give it to me, Alissa. It's too dangerous—"

"Yes," I said. "It's far too dangerous." Those prison tunnels blazed in my mind, and I lowered my voice. "That compass has caused more suffering than you can imagine. Left in the hands of murderers, it'll only cause more."

"I'm surprised you still care about anyone but yourself. Isn't that why you're doing all this?" His eyes darted around the bejeweled room, and I knew he was referring to my marrying Erik. "You know this isn't just pretend, don't you? You'll actually have to go through with it. Marrying him, living with him." His nostrils flared; his throat bobbed. "Bearing his children."

"I'm well aware," I said calmly. "We're considering a winter wedding."

Garret grimaced, surveying me again. "I don't know how you can stand to be around him."

"Oh, it's not so difficult." I returned his assessing glare. "I can stand to be around *you*, can't I?"

He flinched, still pierced by my words because he still cared. I hated my own bolt of satisfaction, because it meant *I* still cared enough to want to hurt him. And more than anything else, I was so tired of spending my emotion on Garret.

"Briar was impressed you'd dug your claws into him," he rasped. "She'd hoped you would be more pliable without your father's influence—that she could work your talent to her advantage. She said it'll be a shame to waste you, because you have the makings of a great Hunter."

"Then let's make it a hunt." I smiled sharply. "The first one to the compass wins."

A feral look glazed his eyes. He grabbed my shoulders and shook. "Don't you understand? The king—"

"The *king* doesn't like when people manhandle his future queen." Erik's voice came, cold and clipped, from behind me.

Garret dropped his hands as if burned.

Erik slid to my side, looping a lazy arm around my waist, and I rested my hand upon his shoulder. *Gods cannot stand alone*, he'd said. Perhaps there existed some truth in those words. Because as Garret looked on in horror, I straightened, drawing strength from Erik's presence. I let the king's power flow through me—*fill* me—until even my specter sang from the force of it.

"Problem, Capewell?" Erik drawled.

Garret snapped from his daze and bowed low. "No, Your Majesty."

"Then apologize."

Garret went taut. With gritted teeth, he turned to me. "I'm sorry . . . *my lady*." It was the first time he'd addressed me with the honorific. It looked as if it pained him.

Erik leaned down, lips grazing my ear. "Your decision, my love?"

Again, a thrill of power rushed through me. That night with Quincy had proved I hadn't yet perfected my influence over Erik, but he was bending to me slowly. In time, I would master his moods. Then, like a compass's needle, I would direct his wrath toward more deserving targets.

I held Garret's stare so he understood the warning: The king held the Hunters' reins. But soon, I would hold the king's.

"Dismissed," I said.

Garret turned into the crowd, hands fisted at his sides.

"As for you—" Erik squeezed my waist, startling me. I looked up to find a slow grin curving his lips. "*You* . . . are beautiful."

My stomach unclenched.

"Do you like it?" he asked, gesturing around the ballroom.

"It's extraordinary."

His smile widened. "It's all for you."

The other nobles knew it, too.

Their eyes trailed me all night—even during the fealty ceremony, when, for a brief moment, every eighteenth-year noble should have claimed the center of attention. One by one, the courtiers of the new generation climbed the wide dais, where Erik gleamed like a sculpture before his silver throne.

Perla was ninth in line, shuffling up the steps and swearing her fealty so quietly that the gentry unanimously craned forward to hear her. Then she inched closer to Erik, the top of her head reaching just below his shoulders, and she fastened a pearl pin to his jacket. She held her breath, seeming to expect his sudden movement. But Erik stood in perfect composure, looking amused as she fumbled with the clasp.

She drew back and curtsied, awaiting dismissal. Erik delayed until her pose began to tremble. Then he said, with delight and good humor, "Thank you, Lady Perla. I gratefully accept your fealty."

Erik's jacket was bespangled with jewels by the time I clicked onto the dais. The idea of this ceremony had once filled me with dread. Now I dreaded all that would happen once it ended.

Knotted with nerves, I fastened a xerylite pin—my own symbol of fealty—to Erik's jacket and said with empty meaning, "Please accept this, Your Majesty, as a token of my eternal service to the Crown."

I was halfway into my curtsy, head lowered, when Erik's finger hooked under my chin. He tilted my face up.

Smiling faintly, he murmured, "Queens do not bow."

Then he dipped his own head to brush his lips against mine—an action that rippled through the gentry in shuffles and whispers.

I spent the rest of the evening agitated, which Erik must have mistaken for nervous butterflies because he took extra care with me—holding me gently while we danced, tucking loose strands of hair behind my ear. The room began to throb with music and laughter, and the crowd grew livelier, buzzing like flies being shaken in a jar.

Was the attacker here already, waiting to get me alone? I tried to spot the anomaly in the horde, but the faces blurred together.

"You're distracted," Erik whispered. Despite the lingering damage to his ribs, he let me lean against him at the edge of the dance floor, his eyes shining with such soft affection that I knew: If he ever discovered I'd been the one to strike him, he would sentence me to an excruciating death.

I mustered a sweet smile. "I'm just thinking."

"Of?"

"A birthday gift for my king."

Erik would turn twenty-two next month, and the servants were already speculating about my role in the occasion. Some had even suggested I hold my seating ceremony on the same week and declare a national holiday.

"You're already giving me everything I want." His hand found mine, and he caressed the spot on my finger where the engagement ring would go.

My insides churned, and I had to look away.

Perla's eyes caught mine across the room. She turned her head instantly, as if she'd been watching.

"She troubles you," Erik said, following my gaze. "Perhaps you could make her your lady-in-waiting."

"I don't desire a lady-in-waiting." Especially one who would want to stab me with my own hairpins.

"Then create a new position for her. The Maiden of Melancholy, or some nonsense."

I smacked his chest, earning his deep chuckle. I didn't realize until a second later that I'd just hit the king of Daradon. I was the only person who could do so without consequence.

He said, more serious, "You were always my only choice. Don't feel guilty for being superior."

Superior. The word struck an uncomfortable chord inside me. "That's awfully blunt."

He kissed my temple and murmured against my skin, "Candor is underrated." Then, with his lips still hovering close, "Didn't you wonder why I told my advisors I wished to find a bride this year? Couldn't you guess whose eighteenth season I'd formed my plans around?"

I blinked, glancing up toward him. Inadvertently putting our faces at a more intimate angle. "But—I didn't—I wasn't going to join court initially."

"Then I'd have waited." His loose grip on my waist turned even gentler, fingers drifting along my ribs. "Only for you." The words were a breath across my lips, but he didn't close the distance. He shifted instead, peering toward the dais.

And I knew. He was going to make the speech. He was going to ask me now.

"Many apologies, Your Majesty."

We turned toward a bowing servant whose hands quivered around a scroll.

"What is it?" Erik demanded.

The boy flicked nervous eyes to me. "A message came for you, my lady."

"Deliver it to the lady's chambers," Erik said. "We're occupied."

"The messenger said it was urgent."

"It's all right." I peeled from Erik and took the scroll. "It's probably from Vereen."

Amarie must have sent this message before Tari had arrived.

I shoved a fingernail under the wax and paused. I didn't recognize the seal. Erik peeked over my shoulder, and I wrapped my hand around the emblem.

"I should tend to this privately. It won't take long."

Erik hesitated, eyes flicking to the scroll. Then he stroked a hand down my back. "Take as long as you need." He offered me a soft, confiding smile. "I'll wait."

I surprised myself by rising to kiss his cheek—an oddly automatic gesture—before I hurried away.

My heart raced with every step through the corridors. I hadn't expected them to draw me out like this, especially so early in the night. But it didn't matter; my specter already teemed beneath my skin. I knew where to go. I knew what to do.

I was ready.

I made it to my chambers and tossed my head around, expecting to find them there. I even lashed my specter out—rustling the curtains, curving inside the bedchamber. Nothing.

I looked again to the seal on the scroll: a sun rising behind a diamond-shaped shield, crossed with two swords. I shakily broke the wax and unrolled the parchment.

My eyes darted over the page, trying to devour the words before comprehending them. Then I saw the swirling symbol and focused. It was the symbol from the underground prisons and those eurium weapons. The copycats' symbol. And underneath, written in Keil's flowing script, was its translation.

The writing slipped out of focus. My specter slackened.

This couldn't be right.

But a deep-rooted instinct told me it wasn't a mistake.

I threw the scroll aside and lurched back into the halls. My legs knew where they were taking me before my mind could catch up.

Hands closed over my shoulders and my specter rushed to the surface. I whirled, primed to run, when Garret hauled me into a parlor and slammed the door behind us. The air left me in a sharp gust.

"What was that?" he said.

"I don't have time for this." I staggered forward, but Garret blocked me.

"I saw you leave with that look on your face," he pressed. "What happened?"

"I don't answer to you," I spat.

But my expression must have betrayed me, because Garret's eyes widened with understanding.

"You know who took it," he said. "Do you have it already?"

My ragged breaths filled the silence.

"Alissa, *where is the compass?*" He reached for me again, but my specter knocked him aside. My hand was on the doorknob when he said gruffly, "Don't make the same mistake as your father."

I faltered, turning. "What are you talking about?"

"Briar visited him after she had me flogged. She saw something she shouldn't have. She returned later to search his study and found research—*years'* worth of journals—documenting theories on how to destroy Spellmade objects. He'd always believed the compass was too dangerous, and if we ever found it, he didn't want it used against you."

My mind was working too slowly and too quickly all at once. The texts in Father's study, the books about Spellmaking...

The last time I'd seen him, he'd emerged from my palace bedchamber. Waiting for me? Or *searching*, in case I'd already recovered the compass?

"Briar's going to claim that Heron was the one who stole the compass," Garret said. "She'll use his research as evidence that he was experimenting with it all these years. She'll say he harbored a longstanding family resentment toward the Capewells and had hoped to draw Erik's wrath upon them. She'll claim that the compass passed to *you* after Heron's death—that *you've* been directing these copycats ever since." His temper guttered, his eyebrow scar slanting low. "Even if Erik doesn't believe her... he will understand what Briar didn't. He will realize why your father wanted that compass destroyed."

I couldn't think past the sudden pounding in my ears.

The gaping wound in Father's chest. His vacant face. The pool of his blood.

She'd hoped you would be more pliable without your father's influence.

His journals had disappeared that night.

"What did she do?" I breathed.

Garret swallowed. "Please. Give me the compass and let this end. I can't protect you."

"What. Did. She. Do."

His eyes swam with regret, and my stomach plunged. A slow-splintering ache threatened to fracture me open. Because with excruciating clarity, I realized I'd killed the wrong person.

My father's murderer was still breathing.

Garret backed away, hands raised. "Briar saw Heron's research as a betrayal—as an affront to the Hunters' Mark. By the time I knew what she'd planned—"

"You held me as I wept." The words were a whisper. A denial.

Briar had cleaved through my father's heart—*his heart his heart his heart*—

No.

Ice spilled into me—freezing my blood, sealing the fissures of my pain before I could rupture.

Briar had cleaved—out of spite—through my father's *tattoo*.

"I don't want you to share his fate." Garret's voice became a distant hum. "I didn't know what she would do—"

My specter snapped around his throat.

He gasped, eyes flaring. He fumbled for his blazer.

I sent another wave rushing into him, and he slammed to the opposite wall. Pinned like a moth on a board.

"*Alissa.*" His body twitched under the rippling force of my specter. "I swear, I wouldn't—"

"Wouldn't what? Lie to me? Threaten my father?" I coiled my specter tighter, ignoring the strangled sound he made. "You've already proved what you are. You would hurt anyone to save yourself."

"Not you," he wheezed. "I would never hurt you like that."

"*Try.*" I stalked forward. "You're a Hunter, aren't you? Fight me like you fought those Wielders. Kill me like you killed my father."

My vision tunneled, stark red, my specter throbbing around me—but not like the night in the ballroom when it had spilled beyond my control.

This time *I* was pouring it out.

Garret kicked at the wall but didn't try for his blazer again. He only begged with those dark, familiar eyes, his pulse raging under my hold.

"*Fight back!*" I shouted.

"Please, Alissa. *Pl*—" He choked on the word.

I was killing him and I didn't care. *I didn't care.*

A *clink* sounded—too far away to matter. Then a slow, steady hiss.

Fog engulfed me before I knew what was happening. It crammed down my throat, clung to my skin, nipped like wasp stings at my specter until the power hurtled back into me.

Garret and I slammed to our knees in the same moment—both heaving and spluttering, clawing at our necks. His figure swam amid ash and smoke, and I instinctively reached for him—a beacon. An anchor.

Something pricked the back of my neck, and my body went loose. I didn't feel the impact of hitting the marble.

Through the haze, I saw that Garret's pleading eyes weren't fixed on me anymore but on the space above me.

"This explains a great deal," Briar said. "What a waste of Capewell blood." Then her last words—chasing me into darkness, suffusing my failing body with fear: "The king will be so pleased."

40

The air was rich with the apricot-golden light of high summer, the sun making rainbow shimmers through my lashes. Our host of Verenian nobles drifted through the scene, full and happy and inhaling the heady scent of roses—for the flowers sprouted everywhere, shedding to the cobblestones in a red-pink petal sea. Fiddle music and laughter tinkled all around.

And heading the congregation was King Erik, his blond hair shining, his cape catching the breeze. He smiled broadly at the citizens of Henthorn, and many were so enthralled that they forgot to bow as he passed. To those, he offered the sweetest smiles.

We turned the corner, and there began the oohs and aahs. Because, though taller and narrower and washed amber under the fierce Henthornian sunshine, the jewel-colored buildings might have been plucked straight from the streets of Vereen.

The citizens fed off the excitement, throwing more roses at our feet. One grazed my ankle. I winced as the thorn nicked skin.

"Can we go now?" I looked up at Father's face, fragmented by the sun's glare.

"Don't be rude, my girl. The Opal shall be the capital's new crafts district, and the people are excited. We must honor them as they've honored us."

I pouted. If they wanted to honor the kingdom's craftspeople, they could've chosen a better song. Judging by the strident voices at the end of the street, half didn't know the words. They certainly didn't know the tune.

Father clasped my hand. I'd told him not to do that. I would turn fifteen this year, and I didn't want to seem like a child in front of the other nobles.

I began pulling away when I noticed a deep groove between his brows. I stood on tiptoe to see what he was looking at.

King Erik's guards were closing ranks around him, their silver-toed boots glinting. Through the gaps of their armor, I saw a thicker jumble of people, moving with more agitation than the celebrators lining the streets. The fiddle music died out, giving way to a thunderous clacking. Because those agitated people were pounding the cobblestones with the butts of wooden staffs, crushing the roses until that heavy scent scratched the back of my throat.

They hadn't been singing. They'd been calling out names. Zelda Jean, Tavis Kimba, Ruby Clay.

"Sympathizers," Father whispered.

The word ignited in the dry heat. I elbowed between the nobles and stopped at the front of the crowd. To everyone else, the sympathizers must have appeared wild-eyed and rowdy. But to me, their faces were blazing and righteous.

These were the sympathizers—the Wholeborns—of Daradon, campaigning for the lives of Wielders. For lives like mine.

A wave of emotion swelled and crashed within me as Father clambered to my side. He gripped my shoulder, about to pull me back, when the guards shifted again.

The king emerged from their formation.

King Erik was only three years into his reign—untested, as Father would say. The people still waited to see how he would manage the Execution Decree and its ripples.

But this new district was proof, wasn't it? That King Erik was different from past rulers, finally channeling funds into the capital again.

As the young king amiably approached the sympathizers, I felt the first stirrings of hope. He would hear their objections. And slowly, he would implement change.

"My friends," he called, quieting them. "There is no cause for animosity here. Please, celebrate this new district with your fellow citizens. Show our guests from Vereen how we pay homage to their craftwork." With one broad sweep, King Erik looked around to our throng of nobles. I jolted as his ice-pale eyes skimmed mine—a bland, brief glance that inexplicably raised the hairs on the back of my neck.

"Or else return to your sacred Backplace," the king went on, "where the monarchy has generously allowed your freedom of speech. This day is for festivity. Join us or be gone."

The citizens yelled in agreement, the fiddler playing a little lick to send them off.

But the sympathizers stood firm. Then one of them walked forward: a rugged, white-haired man who must have been powerfully built before age had worn him away.

"Lilliana Swan," the man boomed out. "She was my wife. Your coward Hunters came for her while she slept and left their heinous mark on our door. I won't rest—we won't rest—until we have our justice."

Another surge of noise from the sympathizers. More discomfort from the nobles. I was breathing so fast through my open mouth that my tongue had gone dry.

King Erik smiled kindly upon the man. "Your wife was a criminal, my friend. And you are a criminal for keeping her hidden from the law. But I see your anguish . . . and I offer you a pardon. Accept it humbly, and take your boisterous companions away with you."

A tense, swollen silence ensued. The man drew a long breath.

And then spat at the king's feet.

A gasp rushed through the Opal, like a whooshing through leaves.

"You are no king," said the man.

King Erik smiled again—a kind of smile I'd never seen on anyone before. Father's hand went rigid on my shoulder.

Then the guards pounced. In a scuffle of boot-stomps and clanging armor, they tied the man to a lantern pole. He panted wetly, his lip bleeding from where they'd been too rough.

"Your words are treasonous," said King Erik, all mildness and composure. "Do you wish to recant?"

The man looked toward his fellow sympathizers—toward those warriors, those criers of justice. They would tear at those ropes. They would make the king listen. I looked with him, already bursting with trust and bottomless gratitude—

And found a sea of gaping mouths.

Their staffs clattered to the cobblestones. The fury drained from their eyes.

The man lifted his chin, resigned. "I won't recant the truth."

King Erik sighed but did not seem disappointed. He nodded, and one of the guards drew a wickedly thin knife from his belt. The blade flashed light in my eyes, and before I'd blinked out the dazzle-spots, the guard had slashed through the man's shirt, baring his torso.

Father's hand slackened, sliding off my shoulder. He stood frozen in horrified attention.

"And now, friend?" asked the king. "Now will you recant?"

The man spat again, the glob full of blood. "I do not fear death."

King Erik laughed, bright and careless, and I wondered how I'd ever seen him as anything but a beast. "And why should you?" he asked. "There is no suffering in death."

The man lasted twelve seconds before the shriek tore from his throat.

They started at his ribs, peeling away the skin as surely as flaying a deer. The man writhed and the crowd writhed with him—at the blood and tissue and gore, all glistening wet and red in the afternoon sun. When asked again to recant, he shook his head, tears streaming. They moved up to his chest.

Someone in the crowd threw up. Someone else was screaming. But the sympathizers only watched in sickened silence as their friend was skinned alive at the Opal.

The minutes spiraled into eternity. His screams grew savage, his sobs breaking. Pinprick flies roved around the open mess of his body. The nobles had pressed their hands to their ears, and Father was crying quietly beside me.

And I knew a single, biting truth: Nobody would save this man.

A numbness spread over me as my specter breached the surface. Distantly, as if through the waterlogged air of a dream, I fed a tendril toward the man. I shuddered when I reached his bloodied skin.

As I looped my specter like a noose around his neck, he squinted into the distance and mouthed the question, "Lilliana?"

Tears misted my vision. I drew a deep breath and tasted the rose stench, mixed with the metallic reek of blood. And though my bones wanted to crack under the weight of the task, I tightened the noose.

The man's next scream broke off with a gasp.

In my periphery, I glimpsed a blur of indigo movement: King Erik stiffening, his face tilting toward the crowd.

But I didn't loosen my hold, even as the man's pulse thundered under my specter. Even as his body convulsed, fighting for air he couldn't inhale.

Ten seconds passed. Twenty. Sweat dripped into my lashes, stinging my eyes. His pulse slowed—the final dregs of his life laboring against my power.

Then his body went limp. His gaze stilled on that point in the distance.

My face was wet. Perhaps I'd been bleeding, too.

I reeled my specter back, but it didn't feel the same inside me. It felt dirty. Tainted.

"His heart gave out," a guard said, his voice far away.

The king waved a dismissive hand as if this entire scene bored him, and he ordered the body burned for all to witness.

I'd killed a man. The fact that it had been a mercy didn't make it any less awful.

I wiped my hands down my dress as if to clean them from the deed. The deed I could never share with anyone, not even my father. The deed that had dimmed something inside me.

The flames consumed the man's body before anyone made out the red marks around his throat.

41

The first thing I noticed was the wrongness inside me. The second was the ice-hard surface under my ribs. My hair hung loose, grazing a sore spot at my nape. I couldn't remember taking out the hairpins.

I opened my eyes, and the darkness stole my breath. My chambers were never this dark. It took several attempts to push into a sitting position. As my shoes skimmed the surface beneath me, I realized the pointed heels had been snapped off. I reached to inspect them, and my bracelets jangled.

I paused. These were too heavy to be my bracelets.

I grasped my wrist and found the weighted iron of manacles. I tugged, and the chains rattled again—not running between my wrists but connecting to a shadowy place behind me. I blinked frantically, willing my vision to adjust.

What had happened?

I'd been killing Garret. *Had* I killed him? Raw panic surged within me at the thought, but—

No. He'd collapsed, coughing, as the room had dissolved. Because Briar had been reproducing the copycats' canisters. As I inhaled the bitter stench of dullroot clinging in my hair, I remembered why I hadn't cared about killing Garret. Why I still shouldn't care.

Briar had killed my father. And Garret had known.

My fury rekindled, and I yanked on my specter to wrench away the manacles.

And the wrongness finally made sense.

That dullroot fog had been a mere echo, like the scent of wine before the first heady sip. Because now, the poison was *in my blood*—throbbing like mercury, sticky and heavy and sickening. My specter bounded around my body, unable to break the skin.

It was trapped. *I* was trapped.

"This isn't the birthday gift I was expecting."

Torch flames burst to life, drenching my surroundings in a sinister orange glow. I was on a cell floor, confined by three solid black walls and one of thick iron bars. For a moment, with the bars' shadows cutting across the harsh planes of his face, it seemed as though Erik were the one imprisoned. But from the way he looked down at me—with bleak, imperious eyes—there was no mistaking which of us was the captive.

"I want you to do something for me," he said, voice chilling in its softness. "I want you to imagine that scene in the ballroom. My anticipation in awaiting your return. The speech prepared. Celebrations arranged. Imagine Briar Capewell approaching to summon me away." The torch sputtered in its holder, light dancing in his eyes. "Now imagine how I must have felt walking into that parlor and seeing *you*—the woman I'd planned to marry—lying in that filthy ash."

I was hardly breathing. To hold Erik's gaze went against every survival instinct; his gaze was one that dominated, that demanded submission from its subjects. I resisted the urge to cower against the back wall, where the trail of my chains began.

"She told me you revealed yourself when you attacked the Capewell boy. Why?"

It was less a query than a demand, and I had to swallow to unstick my words. "They killed my father."

"Hmm, I guessed as much. Yet the boy is still alive. Your father, still dead. So I ask: Was it worth it?"

The first hints of rage glimmered beneath his composure. Still, I held his stare, hands fisted to hide their tremors.

"Briar spouted a fascinating tale." Erik turned to pace before the bars. "She told me that the Hunters' compass—the tracker of Wielders, the object I demanded they reclaim from this copycat group—had been stolen by the late Lord Heron Paine. In part, to draw my wrath upon the Capewells he loathed. But mostly to protect his Wielder daughter."

The back of my neck bristled. It was exactly what Garret had warned me about. Having failed to exploit my influence with the king, Briar had decided to frame my father—and *me*, by extension.

But it wasn't until I'd revealed my specter that she'd realized what a fitting scapegoat I would make.

"Briar brought me ample evidence: Lord Heron's journals, detailing the most remarkable research on Spellmade objects. I doubt Briar understood half of it, but I certainly did. Your father was more brilliant than they realized." Erik stopped pacing, fixing me with his full attention. His jacket still glittered with those fealty pins, my xerylite centered right above his heart. "Briar told me not to fear, for the compass wasn't lost. Lady Alissa had merely stashed it away. Briar was eager to take you to her hold and wring its whereabouts from you. Can you guess what I told her?"

When I didn't reply, Erik chuckled, making me flinch. "Come, now. This is an easy one." His voice dropped. "I told her I wouldn't have anyone touch you but me."

Slowly, he lifted a key and turned it through the lock.

My heartbeat kicked up, my specter shriveling at his approach. His cape pooled as he joined me on the floor, less than an arm's length away. But he didn't reach for me. He just looked me over, disappointed, and sighed.

"You have been so very foolish. What do you have to say for yourself?"

I glared at him—this man I'd nearly married, whose nature I'd tried to sweeten, whose power I'd tried to claim for myself. My face heated with fury and mortification. Leaning as close as the chains allowed, I whispered, "*I see you.*"

The torch flames crackled over a hair-raising silence.

Then Erik's face split with a knowing smile—a smile best saved for people who shared a secret. "I told you. You're the only one who ever could."

He reached into his pocket, and my breathing quickened.

I hadn't understood how the attacker in my chambers had acquired the silver-toed boots of the palace guards.

I hadn't questioned how the copycats had obtained their eurium when Erik had purchased most of the ores at the beginning of his reign.

At my darkest point over the last weeks, I'd pulled away from everyone in my life. *Maybe this is what the keeper wants*, Tari had said. *For you to be alone.*

Yet throughout it all, there had been one constant. One person who had never balked at my pain or anger but had instead fed ravenously from both.

Now a deep dread plunged to my gut as Erik drew his hand from his pocket.

The language wasn't as dead as I'd thought, Keil's note had read. *Someone recognized the symbol after all.* And there he'd drawn the copycats' emblem, followed by the stomach-churning translation:

Gods cannot stand alone.

My specter puddled inside me as Erik slowly opened his palm.

And revealed the bronze case of the compass shining within.

I met his eyes, tears streaking my vision. I now knew why those prison tunnels hadn't seemed suitable to host humans.

Because from the beginning, Erik had called us *creatures*.

"Didn't I say I wanted more than my predecessors?" He spoke slowly, his bright gaze steady on mine. "Didn't I say I couldn't stand alone to achieve such greatness? Our world is on the precipice of an immense change—a new era of conquest, in which every nation shall blaze with the colors of Daradon . . . and this compass will lead us there."

With rising horror, I looked again to the compass's case—ornate yet unassuming, about the diameter of a tealight.

"*How?*" The whisper dropped off my tongue, and I instantly regretted speaking. Because, as if in answer, Erik unclasped the lid.

Blood rushed to my limbs, my specter coiling again as the compass's glassy face reflected the flames. Though Erik had been the keeper all along, he must have never thought to consult the compass around me until this moment.

And now I had nowhere to hide.

The needle stirred anxiously at first, flicking in every direction—and for a moment, I thought my specter had curled itself tight enough that I wouldn't be targeted. That I was safe, that he had no proof, and I needed only to hold out a little while longer—

Then the needle rallied into a swift, all-consuming spin.

And stopped directly on me.

I gasped as my specter gushed toward the needle, rocking me forward. The dullroot dug its claws deeper in response. I swallowed against the ache, panting as everything inside me felt primed to burst.

"Magnificent, isn't it?" Erik murmured, revoltingly calm. "The Ansoran Spellmakers forged this compass from the raw power of molted specters. Do you think such a mighty instrument was created for the mere purpose of Hunting?"

"You Hunted those Wielders," I rasped, fighting the strain.

He laughed under his breath—a sound that made me want to shield my face from his inevitable temper-snap.

"Can't you feel it?" he whispered, almost reverent. He ran his thumb over the domed glass. "This compass doesn't point to Wielders. It points to *specters*." His voice darkened. "Wielders just get in the way."

A primal terror seized me. I couldn't comprehend his distinction. But as my specter leaned all its weight against me, building in pressure with an ear-humming force, I somehow sensed exactly where it ended and I began.

And the power that had always been mine—that should've been *me*—suddenly felt as foreign as somebody else's arm attached at my shoulder.

"Now you understand why I had to take it from the Capewells," Erik said, though I understood nothing except the sudden urge to cling tighter to my specter than ever before. "How could they be trusted with such an object? They descend from mercenaries—*pests*—always scavenging for power, showing no loyalty or dedication." He smiled dryly. "And yet even pests can be leashed."

My eyes widened, pained tears glassing them over. I'd understood Erik's poetic punishment of the Capewells—picking them off individually, as they'd always picked off Wielders. But I hadn't understood the dark extent of those similarities.

Erik was methodically *subduing* the Capewells, just as the Crown had once subdued the Wielders of Daradon. Making them forget their strength in numbers—even eliciting a perverse gratitude in those left behind.

Because fear leashed people far better than chains.

"The rise in Huntings finally scared Briar into a confession," Erik continued. "And I ordered them to reclaim the compass I knew they could never find. They were so intent on avoiding my wrath that they never suspected I'd committed the very murder they'd tried to conceal."

A chill gripped me. Seeing my expression, Erik laughed again.

"Yes, I killed Wray Capewell myself. I was fifteen, newly crowned, and he was my first. The poor man was so stunned that he didn't even try to fight me." Erik's expression turned wistful, caught in happy memory. "It's a power like no other, to hold a life in your hands. To snuff it out like a flame."

The pressure inside me built without release, my taut skin throbbing. Even the compass's needle began to shudder, as though struggling to maintain its vicious hold on my power.

"So get it over with," I said through rattling teeth. Because now that Erik knew what I was, a quick death was all I could hope for.

A little smile inched around his mouth.

Then he snapped the compass lid shut and severed the strain on my specter. I went limp, almost tipping onto him—lowering in an involuntary bow. One hot teardrop spilled over my lashes, *splatt*ing onto his lap.

As he repocketed the compass, my specter buried itself in the depths of my body, quivering from the violation. I wanted to wrap my arms around myself—around *it*—in protection from the torment to come.

A quick death had been too much to hope for. I'd already seen at the Opal that Erik liked to savor every morsel of human suffering. And after the way I'd toyed with him these past weeks... my suffering would be the sweetest he'd ever tasted.

I was breathing wetly, too tattered to resist as he tipped me up by my chin—just as he had during the fealty ceremony—and forced me to meet his eyes.

"What did I tell you?" His voice was soft, lashes low as he took me in. "Queens do not bow."

I froze. Because the way he looked at me now, with a wry smile and a growing air of mischief...

That image from the Opal hurtled back to me—flames licking around the man's red throat, concealing the evidence of my Wielding.

Then another scene, in the ballroom, with Erik's grip around my elbow. *Leave it*, he'd said, saving me from touching the dullroot on those glass shards.

Again—*always*—saving me from exposure.

Now Erik's thumb grazed my mouth and stilled against my bottom lip. He said, with a note of teasing, "You really needn't have worn those gloves."

And I jerked back, air choking up my throat as my specter thrashed inside me.

Because for all these weeks, the king of Daradon had known exactly what I was.

42

Oh, gods—how, how, how—

I didn't know if I'd spoken the frantic words or if Erik had sensed them from my hysterical breathing, but he answered, still smiling, "Wielders believe they can easily hide within society, that a specter's invisibility protects them. But they rarely consider how they look when they Wield—the exertion they display, the intent on their faces..."

He angled closer, and my heart lurched at the hunger in his stare.

"The first time I truly saw you," he said tenderly, "was the day you killed that sympathizer at the Opal. I heard the sounds he made; I knew that someone, somehow, had wrapped a hand around his throat. So, I searched the crowd, and I found *you*—guilty and impassioned, shaking from the effort. I watched, entranced, as you drew his life away. And I thought it was the loveliest thing I'd ever seen."

The chains clinked with my trembling. *A person changes after their first kill*, Garret had said. He'd been right in sentiment but wrong in chronology. The man at the Opal had been my first kill, and his last breath had ripped something vital from inside me.

Now my specter screamed to break the king, as he'd once forced me to break myself.

"Why didn't you kill me?" I choked out. "Why didn't you burn my body beside his?"

Erik's eyebrows turned up in puzzlement. "When you unearth a treasure, do you seek to destroy it? Or possess it?"

You would be my finest conquest, he'd once said.

I shook my head, stomach turning. "You sent your man after me."

"I had to. It was both fortunate and frustrating when the Capewells involved you in their hunt for the compass. While your mission had brought you closer to me, I couldn't have you nearing the truth quite yet. That man was your deterrent."

"He could've killed me."

"He'd been rougher than I'd ordered, yes. But you should know I don't tolerate insubordination. You must have seen his punishment for yourself."

I blinked, remembering my attacker's bruises—not products of a Wielder's defense, as I'd believed. But of the king's reprimand.

Erik's tone became almost playful. "Don't you see why I sent him a second time?"

I stared blankly. My attacker had been remorseless with his violence and eurium blades. He'd almost won our battle. He *would've* won if that dullroot canister—

I made a strangled sound. The canister had been so much lighter than I'd expected.

Because it had never been filled.

"You meant for me to kill him," I said, horrified.

Erik's smile was full of affection. "And did you enjoy it?"

"You were playing with me."

"I was offering you a gift. After your father's death, didn't you yearn for a way to ease your pain? Didn't I give it to you?"

Nausea doubled me over. *A parting gift*, that man had said, not realizing the king had all but wrapped him up for slaughter.

I braced my palms on the cold floor, eyes burning again. I'd believed I could direct Erik like a blade in my hands. But *I'd* been the blade and he'd been the compass's needle, pointing my way—firing my wrath like the arrow he'd almost launched at Perla on the fields. *There's still time to learn*, he'd said that day, disturbingly tender. Because he'd meant it in relation to my bloodlust. My willingness to loose the arrow toward another human being.

All along, he'd been leading me like a puppet toward violence. Toward *murder*.

And I'd let him.

"Don't despair, my love." He clicked his tongue in sympathy. "That man may not have killed your father, but he'd harmed many others."

"At your instruction!" I whipped my head up, dizzy and shivering. "I saw those tunnels. I know you made them suffer. What could you have gained from their pain?"

I imagined Marge as I'd last seen her, overflowing with laughter. How could anyone want to take that joy apart and splatter it inside a prison?

My voice cracked as I asked, "Do you truly hate us that much?"

Erik's eyes narrowed. "You don't mean to compare yourself to them?"

"They're my people."

Those words must have rankled him; he clenched his jaw, cheek fluttering. "Are they?" he asked darkly. "What have they ever done for you?"

My voice fizzled out. I had no answer.

"Exactly," he said. "Do you think *they* would attempt to save *you* in reversed circumstances? I assume that was the intent behind your initiative—to scour Vereen for more prisons. A wasted effort. The Wielders of Daradon are like rats with blades strapped to their backs. Inept. Lethargic. Overwhelmed by having to drag around their own power. If you'd seen *your people* as they were—crawling in filth, weak by their own design—you would realize that you are far above them. That you and I are above everything."

The loathing in his voice spilled over—inflaming his skin, curling his lip. It was a loathing beyond reason. Beyond remedy.

"You and I," I said coldly, "are nothing alike."

Erik's hand shot around the back of my head.

I startled, jolting back—but his fingers fisted through my hair, tugging until I gasped. I'd seen enough of his cruelty that it shouldn't have shocked me. And yet it did.

"Some describe specters as just another limb," Erik said, his face close to mine. "So tell me: Does dullroot produce the sensation of having your hands tied behind your back? Or does it feel more akin to suffocation?"

I craned away, eyes pricking as the hair pulled against my scalp. My hands scrambled uselessly against him; the manacle-chains were too short to shove him off.

"Let go," I said, chest heaving.

"Make me. Strike me away. Thrust your power past the surface."

I slammed my specter to the underside of my skin, twisting against the dullroot until it hurt. But it was like trying to separate water from salt without the heat to boil it off. I couldn't tear through the poison as I'd torn through Goren's specter. I could do nothing but whimper and then curse myself for making the sound.

"You can't do it, can you?" Erik chuckled—a mocking gust that stirred the hair from my face. "And how does that make you feel? Sick to your very marrow, I suspect." He leaned toward my ear, his nose grazing my temple—the exact spot he'd kissed mere hours ago. "Do you see now how we are the same? It's because we are both repulsed by weakness."

"No," I snarled, straining away. "I am repulsed by *you*."

"You think so?" He yanked me close again, making me hiss. "Then you're still lying to yourself. How many other Wielders do you suppose were at the Opal that day? How many watched while the sympathizer who'd been campaigning for *their* rights was peeled raw?"

I stilled. I'd always blamed the Wholeborns—the so-called sympathizers—for what had transpired at the Opal. Even after Garret had revealed the great number of Wielders in Daradon, I hadn't imagined how many must have witnessed that man's torture.

Or how many could have ended his agony.

"Through their inaction," Erik said, his mouth moving hot against my ear, "every Wielder in that crowd handed the burden of mercy to a fourteen-year-old girl. And in doing so, they planted within you the first seed of resentment toward your kind. A seed which, under proper nourishment, I knew could flourish with a destructive force."

I tried to shake my head, but Erik's grip wouldn't allow for my denial; the movement lanced me with pain.

"You're wrong," I breathed, hearing my own wretched uncertainty.

Erik must have heard it too, because his laughter rippled across my neck. "I see how you ache, remember? Don't you know why it hurts you, far more than others? Why you must constantly battle against the strain?" He inhaled against me, and on the cool exhale, whispered, "The greater the power, the greater the need for release."

Goose bumps prickled me all over.

I remembered the dense petal-peeling sensation of reaching into my specter. The waves that had poured out upon discovering Father's body—the startling layers of a power I'd never wanted to explore.

Because I'd been too afraid to embrace the core of myself.

"My only error," Erik said, "was in overestimating how much nourishment you would actually require . . . before you unleashed yourself."

His free hand drifted to his ribs—to the place I'd injured when I'd struck him in the ballroom—and fear gripped me for one knife-sharp second. But as he drew back, I saw none of the icy anger I'd anticipated. Only heat.

"I'd dreamed about your specter." His thumb glided down to caress my cheek. "How it would feel on my skin. How it would taste on my tongue. But"—his thumb stilled, pressing under my cheekbone—"the unveiling was ill-timed. Though it was everything I'd imagined—fierce and full-bodied—yours was not the power I'd wanted to ignite that evening."

A sharp, plunging feeling.

Our world is on the precipice of an immense change.

And thanks to their ambassador's violence that night, the Ansorans—the greatest power-players this side of the world—were exactly where Erik had wanted them: in his debt.

All along, he'd been trying to provoke *Keil*.

"You increased the Huntings to draw Ansoran attention," I said thinly. "You lured them here."

"And your outburst could have destroyed everything for us. In that moment, even your own exquisite fury couldn't match mine." He drew my head back slightly, baring my throat. Something glinted in my periphery. Then Erik lifted Keil's dayglass shard into my eyeline and said, "How fortunate, then, that Ambassador Arcus sacrificed himself for you."

I shook so hard that my breaths kept catching over themselves. He'd seen the fire-sparking glance I'd shared with Keil. But this dayglass shard—the shard I'd forgotten under my mattress, which Keil had *entrusted* to me—proved we'd shared more than glances.

Erik gave a cutting smile. "I recognized his script on that letter." His thumb slunk under my jaw, across my throat. "I know he helped you assemble the final piece of your puzzle. What I *want* to know is this . . ." He halted over my throbbing pulse—reading me in its rhythm. His face darkened with a look both savage and razor-shrewd.

"Did you let that Wielder brute touch you?" His voice rumbled low, his thumb juddering with my wild, treacherous heartbeat. "Did he put his hands on what is mine?"

Mine.

That word fractured my terror. I wrenched back, driving my knees between us until he either had to rip my hair out or release me. Mercifully, he chose the latter.

I skidded to the back wall, skirts ballooning.

"I know why you do it," I panted. "Why you poison us and chain us. Why you keep us long enough to torment and degrade. It's because *you fear us*."

Erik's lips twitched. "Do I look like I fear you?"

"You look like a monster. And all monsters are afraid of something."

The corner of his mouth fell, and I braced for him to grab me again. To heave my head back all the way this time and smash it against the wall.

Instead, he pocketed the dayglass and took out something far worse: a large, oval xerylite rimmed with sparkling diamonds and centered on a silver band.

The engagement ring.

"A king shouldn't fall to one knee," he said quietly. "But I would have for you. There would've been music and merriment. I'd have danced with you all night, then carried you upstairs in my arms." He shook his head sadly. "The time for splendor has passed . . . but the sentiment remains."

He set the ring on the floor—reminding me of Junius, relinquishing his jewelry in submission. And I realized why my plan to corner my attacker wouldn't have worked.

Because Erik had never wanted my head. He'd only ever wanted my hand.

"I'm a Wielder," I breathed. "I'm everything you despise."

"I could never despise strength. You were the only one fearless enough to Wield your power at the Opal. The only one worthy of such a power." His brow creased in a perfect imitation of compassion. "You worried about my finding out, and it kept you from warming to me. So, isn't this a relief—that I've known you and have wanted you anyway? You've always been safe with me, Alissa. Nothing shall ever harm you at my side."

His voice rang deep with such emotion and sincerity that I might have once believed him. But just like Erik had known me since the Opal, I had known *him*.

I would not forget again.

Erik smiled ruefully, seeming to read my answer. "You'll need to digest what you've learned. But you must appreciate, I cannot undo these chains until you reach a . . . *favorable* decision. The Capewells will prove troublesome now that they know your secret, and only together can we manage them. Together, we can carry all the power in the world."

He slid the ring toward me, silver scraping the stones. For the second time tonight, he said, "Take as long as you need. I'll wait."

I stared at the ring, dazed. "I will never marry you," I said weakly.

Erik lifted a hand to my cheek and I recoiled—because I knew it would be a tender touch, and that was somehow worse than a cruel one.

At my reaction, he dropped his hand. The torchlight swooped golden against his blond hair and gilded his outline. All painted in the glow, with his sculpted face drawn in sorrow, he appeared celestial—a portrait of a god in mourning.

"I hate to see you like this," he murmured. "Promise me you'll think about it."

He left the ring on the floor and stood. The door squealed shut behind him.

"I promise," I whispered, and his eyes met mine between the bars. "I promise," I went on, "that I'll be the one to kill you. I promise I'll enjoy it. And I promise that your death will be as painful as the deaths you have granted others. By all the gracious gods, Erik Vard, I swear it."

A formal oath. As binding as any wedding vow.

Erik's face was unreadable as he took the torch and left.

43

As a Daradonian Wielder, a part of me must have always anticipated imprisonment, because I took to it with grim resignation. I bore the hard floors, the cramping muscles, the heavy-lidded chamber pot. I didn't even grumble when the tulle grew scratchy around my legs.

But no matter how hard I tried, I couldn't grow accustomed to the dark.

Relief only came when Erik brought me trays of hot venison stew with hard cheeses and fruits and bread rolls, served in metal crockery and illuminated by a single candle. The first time I woke to the salty-rich scent, I upturned the tray in a fit of rage. The flame went out, and I immediately regretted it.

The candle at my next meal was half the size. I savored the light, not daring to breathe too hard for fear of extinguishing it. For every untouched meal, Erik granted me a shorter candle. On his eighth visit, when my stomach was panging, I succumbed to the entire tray. The next candle was twice the height. I blew out the flame and stewed in shameful darkness.

The way my meals were staggered, I could only track time by his appearance. When he was coiffed and smelling rose-sweet from bathing, it was morning. When his cape was wrinkled or his hair roguishly tousled, it was evening. But no matter the time of day, the dullroot never wore off.

When I noticed the growing soreness at the back of my neck, I realized why.

Erik was administering the dullroot while I slept.

At first, I tried to stay awake; once the poison left my system, I could *run*. Deep down, I knew Erik wouldn't let it get that far. He'd possessed those canisters all along and could easily infuse the dungeon air with dullroot. Still, the idea gave me purpose, and for five meal trays, I didn't even doze.

Then the stones became bitingly cold from what I suspected was the seep-through of an early-summer rain. The chill drenched the fires of my resolve, and I awoke shivering, with my head in Erik's lap and his cape around my shoulders and his hand stroking my hair.

I lurched away so violently that I thwacked my head against the wall. He frowned, reproachful, but didn't try to comfort me again.

After that, the water took on a faintly saccharine aftertaste. Nightmilk—a few drops per jug to ensure regular sleep. I wasn't yet petty enough to die of thirst, so I drank deep from every cup, hating myself with each swallow.

Oftentimes, Erik would serve me and leave. "I have business," he would say apologetically and add something encouraging about how the rolls were still warm.

But sometimes, he lounged against the wall beside me, like we were fugitives made allies by shared captivity. Once, he took the purple grapes himself, nudging one against my fingers every other bite. Trying to trick me into eating absentmindedly, like he had during our first dinner together, when I'd been preoccupied with upholding the conversation.

He ended up finishing the grapes alone, looking vaguely irritated, because the trick didn't work now that he carried the conversations single-handedly. It wasn't for lack of effort; he asked my opinions on various topics, hoping to engage my interest, while I remained mutinously silent. Surely there would come a point at which the thrill of the hunt gave way to boredom, and I would be no more satisfying to conquer than an injured deer on open grass.

But after twenty meal trays—most left cold and unfinished—that point still hadn't come.

During my most restless hours, I dreamed of passageways and trip wires and Briar's tar-treads when she'd caught Garret and me at Capewell Manor as children. My unconscious mind sent me across booby traps again—avoiding tar, leaping over obstacles—until I felt my dry lips moving in slumber, anxiously counting steps I would no longer need to remember.

Then I would jolt awake to darkness, wishing I'd wrung Garret's neck more swiftly. I replayed the scene of his betrayal over and over, my specter pulling against the dullroot until I wanted to tear myself to pieces just to get the power out. There was something perverse in its confinement, like the specter itself became a poison I wasn't allowed to bleed from my system. Soon, it felt exactly as Erik had surmised: like I was suffocating.

This must've been what the Hunted Wielders had experienced before he'd killed them. With the compass still in his hands, many more would experience the same. I'd been their only hope, and I'd failed them—just as I'd failed my father.

Father.

The word formed with a knifepoint, twisting through my naval. I couldn't dissolve the image of Father's face as it surfaced in my mind.

Then, like darkness blotting out the sun during an eclipse, the yearning for my father overrode every other feeling.

I became bleary and vacant and agitated. I stopped eating more than the crusts off the bread rolls and began sleeping more frequently, exhausted to the bone. At one point, I woke atop a pillow and thought I was in Vereen until the rattling chains plunged me back to reality.

Judging from its citrus-and-lavender fragrance, Erik had plucked the pillow off my bed. Not to keep my head off the stones but to fill my lungs with my own scent. To remind me of who I'd been before becoming his prisoner. A girl set to become the queen of Daradon.

If I wasn't chained to a wall, I might've found it funny. Only Erik could weaponize a feather pillow. But that had always been his way: adding kindness into every cruelty and cruelty into every kindness. A voice in my head—a sage, rational voice that sounded like my father—told me to feed gratefully from that kindness. I'd already seen how gentle the king could be with me. And in a strange way, wasn't he still protecting me from the Hunters? Would it be so terrible to yield to him?

It would have to be a real surrender, of course. I couldn't manipulate or bargain or blackmail my way to freedom. Erik would see through me, as he had from the start. Now he would only settle for the truth.

So stop resisting, that wise voice said. *Nothing can be worse than this.*

And I almost believed it. But then I would see the xerylite ring, and I wondered if that voice actually belonged to Erik, burrowing through my defenses like a worm through soil.

Keil once told me that everyone held some kind of power. Now defiance was my *only* power.

I couldn't relinquish it.

I was awake when Erik delivered meal number thirty-something. At the sound of his approach, I pulled the pillow from behind my back and wearily pushed it aside. If he realized how much I valued the wretched thing, he would probably take it away.

My stomach whined upon the tray's arrival, so loud that Erik scowled as he joined me on the floor.

So, this was a talking day. Excellent.

I looked at the food without meaning to. The rolls were golden, the stew thick and steaming, its aroma coating my tongue. To my dismay, he'd even included a slice of lemon cake today.

A stub of a candle sat beside it.

He poured a tinkling stream of water into the metal cup with the same air of serving me wine. I drained it hatefully, returning the cup with a *clang* to the tray. Then I nestled back into the corner where the two solid walls met and turned my face. Hopefully his voice would act as white noise and lull me to sleep.

"You're not eating." Fabric rustled as he shifted closer—a tactic designed to draw me toward his body heat. "If the meals displease you, I could always execute the cooks."

The words worked as he'd intended; I couldn't help but react, my breath hitching as I looked toward him.

He wore a victorious little half-smile, humor playing around the edges. A joke.

"If I'd known how easily I could capture your attention, I'd have threatened to slaughter the entire court by now." Still smiling, he scooted the tray toward me. "Eat. You must remain strong."

I angled away, my crystal-embedded tulle grating against the floor.

For several minutes, I felt his eyes on me and I tried not to touch my wrists. The skin constantly aggravated me now, chafed raw by the manacles. But I wouldn't give Erik the satisfaction of nursing the injuries.

Finally, he sighed. "This is futile. Who are you trying to hurt by starving yourself?"

I dragged my gaze to his and said dully, "Isn't it obvious? *You*."

I hadn't spoken in so long that the words rasped up my throat. But it was worth it for the slow sinking of Erik's face, the jaw-flicker of irritation. I turned away once more, content.

He didn't speak again until half the candle had melted into its holder.

"I looked into Lady Fiona's medical history."

My body twitched—another foolish reaction. But he'd never mentioned my alleged mother before.

He continued, "She was a frail, sickly woman, already in her final months at the time of your birth. She couldn't have carried a child to term."

He paused, awaiting confirmation. I kept my face blank.

"So, your father bedded another, then—a Wielder, out of wedlock. According to Daradon's laws, you never should've inherited his seat of power. You certainly never should have been considered for queen." His voice became a low caress. "Look at the opportunity I'm offering. In Daradon's history, how many bastard Wielders have worn the crown? Who wouldn't love to be the first?"

The candlelight flittered, stretching the shadows on the walls. I could hear my pulse-thrum in the silence.

"I'm not your enemy, Alissa. I never have been. *Briar* did this to you. *Briar* killed your father." His fingers slowly reached for mine, then brushed across my white-clenched knuckles. "What if I let you have her?"

Heat flared up my neck far too quickly. My specter screwed against the dullroot and I gritted my teeth, fighting the sensation.

"I could have her delivered to you in chains," Erik continued. "You could do to her what she did to your father. More, if you'd like." His hand worked steadily over mine, unclenching my fist and cradling my palm. "I could help you. I could make her suffer in ways you couldn't imagine."

I squeezed my eyes shut, and Briar was there—writhing, screaming, begging for forgiveness until her agony filled my head and I realized I liked the sound. My specter would rip her apart like the books I'd destroyed in Father's study. I imagined his claw-foot desk cracked down the middle and wondered how her body would look split in half like that. Would she bleed as much as Father had, or could I make her bleed more?

My skin felt tight, my breathing shallow. I opened my eyes to find Erik smiling at me like he'd already tasted such fantasies and could recognize the desire in my face.

Then I noticed what he held in his other hand. The xerylite ring—the ring I hadn't touched the entire time I'd been here.

I trembled as Erik brought it to the tip of my engagement finger.

"You hold all the power here, my love," he whispered. "Let me take you from this place." He slid the cool silver to my first knuckle. "Let me give you your revenge."

My head rang, and I felt myself bending far enough to snap. Because I *wanted* what Erik offered. I wanted Briar's neck.

No—I wanted her *heart*.

I swayed forward, and the ring glided to my middle knuckle. Erik held his breath, his hand roaming eagerly toward my wrist—

He grazed the raw skin around my manacle, and pain spiked through my reverie.

I gasped, flinging out my hand. The ring clattered somewhere in the shadows.

I slammed back into my corner with what sounded like a sob. "*What do you want from me?*"

Erik was flushed from his near-win, breathing almost as heavily as I was. "You know what I want," he said hoarsely.

"A Wielder pet as your bride?"

He had the gall to look offended. How dare I accuse him of such intentions? He'd only chained me like a dog in a cage.

I opened my mouth to say as much. To run him through with my sharp tongue—the one weapon I'd always possessed.

But as I'd recently learned, silence could be just as powerful a weapon.

So, I huffed a bitter laugh and let my shoulders slump.

"Alissa . . ." The candlelight outlined the hard contours of his face. Was that a flicker of true apology—true sympathy for the girl he'd imprisoned?

It didn't matter. In a flash, the look was gone and Erik stood with all the coldness of a huntsman who'd lost his grip on the prey.

"I can abide this delay," he said, locking the cell behind him. "But I won't abide a hunger strike." He nodded toward the tray. "Finish it. Or there'll be no candle next time."

I wrapped my hand around the empty water cup and hurled it at the king. But it didn't ricochet off the bars as I'd expected.

It flew between a pair of them and struck him squarely on the jaw.

I flinched, but Erik didn't. He stood unmoving as the cup rang against the floor and rolled out of sight.

Then he smirked, satisfied, and ambled away.

By the time I stopped shaking, the stew had gone cold. What had I been thinking? It was only a matter of time before Erik raised a hand to me, and I didn't want to provoke the first strike. But my nerves had been frayed. Did he know how close he'd been to breaking me today?

Of course he did. And now that he knew where to aim, he would redouble his efforts.

I curled over my knees, bundling my hands in my pockets. I'd have to be stronger next time. But I felt foggy with exhaustion, and all I wanted now was that lemon cake, fluffy and glistening in the candlelight—

I reached the bottom of my pocket and froze. Then I drew out my mother's coin. My specter rushed up, tingling to spin the coin as it always did.

But the coin remained flat in my palm.

Tears blurred my vision, streaking the candlelight. For the first time, I realized my greatest asset had been handed to me at birth, no more extraordinary than the color of my hair or the shape of my mouth.

And it could be snipped with a single dose of poison.

It was the truest weakness that existed.

So far, this cell had seemed like a limbo. But now the truth smacked me like a physical blow—that this was it. Just these three walls, the iron bars, and the manacles. Maybe a Wholeborn could've found a way out. But without my specter, I knew I couldn't.

My parents had died for my safety. And this was where I'd ended up.

A bottomless shame settled inside me as the first tear fell. I had barely enough time to cry for my parents, for the burden of their deaths, before the flame sputtered out and I plummeted into darkness once more.

44

I was dozing when tawny light flushed the insides of my eyelids. I instinctively kept my eyes closed and my breathing heavy. Erik never bluffed; he would serve me in darkness until I ate.

Which meant he wasn't here with a meal.

I tensed. I hadn't drunk more water since throwing the cup, and the little I'd had must not have contained enough nightmilk to produce a heavy slumber. I would have to feign sleep as Erik dosed me with dullroot.

Or I could resist. I had no weapons—not even the heels of my shoes—but I had my nails. I could claw him, perhaps draw blood.

But then what?

Erik was far larger and stronger than me, and I couldn't bear the indignity of thrashing beneath him as he forced the dispenser through my skin. My head was still stuffy from crying, my body still limp. I didn't have the fight in me. Not today.

Maybe not ever.

There was a *clunk* as he placed the torch in its holder. The clatter of keys. The cell squealed open, and my pulse quickened.

He crouched, breaths lapping across my face. My own breathing became shallower as I prepared for the pin. *Don't move, don't move.*

A hand touched my shoulder—warm, soft. And smaller than Erik's.

"Alissa."

I jolted upright so fast that my vision spun. But there she was, clear and bright as the rising dawn.

"Perla?" I reached for her doll-like face and saw my fingers shaking.

She grabbed my manacle, making me gasp. And I knew this was real.

I knew what she was going to do.

Before she could unlock the manacle, I shoved her off and scrambled away. "Don't," I croaked.

"It's all right." Perla raised her palms. "Erik's occupied. But he won't be for long." She leaned forward, her black cloak shifting.

I flattened myself against the wall and shook my head. "Stay away." Fresh tears burned my throat.

Because of all Erik's ploys, this was the cruelest yet. This taste of hope—of *freedom*—before he ripped it away again. And to deliver it through *Perla*, the girl whose plans I'd torn apart. The girl who probably considered my fate well deserved...

"Just tell him it didn't work," I moaned, burying my head in my skirts. "Tell him I didn't fall for it."

The tears were streaming now, the dam ruptured from my last bout of crying. She would probably tell Erik how I'd sobbed as she'd dangled the keys before me.

Perla didn't speak for several seconds. Then I heard her shuffle closer.

"This isn't a trick, Alissa. I need you to trust me. Because if Erik finds me here, he'll have both our heads."

The voice didn't belong to the Perla I remembered. This voice resounded low and firm, without a trace of uncertainty.

Sniffling, I lifted my head.

Her face was a contradiction: the dark brows scrunched in pity, the pink mouth tight with impatience. But her large eyes were the strangest of all—cunning and kind and full of strength. I'd never seen that expression on anyone. I almost balked at its intensity.

"But you hate me," I said numbly.

Her brows puckered further. "Whatever gave you that idea?"

This time I didn't protest when she seized my wrist.

"We really must hurry," she said. "I could only find the spare keys to the cells."

She assessed the three locks in the manacle, then reached into the back of her hair. She pulled once, twice, thrice—dark wisps falling around her cheeks—and produced a strange set of jagged hairpins.

It wasn't until she began tinkering with the first lock—producing the first loud *click*—that I truly awoke to what was happening. And I had the sudden urge to capture this scene and somehow show it to Lye. Because these weren't hairpins.

They were lockpicks.

"You're freeing me," I whispered.

Perla smiled wryly. "Still sharp as ever, I see."

She plunged into another lock, pins twirling between deft fingers.

"You know what I am," I said.

"You can say *Wielder*. I promise not to flee."

"How long?"

"Since Erik's coronation. I saw you swiveling a coin in the gardens and led my mother away so she wouldn't see. You were never careful." Perla's eyes flicked up, hard but not unkind. "It seems you still aren't."

You think Erik won't notice? she'd asked when she'd caught me after an evening with Keil. She hadn't thought we'd been spending time as lovers, I realized. But as *Wielders*.

And it hadn't been a threat.

"You were warning me," I said over the *scrape*-and-*clink* of lockpicks.

"Not very well, apparently. I suppose you thought tempting a Wholeborn king into taking a Wielder bride would be poetic." She shook her head. "It's a miracle you hid your specter from the Capewells. I don't know how you expected to trick Erik."

"Th-the Capewells?"

"The Hunters," Perla clarified, as if telling me something I didn't know. "They're in another meeting with Erik now. They seem to be in a tug-of-war with him—lingering in the council room every night, like they want to be here in case he changes his mind. But they always leave angrier than they come. I think they're losing."

So, Briar still wanted my head. And Erik was holding her off.

I shuddered just as the first manacle came apart in Perla's hand. The air kissed my raw skin, and I could've cried again.

"There's a horse by the servants' door," Perla said, starting on the second manacle. "Ride to Backplace. A coach is waiting at the western corner, and it'll take you to the Byrds' private harbor in Avanford. We have a ship that can navigate the waters into Bormia. The coachman will give you the citizenship papers you'll need.

"Now, this is important, Alissa. The coach will depart at midnight with or without you. If it waits longer, the city guards will grow suspicious. Do you understand? You must reach Backplace by midnight."

"I—I understand," I lied. It was too much to remember in my muddled state. Backplace. Citizenship papers. Passage to Bormia . . . ?

I was still dazed at the fact that she could *pick locks*. "How did you do all this?"

She gave a crooked smile. "My father was a naval soldier in his youth. He passed a few things on to me, including his connections." Her smile turned sour. "Mother's the strategist. She'd been preparing my older sister, Petra, to secure Erik's hand in marriage. But last spring, right before her eighteenth season, Petra and I fell ill. Mother fasted for days, imploring the gods to spare at least one daughter—her darling, favorite girl. The gods had a dark sense of humor. They saved me instead. After Petra died, Mother tried selling me off as Erik's bride in her place. But I wasn't going to become a vicious king's toy."

If Perla had looked up, she would've seen my face falling slack. I was remembering her fear when Erik had aimed my arrow at her foot; her wobbly reach when he'd offered her a turn. Then the incongruous stability of her grip, clenching strong around the bow.

Like she'd wanted to make a swing with it.

An invisible hand wiped the haze off my mind like steam off a window.

How often had I seen Perla clinging to the shadows? How often had she startled me with her silent presence? She hadn't been cowering. She'd been listening, noticing. *Performing*.

From the start, she'd thought to save herself by acting too dull for Erik's consideration. When I'd arrived, she'd tried to save me, too.

She was still trying.

"How did you know I was here?" I asked, awed.

"Erik told the court you'd contracted blueneck fever to explain your disappearance. He even brought a high minister to pray for your recovery." She scoffed. "A court of educated nobles, and nobody realized you've already had blueneck fever."

"You realized."

"Well"—she tugged at her neckline—"I recognized the scar."

Between her breasts sprawled the bruise-like discoloration I knew from my own bosom—though hers was a richer blue, suggesting a more recent sickness. The same sickness that must have taken her sister.

She returned to my manacle and released the final lock. The iron clunked to the floor.

I stared at my wrists, bewildered. *Free.*

My knees creaked as Perla heaved me up. I swayed, and she hooked an arm around me.

"When did you last eat?" She looked toward my untouched tray.

"I'm not sure. I don't know how long I've been here."

"Rose Season ended twelve days ago."

I winced. Of course Erik had been worried. Over twelve days, I'd eaten a fraction of what I should have.

Perla propped me against the wall and grabbed a bread roll. "Eat fast. I can't carry you if you collapse."

Each bite slid like a rock to my hollow stomach. As I finished, I caught a glimmer from the shadows. The xerylite ring—tucked in the corner from when I'd flung it away.

Following my gaze, Perla straightened. "Is that a . . . ?" She trailed off, studying the cell anew: the pillow, the hearty meal, the dignified chamber pot with fresh linens on the side. Then she looked at me and seemed to realize I hadn't a scratch to show from my time as Erik's prisoner. She asked, incredulous, "What does he want?"

I didn't have an answer.

She fetched the ring and dropped it into my pocket.

"I don't want it," I said, about to take it out.

"Sell it," she said, then lifted the torch and led me away.

I tottered awkwardly in my broken heels, but Perla didn't grouse, even when I took a whole minute to climb the stairs. At the apex, she produced a key and unlocked the iron door.

The wash of lantern light assaulted me. Through half-closed lids, I surveyed a small armory, its cracked walls adorned with all manner of weapons.

The rest happened quickly.

Perla produced a pair of riding boots and laced me into them. She took a knife from a display case—a short, decorative weapon with a latticed handle—and cut away my crystal cape. "Successful prison escapes don't involve sparkly fugitives," she said, kicking it aside with a scratching sound.

Prison escapes. Fugitives.

This was all becoming violently real.

My pulse ratcheted up as Perla fastened a belt around my waist and sheathed the knife. "Keep this close until the dullroot wears off," she said.

"How long will that take?"

"Your guess is as good as mine." She undid her cloak and threw it around my shoulders. Then she began removing her pearl rings. "The crew at the harbor will only sail for the Byrds. Tell them you are Lady Perla, and use these as evidence." She dropped them into my pocket like she had with the engagement ring.

I gaped. I didn't know what it meant to offer up jewelry in anything except submission. But there was power in the gesture—so much that it humbled me.

"Why?" I asked.

She must've known what I was really asking because her voice softened with something like gratitude. "Because I know, that day on the fields, you weren't going to let your arrow fly."

I swallowed an unexpected rush of emotion.

Then Perla gave a dry little smirk—an expression I was beginning to recognize as her true face—and added, "Besides, who else was going to get you out of there? These courtiers couldn't cut a fish out of a net."

She guided me to the exit.

Fresh air swept over me as Perla steered us through the palace, cool moonlight shafting in intervals down the empty halls. Most of the nobles must have left after Rose Season because our footsteps clicked over a permeating silence.

Perla stopped at a branch of hallways. "You know your way?"

"Yes. *Thank you*," I said, with all the feeling left inside me.

She glanced around the narrowest corridor. "The way is clear. Be well, Alissa." And she dashed in the opposite direction, leaving me with the childlike feeling of wishing she'd stayed.

But with a fortifying breath, I pushed ahead.

Minutes later, I tumbled through the servants' door and inhaled the evening air, savoring its cold bite. The steed was tied to a spoke in the grass, his saddlebag bulging. I clutched the reins and paused to gather my bearings.

This was it. I would live freely in Bormia, as my parents had envisioned. I would finally be happy.

Then why did it feel so wrong?

The moment I'd summoned the question, the answer struck me. However rotten I'd become these weeks, I hadn't yet become a coward.

But this act would make me one.

I wouldn't just be abandoning my province. I'd be abandoning *everyone*. Because Daradon wasn't enough for Erik; he wanted to forge his own blood-begotten empire. He would grow wild with ambition, slaughtering all who stood in his way . . . and somehow, the compass would lead him there.

This compass doesn't point to Wielders. It points to specters. *Wielders just get in the way.*

I shivered, suddenly understanding why those words had terrified me. Because, on a physical level, there *was* no distinction between Wielder and specter; specters only sloughed away after Wielders' deaths, remaining as shreds of raw power.

A power that only the ancient Spellmakers could harness.

I remembered the feeling of violation when the compass had targeted me. The sudden foreignness of my own specter, as if it were being pulled beyond my reach . . .

Was that the compass's true purpose? To grasp the power of a specter before death rendered it intangible?

Did Erik wish to somehow *exploit* that power?

The horse neighed, but I didn't mount. I'd glimpsed the clock in the servants' hall: thirty minutes until midnight. I could reach Backplace in fifteen minutes, riding hard.

That left fifteen minutes to spare.

My specter squirmed, echoing the truth now writhing inside me. The truth that I would carry this gift of freedom like a bitter stone in my heart if I didn't stop Erik now, while I had the chance.

So I whispered to the horse, "Wait for me." Then I turned back toward the palace.

Because the compass had been there all along.

And I wasn't leaving Daradon without it.

45

It was madness. I knew it was. Yet my aching legs plunged me quickly down the hallways, driven by a new spike of energy.

I knew the palace intimately now—where the maids congregated, where the guards were stationed. So although I was a mess of cold sweat and nerves as I reached the first staircase, I reached it unnoticed.

Then came the climb.

I labored up each step, desperately hoping nobody would catch me halfway. I paused at the top, teetering, then pressed onward.

This was the journey I'd started after I'd read Keil's note. It felt strange to finish it from the opposite direction, an exhausted husk of the girl I'd been. But sheer willpower kept me moving until only a few turns remained.

Voices echoed ahead and I faltered, skidding on the marble. I waited. The voices didn't retreat. So, I scrambled backward, catching my breath in a nearby corridor.

The voices droned on, and I mentally counted the seconds. Two minutes passed. Three. Four.

My thighs trembled. How long had I taken to climb the stairs? How long would it take to climb down?

Was I already out of time?

I peeked around the corner, but the speakers were beyond view, somewhere in an adjacent hallway. Maybe if I continued, they wouldn't notice me.

I began to step out when someone clasped my shoulder. Panic flooded me as I turned, knees buckling—

Carmen took my weight against her.

"Alissa?" She held on until I regained my balance, her face stark white with shock. "What happened to you?"

I leaned back against the wall, blood rushing in my ears. This was too much. I needed to forget the compass. I needed to leave *now*.

But Carmen was studying me, a picture of uncertainty. "Erik said you were ill. Is that the same dress—?"

"No." I stepped past her. Maybe I could still reach Backplace in time.

Carmen grabbed my elbow, frowning. "You're clearly not well. I'll bring a physician, and—" She paused as those voices drew nearer. Her eyes sparked with recognition, and I knew she'd heard him the moment I did.

Erik.

"Come, darling." Carmen tugged my elbow. "Erik will know what to do."

"*Don't*," I said, and Carmen went rigid.

She lowered her gaze to the knife I held, its blade pinching into her saffron bodice. "Alissa?" Her voice quivered. "What are you doing?"

"Turn around and walk."

"Walk—but—? Where? Alissa, please—" She was stalling, waiting for Erik to appear.

He couldn't be much farther. I could almost make out his words.

Carmen sucked in a breath—

"Don't call for him," I said, hissing. "Walk to your suite. Now." I pushed the knife until she lurched ahead.

I kept the blade on her spine all the way to the royals' halls. She unlocked her suite, and I pushed her inside. Then I snatched her key, locked the door, and sagged against the wood.

My body vibrated with the remains of terror.

Erik had finished his meeting with the Capewells. How long until he visited the dungeons and realized I was missing?

"What's the time?" I asked. Carmen whimpered, her arms wrapped around herself. "The time!" I shouted, and she jerked into movement, fumbling around the lounge until she found a pocket watch.

"Midnight," she said. "Please, Alissa. I don't know what you're doing, but—"

I didn't hear the rest.

I'd squandered Perla's kindness. There would be no coach waiting for me in the city. No transport into Bormia. I would be stuck in this kingdom forever and Erik would find me—of course he would find me—and I might as well have stayed in that cell—

"Alissa?" Carmen's voice yanked me from my spiral. She trembled in the sea of pink-on-brown that was her lounge. I'd broken into these chambers so often that the mismatched style was familiar now. I looked across the room, those occasions drifting back to me . . .

"It's been twelve days," I breathed. "The ship hasn't left."

I staggered for Carmen's bedchamber and blew around like a storm—rummaging through the vanity, upturning garments.

I hadn't dragged myself through Rose Season to collapse now. I would finish what I came here to do; I would stop Erik's copycats from hurting anyone else.

I just needed another escape route.

"I know you're helping the Ansorans transport Wielders out of Daradon," I called. "The shipping documents were in your dresser, but you moved them. Where are they?"

Carmen shuffled inside, her teary eyes accusatory. "Keil wouldn't tell me who he'd caught sneaking around my chambers. But I knew it was you."

"Yes, very good. Now, where are the documents?"

"Why should I tell you?"

"I'm the one with the knife."

"And I'm the princess of Daradon." She raised her chin. "To threaten me is a prison sentence."

I couldn't contain my burst of laughter. "Look at me." I gestured from my tangled hair to the filthy hem of my gown. "Where do you think I've been?"

Her red lips flattened.

I laughed again, returning to my search. "You're fooling yourself if you think you know everything that goes on in this palace."

She murmured, "I know what you are."

My fingers stilled inside the dresser. I glanced around.

"I didn't want to believe it at first," she said. "You and your father always seemed different from the others. But then you arrived at court and latched onto Erik like a parasite. And when I found the coordinates to those prisons"—she shuddered—"I knew for sure: You Capewells are all the same."

Capewells.

She thought I was a *Hunter*.

In my shock, her other words had almost slipped past me. Then they pierced with a twist of understanding.

"*You* intercepted Junius's note."

Carmen swallowed. "I saw it under your door when I delivered your gown for Budding Ball. I didn't know who'd sent it, but I knew it had to be important. I checked the coordinates against a map, and the location was barren. Then the tall girl—your friend—came to us in the gardens, saying you had a delivery from Vereen. I thought it could be from the Capewells..."

"So, you broke into my chambers to see it?"

"You broke into mine first," she snapped, then glanced at the knife and winced. "When I saw the map of the xerylite mines, I put the pieces together."

"And you told the Ansorans to check the location," I finished, shaking my head.

While I'd suspected Carmen and her mother of building those prisons, she'd suspected *me*. Did Erik realize he'd been playing us against each other, keeping either of us from looking his way?

I didn't know. But I knew what he hadn't planned for: Carmen's secret alliance with Ansora.

The alliance that could still provide my own ticket to freedom.

"I need to know when that ship departs," I said.

"So you can slaughter those Wielders like you tried to slaughter sympathizers with your initiative? If Sabira hadn't called off her mercenaries—"

"Enough, Carmen!" I slammed the drawer and staggered forward. Carmen backed away, eyes fixed on the knife. "Stop pretending to care about the sympathizers and the Wielders and everyone else. I know you're only helping them to further your own agenda."

"You don't know what you're talking about."

"Don't I? You told me you would always remember Erik's mercy toward your mother. Do you think he'll extend you the same mercy once he learns you want his crown?"

Carmen suddenly flushed—but not with fear. With anger. "You mean Erik's *mercy* when he forced my mother from her home? His *mercy* when he turned her friends against her? All to punish her for a crime she committed only because he didn't possess enough *mercy* to spare her from my father's hand?"

I jolted, almost dropping the knife. *Some people are simply cruel. Fathering a child doesn't erase that cruelty.*

Carmen hadn't been talking about Perla's father at all.

"My mother killed him before he could turn his violence on me," she said. "Erik destroyed her for it. So yes, I want his crown. And yes, I would do almost anything to get it . . ." She inhaled deeply, the burst of color draining from her face. "But not this. I swore to protect the Wielders on that ship, and I will die before I let a Hunter go near them."

In the resounding silence, I grappled for any threat with which I could bend her enough to break. But as Carmen folded her hands in resignation, my knife drooped.

For so long, I'd inhaled the stench of Wholeborn cowardice and let it convince me of their collective blame. But hadn't sixty-three Parrians recently died trying to help Wielders? Hadn't the Jacombs risked their lives to bury their Wielder employees while Perla had risked herself for *me*? And Tari and Amarie and my dear tormented father who'd loved my mother more than anything and had drowned in his guilt for years so I wouldn't share her fate?

Under the perpetual heat of his temperament, Erik had forged true sympathizers in Daradon. He'd even increased the Huntings— unafraid of risking rebellion—because, like me, he hadn't realized the truth:

That although the kingdom hadn't always been fighting in a way we'd recognized . . . it *had* been fighting.

Now this was Carmen's time for battle—she who'd suffered under the king's tyranny more intimately than perhaps anyone else. But as this mismatched suite suggested, she'd inherited more from Nelle than people realized. She would defend the vulnerable just as her mother had defended her. She would not help a Hunter.

But astonishingly . . . she would help a Wielder.

With shaking fingers, I transferred the blade to my left hand and extended the latticed handle.

"I'm the one who told Sabira to call off the mercenaries," I said quietly. "The initiative was a ruse. I would never hurt my people."

Carmen eyed the knife suspiciously. I stepped closer.

"You were right about my father. He wasn't like the Hunters, and they killed him for it. Just like they—" I hesitated. I'd trusted Perla blindly in the dungeons, too dazed to consider my choices. But it was with full consciousness that I ignored every instinct I'd honed for eighteen years and chose to trust the Wholeborn princess of Daradon. "Just like they killed my mother," I finished.

"Why would they—?" Carmen stopped. Blinked. She'd answered her own question.

Why did the Hunters kill *anyone*?

"Because she wasn't allowed to exist," I said.

Carmen's realization was drawn out—eyes widening, face slackening—as if she were waking from a dream. I imagined the memories replaying in her mind: Erik flying across the ballroom, my horror when Keil had stepped between us. Carmen had seen it all. But like everyone else, she hadn't really understood.

"It's not possible," she whispered, slowly shaking her head. "Prove it."

Through these agonizing minutes, I hadn't checked on my specter. With a jerk of surprise, I realized the dullroot felt less like a lead weight upon me and more like a burial of smaller stones—still heavy but capable of being shifted with the right movements. I tried to wriggle past the poison, but the more I twisted, the more those stones avalanched onto me.

"I can't," I gasped, winded. "You'll have to trust me." *Like I'm trusting you*, I added silently.

Carmen's gaze skewered me, trying to root out a lie. I held her stare, my knife spanning the gap between us.

Finally, she took the handle and sailed toward her canopy bed. She slashed the side of her mattress and reached into the stuffing-clogged wound.

The shipping documents flapped in her hand.

I exhaled, reaching out, but she flicked them away.

"Who built those prisons under Vereen?" she asked, still wary.

"Erik," I said, unflinching.

Carmen's eyes narrowed, and I felt a current pass between us—a silent promise of alliance against a mutual enemy.

I left her suite with the knife at my hip and the shipping documents tucked inside my bodice.

46

The dullroot was thinning in my veins, and it was the worst possible development. It meant Erik should have administered my next dose by now.

It meant he knew my cell was empty.

I raced through the halls, swinging wide around every corner. My thighs protested; my breaths grew frantic; my specter squirmed painfully for release. But I wasn't leaving without the compass.

My hair plastered my neck by the time I reached the candlelit gallery. I rushed to Queen Wilhelmina's portrait and plunged my hand behind the arch. A *click*—then I heaved the arch open and stepped into the musty room.

The sight of my own royal portrait focused my scattered mind.

Gods cannot stand alone, Erik had said when he'd revealed this crowned rendering of me. Those words had formed his emblem, had cemented a truth in his bones.

So, I wrenched at the frame; like a window, the portrait squealed open on a hinge.

And behind my powerful likeness, within a velvet alcove and glinting under what little light poured from the gallery, sat the compass. As if, after years of preparing for his era of conquest, I was somehow the final piece of Erik's plan.

A piece he would never possess.

My heartbeat thrummed as I palmed the cool bronze case and unlatched the lid. The needle stirred, and I readied for its pull on my specter.

But the pull never came. The needle must have grounded itself in my hands because it whirred on in search of another.

I snapped the case shut before it found its target, then I stuffed the compass beside my mother's coin. With one last gulp of stagnant air, I left the concave room and sighed as my boots hit the marble.

But my sigh hitched, choked with panic, as I saw Erik leaning against his own portrait. His eyes shone like blue flints in the dark.

I staggered back, almost tumbling when my heels caught my skirts. One more minute—just *one*—and I might have made it out.

"I was halfway to the gates," he said softly, his voice skittering over me. "Then I asked myself: Would you use your freedom to flee?" He glanced toward my pocket, where the compass resided. "Or to finish your hunt?"

Cold sweat pricked my forehead. He stood a few yards from the door—too far to block my path but close enough that he *could*. He'd chosen that spot deliberately. A predator toying with his kill.

As if reading my thoughts, Erik gave a faint, discerning smile. On anyone else, it would've looked benevolent. "How long will it take you to decide whether or not to run? I won't wait all night."

I swallowed dryly, the roar in my ears muffling his words. Then I inched forward, quaking like an elk trying not to alert a wolf to its movement. With each step, I tested my specter against the dullroot. The poison wavered in my blood now; soon, I'd be able to push my specter past the surface.

- 429 -

But not yet.

Erik laughed, and my hairs stood up at the sound. "Surely you can go faster than that," he teased. "Or has this excursion truly worn you out? I did tell you to eat."

"I won't be your prisoner," I said.

"Good. I never wanted you to be."

"I won't be your bride, either. You'll have to kill me or let me go."

He smiled wider, bright eyes following my progress. "Are those my only options, or are you open to negotiation?"

Of course this was a joke to him. *I* was a joke to him. Without my specter, I was defenseless.

Another twist against the dullroot. Another tug toward the surface. Nothing.

Erik sighed with the air of humoring a child. "Perhaps I've been too harsh in my methods. I see now that you require a gentler hand. A warm bed, a bathing chamber, comfortable clothing. We'll start from there and continue this in the morning."

"You mean after you've poisoned me again?"

"Ah, is that why you stall? You're waiting for the dullroot to run its course?" He slanted his head, unnervingly calm. "It shouldn't be long now. Then again, you look halfway to fainting. Let's make a bet on which will drain first: the poison or your strength."

He spoke steadily, his expression mild. Yet . . . there was a slight tenseness to his brow. A faint glimmer of worry beneath the mask.

He didn't *want* the dullroot to run dry.

The knowledge fortified me.

The door stood three yards away; nothing obstructed my path. My body tensed to run—

"You know what will happen," Erik said, suddenly serious, "and I don't want to embarrass you. First, you shall rest..." His gaze dropped to my wrists; his voice deepened. "Then you will tell me exactly what power got you out of that cell."

When his eyes lifted again, they'd lost any pretense of kindness. He didn't know how I'd escaped, and the mystery was killing him.

"Come." He smoothed his jacket. "It's growing late."

"No." I unsheathed my knife, and Erik froze.

"Careful," he said darkly. "Your defiance is only endearing in the right context. You must learn when to yield."

I held his stare, my knife juddering. But I didn't let it fall.

"Very well." He drew away from the wall. "You will have to learn through demonstration."

He started toward the door, but I didn't lurch toward it as he expected. I dashed back to the portraits, crashed into King Hoyt's frame, and thrust my hand behind the arch.

Erik growled, his thunderous steps changing course. But I'd already opened the hidden doorway—an entrance to one of the many passages Sabira had mapped out for me all those weeks ago. The passages I'd planned on using to bait my attacker.

Now I bolted through the gap and inhaled the familiar, musty air.

And just as I'd once imagined, I ran.

I frantically hurtled across the stones, slamming hard against each turning, teeth clashing with every stride. The passage was stagnant and narrow, giving the impression of being enclosed within the palace walls. But as I heard Erik pounding after me, I knew I would rather fight for my life in here—would rather *die* in here—than go back to his cell.

Back to the darkness and hopelessness and the rattling chains. Back to the fear of spending forever behind those bars—alone but not alone, because Erik would always be there, wearing me down until I took the shape of what he wanted.

Raw terror bled into my desperation, the pressure of it near bursting as I rounded another corner—

And heard Erik smack to the ground.

My hope flared, sharp and bright, but I couldn't let it derail my focus. Though I'd prepared these passages weeks ago, I'd memorized each route—had even run through the steps in my anxious dungeon dreams.

So, I knew how to avoid the traps I'd set.

Erik did not.

His cool laughter echoed across the stones as he hauled himself up. Stringing twine between the walls had been Garret's favorite trick—one he'd used over and over when we'd set similar traps at Capewell Manor.

But Erik would see the next few coming.

"Very creative, my love." His footsteps clipped onward, more careful now. "How long have you been planning for this chase?"

I pushed my legs to put more distance between us, my palm slippery around the knife. Even in my nightmares, I hadn't imagined that Erik would be the one to hunt me through these passageways.

He paused at what must have been another length of twine and chuckled again.

Then a grunt.

In his arrogance, he hadn't seen the tar I'd avoided. And now his boots were stuck in it.

"What is this?" he called. "A child's game? You've gone to all this trouble, and to what end?"

He didn't understand. Unlike the attacker for whom I'd set these traps, I didn't plan on cornering Erik. I only needed to slow him down.

I only needed to get away.

I heard the clink of glass, then Erik's curse rang out.

Hysterical laughter bubbled in my throat. *Gracious gods, this was actually working!*

"Alissa," he warned, all amusement gone. "I'm growing bored of this."

I refused to hear him. A sliver of light trickled across the stones, growing closer—the door to the kitchens. The door that would lead me *out*.

With victory propelling me, I didn't see the bump in the floor. But I felt it. My ankle rolled and I flailed, trying to regain my balance.

I heard the *thud* before the sensation registered. Then pain all over—singing in my bones, sending sparks across my vision.

The mental image of that cell blazed through my agony.

I had to get up.

My heavy hands scrambled over the stones, and I found the knife. I forced myself to stand. But my eyes watered from the blow; I couldn't see the light anymore.

Where were the kitchens?

Then I heard Erik's sharp breaths—*too close*—and I knew where to turn—I was already stumbling away—

He grabbed my cloak, wrenching me back. I raised the knife a second before he slammed me against the wall.

The air burst out of me. I was blind, my head ringing.

My sight returned in swimming pieces: the pale flash of Erik's eyes, the glint of the blade, the glow from the kitchens. His body crushed me, keeping me upright. His fist wrapped mine so tightly around the knife handle that the latticed grooves dug into my palm.

I panicked, trying to twist free. But Erik's grip was unrelenting as he guided the blade to my throat.

"Enough," he said, quiet but firm. The cool steel pressed my skin. Not to cut me, I knew, but to keep me still. To keep me from fighting anymore.

I should have aimed lower. I should have run faster.

I should have never left Vereen.

I must have been crying because Erik tutted, his breath hot on my face. "Don't give me those eyes," he scolded. "This was your doing."

I tried to squirm away again, but he shifted with me, hissing in discomfort. I looked down and saw his feet bleeding. He'd removed his boots after the tar as I'd anticipated and stepped right into the broken glass.

Still, it hadn't been enough. Because, inch by inch, with unbroken strength, Erik prized my fingers off the knife. I resisted at first, my knuckles clicking under his hold. Then all at once, my grip slackened. The knife clanged to the stones.

My knees folded.

Erik caught me as I fell, my skirts creating a tent around us. He pulled me into his lap, and I yelped as he gathered my tender wrists in one hand. Then he slid his other hand into my pocket and retrieved the compass.

That quickly, it was over. This had all been for nothing.

My first night in the cell, I'd decided not to beg. So, I hated myself now, more than I'd ever hated anyone, as I looked the king in the eyes and whispered, "*Please.*"

Erik sighed. He tucked my head under his chin and began stroking my hair. I was shivering all over.

"You're the last person I ever wanted to hurt." His voice vibrated against me. "I hope you know that."

"Please," I said again. The word hitched on my sob.

Erik just cradled me closer, shushing me as I wept.

I didn't know how long I remained enfolded in his arms, my tears soaking his jacket. How long my specter heaved in great waves under my skin, each smack crashing out into another sob.

But in the cold whimpering aftermath... the last weight of dullroot glided off my power. My specter stilled inside me with the sensation of bated breath.

Slowly, I unfurled a tendril.

It trembled in the open air, straining against a strange, internal grip. Strange, because the poison had run dry; I *knew* it had. So I couldn't understand why, as my power dragged itself toward the fallen knife gleaming in my periphery, Erik had worried about the dullroot wearing off.

My specter was too weak. This tendril could barely cling around the latticed ridges, let alone lift the weapon.

I sagged from the attempt.

"All cried out, my love?" Erik cupped the back of my head and gently angled my face for his assessment. He caught my last tear with the pad of his thumb and brushed it against my cheek.

Then he released my wrists. With his eyes still on me, he would see if I reached for the knife.

He curved his arms under my knees and around my back, ready to carry me away. He would put me back in manacles. He would flood me with dullroot again.

This was my last chance.

As his muscles tensed to lift me, I directed that strand of my specter toward my pocket. Toward my mother's coin. My specter buckled under the little weight, but I lifted the coin as high as I could endure. Then I did what I'd always done.

I set it twirling.

Erik's head whipped up at the glimmer, his attention narrowing on the coin. The moment his eyes turned, I stretched my hand out behind him. My fingers connected with the knife handle.

Then Erik stood to get a closer look, carrying me up with him. The coin swiveled harmlessly in his eyeline, bobbing with every splutter of my power. He exhaled—with something like relief. He opened his mouth as if to laugh at the feeble display.

And I rammed the knife into his back.

His breath snagged. He looked down at me wide-eyed, with the expression of someone betrayed.

Then the king's blood warmed my fingers, and the fight rushed back into me.

I yanked out the blade, and Erik's roar shook the walls. He dropped me. I cried out as I tumbled, losing the knife. My forehead smacked the floor. Blood dribbled into my lashes.

But up ahead, I could see the light of the kitchens. I clambered forward, breathing fast.

His sticky hand seized my calf. "It will take more than that," he growled.

As he hauled me back, I looked over my shoulder so I would know where to aim. Then I drove my heel into his nose. He bellowed again, spraying red. I wrenched away with a final kick.

In a hot, heaving scramble, I pushed to my feet and staggered ahead.

I charged into the kitchens and light stunned me, the blast of fresh air drying my sweat. His breaths echoed a few paces behind, relentless.

I whipped around. Cleavers, carving knives, kitchen shears—all gleaming for the taking. But as the passage door swung wide, I darted to the shelf of nightmilk vials beside it. If I could smash them at Erik's bare feet, release the sedative into his wounds—

I reached out too late.

Because his hand snapped around my throat—*squeezing*—crushing in harder when I tried to claw him away.

He slowly drove me back—away from the nightmilk vials, the passageway, the kitchen blades. He loomed over me until his ice-glazed eyes reflected my own terror. Until his face—as cold and hard as marble—was all that would ever exist. And as my lungs spasmed, burning for air, I realized I'd never seen him truly angry until now. Not at the Opal, not in the dungeons, not in the ballroom after I'd struck him.

This was the king's wrath. A wrath so fierce—so blind—that he really would kill me, whether he meant to or not.

And he would send with me every life that had ever fueled my own.

Tears scalded my eyes as I saw Lady Fiona, signing her name onto my birthing papers; the blurred faces of every Wielder my father had condemned; my mother's smiling face, rendered in Father's hand; my father, wrapping his arms around me, kissing the top of my head.

Father again, teaching me to swim.

Father, stirring honey into his tea.

Father, looking up from his book, eyes creasing at a joke I'd made.

My specter was corkscrewing tighter and tighter inside me now—but not to hide. This was the rapid recoil of a backswing. The inhale before a scream.

I saw myself at seven years old, threading strands of my power through the eye of a needle while holding the rest within.

I saw the spectral waves heaving free around my father's body—the layers I hadn't known existed because I'd *kept* them within for all those years.

The dullroot had left my system; it wasn't the poison tethering my specter now, thinning it out into fragile ribbons. It was years of habitual control. It was instinct, rekindled by my fresh fear.

It was *me*.

The greater the power, the greater the need for release.

I remembered the compass's needle, shuddering to maintain its hold on such a power.

And as Erik's face fragmented in my vision, as I weakened in his hold, I painfully unclenched the long-calcified fist inside me.

My body shuddered.

Then the room shuddered with it.

47

Erik was the first to feel the force.

He flew backward, his hand tearing off me, as glasses and trays and kitchen blades clashed out as if from a shockwave.

I wheezed, hurtling against a counter. My power lashed back toward me but didn't return to my bones. It shimmered around me in a fog, undulating with rampant energy, rolling hot against my skin.

I took a painful, blissful inhale—truly *breathing* for the first time—when glass clinked, and I looked up.

The king of Daradon sat slumped against the wall.

His nose dripped red; the wound in his back gushed freely; his drooping lashes cast shadows down his cheeks.

Because those nightmilk vials had smashed into him, the milky liquid now marbling with his blood.

Through the thick ripple of my power, I held his fading gaze and crunched across the broken glass. I squatted before him, our heavy breaths roaring in the silence.

Then I slipped my hand into his pocket. As I brought out the compass, he snatched the hem of my skirts—a last cumbersome effort. He turned his head just enough to whisper in my ear.

Footfalls pounded in the distance. The guards must have heard the commotion.

So, I left Erik in the pool of his blood and hurried back into the passage, his last words replaying in my mind.

I'd stopped only to retrieve my coin and the knife, and my power was still churning free as I pitched into the night. I couldn't have it pouring around me while I rode, so I pulled it back inside, preparing for that familiar, stifling ache.

But there was no ache. Just a soft melting against my bones.

I mounted the steed clumsily, wiping the hair from my eyes. Then I kicked him into a gallop toward the hidden servants' gate. I was scanning the grounds for movement when an arrow whizzed past my ear.

The horse screeched and reared his front legs. I clenched tight, leaning forward to keep mounted. He slammed back on all fours, and my body shook from the impact. I whipped my face from side to side, frantically searching for the archer.

There—a shadowed figure several yards ahead, positioned on the diagonal. As the archer drew another arrow and stepped forward, the glow from the palace spilled over a tailored leather uniform and long straw-blond hair.

Briar.

With a jerk of horror, I snapped the horse's reins, urging him toward the exit. Cold air rushed down my throat. I reached for my power again but it rolled thickly off my back—an unwieldy cape spilling out in the wind.

Another arrow zipped past, just missing me.

Briar was aiming for the kill.

She sprinted for the servants' gate, hair streaming, presumably trying to head me off. We would meet like two lines intersecting on a grid.

No—the horse was faster, but Briar was closer. She would reach the gate first.

And she did.

Facing me head-on, Briar nocked a third arrow. My heartbeat kicked in a wild, desperate rhythm as she pulled the bowstring to her smirking mouth.

Then a figure tackled her. And her arrow whistled, flying wide.

My body jolted, my specter shuddering from a slice of pain.

The horse reared again, and this time I almost toppled off. Warmth trickled down my left arm. I'd been clipped.

I grappled for purchase amid the stomping and shrieking, and saw the figures wrestling in the dark. Briar was stronger than her opponent—more skilled.

But Garret had more incentive.

He pinned Briar under him, crushing her face to the ground. "Go!" he shouted over his shoulder. Our eyes met, and for a split second I saw the boy he used to be. Passionate. Determined. Blazing with love. "Go!" he yelled again as Briar bucked beneath him.

I charged on, and the scuff of their battle continued as the horse kicked down the gate and plunged us into the city.

48

It was long past midnight, and no coach waited for me at Backplace. Though I didn't want to stop before leaving the capital, my left arm throbbed and my bloodied hands kept slipping from the reins. So, I dismounted behind a tavern, where textured-glass windows diffused enough murky light to see by. Then I assessed my arm.

I told myself it could've been worse; the arrow had skimmed me rather than piercing through. Still, my eyes watered at the sight—the open skin flaps, the gruesome slash of red. The more I looked, the less I believed that this was *my* arm, *my* wound.

But the pain was hammering now, tethering me to reality, so I rummaged through the saddlebag for something to stop the bleeding.

Perla had supplied me well, with a waterskin, a food parcel, and several items of fresh clothing. I'd learned enough from Tari to know that the wound would fester without a proper cleaning.

A mediocre cleaning would have to suffice.

Biting a mouthful of my cloak, I poured water over the gash. The pain doubled me over. I groaned around the fabric, eyes rolling back. Water ribboned down my arm and splattered my boots. Hot breaths sawed through me for several long seconds.

Once the nausea subsided, I tore a strip from a clean blouse and wrapped it around my arm, using my teeth to secure the knot. Then I rinsed my hands, unbuckled the sheath belt, and peeled off the gown I'd been wearing for twelve days. I transferred everything to the saddlebag—the rings, the shipping documents, my mother's coin, the compass—and I was buttoning a new blouse when a tavern window cracked open.

I froze at the shock of light. Laughter streamed out with the fatty smell of cooking meat, figures drifting behind the glass. But none turned their heads toward me.

After five heart-racing seconds, I left my blood-soaked gown deflated over a bush. Then I rode on.

If I'd been more alert, I might have worried at the sudden influx of guards sweeping the streets—pulling over coaches and searching citizens at random, their whispers catching on the wind. *An intruder. An attack at the palace.*

But I was wilting in the saddle, bleary-eyed and aching.

And maybe that was precisely why the guards didn't spare me a second glance as I rode right past them beyond the city border.

Sunset boat rides along Emberly River were a staple of Verenian summers. Father and I had boarded a streamlined vessel every evening last year, carrying ripe apricots and olive loaves and a palette for his watercolor paints. He'd painted the pink-and-amber sky, losing himself in his art, and I'd secretly wished for a craft worth losing myself in too.

The vessel I was currently trying to board in the dead of night was more beast than ship, and the open sea behind it was a far cry from the crystalline river that weaved around my province. The roaring water muffled the sharp hiss of my words, the misted air plastering my furrowed forehead.

I'd thought, after besting the king of Daradon and escaping the leader of his Hunters, that I'd overcome the last obstacles stopping me from reaching the ship secretly bound for Ansora. The ship that would carry me—and the compass—out of this stifling kingdom for good.

As it turned out, my last obstacle was an overseer named Ed.

And Ed was proving difficult to defeat.

"Your name's not on the list," he said, stroking his black goatee. "No name, no entry."

"I was a last addition," I insisted for the third time, flapping the shipping documents in his face. "Here. I have all the right papers."

"You could've stolen those from anyone."

A young man started elbowing ahead of me. At my glare, he retreated.

Ed snapped shut his book of names. "Listen, girl—"

"No, *you* listen. See that alley over there? Yes, the one behind the fishmongers, where they throw out the guts? I've spent two nights camped in that alley so I wouldn't miss this ship." Truth. "I had to sell my steed to avoid attention"—also truth—"and I wasted half my coins on a physician who wouldn't know how to stitch a flesh wound if it opened its mouth and gave him the instructions." Another miserable truth. "So *you*"—I slapped the documents against his broad chest—"can either let me aboard or I will let myself aboard."

A lie.

The only time I'd used my specter over the last two days was to reach for an apple. No longer confined to my internal grip, the power had gracelessly blasted the apple into the alley wall with a force that could've dismembered a full-grown man.

I wasn't about to Wield that power against an *actual* man,

no matter how irritating he was.

So, I maintained the arrogant sneer I'd perfected at court, and eventually he sighed.

"What was the name?"

"Dinah Summers," I lied again.

"Proof?"

"I don't have identity papers."

"Not proof of identity," he said, impatient.

Then I understood. So I took a tight breath—he really was pushing his luck—and aimed one hard blow toward his book of names.

The book shot fiercely out of his hand. Skidded across the dock. Would've fallen into the water if another power—probably his own—hadn't kept it from slipping over the edge.

Ed rolled his eyes, seeming neither surprised nor impressed. "On you go, then. You're holding up the line."

I hurried aboard, wobbly with relief, and followed a deckhand's instructions toward the hatch.

Dust spun through the beige-washed cabin—so vast it must have once been a cargo hold. Sleeping mats scattered the wooden panels, and a dozen people already sat atop them, wringing their hands and whispering nervously. The smart ones would stay vigilant until we departed, to make sure this voyage wasn't a trick—a *trap*.

I was too exhausted to be smart. So I chose a mat, propped my saddlebag under my head, and collapsed into sleep.

I didn't open my eyes until my stomach growled loud enough to wake me.

For a moment, I was disoriented. My tongue felt fuzzed with a sawdust taste, and a rumbling filled my ears. Then I remembered where I was, and I jolted upright.

The ship was moving. We'd left Daradon.

"The overseer handed those out while you slept," someone said. A young curly-haired woman on the mat beside me pointed toward a brown-paper bundle. Inside I found corned beef, bread crammed with seeds and raisins, and a warm bottle of ale.

I was halfway through the food when I had to stop and blink at my surroundings.

With so much talking and moving, it was impossible to keep count. But I reached over a hundred before I lost my place.

Over a hundred Wielders that Carmen had helped liberate from Daradon.

I wish I'd asked her how she'd found them all—the people I'd waited eighteen years to meet. A few months ago, this sight alone would have sent me careening out of my body.

It might still have, if a slow throb wasn't radiating down my arm, dampening every other feeling.

My wound had been a gory mess by the time I'd reached the Avanish harbor, and I'd had to visit a back-alley physician who may well have been a butcher for all the bloodstains on his overalls. He'd handed me a bottle of white spirit and told me to drink while he stitched. Then he'd given me a tonic to stave off infection—though I suspected it was mostly water—and I'd staggered from his workroom to empty my stomach in the canal.

Now I shimmied up my sleeve and peeled away the bandage. The tender skin pulled, and I hissed. Even in my drink-muddled state, I'd known that stitches shouldn't look like this—bumpy and ugly and flaking dried blood.

"Need help?" the curly-haired woman asked.

"No." I cleared my throat and added, "Thank you. I'm fine."

The physician had been a necessity. I didn't want anyone else's hands on me for a while.

As I rewrapped the bandage, the woman glanced at my wrists—at the bruises and chafe-marks distinctly produced by manacles. I shouldered my saddlebag and labored above deck to escape the pity in her eyes.

I wasn't the only one who'd needed escape. More people—*Wielders*—crowded the deck in groups, their voices lost over the rushing sea. Salt-fresh air blustered against me as I approached the rail, sunlight glaring across the water.

The coastline of Daradon was a smudge on the horizon.

I should have felt victorious. But I mostly felt tired. I was leaving so much behind: Tari and Amarie, my province, my people... and Garret. Garret, who'd chosen me over Briar when it had mattered most. She would kill him for it, if she hadn't already. His death would be another weight on my conscience.

But right now, no weight seemed heavier than the weight in my pocket.

Slowly, I brought out the compass.

I'd seen no signs of mourning during my days in Avanford. No black pearls strung across the windows.

Erik had survived.

I will find you, Little Thorn, he'd whispered as he'd bled. *It will be in my hands again.*

The words had chilled me because I'd felt the truth in them. As long as I remained keeper of the compass, Erik would search the world for me. I was tempted to throw the accursed thing into the sea, just to be rid of it.

But... I couldn't.

This compass didn't simply identify Wielders, as the Capewells had believed. It possessed a greater purpose—a greater *power*. And though I was still assembling theories regarding that power, I knew one fact for certain: My father had believed that its power could be destroyed. Not lost. Not hidden away. *Truly* destroyed.

His conviction had gotten him killed—which convinced me, more than anything, that he'd been close to finding answers. That the only way to stop Erik—to stop *anyone* who shared Erik's goals—was to finish what my father had started.

But I couldn't do that without first understanding the true nature of the device in my hands.

I ran my thumb over the bronze case. Then I unlatched the clasp.

I hadn't viewed the open compass since the first afternoon of my campout in Avanford. And now, just like then, the flash of light glanced up my blouse, across my vision, as I eased back the lid.

It's as strong as diamond, Keil had once told me, with that dayglass shard in his hand. *Under sunlight, it glows as if a rainbow has been captured within.*

He was right. Beneath this open wash of sunshine, the glossy dome of the compass shone in vibrant hues.

Because, as I'd realized on that sunlit afternoon in Avanford . . . it was formed from dayglass.

The color shifted with every angle, radiating a dazzling light above its surface—the soft shimmer reminding me of a spectral ripple in the air. It was so entrancing that Keil had worried about Erik seeing a specimen of the material—not realizing that the king had possessed this one all along.

And now, under its translucent watercolor-swirl, the compass's needle was beginning to stir.

I shut the case, snuffing out the haze of rainbow light. Stilling the needle before it could spin.

Ansoran Spellmakers had forged this compass from a material native to their lands. Erik had rendered his emblem in ancient Ansoran—had emblazoned it across his weapons and his Wielder prison. At first, I couldn't fathom the reason. But for the last two days, the words on Keil's note had bounced around my head: *The language wasn't as dead as I'd thought. Someone recognized the symbol after all.*

Recognized, he'd said. Not *translated*. It seemed an important distinction.

And it was the only lead I had.

So, I tucked the compass into my pocket and turned, squinting across the opposite horizon. The secrets of the compass began in Ansora.

I would begin there, too.

EPILOGUE

Marge had come to learn that terror was a wet emotion. It was sweaty palms and watery bowels. It was tears and urine and hot, rising bile.

But mostly, *mostly*, it was blood.

This new prison already reeked of it. Judging by the amount of stale bread the wardens tossed into the cells at regular intervals, Marge had been here longer than she'd been in the last prison before it had started to collapse.

But in all the weeks combined, this was the longest *he* had waited between visits.

The trials, as the wardens called them, usually took place once or twice a week. He never came in his finery. He dressed in a light shirt and trousers and walked up and down the rows of cells as if choosing a dog from a kennel.

On Marge's first night, he'd picked a Parrian woman in the opposite cell. Marge had watched open-mouthed as the wardens had dragged the woman out screaming, her bare feet kicking up dirt as she tried to break free. The other prisoners sobbed and Marge had joined them, caught up in the horror of it all. Only afterward did she realize they'd been sobbing with relief.

The wardens returned from the trial hours later and flung the Parrian woman back into her cell, her tunic stained red.

Marge didn't understand. Hadn't they reached a verdict on the woman? Couldn't they prove she was a Wielder?

He turned the corner then, wiping the blood off his hands with a silver-embroidered handkerchief. He noticed Marge watching and smiled at her, slow and wide, his pale blue eyes creasing at the edges.

He chose Marge for the next trial.

She confessed immediately, pleading guilty to the crime of Wielding before they'd finishing tying her to the table. Better a quick execution than an agonizing survival.

But he only laughed at her confession. And then he began.

He sliced her skin all over, first with a silver blade, then with obsidian, then with an iridescent metal he called eurium. He frowned while he worked, clearly disappointed, as though he expected something other than the steady trickle of her blood or her wild screaming filling the room.

That was when Marge understood what sort of trial this was. Not a criminal trial.

An experimental trial.

There would be no verdicts or executions. There would be no reprieve. She couldn't even hope for an accidental death because he made the cuts with expert precision, minimizing blood loss. The wardens sealed the wounds afterward with a thick salve, and the subjects were left to heal for at least a week before he chose them again. It was a clinical kind of torture.

But his absence had been the worst torture of all.

The wardens stroked the bone-white handles of their weapons, itching for bloodshed. The prisoners didn't mention him, from a shared and unspoken fear that his name might summon him sooner.

But superstitions were wasted here. Eventually, a door squealed open in the distance. And because Marge had grown accustomed to the sickly taste of terror, she knew that those lazy, predatory footsteps didn't belong to a warden.

The whispers died out. The rattling chains stilled. The silence became an anxious, bloated thing, as if the very air knew it too.

That the wick of their luck had burned through.

The king had arrived.

ACKNOWLEDGMENTS

I feel incredibly fortunate to be writing these acknowledgments, and even more fortunate to have been surrounded by such wonderful people on my journey toward publication.

I'd like to begin with an immense thanks to my inimitable agents, Claire Wilson and Pete Knapp. Diving into the publishing industry as a debut author means experiencing a lot of firsts, and I am extraordinarily lucky to have had your kindness, guidance, and continuous belief in my writing to see me through every step. Thank you for lending your hard work and talent to all areas of this project and for making this adventure what it is.

Thank you to all the amazing people at RCW and Park, Fine & Brower Literary Management who have helped bring *Thorn Season* into the world. A massive, very special thanks to Safae El-Ouahabi, who first flagged my manuscript in the query inbox and who has been championing this book ever since. My heartfelt thanks to Stuti Telidevara and Danielle Barthel for all your incredible work and support; I'm so grateful to have you on my team.

An enormous thanks to the brilliant Sam Coates for your phenomenal work in introducing this book to publishers around the globe. I'd also like to thank the coagents who have helped take this story far and wide, as well as everyone on the foreign rights team at RCW. Special thanks to Maddie Luke and Sampurna Ganguly for all your assistance.

To my film agent, Emily Hayward-Whitlock at the Artists Partnership, I'm incredibly grateful for the work you're doing to bring the world of *Thorn Season* to the screen.

I am fortunate enough to be working with *two* wonderful editors on this series; a very deep thanks to Tom Bonnick and Kristin Daly Rens, for not only welcoming *Thorn Season* into your publishing houses with exceptional passion and ambition, but also for enriching my first publishing experience with your insight and inexhaustible kindness. I'm privileged to be one of your authors and so thrilled to be going on this journey with you.

So much behind-the-scenes magic goes into launching a book, and I am extremely grateful to my publishing teams on both sides of the Atlantic, who have been working their magic on *Thorn Season*. To everyone who read, rooted for, and/or helped to release this book: Thank you!

Over at HarperFire, I'd like to give particular thanks to Cally Poplak, Hannah Marshall, Charlotte Winstone, Elisa Offord, Laura Hutchison, Jasmeet Fyfe, Aisling Beddy, Dan Downham, Caroline Fisher, and Sandy Officer. Nick Lake, thank you for cheering me on from the very first meeting. Huge thanks to Andrew Hodges for copyediting and Mary O'Riordan for proofreading. Tom Roberts, thank you for your incredibly gorgeous jacket illustration.

To my US team at HarperCollins, I'm so thankful that Alissa's story has found a home across the ocean with you. I especially want to thank Laura Mock, Joel Tippie, James Neel, Kristen Eckhardt, Michael D'Angelo, Audrey Diestelkamp, Jenny Lu, Jenn Corcoran,

Sam Fox, Patty Rosati, Mimi Rankin, Kerry Moynagh, Kathy Faber, Jennifer Wygand, Jessica Abel, Susan Yeager, and Christian Vega. A huge thanks to Jessica Berg, Mary Magrisso, and Marinda Valenti for your work on copyediting and Stephanie Evans for proofreading. Thank you, Bicem Sinik, for your absolutely epic US jacket illustration.

I am continuously amazed that *Thorn Season* will get to travel the world, and I'm beyond grateful to all the overseas publishers who loved Alissa's story enough to invite this book into your publishing houses. Thank you so much for your passion and belief.

This story began its life in a dream journal and somehow ended up taking me on the most joyful and fulfilling journey I've ever embarked upon. So I want to thank my past self for first writing down this concept and then finding the courage to explore it.

To the writers and industry professionals who share their knowledge and experiences in books, articles, blog posts, and videos: thank you for demystifying the route to publication, so that a Biomedical Science graduate could learn how to become an author.

Thank you to all the women who have been writing books throughout history, whose journeys made mine possible.

Thank you to the wonderful family members and friends who have been encouraging me through all my ventures, from every corner of the world. To my grandmothers and grandfathers, for your infinite love and support; to those who are no longer here to experience this with me, I know you would have been so proud. To Juliette, for all the laughing-until-we-cry moments and the endless joy you bring me. To Laura, for nearly two decades of fabulous friendship.

Thank *you*, reader, for allowing these characters into your life.

And finally, my greatest thanks will forever go to Mum and Dad.

There are not enough words in any language or dictionary for me to truly express the thanks I want to give you, but I will begin with all the words that make up this book, dedicated to you. Thank you for inspiring me every day and raising me to believe I can do anything. For standing beside me on each journey I take and holding me up whenever I stumble. For being my first readers, my first supporters, my first (and eternal) heroes.